THERE'LL ALWAYS BE AN ENGLAND

Also by David Pinner

Novels

RITUAL
WITH MY BODY

Plays

DICKON
FANGHORN
THE DRUMS OF SNOW
THE POTSDAM QUARTET

THERE'LL ALWAYS BE AN ENGLAND

A Novel

DAVID PINNER

First published in Great Britain in 1984
by Muller, Blond & White Limited, 55/57 Great Ormond
Street, London WC1N 3HZ

Copyright © 1984 by David Pinner

All rights reserved. No part of this publication may be
reproduced, stored in a retrieval system, or transmitted, in
any form or by any means, electronic, mechanical,
photocopying, recording or otherwise, without the prior
consent of Muller, Blond & White Limited.

British Library Cataloguing in Publication Data

Pinner, David
There'll always be an England.
I. Title
823'.914[F]   PR6066.15

ISBN 0–85634–152–5

Phototypeset by Input Typesetting Ltd, London
Printed in Great Britain by
Billing & Sons, Worcester

For Stephen Haseler
Roger Fox
and Elspeth Cochrane

'There'll always be an England'

'British Communists should support the Labour Party leaders as the rope supports the hanged man.'
Vladimir Ilyich Lenin

MARCH

The wind shrilled through five hundred and fifty-two aerials which lined the roofs of rows and rows of grey-fronted houses. It swirled sweet-papers, plastic cups, cigarette butts and empty Coca-Cola cans along the dismal arteries of the Eden Council Estate. Every house the clattering garbage passed was identical. The doors were sun-blistered, the curtains in desolate, bright colours, and the occupants, with their heads lowered against the biting wind, had drawn faces and not enough in their shopping bags.

As Roy Hampton edged into Angel Street, the central thoroughfare of the estate, he could not help thinking that perhaps Jean-Paul Sartre was right when he said: 'Hell is other people'. Well, maybe not quite right. It was not these hunched-up people who were hell. It was the other people, in the brighter world, who did not care about these people who were the real incubi and succubi.

Roy stopped and glanced upwards. It was now so cold in the Borough of Lamberton North that the clouds above him were spitting out chips of hail. He pulled his overcoat collar round his ears as the icy tin-tacks stung his forehead. The hail became more persistent so he stepped into a dilapidated shop doorway.

What the hell am I doing here? he thought. Must be some kind of penance for the years of guilt. It's not that I haven't tried to help these people but 'What can an ordinary Member of Parliament do?'

Roy coughed, realising he had spoken out loud. He was embarrassed to see a black youth in an orange woolly beret. The youth was leaning against the bus stop and laughing. Roy could only shrug helplessly and laugh back. Then, adjusting the pale-blue scarf that his wife Liz had knitted him last Christmas, he ventured into the hail.

'That's what happens to you when you've been an MP for fifteen years.'

'Oh, you're de MP round here, are you, man?' jeered the black youth, his face almost obliterated by his perfect white laughing teeth.

'So rumour has it,' returned Roy. 'That's why you caught me talking to myself.'

'An' you talk to yo'self because no one else will listen to you, right, man?'

Roy laughed. 'I don't think it's quite as bad as that. I've done everything I can to improve things round here, you know.' But as he said it he knew how lame it sounded.

'What things you improved round 'ere, then?'

'Well, despite the Tory cuts, the two hospitals are still open. I stirred up a hornets' nest to save St Michael's. Most of the schools have still got books despite Sir Keith. And I stopped them building the motorway through Norman Point.'

As Roy ran through his 'successes', he could hear the bleak irony in his voice, but he retreated behind his upturned collar and continued with the litany of his accomplishments: a new school for the subnormal, another ward added to the reconverted Early-Victorian 'Bedlam', three new Job Centres. . . .

The youth went on smiling with his glistening teeth.

'So I trust I can rely on your vote when the time comes.'

'What's the point of votin' for you, fat cat? All that stuff you said you gone an' done ain't changed nuthin'. This still the same ol' shit-hole it always was. When my folks come over from Trinidad, they say it were just as bad then. Nuthin' ever changes round here except more an' more folk end up on the dole. Well, ah got to go now, Mr MP. This 'ere my bus.'

The youth thrust out his arm and a bus lurched towards the kerb.

'Things could be worse,' Roy shouted as the bus moved off again. 'You could have a Tory MP!'

He did not catch the youth's reaction through the window but he was sure those teeth were still laughing. Roy shrugged, then returned to the shop doorway. On the third attempt he managed to light a cigarette. Earlier that week he'd promised Liz that he'd give up smoking but the hopelessness of this particular council estate always affected his nervous system the same way. Nicotine was the only drug that could calm him. He gulped the filtered smoke into his lungs, which triggered his latent cough.

When he recovered from coughing, he stubbed out the cigarette and moved back into the street. He would have liked to have gone on smoking but felt it was bad for his image.

I really must take up the pipe again, he thought. People approve of pipes. Despite Harold Wilson!

Chuckling, he walked on as the hail died down. He decided it was time to leave what was laughingly known locally as the 'Shopping Centre', and patrol the grimness of Eden Council Estate proper. Every month he made this perverse pilgrimage through one of the highest areas of unemployment in his constituency. Every month he stopped and talked to any passer-by who would listen. He knocked on doors and asked sour-faced husbands and wives if they would like to talk to him. He patted spotty children on their heads and made goo-goo noises at milky-breathed babies. Then he would go to the local pub and listen and talk and listen some more.

What else can I do? he asked himself again. We can't change anything while we're in Opposition. And when we get into power, half the things we want to do are crazy. Which is why less and less people believe in us. Why should they believe in us? Despite the Shadow Cabinet's protestations of 'unity', the public aren't stupid. They know that the only thing which 'unifies' the Parliamentary Labour Party is mutual hatred! And though periodically the right-wing camp and the left-wing camp declare their desire to 'join forces to throw out the obscene Tories', that doesn't fool the man in the street. He still remembers the years of acrimony, the barely-disguised loathing between the warring participants, and the trumpeting ambition of men like Kinnock, Hattersley, Healey, Heffer and Benn. The battle will go on until one side or the other is destroyed. And the way things are going at the moment I know who is going to win that battle. And if I'm right, God help us all!

What chance have these people living in these houses? Yet there are certain comrades in the Party that, if they had their way, would one day soon make it compulsory for everyone to live in houses like these! Except the comrades themselves, of course.

Roy paused under a bedraggled plane tree. After checking

that no one was looking, he cupped his chilled hands together to light a cigarette. The wind was too strong so he gave up.

I suppose I ought to knock on a few doors and tell them that all's well with the Party. Our great leader is doing his balancing act, and Tony B. still loves everybody. God, I really must do something about my cynicism.

Roy was now on the edge of the council estate. Stretching before him was a large expanse of wasteland and, to his right, two monstrous tower blocks.

To my eternal shame, he thought, I didn't stop them being built in the late sixties, and now understandably those poor rabbit-people in their Tower of Babel find it hard to forgive me. So the least I can do is visit them.

The hail was only intermittent as he trudged away from the road. Soon he was on the flagstone path which bisected two unkempt grassy slopes, leading up to the paved square in front of the first tower block. The square was deserted. Roy looked up at the vast building which loomed over him. Any moment he felt the whole structure would come tumbling down and he would be buried under countless protesting husbands, wives and children. He shook his head, trying to escape the enormity of the desolation above him. As he approached the shadowy, neon-lit tunnel leading to the lift shaft, he heard a woman cry out in the square behind him.

Roy whirled round and saw two fifteen-year-old schoolboys snatching an elderly woman's shopping bag. Then the boys raced off up the grassy incline and Roy heard himself yell: 'Stop, thief, stop, thief!' like a Bow Street Runner in a fifties movie. Moments later he found he was running across the grass in pursuit. It was hard going because the surface was uneven. He had only pounded four-hundred yards when his bronchial cough returned.

Christ, he thought, here I am just turned forty-five and I've still got most of my hair but I'm wheezing like a clapped-out Puffing Billy.

Then the boys heard him and realised they were being chased. The leaner of the two shouted over his shoulder: 'Fuck off, Grandad, you'll 'ave a heart attack before you get your mitts on us!'

Still running, the boy gave the obligatory V-sign, crossed the road and raced ahead of his friend into the council estate.

Together the two thieves sprinted along the street and were soon swallowed up in the bustling thoroughfare.

Roy was now so far behind that by the time he reached the estate there was no sign of them.

He stumbled against an empty dustbin. For a long moment he clamped his hands on the dustbin lid and coughed and coughed until he thought his lungs would haemorrhage. Eventually the terrible coughing subsided. He paused to gulp some air, then hacked up the last of the phlegm that was torturing his chest.

My God, what a day! Six boring hours in the Commons and now this. Anyway, what use is an MP who hasn't even the stamina to make a citizen's arrest of two snotty schoolboys? I'd better find that poor old lady and try and comfort her. Then we can go to the police together. Not that the police will ever catch them, but at least I can tell her I tried to catch them.

He laughed out loud at his next thought. What I really need now is a drink!

Then his public conscience returned and he headed back to the square. From a distance his broad shoulders and the slight splay-footedness of his walk made him seem older than he was, but his pale-blue eyes, his full mouth and the boyish roundness of his face altered this impression. On a good day, when he was smiling with his children, he could be mistaken for a mere thirty-five-year old. However, today was different—as was nearly every day after being in the House of Commons.

It's the lack of achieving anything in that place that's so dispiriting. We seem to have done nothing recently but oppose Maggie whenever she opens her mouth. Mind, there's a lot to oppose her about. But even when we secretly agree with her, we still oppose her because that's what being in Opposition means. Not that if she were in Opposition, she'd behave any differently! So the country is being destroyed by default because both we and the Tories react to everything on strictly Party lines. And as we're in Opposition at the moment, we must go on bitching about everything that's Tory until we've toppled the Queen Bitch from her Parliamentary Throne and set up in her place – who? Crusading Kinnock? Huffing Hattersley? Or, God help us, Lord Protector Benn!

Roy strode into the middle of the square but it was deserted. The elderly lady whose purse had been snatched was gone.

Perhaps she was lucky enough to find a policeman and he's taken her to the station. But that's not likely. Despite Tory promises there are never enough cops to go round, especially in areas like this: the Muggers' Paradise. Christ, I really do need that drink!

Still wondering where the old lady had gone, Roy set off for the Builder's Arms, which was an ironic name for a pub considering the state of the building industry in Lamberton.

Yes, you can almost smell the despair in this Garden of Eden. Sometimes I wonder whether Liz isn't right when she says we need a revolution to forcibly take from those who have too much and give it to the poor devils round here who palpably have too little. But that wouldn't work either. When Lenin tried it in Russia, he ended up with a police state that made the Tsar's Secret Police look like French gendarmes. Well, that's what the first Bolsheviks, the Kronstadt sailors, said about Lenin, and they should know because he crushed them like bugs. Mind, it was Trotsky and the military that did the actual killing.

Roy stopped in his tracks. His ramblings on the Russian Revolution were abruptly snuffed out.

I don't believe it!

But it was true: there were two intertwined chains stretched across the lounge bar doors, barring his way into the Builder's Arms. Irritably he rattled on the heavy padlock. Then the large sign in one of the opaque windows caught his eye: 'Closed for Renovation'.

What a pig of a world! There are nearly twenty-three per cent unemployed round here. Their only solace is to come and sit in the Builder's Arms and drown their sorrows. Now even that's denied them! I haven't the energy to walk up to the Red Cock so I'll have to make do with a cup of tea.

He walked on, passing the shabby electrical shop on his left and the shabby barbershop on his right, until he reached Zorba's Café, the shabbiest of the lot. As he stepped inside and closed the door behind him, he realised he had made a mistake. But his 'enemy', for that was how Roy Hampton regarded Terry MacMaster, at first did not notice the new arrival. Terry was too busy haranguing his troops in the far corner of the café.

Quickly Roy seated himself by the café door. His instinct was to leave before Terry saw him.

But it's too risky, he thought. If Terry looks up and sees me beating a retreat, before the morning is out the entire constituency will know that their diligent MP is a coward. Maybe I am a coward but I'd prefer not to look like one!

The Greek proprietor came over to Roy's table and grudgingly asked Roy what he wanted.

'Cup of tea, please. A little milk and no sugar.'

To his embarrassment Roy realised he was whispering his order. The Greek grunted, then returned to the counter to make the tea. While Roy was waiting, he craned his neck in the hope of catching some of Terry's conversation. The café was empty but for Terry and his companions, yet Roy could make little sense of what was being said. Then Roy caught a comment affirming the political astuteness of Lenin. One of the girls at Terry's table started laughing. Then MacMaster made another witty jibe at the expense of Maggie Thatcher. This set both girls off.

A mug of doubtful-looking tea was slopped on to the ageing formica-topped table in front of Roy. He tried to drink the tea but it was too hot. As he blew on the cloudy liquid, he heard Terry utter his name. One of the girls made a spitting noise. Then there was the unmistakeable sound of a man's fist being slammed down on the far table.

'Joan, that kind of behaviour's not very helpful! Whether you like it or not, Roy Hampton is still the bona fide MP in this constituency. So whatever we do, must be done by the rules. Otherwise we'll all be shunted into a siding, and so will the Cause! That's why it needs proper planning and . . . .'

Terry trailed off as Joan, an attractive redhead, whispered something in his ear. Out of the corner of his eye Roy saw that the girl was whispering and pointing at him, but he couldn't hear what she was saying. Before he could address himself again to his hot tea, Terry turned his unblinking gaze on him.

For a moment the two adversaries stared at each other. Then Terry allowed the left corner of his mouth to smile and stood up. Roy was always surprised how handsome Terry was, with his sea-grey eyes and cropped curly black hair. He had pronounced Slavic cheekbones, offset by a straight nose and a purposeful lower lip, but it was his deep-set, laughing eyes that unnerved Roy.

As the younger man crossed the eight yards separating their

tables, Roy found himself admiring the leanness of his adversary's body.

If only he didn't always wear that predictably battered, black leather jacket and those carefully paint-stained jeans, he thought. Yet despite these social affectations there is something appealing about Terry. I suppose if we were on the same side of the fence, we might even have been friends. We both come from the same working-class background. My dad was a meter reader for the gas board, and Terry's is a milkman. We both went to grammar schools in those good old days when they still existed. Then we both went on to the London School of Economics, though there was an eight-year gap between us. So we belong to the same world. Yet he regards me as bourgeois and middle-class – which I suppose is partially true. Though much of me hates being middle class. Mind, Terry could be middle class if he wanted. Instead he prefers to affect a cockney accent and ferment revolution on the dole.

Then Terry's physical presence intruded on Roy's reverie. He refocussed on his adversary.

'Mind if I join you, Roy?'

'My pleasure, Terry.'

The thirty-six-year-old pulled up a chair and sat down opposite the forty-five-year-old. The younger man was still smiling but now with both sides of his mouth.

'Nice to see you slumming, Roy,' Terry said.

'And I'm glad to hear you're still using my name in vain, Terry,' countered Roy, aching for a cigarette but determined not to show weakness.

For a right winger, Hampton, you're quite a decent bloke, Terry thought to himself, as he continued to gaze good-humouredly at the parliamentarian. But unfortunately for you, after my lunch tomorrow at County Hall you're going to have real problems, my friend. . . .

Wonder what he's thinking? Roy thought, his fingers teasing the cellophane off the cigarette packet in his pocket.

Terry smiled. 'I trust you're going to drop into our local General Management Committee next week to give us your Parliamentary Report, Roy. You know how much we look forward to listening to your legendary quips.'

The bastard's taunting me and there's nothing I can do about it, Roy thought. Sometimes I wish I shared his blind faith in full-blooded socialism. Unfortunately I don't have a clear-cut answer to the future, but I'm sure if we change things too precipitately, we could end up destroying more than we create. Or am I simply making excuses again?

His thoughts trailed off as he imagined himself as an elderly walrus, flapping along in vain pursuit of two errant schoolboys.

'Roy, I know it can be a bit tedious talking to yer actual rank-and-file,' Terry said, still smiling. 'But I must say I find it marginally insulting that you're so obsessed with your thoughts that you can't answer a comrade's question.'

'Sorry, Terry. Been one of those terrible days. But don't worry, I'll be there a week on Wednesday with my Parliamentary Report.' Roy couldn't bear the tension any longer so he pulled out the cigarette pack. 'You of course don't smoke, do you, Terry?'

'No, and if you knew what was good for you, you wouldn't either. But you don't know what's good for you, do you?'

Roy ignored this. 'Am I right in assuming, Terry, that there'll be even more delegates – of your persuasion – at the GMC next Wednesday? You have been recruiting like crazy recently, haven't you?'

'Have I?'

'Yes, but even if you flood the GMC with your Trots, you'll never kick me out as an MP! Never! Do you understand that, you sonova . . .?'

Roy clamped his mouth shut abruptly.

God, I never meant to say any of that! he thought. Talk about playing into his hands. Shows what a state I'm in.

Furious with himself, Roy stubbed out his cigarette. MacMaster continued to examine his fingernails. When he looked up, there was genuine pity in his eyes. The sense of triumph which had flooded through him was overwhelmed by a feeling of compassion for his political enemy. For Terry was certain that Hampton was the enemy of the working class. It was Hampton's bourgeois, wishy-washy thinking that was holding back the socialist deluge – and only the deluge could sweep away all the privilege, the monetarism, the big corporations, the public schools. . . .

Terry's eyes clouded over as he tried to disguise the fury of his thoughts. Well, there's no point in me pitying Hampton just because he has no self-control. I must get onto the streets, knocking on those doors, because the night's the best time for recruiting new members to the Party. First I'd better get my troops back to the office to lick all those lousy envelopes.'

Terry was now so engrossed in his plans that to his surprise he found he was standing. Then he realised Hampton was waving a truce-like arm at him.

'Listen, Terry,' Roy muttered. 'I didn't mean to be insulting. What I'm trying to say is that all of us in the Party here in Lamberton have got to find a way of working constructively together. Because I'm sure we can work together – if we try hard enough. Well, whether we like it or not, Terry, we are both on the same side of the fence. We're not stinking Tories! Let's face it, if we don't try to co-operate, it's those poor bastards out there who are going to suffer!'

Roy jabbed his thumb at the steamed-up window. As he did so, the diffused yellow light from the street lamps transformed the passers-by into hump-backed shadows in a ghost world.

'It's our job to try and make life better for those poor devils out there, Terry. That's why we've got to compromise to some degree, or all we'll end up with is a political bloodbath! So what do you say?'

Roy thought MacMaster was not going to respond. Then Terry turned back.

'Don't you see, comrade, that your entire problem is compromise? And it's too late for that now. Oh, I've nothing against you personally. You're just an historical anachronism. There's only one way to help the working class, and that's Tony Benn's way. And my way.'

The younger man didn't wait for a reply. He beckoned peremptorily at the two girls and the youth at the far table. Joan nodded and went to pay the bill.

Terry paused in the half-open doorway. 'No hard feelings, comrade. We've both got a job to do, and we see our mission in different ways, that's all.'

Without glancing at Roy, Terry's companions filed out past their leader into the street.

'Oh, Terry?' interjected Roy. 'There is one question I'd like to ask you.'

'Which is?'

'Do you hate Mrs Thatcher and her crew as much as you hate me and the rest of us so-called right wingers?'

The younger man thought for a moment, then laughed good-naturedly.

'You don't understand anything about being a Marxist, do you, Roy? Hatred doesn't come into the equation. If there are persons or institutions that stand between the working class and their rightful inheritance, they have to be swept aside. But it'll all be done quite impersonally, and strictly following the Party Rules. It's simply a question of the natural justice of history catching up with bourgeois tyranny. So, as I say, you shouldn't have any hard feelings, comrade.'

For a moment the quiet confidence in Terry's eyes was replaced by a cold glitter, but it passed as swiftly as it came. Then the revolutionary smiled warmly and strode off into the night.

He is a true believer, thought Roy as he paid for his tea. And like all true believers, despite his charm there is a fanaticism bubbling inside him. It's disconcerting that it rarely shows in his face. Or even in his eyes. Strange, because in his own way Terry is as dedicated and as obsessed by his cause as his hero Tony Benn, or his *bête noir* Enoch Powell. And their inner frenzy positively streams from their eyes.

Before he was aware of it, Roy had stepped out in the street. In the moonlight, the bleak architectural lines of the council estate were softened. Dazed-looking people shuffled by him and were swallowed up in the dark, but for a moment Roy was able to obliterate from his consciousness the ever-present sense of misery and deprivation. He was so overwhelmed by the night sky that he stopped in mid-step on the kerb and stared at the moon. Despite its luminous barrenness, he found its impassive presence in his world inexplicably reassuring. He couldn't understand why he should find it so reassuring. Then he remembered that it reminded him of a momentous evening twenty-one years ago.

It was on such a night he had asked Liz to marry him as they stood beside the railway siding in their home town, Peterborough. To his surprise she had said yes. They had made love on a bench by the River Nene and he was walking her home to the railway cottage where she lived with her parents. There had been a crisp March wind blowing then like tonight. It whipped her long flaxen hair out behind her, and her face was flushed with contentment. She stopped by the garden gate before he could open it and pointed up at the moon.

'Did you know the moon is really an enormous precious stone?' she murmured. 'And like all precious stones, although it's dead it still has a cold fire at its heart. That is why it's the central jewel on an invisible necklace – on which God has threaded all His stars.'

As Roy remembered the details of his engagement night, he smiled in the dark because he always prided himself on his memory. Something inside him insisted he train it diligently. It began at the age of eight when in one night he learned the part of Joseph in the school nativity play. That 'sacred moment of glory', performing Joseph in front of his admiring parents, spurred him to even greater acting heights over the years. That was why he inveigled his teachers to let him star in every school play that followed, culminating in the title role in *Hamlet* while he was in the upper sixth. Often during his school years he wondered whether he should be an actor, rather than a politician. But his father continually warned him that an actor's life was bloody insecure, so he decided it was safer to go to the London School of Economics rather than to the Royal Academy of Dramatic Art.

Roy walked on, no longer aware of the council house misery around him. Instead he recalled his years at the LSE where he spent most of his time playing leading roles for the college's Drama Society. When he left the LSE, it wasn't surprising he went on to the London School of Music and Drama to gain a Drama Teaching Diploma. Then from the age of twenty-five to thirty, when he became an MP, Roy taught drama at the local polytechnic.

As he skimmed over his past, he experienced a tremor of guilt about his years at the LSE, during which he'd almost destroyed another human being. To exorcise his guilt he stopped again to stare at the moon, because since the night of his engagement to Liz he had always believed that the moon belonged to his wife. He needed to picture her face so he could hide from his guilt and forget the other face.

I wonder if Liz still remembers what I said to her on our engagement night as we stared up at the moon? 'Well, Liz, your husband-to-be is not dead like the moon. Whatever "fire" is inside me isn't a "cold fire", it's a volcano! For I'm going to be at the forefront of a socialist crusade because I'm determined to help as many people as I can to have better lives, better jobs and better prospects!'

Roy was now walking rapidly to try and escape the implications of his crusading words. For he knew that whatever banners he had waved in his life, though they had cracked in the wind on occasions, they had failed to add up to a crusade. He was now on the outskirts of the estate, close to where he had parked his car. On his right, the tower blocks, with their cavernous car parks, were howling like the damned, strummed by the incessant wind. On his left, old newspapers flapped against a gutted Austin-Morris on a patch of wasteland.

Suddenly MacMaster's messianic face materialised in his mind's eye between the wrecked car and the moon. The storm-grey eyes were asking him the same question over and over: 'What can your eternal compromise and moderation do to change all this, comrade?'

Roy's tired brain tried to provide an instant answer, but as he knew that everything instant was political nonsense, he gave up. Then, to his surprise, he heard himself shouting to the deserted wasteland: 'Fuck politics!'

As he unlocked the car, the wind jeered at him.

So what! he thought. All I want to do now is to go home to Liz and the kids. At least whatever they say to me, they'll mean.

The room was small and unloved. Greyish walls, with faded ochre roses stencilled on them, converged on two battered armchairs, a lumpy forties sofa, a chipped coffee table and a narrow double bed. Threadbare lace curtains allowed the nine o'clock sunshine to stipple the air between the bed and the window with sparkling motes of dust. In the distance the town hall clock chimed the hour. The two occupants of the bed stirred. Terry fumbled on the wicker chair beside the bed in search of his black-strapped digital watch. He cursed as the watch eluded his fingers, then cursed louder as he knocked over an empty glass. As the tumbler rattled against the foot of the bed, the other occupant jerked awake.

'Wot the bleeding hell's going on, Terry?'

'Sorry, luv. Trying to get me bleeding watch and knocked over a bleeding glass!'

Terry, who always slept in the nude, rubbed his sleek torso against the girl's breasts.

'I think you've got the world's greatest tits, Angie. Always remind me of my Uncle Sid's fruit stall in Peckham. And he does the best line in yams this side of Trinidad.'

Angie giggled. Then before she could stop him, Terry tongued her nipples while his hand slipped eel-like between her thighs.

'Ain't you had enough, Terry? Your chin's all horrible and bristly. And you know I'm never over-keen of a morning. Hey, where you going?'

'To have a bath, aren't I?'

Terry was already halfway across the room. Then as he opened the door Angie sat bolt upright in bed. The sight of her extraordinary mouth-watering breasts brought him up short.

'Oh cover 'em up, for chrissake, baby, or I'll have to come back and molest you.'

Angie laughed, tossing her amber curls so they bounced on her shoulders. Terry continued to eat her with his eyes. He grabbed a damp towel from the back of the door to cover his growing excitement.

Shit, if I wasn't committed to changing the world, he thought, I'd spend the rest of my life kissing her lovely mouth. Actually, when you come to think of it, it's pretty ironic. Here am I, a dedicated, energetic Marxist, who is supposed to be as cool and detached as the proverbial cucumber, and yet just looking at her drives me crazy. Well, how many other Marxists have got an erotic-Big-Businessman's-Wet-Dream-Masterpiece as a girlfriend? Marx and Lenin weren't so lucky for a kick-off. She's the Marilyn Monroe of Lamberton North. Her every movement, whether it's that little pout or the spring of her breasts, is an invitation to an orgy. And what makes her so delicious is nearly all her sexuality's unconscious. God, if I go on looking at her, I'll have to have an orgy with her now. Trouble is, once I've got my hands on that superb body, I'll be helpless. To make things even more difficult, she loves me! Then, I suppose in my own way – God help her – I love her. Jesus! If she stretches like that again I've had it! And if I didn't have to get to County Hall by twelve....

'Stop looking at me like that, Terry. Your hard-on's showing under the towel. You know once you start, we'll never get any breakfast.'

'Yeah, and even worse, I'll be late for the Revolution.'

Minutes later Terry was lying in the badly-stained bath on the next landing. Streams of condensation ran down the walls of the bathroom. As always the bath water was tepid and someone had stolen most of the soap. Terry scrubbed his thighs with a pink plastic brush and enjoyed the sensation of his skin tingling.

Yes, it's going to be a good day, he thought. Lunch with Ken's friend at County Hall is going to be very interesting. Especially as the main subject on the agenda is Mr Roy Hampton. Oh shit! Almost forgot. I've got to go and sign on first. If only they'd just pay out the bloody dole money without all the rigmarole. Mind, living off the dole does have a nice irony to it. I mean, here I am working full-time to dismantle this rotten Capitalist System – and yet I'm being financed by the very system I'm dismantling! Still, all revolutionaries have to live off someone. And if Marx could live happily off Engels and drink Engels' champagne while he did a lot of his most constructive thinking, the very least I can do is live off the Welfare State while I put some of the Great Man's ideas into practice.

Terry stood at the middle of Wordsworth's favourite bridge, but he did not have Wordsworth on his mind. He was wondering what kind of day Roy Hampton was having in the sprawling Gothic pile on the north side of the Thames. Whenever Terry glimpsed the Mother of Parliaments, he always regarded her with the true Marxist-Leninist's contempt. In the dazzling April sunshine the building that housed the governors of the kingdom was to him merely an insubstantial, half-cleaned cut-out, with its elaborate towers, ornate spires and Big Ben swaddled in scaffolding. Then Terry peered down into the murk of the river where he made out Parliament's hazy reflection in the water. A police launch zoomed under the bridge and the spray from its bow cut the reflection in two. This amused him.

He turned back to look at the warm solidity of County Hall on the south bank. The well-proportioned, oblong seat of power of the Greater London Council always had an appeal for Terry.

There is nothing silly, fustian or faded Gothic about County Hall, he reflected. The building has a no-nonsense, down-to-earth look to it. I especially like that vast banner which stretches right across the building. What a brilliant idea of Ken Livingstone's it is to proclaim the exact numbers of London's unemployed in such a startling manner!

Yes, in fact, since Livingstone and his friends took over London, County Hall, for the first time in its history, has started to become the genuine political powerhouse of the working people of this godforsaken city. Which is why the Bitch wants to abolish it!

Terry was now on the Embankment and walking quickly towards County Hall.

Yes, there's no doubt that Ken's got a lot going for him. For as Lenin advised, Ken will change tack, reverse his argument without blinking, say yes when he means no, and no when he means yes. He'll do anything, everything, so long as the socialist cause goes forward. Also to his credit, unlike most Marxists, Ken's got a sense of humour, charisma, and is nearly always smiling. But most important of all, even at his most radical, say on the subject of squatters or the IRA, Ken always sounds plausible. In fact he's just the kind of man we need to charm the populace into accepting some of the more unpalatable changes that this country will have to undergo, in order that true socialism can be established once and for ever!

Terry paused on the third step leading to the entrance of County Hall. He realized he was still wearing his paint-stained jeans and his second skin, the black leather jacket.

Maybe I should have worn a tie? Ken always does. And in a way I've modelled my cheery personality on Ken's. I'm brighter than him, of course, and probably genuinely more likeable. Oh screw it! So I don't have a tie and I look a bit scruffy. So what! As Ibsen rightly said: 'There's no point in starting a revolution in your best suit!'

'I reserved us this table here by the window, Terry. So you can have a butchers at the river if you get bored with our little chat.'

Phil Wright grinned, showing his gold fillings, and indicated that Terry should sit facing the Thames. Terry grinned back and sat down, but behind his smile he felt out of place. County

Hall's palatial dining-room, with its plush curtains and crisp, white linen on the tables, made the social revolutionary uneasy. There was something vaguely indecent about eating an expense-account lunch, served by over-worked, middle-aged waitresses in starched blouses and black skirts, especially as it was being subsidised by the ratepayers. But Terry was certain he was the only one in the restaurant that felt that, because wherever he turned there were tables crammed with fat-arsed councillors, of every political persuasion, cheerfully ploughing through vast lunches.

'Why don't we order first, Terry? Then we can get down to some real intriguing, eh?'

Terry turned to face his host. The councillor was bulging out of a black polo-neck sweater, and he sported a gold chain with a St Christopher's medallion on the end of it. The doubtful combination worried Terry as to the ultimate seriousness of his host. However, Terry suppressed this feeling of unease because he knew the councillor was a very useful man – as long as you didn't get on the wrong side of him.

Terry had first met Phil at the Labour Party's Greater London Regional Council Annual Meeting two years earlier. Ever since, he had found Phil's advice invaluable, as far as what Phil called 'political intriguing' was concerned. Terry wished intriguing wasn't necessary, but during his tempestuous years at the LSE in the troubled sixties he had learnt that it was the only way to get anything done, certainly at local level.

'If you'll take my advice, Terry,' murmured Phil, having ordered a carafe of house burgundy for himself, 'you'll have the avocado and prawns for starters. Not even our chef can screw them up. Then the porterhouse steak's not too bad. As for the veg, well, that's in the lap of the gods. Sometimes it can be nice and crisp, but often as not the cabbage tastes like piss-water.'

Terry let Phil order for them both. He was rarely interested in food, especially at lunchtime.

'You sure you don't want anyfink to drink, Terry?'

'No, thanks. I'm a teetotaller.'

'Blimey! Had a bit of a problem with the sauce in the past, did you?'

'No. I've not had an alcoholic drink since I was sixteen. Then I was so sick on gin, I decided booze couldn't be good for me.

I've always been partial to certain kinds of discipline, so I've never touched a drop since. Though I have developed a penchant for grapefruit juice.'

'Holy shit.'

Moments later a tumbler of iced grapefruit juice was placed in front of Terry as he glanced surreptitiously at his watch. Phil noted the glance.

'OK, Terry, I know you find relaxation almost impossible.'

'That's nearly true but not quite,' Terry rejoined, instantly conjuring up Angie's superb breasts. 'It's just when I'm out for a working lunch, Phil, I like to work.'

Terry gestured to the other councillors in the buzzing dining-room who were variously contemplating the wine lists and savouring the dessert trolley. 'Which is more than can be said for this shower.'

Phil snorted and refilled his glass. 'Wait till you have power, Terry, and then we'll see whether you're so bloody pure when it comes to the fleshpots.'

'I wasn't casting aspersions, Phil. I simply want to get Roy Hampton out of the way. And quickish. You said you might have some ideas.'

'All right, Terry, I can see you're getting itchy. Let's get down to cases. Now you want to ensure, via your local General Management Committee, that Roy Hampton will cease to be your MP come his reselection in December. Right?'

'In a nutshell.'

'Then let me refresh my memory as to the various elements that make up your current General Management Committee. Oh, but don't hesitate to put me right if I go wrong. Ah, here's our nosh. Well, *bon appetit* – as we're still forced to say in the Common Market.'

Phil refurbished his glass with wine and swigged it back.

'Now I think I'm right in saying, Terry, that your local GMC is at this moment composed of forty delegates from the various wards in your constituency, plus five delegates from the trades union branches, and one delegate each from the Co-operative Party, the Society of Labour Lawyers, the Fabian Society and the Socialist Education Association respectively. That's about the lot at present, ain't it?'

'Not quite, Phil. There are two delegates from the Socialist

Feminist Movement who always vote our way. Officially they're in the Women's Section, of course.'

'Of course. But according to what you told me on the blower last week, you and the comrades still ain't got the majority you need on the GMC in order to stop Hampton being reselected, right?'

'Yeah. You see, quite a few of the delegates from the wards are still right-wing Labour, plus half the trades unions. So we need at least six new delegates on our side to have an overall majority. Then we can relegate Hampton to the dustbin of history where he belongs!'

'Hey, Terry! Watch all that dialectical rhetorical stuff in here. Ken prefers us to keep that stuff outside County Hall. In the dining-room he likes us to talk wiv a little more finesse.'

Terry smiled with the left side of his mouth. He wanted to smile with both sides but restrained the impulse. He picked at the overdone steak. Phil attacked his steak like an apprentice in a butcher's shop, which under the circumstances wasn't surprising as his was beautifully underdone.

'But am I not right in saying, as far as the wards go in your constituency, Terry, for the first fifty people who are recruited as members of the Party, four of them come as delegates to your GMC? And then for every twenty-five people who are recruited to the Party thereafter, only one of them comes as an actual delegate?'

'Yeah, this is all true, Phil, but I don't see . . .'

'Now don't get impatient wiv me, Terry. Impatience leads to cock-ups and bad politics! If you want Hampton by the balls, you've got to do it carefully, and thoroughly. So what I'm recommending is this: in the next few days you and your like-minded comrades should go out into the council estates and the tower blocks, and you should concentrate entirely on recruiting old-age pensioners.'

'What?'

'Will you just shut up and listen to your Uncle Phil a minute, Terry? As I was saying, you should concentrate your efforts on recruiting OAPs as members of the Party. See, OAPs only have to cough up a mere fifty pence a year subscription to become members. Anyroad, they live such rotten lives that you'll easily recruit 'em. Well, you just think of the old folks' grievances. If it's not hypothermia, it's damp, bad pensions, the blacks as neighbours and smells of Indian cooking. So you name it and they'll moan about it.'

Phil paused to spit out some gristle. 'Then when you've recruited all you can of the OAPs, you next want to turn your attention to the long-term unemployed. Again, in the council estates and the tower blocks because that's where you'll find most of 'em. And they're filled with even more hatred and disillusion than the OAPs. You'll only have to mention the word Tory, and anyone who's unemployed will immediately tell you what uncaring fascist pigs Thatcher and her heavy mob are! Also, Unwaged Persons only have to pay two quid subscription a year.'

Terry put his knife and fork down and stared at a bluebottle on the curtain. Then he nodded at Phil who was now on his fourth glass of burgundy.

'You really think that we can recruit enough OAPs and unemployed to . . .?'

Irritably Phil cut him short: 'With your soft-soap and charm, Terry, it'll be a walk-over. I mean, Christ, look how Ted Knight and the boys in '76 got them licensed squatters to take over the derelict property in Lambeth that the Lambeth Council couldn't afford to renovate. And why did Ted do that? He did it because he knew most of them squatters would be disillusioned, middle-class drop-outs, wiv a distinct leaning towards the left. So once Ted got 'em into the derelict properties, he immediately recruited 'em into the Party at ten pence per head. Then he persuaded them to help him oust the right-wingers off the Council. Which, as you know, is why Lambeth has been left-wing ever since. But that's the beauty of working for the Labour Party, Terry, ain't it? You're allowed to recruit anybody that takes your fancy. It don't matter whether they're on the electoral roll or not. Or what their nationality is. Or even if they're only over here on holiday!'

Phil laughed, then prodded an ivory toothpick between his rear molars.

'So what Ted did with the squatters in '76, you've got to do with your down-and-outs now! It's important you follow in Ted's inspiring footsteps because Ted's always been a shining example of applied socialist initiative. It's the duty of all true socialists to recruit the most promising type of person, which in your case is the most demoralised and fucked-up type of person. Then if some of the most fucked-up ones should happen to become delegates – and I'm sure you can fix it that they do become delegates on your GMC – they can always be relied on to vote for your candidates come Hampton's reselection. They'll be only too happy to help you kick Hampton out on his ear!'

Phil waved his fork at a waitress.

'Can I have another jacket potato, luv? This time with sour cream and chives, and not that rancid butter, OK?'

The waitress gave him an inscrutable grimace.

'Hey, you all right, Terry?' Phil asked, seeing him frown.

'Yes, thanks. I was just thinking . . .'

Terry trailed off and peered out of the window at the sunlit river.

'Wot were you finking?'

Terry was too embarrassed to tell the councillor, because he was thinking how radiant the embankment looked in the sunshine, with the fresh spring green stippling the branches of the trees. As an avowed Marxist-Leninist, Terry chided himself for allowing romantic sentimentality to blur his concentration. But the sight of the wheeling birds, the shiny leaves and the legendary London skyline made him wonder if there wasn't another way of recruiting membership to the Party. It went against the grain to have to recruit the old, the decrepit and the dispossessed. Especially as the only reason he would be recruiting them was because they *were* the old, the decrepit and the dispossessed. Worse, he was going to have to recruit them in a hurry.

'Hey, Terry!' snapped Phil. 'You're not going soft on us, are you? You've got that milky faraway look in your eyes. Bit like my missus when she used to get broody.'

Terry refocussed on Phil's chewing mouth.

'No, don't worry, comrade, I'm not going soft. I was only thinking about how unfortunate it is that we have to use pensioners and folk who are out of a job, simply to put our reactionary MP out of *his* job.'

Phil laughed. 'It's quite natural to have scruples, Terry. You've just got to be careful never to let 'em cloud your political judgement. In order that we can help the working class to help themselves, we must use every weapon in the Party's arsenal.'

'Of course you're right,' assented Terry, pushing his scarcely-touched plate of food to one side. 'As always, Lenin put his finger on it, didn't he?'

'Did he?'

'Absolutely. Vladimir Illyich once wrote: "Those who are engaged in the formidable task of overcoming Capitalism, must be prepared to try method after method until they find the one which answers their purposes best. For to be afraid of the dictatorship of the proletariat or of conspiratorial organisation, and to sigh for democratic liberties, is mere opportunism".'

The councillor looked worried and for the first time stopped eating. He cocked an eyebrow towards the other councillors in the dining room.

'Look, I know you've had the doubtful advantage of a proper education at the LSE, Terry, but for Pete's sake, keep your voice down!'

'Why should I keep my voice down?'

Phil leaned over his glass of wine and whispered: 'If any of these councillors hear you quoting from Lenin, they could easily get their pink frilly knickers in a twist. Lenin may be right about many fings – which of course he is – but he ain't British, is he? And anyfink that ain't British makes a lot of our softer comrades round here nervous. Which reminds me, we ain't discussed what you should do about the trades unions in your parish.'

'Well, some of *them* are ultra keen on Lenin,' smirked Terry, inwardly congratulating himself that he was the only person in the dining room without a tie.

'Very funny, Terry,' rejoined Phil without smiling. 'All I've got to say about the unions is this: make sure you recruit as many delegates as possible from the right unions – or should I say the left-left unions?'

'Don't worry, we've already done well with the ASTMS and NUPE. Then of course there's ASLEF. And we've even got a crazy-crazy from TASS. He's so far to the left he even takes *my* breath away.'

While the waitress was removing their plates, Terry paused because he noticed his host was no longer listening to him. The fat man had been distracted by the approaching vision of the sweet trolley.

'Oh, miss,' drooled Phil. 'D'you fink I could have some of that delicious looking trifle? Oh, and put a couple of them figs on the side. I'll come back later for the profiteroles. And when you've done, I'd like a large glass of Sauternes. The chateau-bottled Sauternes, mind. Not the rubbish.'

Terry was now feeling distinctly ill. Although he had hardly eaten anything himself, simply watching this socialist Falstaff at work was enough to make him feel as if he had swallowed a mountain of food. Not only was the sheer quantity that the fat man consumed daunting, but the speed with which he shovelled it down should surely be in the *Guinness Book of Records.*

And I've got to go out into the streets, he thought, to recruit people to the Party who would give their right arms to even gaze at food like this, let alone be allowed to eat it!

Terry pushed his chair back abruptly.

'If you'll excuse me, Phil, I think I'd better be going. I'm very grateful for all your advice but . . .'

'You don't have to go yet, Terry, surely? I thought we'd nip back to my office for a cigar and some brandy. Or, in your case, fruit juice.'

'That's very kind of you, Phil, but I ought to be getting back.'

'Well, I hope I've been of some help,' sulked the councillor, as he turned his plate of trifle into a veritable wasteland. 'Oh, before you go, there is just one other fing. I forgot to mention that you should also try to fix the votes for the Co-op and Fabian Society. And also organise all the other branches of Socialist Societies to send sympathetic delegates to your GMC.'

'Don't worry, we got our active left wingers to join the Fabian Society and the other affiliated Socialist Societies. Then when they go to the Annual Meetings of these societies, they naturally ensure that our candidate gets elected as the delegate to our GMC.'

'Excellent. Then it's only a question of time, Terry, and you'll clean up. Well, it always works, dunnit? This fixing. The other side, thank God, are too stupid and too lazy to fix anything! That's why most right-wing Labour MPs have such a miniscule membership in their constituency. They simply haven't bothered to fix anyfink. Oh, I know Roy Hampton bothers but not in the right way. He's so busy trying to get his constituents to like him, he doesn't spend enough time protecting his home base.'

Terry stood up. He looked round the room. Everyone was still scoffing and boozing. He felt that if he didn't leave immediately, there was a chance he'd puke up his breakfast over Phil's rapidly-diminishing profiteroles. The fat man belched and placed a clammy paw on Terry's wrist. He had been aching to touch his guest throughout the meal but this was his first legitimate opportunity.

'Just thought of something very humorous, Terry.'

'What's that?'

'Well, although numerically there's still so few of us real socialists who have any genuine power, it's extraordinary how the few of us have been able to fix so much in so short a time.'

'What's so funny about it?'

'It's the only thing that Churchill was ever right about.' The councillor guffawed as he mimicked the Great War Leader. 'Never before in the course of human history . . . has so much . . . been owed by so many . . . to so *few*!'

APRIL

It was a quarter to seven on a Wednesday evening in the second week of April. Wilberforce Close was deserted as the five-year-old, navy-blue Ford estate shuddered to a halt outside Number Twelve.

Roy Hampton grunted, switched off the engine and then cursed: 'God damn this bloody safety belt! Why does the sodding thing always get stuck on my Parliamentary Report night?'

He was disturbed in his fight with the seat belt by a tap on the window. Roy scowled and wound it down. A smooth-faced City gent in his mid-forties was grinning at him.

'Why don't you do us all a big favour, Roy?'

'Such as?'

'Why don't you buy yourself a decent car for once?'

'Because I can't bloody afford one, Adrian!'

Using all his strength Roy yanked at his recalcitrant safety belt for the umpteenth time. To his amazement he pulled it out of its socket. Shaking his head in disbelief, he reached over the back seat and collected his briefcase. Then he got out of the Ford and locked it. Adrian Royce, his next-door neighbour, was still smirking.

'Yes, I know, Adrian. You wonder how I can afford to live round here at all. Especially on an MP's salary.'

Adrian followed Roy's sweeping glance to take in the row of elegant Georgian houses in which they both lived.

'You see, what you're always forgetting, Adrian,' Roy explained patiently, 'is that I bought my house long before the rest of you rich City whizz kids bought yours. In the early sixties when we first came here this part of Lamberton was still pretty much of a slum. That's why I was able to get it comparatively cheaply. My problem now is I can hardly afford its upkeep.

You've only got to compare my place with yours to see who is in fiscal clover. You've ponced your place up so much, like the rest of the high-fliers in this road, that Wilberforce Close is now known as Nobs' Row. Though I do realise, of course, my dump doesn't look as nobby as the rest.'

Roy grinned and pointed to a section of guttering, precariously suspended thirty feet above his small, untidy front garden. Then he indicated the front of the house which needed a fresh coat of paint.

'Yes, I must say, Roy, your place in its present state does rather lower the tone of the neighbourhood. It's not that I like saying this, you understand, but . . .'

Roy interrupted him: 'Now don't be a fibber, Adrian. Nothing gives you greater pleasure than reading me the Tory-House holders' Riot Act.'

'There's no need to bring politics into it, Roy,' Adrian muttered, self-consciously adjusting his silk tie.

'How can I not bring politics into it, Adrian? Whether you like it or not, politics influences almost everything we say and do.'

'Hm!' sniffed his neighbour, now on his guard, and wanting to beat a dignified retreat but not knowing how.

'Now don't get your knickers in a twist, Adrian. I promise the minute I've got some spare cash, I'll have the place painted and some new guttering put up. As a bonus, I may even splurge out and have a bright-red burglar alarm attached above our bedroom window. Well, it will make a nice contrast to your blue one, won't it? And once I've got my burglar alarm I'll no longer be the odd man out in the Close. What's more important, I'll look as rich as you obviously all are!'

Adrian was not amused but he couldn't think of a crisp rejoinder, so he executed a superior sniff and turned on his heels. Then he walked the length of his freshly painted garden wall, opened his freshly painted garden gate and strode up to his freshly painted front door. Then to his chagrin he discovered he had left his key in the office and was forced to ring his own bell.

Roy smiled. Well, I might as well smile now, he thought, because the rest of the evening is likely to be a nightmare.

He was pushing his front gate open when suddenly he remembered what he'd forgotten. Cursing, he ran back to his car, unlocked it, fell into the driving seat, and without fastening his safety belt, drove out of the Close.

Liz Hampton always preferred marking homework in her red-and-white-tiled kitchen. It was the one room in their otherwise ramshackle house that had been modernised. Unconsciously she stroked the pine table as she wriggled her bottom into a more comfortable position on the pine bench. Then she scratched the tip of her ear with a ruler, wrinkled her nose and refocussed on Roland Kimble's homework. She was about to correct another spelling mistake when the ear-shattering sound of heavy rock music erupted from the living room.

'Will you please turn that record-player off, Alexa, and do your French and biology homework.'

The music continued to pound through the house.

'Alexa, I won't tell you again! Switch that bloody racket off!'

In response, the kitchen door clicked open and Alexa, Liz's daughter, appeared framed in the doorway. Alexa was fourteen years old but looked eighteen. Her oval face was framed in a mass of blonde hair, highlighted with silver streaks. Her mouth was overpainted with a shocking-pink lipstick and her eyelashes were so weighed down with purple mascara that she could hardly keep her huge brown eyes open.

I do wish she wouldn't stick her breasts out like that, thought her mother. And if her jeans were any tighter, she wouldn't be able to walk at all! No wonder the boys buzz round her like wasps round a jamjar. Trouble is, girls develop so quickly these days.

Liz remembered herself as a teenager when she was at the County Grammar School for Girls in Peterborough. She saw herself in her chocolate-brown uniform, her satchel over her shoulder, as the King School boys rode by her on their bicycles, waving and blowing kisses.

Mind, I'd hardly developed bust-wise at all when I was fourteen, she thought, relieved that her youth was over. Then she returned to the present, and to her daughter who was pouring herself some milk from the fridge.

Alexa's already nearly as tall as I am, she thought. She must be all of five-foot-seven. Yet beneath that gaudy sophistication she's still a child, though she thinks she's a woman. So whenever we treat her as a child, which we do when she's cheeky or lazy, she bursts into tears and hates us.

'Why you always starin' at me critically, Mum?' scowled Alexa, refilling her glass with milk.

And why's she got that bad Cockney accent? Liz sighed, drifting off into her thoughts. I know she's picked it up from her comprehensive, but I still believe she deliberately flaunts it in front of Roy and me because she know it irritates us.

'You're doin' it again, Mum!' her daughter protested, gyrating round the kitchen in time to the heavy beat of the rock music, which was still blaring from the living room.

'Doing what, dear?'

'Starin' at me!'

'Sorry, dear, it's just, well, you look so tarty with all that make-up.'

'I'm not a tart!' Alexa screeched in her most refined Billingsgate manner.

'I didn't say you *were* a tart, dear. I said you *look* tarty. For godsake, stop grinding your hips! Can't you see I've got this pile of marking to finish? I can't even think with the noise of that record!'

'It ain't a record! It's Charlie an' his Bangers on the telly.'

'I don't care what it is, Alexa. Switch it off and go up and do your homework. You'll never get your O-levels at this rate. And your father and I are sick of going up to your school to listen to your teachers' complaints.'

Alexa laughed. 'OK, OK, Mum, don't get your knickers in a twist. Anyroad, you should count yourself lucky.'

'Why?'

'Well, at least *you're* not one of the teachers who has to teach me, are you?'

Still laughing, Alexa danced out of the kitchen and banged the door behind her.

'How many times have I told you not to bang that door?'

Wearily Liz returned to her marking. She didn't look up as her husband dumped his briefcase on the far end of the table.

'Your curry's in the oven, darling. I'm afraid the rice is overdone but there's some dahl.'

'Oh I'm not up to curry, Liz, thanks.' He glanced at the electric clock. 'Discovered I was out of fags so I had to nip to the off-licence and I'm running late already.'

'Yes, don't you have to deliver your report to the GMC tonight?'

'Afraid so. The time I waste is unbelievable. I mean, there I was, teasing Adrian when I should've been in here grabbing a bite.'

'Don't know why you always have to be so awful to Adrian, darling. He can't help being a Tory. Everybody has to have some disease and that's his.'

Roy laughed and studied the slender nape of his wife's neck as she continued marking. He counted five white hairs in her flaxen locks which she had bound up in her habitual schoolteacher's bun. He admired her determined, high cheekbones, the little nose and the sad, brown eyes.

His wife looked up: 'Have you been boozing at the Commons?'

'Why do you ask that?' Roy growled.

'You've got the beginnings of a double chin, dear, and your collar looks a bit tight round your neck.'

'So I've been drinking a little more than usual? Spending the hours I do on that lousy Select Committee is enough to drive a nun to drink.'

With a smouldering cigarette in the corner of his mouth, Roy yanked a three-quarters-empty bottle of Teachers from the shelf reserved for cookery books. Liz gazed at him steadily.

'There have been several calls for you,' she said.

'I'll deal with 'em later. Just having this drink and then I'm off.'

He had hardly finished pouring himself a large Scotch when to his consternation he discovered he had drunk most of it.

'Where are the kids?'

'Sebastian's upstairs doing his homework and Alexa's watching the telly but ought to be doing her homework.'

Roy slammed his glass on the table.

'Someone should smash that bloody telly! All there is night after night are American cop movies and *Dallas*! No wonder everybody's so full of violence and envy!'

'God, you're in a foul mood.'

'Sorry, love, but I've got this bad feeling about the GMC meeting this evening.'

'Should you drink like that on an empty stomach?'

'No, but it might settle the queasiness I've had all day and give me the courage to deal with those Trot bastards tonight!' he rasped, gulping down another mouthful.

'Why do you always call the Trots bastards? They're not really that bad,' Liz said, meaning it. 'Anyway, what harm can they possibly do you tonight? They know damn well you're as good a constituency MP as any of the others around. Actually you're a sight better than most.'

'That's not what my local Executive thinks, and they're the "comrades" who matter,' Roy snapped back, finishing his Scotch.

Then he dragged his briefcase across the table and shuffled through its contents. Liz poured herself a glass of tonic water. Then, with concern in her eyes, she came over to him.

'You really are worried, darling, aren't you?'

'Yes. There's bound to be a lot of new faces there tonight.'

Liz laughed: 'So there are some new faces?'

Roy glanced at the final paragraph of his parliamentary report, then thrust it back into the briefcase.

'MacMaster's such a cunning sod. Every month he brings on new, hand-picked delegates, and they're all of a like persuasion.'

'You mean they're all real socialists?'

'They're not socialists, they're lousy Trots!'

'Maybe they'll give the Party some long-overdue backbone.'

'Some backbone! Jesus God!'

Still smiling, Liz returned to the pile of exercise books. 'Where is your radical spirit?'

'Not with Leon-bleeding-Trotsky! Trouble is, I don't know where half of MacMaster's so-called delegates come from. Except out of the woodwork.'

'Why don't *you* go recruiting yourself and find some right-wing delegates?'

'Haven't the time to recruit. I've been in the Commons for nearly twelve hours a day for the last six weeks. But I can't stand here jabbering, I'm going to be late as it is. And for every minute I'm late, you can bet that MacMaster will produce another new Trotskyite bunny out of his hat!'

'If the Trots are soon going to be in a majority on the Executive and you haven't got time to recruit right-wingers – well, if you can't beat 'em, darling, don't you think perhaps it would be wiser to . . .?'

'To join 'em?!' screeched Roy in disbelief.

'There's no need to burst a blood vessel. You know perfectly well that during these last few months you have moved farther and farther to the right of the Party, and now you're out on a limb. All I'm saying is, if you don't want to be chopped off, it might be more sensible . . .'

'No, no, no!' Roy raged. 'Someone's got to stand up to Tony Benn and his craziness! And most of them who'll be there tonight support Tony Benn.'

'You're not thinking of standing up to them tonight, though, are you, darling?'

'God knows! But if those bastards are as rough on me as they were last time, I might go crazy and tell them exactly what I think of them. You've no idea what it's like in that place.' Roy broke off and wrenched open the door. 'Why don't you join me for a drink at the Red Cockerel after? That's of course if I'm still in one piece.'

His wife half-rose from her seat. 'I'm sorry, darling, I didn't mean to upset you.'

But Roy had gone. Liz followed him into the hall, only to see the front door slam. Now upset herself, she ran down the steps and called to Roy as he climbed into the car.

'Darling!'

As he turned on the ignition, he barked: 'Yes?'

If only I can make him laugh, she thought. That always lowers the temperature and makes marriage bearable.

'If I were you, darling, I'd run a comb through your hair,' she said.

'Why?'

'Because it's standing on end in protest.'

But Liz's quip didn't work and the car hurtled off into the growing dusk. As she went back to the house, she glimpsed her seventeen-year-old son, Sebastian, behind the second-floor window. He was doing his homework in a pool of light from the lamp on his desk. His long, sad face was rigid with concentration. His untidy mop of hair flopped across his eyes. Impatiently he brushed it back, then flicked through another reference book, found what he wanted and wrote furiously.

Suddenly Liz felt tired. What is going to become of us all? she thought as she went back into the house. She sighed outside the closed door of the living room. The heavy rock music was no longer so loud but was still apparent. She paused at the foot of the stairwell. Half of her wanted to run upstairs and throw her arms round her work-crazy son, but she knew it wouldn't be appreciated. Sebastian was desperate to do well in his A-levels, so he generally worked until one in the morning. As he explained to his mother: 'You have to work twice as hard in a comprehensive as they do in the public schools, especially if you want to go to Oxbridge. Oh, I know that you and Dad, as traditional Labour, disapprove of Oxford and Cambridge, but I still believe it's the best education going, so I intend to get a place there and do chemistry.'

That's all very well, thought Liz, wearily returning to the kitchen, where she poured some gin into her tonic. But even if you do get a good degree, it won't guarantee you a job. And if your father decides to make his stand against the Trots tonight, he might also end up without a job before the year's over. I suppose I can keep us all on my part-time teacher's salary. Though knowing my luck, the Local Education Authority will probably dispense with my services, too. Then what will become of us all?

Then in her mind's eye she saw into ten million kitchens simultaneously, where ten million housewives were forever washing dishes, cooking dreary meals, ironing ragged shirt-collars and worrying about their husbands and children – as she was at that moment. They were all saying over and over again: 'With all this unemployment and hopelessness and helplessness and everlasting drudgery, what will become of us . . . ?'

As the first smarting tears pricked the corners of her eyes, Liz buried her head in her hands. As she wept, she knew she was being indulgent and foolish.

I'm probably just overtired. There's nothing I can do to help those desolate women, especially those who have husbands who are unemployed. Weeping helps nobody, but it brings temporary release. Though if the truth were known, perhaps the only person I'm really crying for is myself.

With a startled cry, she whirled round, sniffing the air.

Wherever's that dreadful smell coming from?!

Then she recognised the pungent odour of burning spices and wrenched open the oven door, only to discover the smoking remains of Roy's chicken vindaloo. Liz thought about crying again but decided it was too exhausting. Instead she burst out laughing.

It's only too obvious what's going to become of us all, she thought, with tears of laughter in her eyes. Only too obvious. . . .

The Labour Party Hall in North Lamberton, with its grey walls and creaking floorboards, was in its habitual state of disrepair. The huge, yellowing photographs of Keir Hardie, Nye Bevan and the other stalwarts of the left, interspersed with old election posters, could not hide the thousands of spidery cracks in the plaster, or bring any genuine good cheer into the long, depressing room. In the hall there were sixty-six uncomfortable wooden chairs, forty-three of which were occupied by restless young men and women with angry faces and smouldering cigarettes. The older folk sat at the back by the main door. They were also smoking and coughing but bored by the proceedings.

At the far end of the hall was a two-foot-high rostrum, dominated by a heavy oak table covered with a red tasselled cloth. Terry MacMaster, as the chairman of the GMC, sat in the central position behind the table. To his left was Joe Smithers, the Party secretary. To his right, at the far end of the table, stood Roy Hampton with his hands in his pockets. Roy was trying to deliver his parliamentary report, 'trying' being the operative word because few of the delegates were listening. They were too busy laughing at their own derisive jokes. Roy noted there were several of his friends dotted about the hall but they were cowed into silence. Many of his supporters had not turned up because they were sick of the in-fighting and the relentless pressure from Terry and his acolytes.

Roy cleared his throat again in an attempt to make himself heard, but the continuous jeers and insults from the floor soon reduced him to silence.

Every month it gets worse, he thought, clumsily pouring himself a glass of water. He tried to drink it but his hand was shaking so much that he only succeeded in rattling the lip of the tumbler against his teeth and pouring more than a quarter of its contents down his red tie. Hastily he put the tumbler down on the table. He opened his mouth to continue but the delegates again commanded him to sit down and shut up.

Then Roy's old right-wing Labour friend, Councillor Harold Bunting, wheezed to his feet to offer support but instantly was shouted down and shoved back into his seat. The councillor gave the MP a despairing look as he put his hands over his ears to shut out the clamouring voices.

Inwardly sighing, Roy squinted into the smoke-filled hall, noting the new faces.

I certainly don't remember those two old ladies, he thought, or that tramp with the pipe. And those new younger ones have a gaunt, unemployed look about them. No question about it. This time MacMaster's moving in for the kill.

As there was an unexpected momentary lull in the abuse coming up from the body of the hall, Roy launched into the tail-end of his report.

'So I'd like to conclude, comrades, by reiterating what I tried to say earlier, and that is, we in the Parliamentary Labour Party have been having a great deal of constructive discussion on the whole nuclear issue. . . .'

Roy hardly got the word 'nuclear' out when the heckling started up. It was lead by Dave Pickles, an over-earnest wood-work teacher in his mid-twenties.

'Look, why don't you cut the crap, Hampton, and stop sittin' on the fence and flanellin'.'

'The kind of heated discussion we're having in the PLP on Defence can hardly be termed flanelling, Comrade Pickles,' Roy flared back, trying to keep a rein on his temper.

As he snapped at the woodwork teacher, he caught a glimpse of Terry MacMaster's famous half-smile. Then Geraldine O'Hara, a dumpy social worker, leapt to her feet.

'Question is, Comrade Hampton, do you or do you not support the Annual Conference's decision to go completely unilateralist?'

'As you well know, Comrade O'Hara, in the PLP there are still many of us who favour the UK maintaining a multilateral nuclear policy. And I think it's the only sensible course, faced as we are with potential Soviet aggression.'

Her eyes blazed: 'Are you saying that you categorically refuse to uphold the decision of the Annual Conference?'

Roy shook his head. 'Of course I'm not refusing to uphold the decision of the Annual Conference. But as there are many of us in the Party that passionately believe in multilateralism, we are trying to find a way of making our views compatible with those in the unilateralist lobby.'

Again Dave Pickles was on his feet, waving his arms: 'And you don't call that a load of old flannel?'

Before Pickles had finished, several other delegates were jeering and waving. Roy noticed a new delegate in particular, a wiry bearded man, who pointed an imperious finger at him.

'Yeah, comrade, if you don't accept Conference decision, you should resign your seat so we can select a real socialist to represent us here in Lamberton North!'

Everyone had been waiting for this. Within seconds most of the delegates were waving their fists at Roy and chanting their litany of hate. Roy made a soothing gesture over the angry groundswell, then shouted out his defence.

'Comrades! Just because I don't agree with Conference on this particular issue, it doesn't make me any less of a socialist. Indeed, if you knew the history of our Great Movement, you'd be the first to acknowledge that all Labour administrations since the Second World War have consistently been multilateralist – like I am! It's true: Attlee, Gaitskell, Wilson and Callaghan always had a multilateralist policy.'

This brought on another storm of abuse, but the wiry man made his ringing tones heard above the clamour.

'Yeah, you're right about that, Comrade Hampton. It's scum like Gaitskell and Wilson that have continually betrayed the working class! Gaitskell was just a dirty warmonger who betrayed us every time he opened his middle-class mouth! Look how he was always trying to stop the CND marches!'

'There's betrayal and betrayal, comrades,' Roy shouted back.

'Are you accusing us who support CND of betraying the working class, then?' challenged a gaunt woman from the centre of the hall.

The noise subsided as the delegates waited impatiently for Roy to answer. The MP downed the last of his water and again shook his head.

'Oh, I'm not saying that most of you who back CND aren't genuine, peace-loving democratic socialists. But I don't need to tell you that there are a fair number of so-called "comrades" who march beside you who are in fact fully-paid-up members of the Communist Party.'

This assertion was countered by a barrage of cat-calls and

cries of 'Slander' and 'Stop smearing!' But Roy was determined to finish his reply and pounded the red tablecloth with his fist until his empty tumbler jumped onto its side.

'And whether you like it or not, comrades,' Roy roared above the tumult, 'those CND communists are not interested in peace at all. Because they take their orders from the Kremlin! Well, it's a known fact that from Stalin's time onwards, the Soviet leadership has always used the peace movements in the West to undermine our internal security. So the CND communists in your midst are Moscow's tentacles. And they're working towards the Finlandization of our great country. So if you're talking of *real* betrayal, comrades, why don't you ferret out the real enemies of the working class, and pour your righteous indignation down on them for once?'

The end of Roy's speech was drowned by the delegates baying for his blood.

'Why don't you go back to Nobs' Row where you belong, you two-faced bastard?' screamed a frenzied intellectual from the side aisle. He was immediately capped by a bald giant in a faded blue duffel-coat.

'Don't worry, Comrade Peters,' he thundered. 'Our beloved MP won't be around us much longer!' Then he scythed his arm round until his forefinger was pointing at the MP's forehead. 'Can't you see Hampton's got the Mark of Cain on him, comrades?'

Roy had had enough. He picked up the fallen tumbler and stood it back on its base. With an exhausted smile, he made a final placating gesture towards the convulsed faces below him.

'Yes, well, thank you, comrades, for yet another vote of confidence. As always it gives me profound pleasure delivering my parliamentary report to such sympathetic ears.'

'Class traitor! Class traitor! Class traitor!' was the response to his weary irony. Roy shrugged and sat down.

As he poured himself another glass of water, he noticed a religious hush had fallen on the hall. The delegates had gone quiet because the person addressing them was the GMC's chairman, Comrade Terry MacMaster.

'Well, thank you, Comrade Hampton, for yet another succinct, if marginally ambivalent, parliamentary report.' Terry beamed at Roy. 'And now you've heard it, comrades, I'm sure some of you might like to question our MP about it?'

Oh, not more bloody questions! Roy thought, closing his eyes and wishing to heaven he was asleep and this was a nightmare from which he could wake up. Biting his lower lip, he forced his eyes open to see Terry pointing at a redheaded girl in the second row. As she stood up, Roy realised he had seen her somewhere before. Then she smiled radiantly at the chairman and he remembered where. She was the girl who had warned Terry of Roy's presence in Zorba's Café last Monday.

'Yes, Comrade Keithley,' the chairman murmured, 'As you're one of our new delegates, perhaps you'd like to kick off?'

Joan Keithley turned her large grey-green eyes onto the MP.

Jesus, Roy thought, what an attractive girl she is! He even liked the way her red hair was cut short like a boy's. Then he noticed the cigarette which smouldered habitually between her elegant fingers. To his surprise, she acknowledged his appreciative stare with the beginnings of a smile, but the sexual undercurrent evaporated as she posed her first question.

'All I want to ask is whether our Member of Parliament is on the side of progressive socialism or not?'

Here we go again, he thought, the usual honest-sounding trick question. Well, the only thing I can do is give her the usual honest-sounding evasive answer.

'It depends what you mean by progressive socialism, Comrade Keithley.'

Instantly a wave of restless hostility washed round the hall. The cigarette smoke was now so dense that Roy felt as if he were the Ancient Mariner and the Labour Party was his albatross, and they were both lost and drifting helplessly through miles and miles of sea-fog.

'Well, either you are a progressive socialist or you're not, Comrade Hampton! And the quickest way for us to find out whether you are is for us to hear your cogent thoughts on foreign policy. I choose foreign policy as you're always going on about it in the Commons. So presumably you regard yourself as an expert on the subject?'

'Yes, it's true I've always been interested in foreign affairs, but I'd never call myself an expert.'

'No buts, comrade! Let's just have a straight answer for once.'

'Yeah, let's 'ave a straight answer! It'll make a change,' chorused jeering delegates.

Joan took a quick drag on the remains of her Gauloise, then launched her Exocet straight at Roy.

'Why have you never supported us in our campaign to have cruise missiles and their bases dismantled?'

Roy groaned inwardly. He felt too tired to answer and his mouth was parched because of the tobacco smoke. He croaked: 'As I keep telling you, Comrade Keithley, some of us in the PLP still believe . . .'

'Your beliefs have nothing to do with it! Conference has made its views abundantly clear on this matter. And either you are going to uphold Conference Decision and support us in this constituency in our determination to kick the Yanks and all their bases out of this country, so that we can set up a nuclear-free zone here in Britain, or you're not! And if you're not, come your reselection . . . Well, need I say more?'

'Apparently not,' murmured Roy, as her challenge was greeted by applause and shouts of 'You tell the bastard, Joanie, you tell him!'

'Yes, you can't get out of it, Comrade Hampton. Either you're wholeheartedly *for* us, or we're going to be wholeheartedly *against* you!'

Roy surged to his feet. Despite his weariness and the tightness in his throat, he knew he had to fight back.

'Listen, comrades. Please listen, will you?'

The din persisted as the delegates became more frenzied and vociferous. Then, to Roy's amazement, Terry, in his role as chairman, waved an imperious arm to quell his fanatical troops.

'Comrades, comrades! Give the man a chance. He is about to make an historical statement as to his views on America's military involvement in the internal affairs of our beleaguered country.'

Reluctantly the troops obeyed their commander's order. Within seconds there was silence in the hall.

'The floor is all yours, Comrade Hampton,' Terry whispered with a twinkle as he sat down and folded his arms.

Unsuccessfully Roy tried to clear his throat before turning to address the enemy.

'Comrades, if we kick the Americans out of the UK, to all intents and purposes we might as well not be in NATO ourselves. . . .'

Again he was interrupted by the wiry man: 'Who wants to be

in NATO, anyway? NATO's only the military arm of Reagan's imperialistic ambitions!'

'That's right, comrade,' interjected Joan. 'As I've said on many occasions, the only hope for this country is for us to become a nuclear-free zone, get out of the Common Market, put on severe import controls and implement full-scale nationalization!'

'Why don't you just join the other Warsaw Pact countries and be done with it?' Roy asked with a smile.

Instantly the baying started again. Delegates leapt to their feet, waving their fists and stamping on the creaking floorboards as they jeered and howled. Through hooded eyelids the chairman watched the pandemonium. Then he inclined his profile towards Joan who waved her arms to get the hall's attention. Eventually the noise died down again. Joan turned back to face the chairman who still had his arms folded.

'I'm sorry, Comrade Chairman, but it's absolutely hopeless questioning our MP. He's more reactionary than Gaitskell. And about as much of a socialist as Margaret Thatcher!'

Then she turned to Roy himself and smiled wistfully. 'It really doesn't matter what you are, does it? Because come your reselection in December, we will be free of you!'

Before Roy could respond to this final barb, the hall erupted into a spontaneous standing-ovation. It was as if Joan had just sung *Aida* at Covent Garden. The only thing missing were the flowers.

This can't be happening, he thought. But it was.... And Roy knew it wasn't the beginning of the end either. As the Great Bulldog once observed: 'It is only the end of the beginning.'

The moment the meeting was over Roy collected his briefcase, stuffed his parliamentary report inside and headed for the urinal. Two delegates tried to head him off but he stared at them balefully, so they let him go in unaccompanied. As the door swung to behind him, he turned on the tap in the grimy washbasin and cupped his hands, like he used to as a schoolboy, until they were running over with water. Then he drank as much as he could. It didn't matter that he was soaking his shirt cuffs. He needed to assuage his terrible thirst. He heard the door swing open behind him but refused to look round.

The intruder cleared his throat, then said hesitantly: 'Mr Hampton?'

'What do you want?' Roy demanded without turning his head.

'It's me, Dave Pickles, Mr Hampton.'

The MP turned round slowly. He remembered Pickles heckling him in the hall.

'So what's your problem, Mr Pickles? You can't accuse me of "sitting on the fence and flannelling" in here.'

Embarrassed, the young man avoided Roy's gaze.

'I just wanted to say that I'm sorry if we, well, hurt you, Mr Hampton. We all get so carried away. Oh, I'm not saying we don't mean it at the time. But we don't mean it personally.'

'You could've fooled me,' grimaced Roy.

'I know it sounds personal but it isn't really,' Pickles said, shifting his weight and wanting to leave, but not knowing how to. 'You look done-in, Mr Hampton. Sure you're safe enough to drive yourself home?'

'You're right. I did drink more than I should on an empty stomach. But other than a little world-weariness, I feel fine. Anyway, I appreciate your apology.'

Dave laughed, then unconsciously stroked his Che Guevara moustache.

'I wish I could say it won't happen next time. But at least you'll know it's not personal.'

Then, because he had nothing else to say, Pickles made his way out into the night. Roy turned back to the sink. The tap was still dripping. He was turning it off when a podgy finger and thumb squeezed his elbow. He was about to challenge whoever had touched him when he recognised his old friend Councillor Bunting.

'I wouldn't've blamed you if you'd slammed that little sod in the face, Roy.'

'You mean Pickles?'

'Yeah. His sort are always the same. Bloody brave when they're with their scummy mates but once you get 'em alone in a bog, butter wouldn't melt in their mouths.'

'He's just young and impulsive, Harold. Like so many of them today he never thinks anything through, which is why he's all mouth and theories.'

'That's as maybe, Roy. But it still weren't nice in there, was it?' wheezed the councillor as he unzipped his flies.

'You can say that again.'

Roy joined his friend at the urinal. The smell of stale ammonia permeated his nostrils.

Christ, it even puts you off pissing, he thought, as he absently urinated into the overflowing trough at their feet.

'Anyway, Harold, why didn't you back me up in there?'

'I tried to, lad, but I got shouted down and manhandled, didn't I? Anyroad, I'm not up to all that rough stuff any more. Nor are the rest of the lads. These young bastards are so bloody strong, they could break your bloody neck!'

Roy watched Harold wash his hands.

He doesn't look at all well, Roy thought. How bloated and blotchy his face is, and he's got such a huge pot on him. Yet he used to be so slim and dapper. It's as if he's deliberately letting himself go to seed.

The act of washing his hands made Harold wheeze badly.

'Why's this place never have any bloody soap?'

'It doesn't even have a towel, Harold, so you can hardly expect soap.'

'Yeah, it's funny how all Labour Party bogs never have soap or towels. Yet they say if you go into a Tory shithouse that it's not only got soap and towels, it's even got a bleeding bidet!'

Roy laughed and finished washing his hands. Then, suddenly serious, he turned to the councillor.

'Isn't there anything we can do, Harold, to stop Terry and his Trots taking over this constituency?'

Bunting thought a moment, then muttered: 'Not a lot, lad. Our type of Labourism ain't popular any more. The young 'uns and some of the punters find us too wishy-washy. We're not fashionable. Whereas Trotskyism, Marxism, Leninism and every other revolutionary "ism" are the "in" things. At least among local activists. Look, it's hopeless trying to dry yer hands on yer hankie, Roy. Let's get out of here, for Chrissake. Stench in this place is enough to make you heave.'

As they made their way into the street, Roy was relieved to see that most of the delegates had already gone home. There was a thin drizzle and the uneven pavement was black and shiny. Together the two friends ambled towards the Red Cockerel.

Roy was about to reiterate his political concern when Harold started to reminisce.

'You know, Roy, I can still remember when you came to live here in Lamberton. In March '62, wasn't it?'

'Yes. That's when I bought my house for a song while I was teaching drama at the poly.'

'You were a live-wire, then, lad. God, the hours you used to put in when you first joined the Party down here. Talk about a glutton for punishment!'

Roy laughed: 'That's what Liz used to say.'

'It were because you were such a glutton that I kept telling my old mate, Reggie Sparraton, that when he retired as our MP, it was young Hampton who should take his place. Mind, Reggie took a bit of persuading, because he was pretty right-wing Labour. And in them days you were still pretty leftish, weren't you?'

'Yes, but the left was different in the sixties, Harold,' Roy said, doing up the top button of his raincoat.

'You don't have to tell me, lad. In them days even I were a bit of a leftie meself!' chuckled the councillor. 'Though I bet you don't remember how Sparraton and me got you into becoming a member of the GMWU by the back door, do you?'

'Of course I remember, Harold! Though I must say I'm glad I didn't have to be a union-sponsored MP like poor old Reggie Sparraton.'

'I doubt whether there's even thirty per cent of Labour MPs who are sponsored today. Still, them sponsored MPs do have one advantage.'

'What's that?'

'The Unions pay for the MP to have a full-time agent, don't they? Whereas you had to make do with a lousy part-time agent like Fred Crowne. Well, let's face it, Fred's been a complete disaster for you, ain't he? I mean, if he's not ill, his wife is! So he's never here when you need him. And even when he is, he's bloody useless!'

Roy nodded glumly, then switched his briefcase to his left hand so he could put his arm round his friend's shoulder.

'You should've been my agent, Harold.'

'I'm soft in the head, lad, but I'm not that soft.'

Roy laughed, then gave Harold a hug.

'I want you to know, Harold, I shall always be extremely grateful for what you did for me in those early days.'

Embarrassed, the old campaigner pushed the younger man away.

'It were nothing, lad.'

'Bollocks! If you hadn't gone out of your way to get all the old guard on the GMC to vote for me on my selection night, I wouldn't be an MP today.'

'Ah, but now you're hanging on by the skin of yer teeth, ain't you? I'm not just talking about the pressure from MacMaster. I'm talking about your miserable majority at the last election, when the Bitch got a landslide and you only got in by – what was it? – 927 votes?'

'No. 926. And I wouldn't have had some of those votes but for the odd boundary change in my favour. Still, I agree it's one helluva drop from the 6,372 majority I got in '79 and the 13,871 majority I got in October '74.'

Roy paused as he skirted round a large puddle between two crumbling flagstones.

'But that's not what's bugging me tonight.'

The councillor grunted and wiped the rain off his face.

'Well, spit it out, lad.'

'What I really can't get over, Harold, is the way MacMaster is so cleverly engineering a majority on the GMC.'

'Well, me and the lads've done all we can to support you, Roy. Trouble is, MacMaster keeps them sodding GMC meetings going till two or three in the sodding morning! And me and the lads are getting too old for all that carry-on.'

'The last person I'm blaming is you, Harold.'

'I know, lad.'

The councillor shivered and huddled further into his old overcoat. Then gasping for breath, he leant against an illuminated, wet shop window.

'Hey, you all right, Harold?' Roy said with concern.

'I'm fine,' wheezed the councillor as a second sharp pain stabbed him in the chest. 'No, I don't need any help, lad, but I need to rest a minute.'

In the neon light of the shop window, Harold's face looked even blotchier than usual. For a full minute the elderly man pressed his cheek against the glass, savouring the cool rivulets of rainwater running down his face, until the pain in his chest receded. Then he pushed himself away from the shop window and shambled off into the dark. Dismayed, Roy shook his head, then quickly caught up with his ailing friend.

'Are you sure you're all right, Harold?'

'Yeah. Just get these twinges in my chest. Mind, they used to be a sight worse before I had my pacemaker put in.'

'Of course, I keep forgetting . . .'

Impatiently the councillor cut him short: 'Oh, for Chrissake, don't go on about my ailments, lad. You're worse than Olive. She's always saying I should do this and I should do that. Still, I suppose that's at least better than my son. Charlie couldn't give a bugger what I do. Doubt whether he'd care if I dropped dead.'

The councillor was no longer aware of his feet splashing through the puddles. His secret once more possessed him. He wanted to grab Roy by his lapels and confess his guilt. Then another sharp twinge knifed into his chest, cutting away his sense of guilt and forcing him back into the present.

'Stop fobbing me off, Harold. You're in real pain, aren't you?' insisted the younger man.

Harold shook his head, then gasped as a tall punk with a mop of rainbow-streaked hair jostled against him. The old man only retained his balance by grasping hold of a lampost. Roy was about to challenge the punk when to his surprise the lad shouted: 'Sorry, grandad, didn't mean to knock you, but I lost my balance on one of them loose flagstones, didn't I?'

'That's all right, lad,' gasped the councillor, still clinging to the lampost. 'Pavements round here are bloody death-traps!'

Despite Harold's protests, Roy took his arm.

'Now stop playing silly buggers, and let me help you.'

'All right, lad. Just don't fuss,' muttered Harold, gratefully leaning on the younger man's arm as they approached the Red Cockerel. The councillor was about to push open the lounge door when he changed his mind and fiercely gripped the wet sleeve of Roy's raincoat.

'I wish to hell I could help you fight them Trot bastards, Roy, but I'm afraid I ain't got the energy any more.'

'Look, I really think you ought to be at home in bed, not. . . .'

'Will you let me finish what I'm trying to say? It's because we've been good friends for so many years that I don't want you to be under any illusions about the trouble you're in!'

Roy attempted to calm the councillor but Harold insisted on finishing.

'Oh, I know you think you can deal with the Trots, Roy, and perhaps you can deal with 'em. But if you are going to beat 'em, I feel you should know that you're going to have to beat 'em on your own. Y'see, lad, it isn't just me who hasn't got the energy to help you fight 'em. Most of the old right wingers in that hall tonight haven't got the energy, either. Well, can you blame 'em? This ain't the same Party we joined as youngsters nearly fifty years ago. In the old days there weren't all this moral intimidation going on. In them days when it were your turn to speak, you weren't told to shut up and you didn't get manhandled!'

The councillor's eyes glistened with angry despair.

'So what I'm getting at, Roy, is we're all sick of being screamed at by fanatics, because that's what most of MacMaster's mob are. Sure, a lot of 'em have got intellectual pretensions, but underneath all their blather some of 'em are real vicious sods who are bursting with ambition and riddled with envy and spoiling for a real fight. Just like those racist shits in the National Front. Oh, I know there's a big difference, Roy, because the Trots and all the hard-line lefties are far too smart to go out fighting in the streets. So they do their intimidating and "comradely" thuggery by using threats and abuse to steamroller their policies through meetings. In the process they frighten their elderly opponents into silence. That's, of course, when they're not crucifying their MP upside down!'

To the councillor's amazement, Roy laughed.

'Now stop worrying, Harold. It's going to take more than a fly-by-night sonovabitch like MacMaster to unseat me. I've still got a trick or two up my sleeve.'

Harold was not impressed. 'Well, you'll need to be sodding Houdini to trick your way out of the coffin they've got lined up for you, laddie!'

Then the councillor disappeared into the Red Cockerel.

Roy walked into the lounge bar and a tremor of relief passed through him. Here at least he was safe from MacMaster's stratagems.

That puritan teetotaller will never come in here, he thought as he waved to his wife, who was sitting at a small table in the far corner.

Liz waved back, then blew a kiss at Harold. The councillor grinned and pretended to swoon. As they crossed the crowded bar to join Liz, Harold muttered under his breath: 'Roy, don't tell Liz I've been feeling badly, or she won't flirt with me.'

Roy laughed, then tentatively edged his way past three wrestling-types downing their beer, until he reached Liz's corner table. Trying to control his wheezing, the councillor joined them. Appreciatively both men stared at the two pints of beer beside Liz's gin and tonic.

'Thank God you got the beer in, darling,' Roy said, indicating to Harold that he wanted the councillor to sit next to his wife.

There was a pause while Harold wedged his stomach in between his chair and the edge of the table. Liz, who was very fond of the councillor, tried not to giggle. As Roy lifted the glass to his lips, he saw that Liz's attention had been distracted by someone at the opposite end of the bar. Then he realised she was smiling at the 'someone' in question. Irritably he turned round to see who it was. He couldn't believe his eyes. Terry MacMaster was toasting his wife with a pint glass of iced grapefruit juice.

Liz nudged her husband. 'Why's he winking at me, darling?' she whispered.

'Presumably because he wants you to know that he has put a noose round my throat. What's more, he gave it a discreet little twitch tonight – which is why I've developed this pain in the neck.'

Liz smiled sympathetically.

'Your report didn't go well then, dear?'

'It went beautifully. They just want me hanged, drawn and quartered.' Roy turned to Harold, who was staring into his beer dolefully. 'What's the matter with you? It's my head MacMaster wants to stick on Traitors' Gate, not yours.'

'Exactly!' the councillor agreed. 'So what is this trick you've got left up your sleeve, Roy? Because you're certainly going to need it.'

'To be honest, I'm not clear yet which trick to use. But I'm going to have to pull something out of my sleeve, aren't I?'

Liz, who had been nibbling her lemon rind, tossed it into the ashtray and glared at both men.

'You two make me sick.'

For a moment the men couldn't believe their ears.

'Well, you do!' Liz reaffirmed as she finished off her gin and tonic.

'Liz!'

'I'm sorry, Harold, but when you two get together you should hear yourselves. You're always on about needing "tricks" and "having to pull something out of your bloody sleeve". No, don't interrupt, Roy. I've been wanting to say this for weeks.'

Roy closed his mouth and gripped his glass with both hands.

'What I'm trying to say to you, Roy – and I know your wife agrees with me, too, Harold – is that if being in politics is nothing more than "playing tricks" and "pulling things out of your sleeves" you should both give it up now! How can we wives hold up our heads with our friends when they challenge us about what you are doing with their lives? They often do challenge us, you know. And they've every right to! Because it's their lives and the lives of their families that are forever being manipulated by you politicians. It wouldn't be so bad if you both spent your time discussing new radical policies that would improve everyone's lives. But I never hear either of you discussing radical policies.'

The councillor laughed and jerked a thumb at MacMaster, now surrounded by half a dozen of his acolytes.

'I think you can safely leave the discussion of radical policies to our friends over there, Liz.'

'Yes, and they're really radical, darling,' interjected Roy, with a twinkle. 'Because they include such delights as a siege economy, and leaving the Common Market and NATO. Not to mention barricades in the streets. In fact, you name it, they want it, and the Kremlin will love it.'

Liz was not amused.

'You should hear youself talk, Roy. You're turning into a reactionary cynic!'

'You'll be telling us next, Liz, that you agree with us coming out of NATO and setting up a siege economy here in the UK?'

Puzzled, Liz wrinkled her brow. 'You're always going on about the horrors of a siege economy, but what the hell *is* a siege economy?'

'It's what will happen to this country if full-blooded socialism is ever implemented.'

'Yes, but what does that mean?'

'It means if we come out of the Common Market and put on severe import controls, and at the same time prevent anyone taking money out of this country, we will eventually turn ourselves into a *besieged* island.'

'I don't see how coming out of the Common Market, putting on severe import controls and . . .?'

'If we put on severe import controls and stop the flow of money to and from this country, then the other countries in Europe, and the Americans, will immediately take retaliatory measures against us. This will interrupt all our trade arrangements, and we will be left with what dear old Michael Foot used to advocate in the *Daily Herald*; i.e., bilateral trade arrangements with the Soviet Union and its satellites. Of course, by that time our siege economy will have pulled us out of NATO and the Western Alliance, and we'll be left in the Russian camp.'

'That will never happen!' countered Liz, tossing her head back scornfully. Several strands of hair jerked free from her bun and she brushed them away from her eyes. 'Anyway, I'm sure we'd be much better off without the Americans influencing us all the time. I still believe that Conference is right. All US bases should be dismantled in this country!'

Grabbing the empty glasses, Roy got to his feet.

'All I can say, darling, is I hope to God you're not drilling this nonsense into the heads of those poor kids you teach up at Eden Comprehensive.'

Before Liz could retaliate, Roy headed for the bar. As he ordered a fresh round of drinks he was conscious of Terry's amused eyes on the nape of his neck.

Terry was not the only one watching the MP. His girlfriend, Angie Robinson, and the redhead were also looking on. Sitting beside the girls there were other worthies of the hard left: Alf Spencer, the wiry man, Dan Peters, the frenzied intellectual, and the bald giant, Les Normington, who as usual was spilling beer down his tattered duffel coat. At the far end of the table, sipping grapefruit juice in homage to her hero, sat Geraldine O'Hara, with her adoring eyes forever fixed on MacMaster's profile. But it was Angie, Terry's 'Marilyn Monroe of Lamberton North', who was dominating the conversation.

'I don't care wot you say, Terry! I fink Roy Hampton's got a nice face.'

Terry's comrades dissolved into laughter.

'I also fink that he and that fat codger are talking about us.'

Terry snorted, then stroked his eyebrow.

'Of course they're talking about us! What else have they got to talk about? Mind, anything Hampton says is bound to be irrelevant.'

'Why d'you say that?'

'You should've seen him in there tonight. He was shitting bricks. But that's what happens when you're a political anachronism who is about to be relegated to the dustbin of history.'

Angie giggled and sipped her St Clements.

'I do wish I had your way wiv words, Terry.'

Joan Keithley laughed.

'Trouble with you, Ange, is you've never taken the time to familiarize yourself with Marx's dialectical materialism.'

Angie's baby-blue eyes grew larger.

'I don't need to, Joan. Terry knows it all. It just pours out of him. Dunnit, Terry?'

Terry, feeling pleased with life and expansive, responded to her rhetorical question with an off-the-cuff speech.

'The trouble with the Tories, Liberals, SDP and right-wing Labour is they're all so bloody illiterate. Many of 'em have never even read Marx or Engels, and certainly not Lenin and Trotsky. So it's no wonder they get crushed whenever they try to argue with us. The only way they know how to deal with us is by shrieking out mindless bourgeois propaganda which they've pinched out of the *Telegraph* anyway. Or in the case of most of 'em, out of the *Sun* and the *Star*. That's why, in the end, they're all going to be relegated to the dustbin of history. That's the penalty you pay for being shrill, English and ignorant.'

'Bravo, Terry, bravo!' shouted the comrades in ragged chorus.

Roy returned to his seat in the opposite corner, but Liz was still disgruntled and refused to thank him when he set a fresh gin and tonic in front of her. So as he blew the froth off his beer, Roy glanced at Harold, then gestured towards MacMaster.

'Doesn't that sonovabitch ever stop pontificating?'

'No use blowing a gasket, Roy. That won't solve nothing. It's obvious you ain't got no real tricks up your sleeve, so your only hope is make a deal with MacMaster.'

'Make a deal with that bastard?'

'Yeah, and you'd better do the deal quickish.'

Roy was about to make an acid retort when he noted the grim look on his wife's face, so instead he shook his head at Harold.

'There's nothing in my limited patronage that would interest MacMaster.'

Harold smiled, then pulled his old Dunhill pipe and his blue tin of tobacco out of his overcoat pocket.

'There must be something MacMaster wants that you can give him. Because if you don't make a deal with him, he's going to put you through the meat-grinder. Where you going, Liz?'

'Home, Harold!'

Bewildered, Roy put his hand on his wife's wrist to restrain her, but she shook him off. As she tied her scarf under her chin, Roy stood up to challenge her.

'Why are you going home?'

'How many times do I have to tell you? I'm sick of hearing you talk of dirty tricks and tacky deals!'

Roy thrust out his hand to bar her way.

'I hate dirty tricks and tacky deals as much as you do, love. Half the trouble I have in the Commons is I'm not good at them. That's why I'm always getting roasted by the Whips.'

The councillor screwed up his eyes and waved his pipe at the arguing couple.

'Now, now, you two, calm down. Can't you see that MacMaster and his crew are laughing at you? Oh, for Christ's sake, Liz, sit down before you burst a blood vessel.'

Liz glared at both men, then sat down. But she refused to take off her scarf.

'There's no need to get on your high horse, gal. Whether you like it or not, your husband has no choice but to be tricky and make deals. Otherwise he'll go to the wall as sure as I've got high blood pressure. Anyway, deals are the lifeblood of democratic politics.'

'Yes, I know they are, Harry,' interjected Roy, lighting up a cigarette to bring some calm back into his life. 'But in one sense Liz is correct. Whatever deals we make with the hard left, it still doesn't change the fact that the bastards are winning! W. B. Yeats was right.'

'W. B. Who?' demanded the councillor.

Liz laughed.

'Surely you know *The Second Coming* by now, Harry? Mastermind here is always trotting it out. No pun intended. And when he isn't, Roy Jenkins is.'

Roy refused to be put off and chanted the poet's words like a religious incantation.

> 'Turning and turning in the widening gyre,
> The falcon cannot hear the falconer. . . .'

The councillor cut across Roy's recitation.

'What the hell's a ruddy falcon got to do with MacMaster?'

Roy closed his eyes and, oblivious of his surroundings, submerged himself in Yeats' music.

> 'Things fall apart; the centre cannot hold;
> Mere anarchy is loosed upon the world,'

'That's true enough,' chimed in the councillor.

> 'The blood-dimmed tide is loosed, and everywhere
> The ceremony of innocence is drowned;'

'Stroll on!'

Still with his eyes closed, Roy cocked his head in MacMaster's direction.

'But here's the killer line, Harry. In fact it's probably the most politically prophetic line in twentieth-century literature.' Roy took a deep breath and then intoned:

> 'The best lack all conviction, while the worst
> Are full of passionate intensity.'

He was so possessed by the profundity of the poet's lines that he didn't notice his audience had increased by one. Then the intruder's shadow slid across his face, jolting him back into the present. Startled, he turned his head to see who was casting the shadow, only to look up into the amused eyes of Terry MacMaster, who was standing behind him with a tray of drinks.

'But if my memory serves me right, comrade,' Terry said, his smile widening, 'Yeats, that great supporter of the IRA, went on to say, in his next line: "Surely the Second Coming is at hand?"'

Roy was ready for him and snapped back: 'Right! But Yeats ended with:

'And what rough beast, its hour come round at last,
Slouches towards Bethlehem to be born?'

MacMaster raised an eyebrow, then beamed at Liz.

'Yes, you're right, Roy, Yeats always did have a thing about "rough beasts slouching", didn't he? But even though, to his credit, he was a passionate supporter of the Republican Army, unfortunately Yeats is dead now, isn't he? Whereas Marx is still very much alive. And he's certainly kicking!'

Then the revolutionary winked at Liz and was gone.

Elated, Roy jogged down the path of his front garden to unlock his car. The heavens were endlessly blue, and the long fluffy tail of a passing jet did not destroy their radiance. Then the magnolia tree in the next garden but one caught his eye. Its white petals were drinking the sunlight. Roy was so absorbed by the beauty of the tree that he stood by his car and gazed. He didn't notice a neighbour waving at him, or hear the cries of three children in pursuit of their runaway puppy.

Wouldn't it be wonderful to be a tree for a season instead of being a human? he thought, as he opened the boot of his car and threw in a case containing his dinner jacket and cricket whites. Though I suppose being a tree must have its drawbacks. I wouldn't fancy having a high wind tearing all my petals off, or being rained on during February and most of March. Though it would be glamorous to have snow in my branches. At least if you're a tree people stop and stare at you, which is more than they do if you're a human. That is, unless you're a pretty woman or a dwarf. They chop trees down, of course. Though not quite as regularly as they chop people down.

His fantasy was obliterated by the demonic vision of Terry MacMaster wielding a two-headed axe. Roy shook his head, because he knew, whether he was a tree or a human, MacMaster would still try to chop him down.

God, if anyone could hear what goes on inside my head half the time, they'd have me certified.

He looked back at the magnolia tree. He wanted to smother himself in its petals so that he too could be radiant for a moment.

What the hell's happening to me? Just because I've suddenly been invited down for a luxury weekend in the country it doesn't mean I should let spring-madness drive me crazy. But, I desperately need to get away. To escape from my responsibilities, my constituency, the Commons. And from my family. And even – God help me – from Liz. I need time to think about something other than politics and family life. The reason I feel excited is because I'm escaping for a whole weekend, and by myself. It's not my fault Liz has promised my in-laws that she'll take the kids up to Peterborough to see them. I don't feel guilty at all. I can't wait to join Freddy and Nancy's house-party in the Chilterns. Ufferton Hall always beguiles the senses. Then, to crown it all, there's going to be a charity cricket match, with me as the guest-of-honour fast bowler. There's no doubt about it. This weekend is going to be heaven on earth!

'Darling, are you all right?' Liz said as she waved a hand in front of his face, making him blink.

'Sorry, sweetheart, I was day-dreaming.'

'So that's why you've got that stupid grin on your face?'

Roy laughed to hide his embarrassment. Then he kissed his wife lightly on the cheek.

'If I'm going to be there for lunch, darling, I'd better go now,' he said, getting into his car.

'You're staying with Freddy and Nancy tonight and tomorrow night, aren't you?'

'Yes. We don't play the cricket match till Monday afternoon, so obviously I can't come back till Monday evening.'

'No, I suppose not,' Liz said, suddenly feeling depressed that she wasn't going with him.

'Well, have a good time, darling,' Roy said. 'And give my love to your mum and dad.'

He was about to drive off when Liz tapped on the car window.

'Did Nancy say who else was going to be staying at Ufferton?'

'Yes, she said an old friend of mine from the LSE was coming for the weekend but refused to tell me his name because she wanted to surprise me.'

'That's typically Nancy,' retorted Liz, now pleased that she wasn't going with him. There was nothing she found more boring than her husband's old LSE chums, especially as Roy always got drunk with them and then ended up rowing.

'Well, give your friend my regards, won't you? And don't get so drunk you make a fool of yourself.'

'Not a chance, darling,' Roy shouted cheerfully and drove out of the Close.

As Roy steered round the long, curving drive towards Ufferton Hall, he knew his battered car was creating an incongruous impression, for either side of him stretched vast expanses of green lawns, flowering bushes and ancient trees. Roy was dazzled by the pristine brilliance of the landscape with its bluish hills in the distance and, nearer, the oval lake with its four black swans.

Then Ufferton Hall itself came into view. Every time Roy visited Nancy and Freddy he was always taken aback by his first sight of this jewel of a Palladian house. The flight of stone steps led up to six stone pillars, then through a mahogany door into the echoing hall.

Still in a trance, he swallowed his first glass of champagne in the Great Room.

'I don't know whether I ever mentioned it, Roy,' murmured his hostess, 'but the Great Room was inspired by Inigo Jones' Cube Room at Wilton. I understand that this came about as the result of Freddy's inestimable forebear, Sir Beverly, and his Grand Italian Tour in 1720. For, as you know, Ufferton was modelled on Palladio's design for the Villa Rotonda.'

Although Roy was overwhelmed by the perfect proportions of the Great Room, with its reddish columns painted to look like marble and its Chippendale and Sheraton furniture, he found that his thoughts drifted whenever Nancy lectured him about them. And when he visited Ufferton, which he did about once every two years, she always lectured him. It was obvious why. Nancy was brimming over with acquired affectation and the need to impress. Though she had married into the upper echelons of the landed gentry, she still had a lower-middle-class, daughter-of-a-grocer's soul. Everything about Nancy was slightly false, from her pinched yet elongated vowel sounds to her magenta fingernails.

Yes, thought Roy, while he sipped his champagne and Nancy

continued to lecture him, she is a bit of a walking disaster, whereas I've been fond of old Freddy ever since he befriended me when we were at the LSE together. Mind, I've never come to terms with Freddy's indolent lifestyle, which he can only enjoy because he owns ten thousand acres of the best farming land in Buckinghamshire. He wouldn't be able to live in such splendour if his infamous ancestor hadn't made a fortune out of sugar, tobacco and slaves in the West Indies. As a result, Freddy's estate is now worth millions, of which he and Nancy pocket two per cent per annum, thank you very much! So over the last fifteen years, as the price of land has gone through the roof, they've grown richer with every day that passes.

Dazed by the magnificence of his surroundings, Roy let himself be led into the gardens. Nancy was still going on, only now in his right ear, about how the grounds had been laid with the personal advice of Alexander Pope: 'Or at least it was the advice of one of Pope's closest friends, Roy.'

Poor old Nancy, he thought. Despite living amidst such classical symmetry, the years have not treated you well and your voice gets shriller every season.

'Ah, excellent!' Nancy called out as the butler came up the steps carrying two huge suitcases. 'Our special guest has arrived.'

Roy squinted into the sunlight, hoping to see which of his old chums from the LSE he was going to get magnificently drunk with. To his surprise a slender-waisted woman, with long, dark hair, walked up the steps towards him. There was something he recognised about her eyes. Then she looked him straight in the face and their translucent greenness enveloped him. She stretched out and touched his cheek with her fingertips.

'Helen!' he gasped. 'It's you, isn't it?'

'Of course it's me, you silly billy,' Helen whispered.

Before he could prevent it, Helen slipped her elegant arm into his and propelled him across the sunlit lawn down to the lake. He turned back to see Nancy laughing and waving.

'As you two obviously need a few minutes to get reacquainted,' Nancy called out, 'I'll go and see if Freddy's returned from the pavilion. As it's such a beautiful day, I thought we'd have a picnic lunch over there.'

Nancy pointed to the honey-coloured Palladian summerhouse overlooking the lake. Then one of the black swans clashed its wings, churning up the water as it attempted to fly. The sun was now at its hottest and the swan only beat the surface of the lake with its black pinions a dozen times, then gave up the struggle and ploughed back into the water. For a long moment the humans watched the swan's progress in silence. Then Nancy's shrillness broke the spell.

'So why don't you two make yourselves at home by the summerhouse, and in a few minutes Freddy and I will come and join you?'

For a long while Roy stared out across the lake, not knowing what to say. Helen sensed what he was feeling; she too was now gazing silently at the sunlit water. As they stood beside the bullrushes, together yet apart, they remembered their shared past. Those hectic, forbidden days and nights in each other's arms, all those years ago at the LSE.

As the images surged back from the depths of Roy's memory, he experienced a tingle of guilt. He had been engaged to Liz throughout his affair with Helen. Liz had been forced to live at home with her parents in Peterborough in order to get her teacher's diploma at the local college, so he was left in London to his own devices.

To this day Liz doesn't know of Helen's existence, he thought. And that's the way it must remain.

Helen smiled to herself and watched a huge carp lazily break the surface of the lake. To her delight the carp refused to submerge. Instead it sunned its glistening brown back as it glided away from the shallows. It was as if time had stopped. The hot spring sunshine and the calm water laving the feathers of the black swans were part of the essence of the England they both loved. Then the faint perfume of bluebells stole upon their senses from a nearby copse. Instantly they remembered another weekend by another lake, when they had made love among the bluebells. It was not long after their erotic war in the woods that Roy told Helen their affair was over. For two hours she wept, naked in his arms, her tears scalding his chest. He hated himself for a long time afterwards, but whenever she called him he refused to see her.

Christ, I was a real bastard in those days, he thought, as the memories overwhelmed him. Talk about being a typically ambitious grammar-school Englishman. What would have happened if I'd married Helen instead of Liz? It wouldn't have worked. Helen's always been too competitive. That's why she's such a successful political historian, and why I have deliberately avoided seeing her all these years. Yes, I'm a true Englishman all right. Because only a true Englishman always lives in awe of a strong-minded woman. In that respect I'm not unlike the present Tory Cabinet, and their timorous relationship with Maggie. Mind, my Liz can be pretty strong-minded when she wants to. Though, thank God, Liz has never been consumed by an ambition to change the world. Or, as in Helen's case, consumed by an ambition to record for posterity the dangerous mistakes of those who tried to change the world.

Helen remained motionless beside him. She knew he was suffering and part of her enjoyed knowing that he was. As they heard the approaching voices of Freddy and Nancy, they turned to face each other for the first time. Again her eyes overpowered him, forcing him to look away.

If only she wasn't so silent and so sure of herself. If only I wasn't here!

As the thoughts jumbled through his head, he knew he was lying to himself. Because in truth he was thrilled that Nancy had deliberately tricked him into coming down for the weekend to meet her surprise guest.

'You're a real sly-boots, Nancy, aren't you?' he said, turning to wink at his hostess.

Freddy, his host, a small, dapper man, laughed. Then he kissed Helen resonantly on the cheek.

'I'm glad you're still talking to each other, children, otherwise we could have been in for an embarrassing weekend. Well, there's no point in standing on ceremony, is there? The picnic is calling by the summerhouse.' Freddy took his guests firmly by the arms and guided them towards the picnic. As they moved over the grass, Helen breathed in deeply and savoured the thought of an after-lunch stroll among the bluebells.

After lunch, Helen and Roy slipped away from their snoring hosts in the summerhouse. Then Helen stopped in her tracks.

'Just a minute, Roy. I've forgotten something!' she said, turning and running light-footed back to the summerhouse.

What the hell am I doing here? Roy wondered, enjoying the

vision of Helen's long, brown legs running through a carpet of cowslips. There's no doubt about it, unless I'm very careful I'm going to make a fool of myself. If only she didn't have such an athletically slim back.

As he watched her lithe shadow run between the statues of two Classical nymphs, he undid the second button of his striped shirt.

If I had any sense, I'd start running, too. In the opposite direction. Unfortunately I seem to have run out of sense. Still, Liz will never know. No one will. Except me. And Helen. And maybe our inebriated hosts. Not that they'll mind, of course. They're so rich and have so little to do that they're always going out of their way to encourage salacious goings-on in the shrubbery.

Mind, it must be wonderful to be rich. What was it Stalin said once? 'The whole world wants to be bourgeois till it's knocked out of 'em!'

Not that Freddy and Nancy are what you call 'bourgeois'; they are more 'faded aristocracy'. And how MacMaster would love to tear all this down! But then I suppose there's part of me, the fenland peasant part, that envies Freddy his wealth and his endless comfort. And being rich and canny, Freddy has discovered that the best way to avoid paying Capital Transfer Tax, and to keep his roof in good repair, is to open Ufferton to the general public for thirty days a year during the summer, because any profits that accrue are tax-deductible. Christ, the rich in this country get away with murder. Only as long as the Tories are in power, of course.

Roy smiled sardonically.

Still, it's strange to think in a few weeks' time there'll probably be some runny-nosed toddler standing where I'm standing now. Only he'll be dreaming of the monster ice-cream that his parents are going to buy him when they leave the grounds. Whereas I'm dreaming about a different kind of ice-cream. . . .

Shaking his head to dispel his guilt, Roy slumped into the grass. He smiled as some pollen dust settled along the crease of his lightweight, navy-blue trousers. Unhurriedly he took off his shoes and socks and tossed them into the buttercups.

God, I love England! And this Italian landscape is somehow very English. It combines pastoral lyricism, historical perspective and, above all, the English tranquillity which still exists in most of our souls, waiting to be tapped. Waiting to repossess us and bring us the peace from that imaginary Golden Age when England was always like this . . . Even though, in reality, it has only ever been like this for the Nancys and Freddys of this world.

I should abhor Ufferton and want to destroy it. But what could I put up in its place? A high-rise block? A council estate? A car plant?

A Red Admiral flitted past Roy's nose, so he lay back in the grass, hoping the butterfly would return and settle on his shirt. To his surprise, it did. For several enchanted seconds he watched its black and crimson wings pulsating.

If only everyone could idle afternoons away like this, then there'd be no envy. Or Socialism. Or Fascism. Or Communism. But the perpetual enjoyment of eternal springtime only exists for the privileged few. Most people rarely glimpse loveliness such as this, except through the wrought-iron gates of other men's gardens.

Jesus, what is a blatant romantic doing in politics? Yet without romance and love of nature, how can you love your fellow men? If we tear this down to make every man equal in his envious despair, and then replace Ufferton with a wilderness of concrete where more men and women can become more disillusioned, then our children's children will point accusing fingers at us. 'You destroyed what was left of our green and pleasant land. Now we are all equally bereft. You lived in the last Golden Age, Roy Hampton, but you did not know it. You and your reforming friends believed you could play games with the environment. You thought as long as more people had more houses and less children, and more money for less work, then the Democratic Socialist Age would come into being.'

Then, sensing that someone was watching him, Roy leapt to his feet, only to see Helen holding a bottle of champagne in one hand and two glasses in the other. She was standing under an oak tree and laughing. Her laughter made her small breasts shake under her white summer dress.

'Don't just stand there looking at the menu, Roy. Let's see if the bluebells are as tempting as they used to be.'

Still laughing, she ran on ahead of him until she was lost among the silver birches in the wooded copse. Roy ran after her. To his relief he didn't collapse against a tree trunk and cough up his lungs. For on the night of his parliamentary report to his local GMC, he had made a resolution to cut back on his smoking. Now he was glad to find the discipline was beginning to pay dividends.

Then he brought himself up short. Panting, he surveyed the woodland, but there was no sign of Helen. He looked over his shoulder, for he knew how fond of playing hide-and-seek she had been in the old days. Still no sign of her.

Recovering his breath, he edged into a sunlit glade. Bumblebees hummed past him. Then he heard a sharp, repetitive knocking at the other end of the wood. He smiled, realising it was a woodpecker chipping its initials into the bole of a tree. There was a stealthy rustle to his left. Something was gliding through a bank of bluebells. As their stalks swayed to one side and the bluebells' perfume assaulted his senses, he knew that Helen was the snake in the grass. She could never resist being a serpentine Eve. Her fingers uncurled like a waking flower above the bluebells. Then her forefinger beckoned him seductively.

She certainly hasn't lost any of her skill, he thought, as he allowed himself to be lured into the misty blueness.

As the cool stalks of the bluebells stroked his ankles, he remembered he had bare feet. Hidden blackberry thorns pricked his toes. He was pulling one of the thorns out when Helen's long hair whispered against his cheek. Before he could resist, her mouth was on his. Involuntarily he sucked her tongue into his throat. Then she pulled him onto her and he felt himself harden against her thigh. Her free hand slid down his chest as she undid his remaining shirt buttons.

The greediness of their kissing increased. He felt he was swallowing her alive as his desperation matched hers. Then her determined fingers tugged at his trouser belt and he wrenched his mouth away from her lips. She was the sea and he was drowning in her. With her other hand she pressured the nape of his neck and tried to force his mouth back onto hers, but he continued to resist.

Then, as she deftly unzipped his trousers, the Cromwellian part of his nature forced him to push her away from him. Even the look of hurt on her face and the bewilderment in her eyes couldn't lure him back into her arms. For a long moment, he sat waist-deep in blue petals and stared in front of him, unaware he had wrapped his arms round his knees. A ladybird landed on his eyebrow. As he flicked it away, he realised Helen's reproachful eyes were still gazing at him. He was about to protest when she laughed.

'Did anyone ever tell you, Roy, that your approach to having sex with someone like me has got a great deal in common with Harold Wilson's 1964 approach to having political sex with the left?'

Roy's mouth fell open: 'I beg your pardon?'

'It's not such an obtuse parallel as it seems, darling, because when you kissed me just now....'

'*You* kissed *me*, Helen!'

'All right, when I kissed you just now, you didn't resist, did you? There's no point in denying it, Roy. You know perfectly well that every part of your little puritan body was urging you to screw me.'

'I still don't see what that has got to do with Harold Wilson and the left in 1964!'

'Simple, darling. During the first moments that our bodies were touching, you were only too eager to have me. In the same way, Harold Wilson, after the death of Gaitskell, was only too eager to join forces with the left, in order to establish for himself an unassailable power-base in the Labour Party. And just as you, as a self-professed happily married man, know that I am dangerous territory into which you shouldn't venture, so Harold, as a self-professed Democratic Socialist, knew equally well that by letting the *romantic* left into his Cabinet to further his career, the Marxist-Leninist *hard* left would come in on the romantic left's petticoats! But I suppose the main difference between you and Harold is that at least you have some kind of conscience. Whereas Harold has always put his party before his country, and his own position as head of the Party before everything. Yes, there's no doubt about it; Wilson is the guilty man of his generation. And I should know, darling, because at present I'm researching the gentleman in question. With or without his permission, I intend to write Wilson's biography – which I'm going to call *The Great Careerist.*'

'Oh?' said Roy.

'Yes,' said Helen. 'Don't you see, darling? It was only to further his career that Wilson brought romantic utopian socialists like Barbara Castle, Crossman and the like into his Shadow

Cabinet. And the first thing those worthies of the left did was to gain control of the Labour Party's National Executive Committee, so they could crank the Party machinery even further leftwards. Then they not only opened up contacts with the Eastern European Communist Parties in relative secrecy, but they also abolished the Proscribed List. And, unfortunately, the Proscribed List was the only thing that prevented the communists and Trotskyites from infiltrating the Labour Party!'

Roy tried to interrupt her but she plucked a handful of bluebells and impatiently waved them in his face.

'As you can't finish what you started, darling, the least you can do is let me finish. Especially as what I'm saying affects you directly. You see, I've heard all about your tussle with MacMaster, on the political grapevine. It's obvious you find it hard to understand how the left have taken over the Party apparatus so thoroughly – and so quickly. Now don't interrupt, darling! And don't say you already know all about it, because if you do know, then you're an even greater fool than I thought. For the knowledge should have given you the strength to fight the bastards, instead of just whining about them, which is all you've done so far!'

Helen was now on her feet, with her nostrils flared and her fists clenched. The aggressive look on her face and the tautness of her breasts made her look very sexy. As Roy watched her standing over him with her legs apart, he had an instant erection. Embarrassed, he placed his elbow casually over his throbbing groin, but Helen was oblivious and went on.

'And it is because of Wilson that *you* are now in big trouble, Roy. If he hadn't allowed the left to destroy the Proscribed List, then avowed Marxists couldn't have swamped the constituency Labour Parties and taken them over as they have done. Nor would we have a growing number of young far-left Labour MPs in the House of Commons like Robin Cook, Ron Brown and Clare Short. And the combination of communists in the unions, with the growing number of MPs of a Marxist-Leninist persuasion, was more than enough to force the Party into approving an extremist programme.'

She curled her lip: 'Perhaps Wilson thought that "the sweets of office" would temper the MPs' radicalism. Like you thought by kissing me just now, you would somehow be able to neutralise me and placate the itch in your loins. Because if you were at all honest, darling, you'd admit you do have an itch. Still, who knows? If you prove a good listener, I might overlook your previous grammar school manners – and you may yet get your just desserts.'

She knelt beside him. Her cool fingertips brushed a fly from the back of his hand. The moment she touched him, she electrified his skin. The wildness inside him demanded he rip off her dress, then mount her and explode his anguish inside her. But being English, he pressed his elbow harder into his groin, hoping the resulting pain would dissolve his lust. It didn't. So he went on trying to possess her with his eyes, while she went on trying to possess him with her mind.

'Yes, the more I think about it, darling, the more I'm sure that you and Harold have a great deal in common.'

He wanted to refute her, but like most men faced with a desirable woman, Roy was the prisoner of his penis. He knew that if he was foolish enough to argue with her, he would only end up railing at her, and then finally ripping her clothes off. The need to satisfy his growing sexual appetite was becoming more urgent by the second. Helen was the only woman who had succeeded in triggering such feelings in him. He could never forgive her for it. She was his Circe and he her swinish Ulysses, and her probing intellect and her passionate sensuality made her a formidable enchantress.

As she peered down at him, a shaft of sunlight gave her seagreen eyes an even greater iridescence, and he knew he was at her mercy. Then she smiled the same mocking ghost of a smile which she had bewitched him with in their youth. Reluctantly he acknowledged that for over twenty-two years in the recesses of his dreams he had hungered for such a moment as this. Yet now the moment was closing round him, he felt like a hedgehog dazzled in the lights of an approaching car. On the one hand, he was too aroused to scuttle away from what was likely to be an emotional catastrophe; on the other, he knew that to huddle up in his protective spikes would solve nothing. And the erotic headlights were getting nearer and nearer. . . .

He tried to drag his conscious mind away from the blood pumping in his groin in an attempt to focus on what Helen was saying.

'You know the reason you and Wilson have so much in common, darling? The reason is: you both leave things until it's almost too late. It's true. You wait until you have an erection, and then you cry out like a puritan virgin: "Down, Wanton, down!" And Harold, in his own inimitable way, did exactly the same thing. Only his was political hypocrisy. You have to be a professional hypocrite if you wait until after you have resigned, like Harold did, before you start pontificating from the back benches about "the growing dangers of Trotskyite infiltration". Well, it is a bit cheeky, considering Wilson was responsible for pulling the Reds out from *under* the Labour Party bed, and then inviting them *into* it! Yet although the great Harold has a phenomenal memory for dates and facts, obviously he suffers from amnesia when it comes to his left-wing bed-partners.'

Roy could bear it no longer. He leapt to his feet to confront her.

'Have you finished, Helen? Have you finished lecturing me?'

To his consternation she started laughing again.

'I don't see what's so bloody funny! To be harangued on Wilson's chicanery, in a wood full of bluebells, has an air of bathos about it, but I'd hardly call it witty. And stop pointing down there! It's not the kind of thing a real lady should do.'

'I'm only pointing at your cock, darling, because that's what's making me laugh. You should see yourself.'

With both his fists clenched, Roy glanced down at his groin and saw that his penis was still fully erect.

'Well, you must admit, darling, that a man who is shaking his fists and his cock about, at the same time as he is ranting about Harold Wilson among the bluebells, would make even a "real" lady laugh.'

'All right, all right, point taken!'

His unintended pun made Helen laugh louder.

For a moment he thought he would deal with this derisive assault on his male pride by ripping off his trousers and forcing his penis down her laughing throat. But he was no longer the sexual stallion of the LSE. As he pondered on what to do with his erection, her continuous laughter cut away the remnants of his self-confidence. Blushing, he swung his body away from her and headed back through the wood. When she called after him, he went on walking.

Thorns latched their hooks in his bare feet but he didn't stop to pull them out. He was too humiliated. For he was no longer even Circe's besotted Ulysses. She had reduced him to one of

Ulysses' followers, a pink-faced hog, rooting for the acorns of his self-respect.

'Roy! Roy!'

Helen's shout rang out, but still he did not waver as he forced his legs through the undergrowth. Then Helen ran after him, calling his name. She caught up with him among the silver birches. She grabbed his arm and forced him to a standstill against one of the trees. She thought he was going to retaliate by hitting her, but the first flush of fury in his eyes faded to a cold sadness. Then the final echoes of his youth died away and he was left only with the confused reverberations of a half-remembered melody.

'I didn't mean to humiliate you, Roy, but because you were so angry with me, and also so erect, well, it struck me as funny. I know I shouldn't have laughed, but sometimes you men are so pompous about your virility. It's true we women appreciate a good lover but it's nowhere near as important to us as you seem to think it is.'

Roy waved his hand in front of her face.

'Will you stop talking for a minute and give me time to express myself?'

Helen could barely restrain a smile.

'Roy, I never thought I would hear a politician of twenty years standing admit that he needed "time to express himself".'

'But I'm not a politician when I'm with you! Jesus Christ, I came down here for some peace and quiet. Not for sex in the bluebells! Or for the précis of your forthcoming book on Harold bleeding Wilson!'

'Stop lying to yourself, darling, and admit that you still want me. Well, you do, don't you? You only have to touch me, or let me touch you, and before you know where you are, you'll be deep inside me.'

Roy closed his eyes. Her unwavering gaze always had an hypnotic effect on him. He remembered those moments in the past when he was about to make love to her. She still had the same honest fervour. Liz was the only other woman he'd known who had an equivalent sexual strength. Neither woman ever played the coquette. Their natures were too passionate and too committed. And *I* used to be like that, he thought, in the good old days. . . .

He opened his eyes as he felt her forefinger trace the contours of his profile.

'Roy, why do you fight me? I've always loved you more than any other man and I'm proud to admit it. Oh, don't get me wrong, I've had a sexy life and lots of sexy men. Even a sexy husband. But he didn't want children, so we parted. Though I suppose I've never been really fair to my men. I've always compared them with you. Oh, not the "you" that you've turned into. But the young crusader at the LSE who was going to change the world, or at the least make Britain a decent place to live in.'

'For Christ's sake, Helen, stop talking!'

Impulsively he took her hands in his. She thought he was going to kiss her into silence like he used to in their halcyon student days. But he didn't. He clenched her fingers, then shook her like a wet spaniel. She found she enjoyed being shaken. It was good to feel the latent violence in her old lover again, though she would have preferred to have been kissed. Then Roy realised what he was doing and stopped shaking her. Bewildered, he unmanacled his fingers from her wrists. Again she resisted the impulse to laugh.

'Why don't you join the Social Democrats, darling?' Helen asked, massaging her wrists as they started to walk back towards the house.

'You haven't joined the SDP, have you?'

'Certainly. Oh, I know they're a motley crew, but at least they're not crazy.'

'Um! "Motley" is too complimentary a word for arrogant sods like Owen, port-imbibers like Jenkins, and scatty, knicker-wetting school-marms like Shirl-the-Pearl. Anyway, what the hell have the Social Democrats and their electoral "cot-death" got to do with us meeting after all these years?'

'Well, as the idea of us having sex obviously embarrasses you, Roy, we've only got one thing left to talk about, haven't we? And that is: what the hell are you going to do about your political future? Let's face it, you've no real future in the Labour Party, because you're not going to be reselected.'

'That's where you're wrong! I've got a trick or two up my sleeve. . . .'

As he said the word 'trick', he checked himself, seeing his wife's disdainful face in his mind.

Is a political trickster all I've become? he thought, as they paused in the grass to collect his discarded shoes and socks.

To his dismay, he realised his eyes were watering. He shaded them to peer at the sun-drenched landscape.

If only I had the guts to take this woman in my arms and pour myself into her sweet body. Perhaps then I'd find the courage to take my life by its throat and squeeze some resilience into me.

But though she was waiting for him to possess her, and though she knew he wanted to make love to her, she did not press her taut breasts against him. She simply said, with a great sense of sadness: 'D'you know what Blake wrote about you, darling?'

'No, and I don't wish to.'

> 'He who desires and acts not, breeds pestilence.
> He whose face gives no light, shall never become a star.
> Shame is Pride's cloak.
> Exuberance is Beauty.'

But I think the killer line is probably:

> 'Sooner murder an infant in its cradle than nurse unacted desires.'

Then, before he could respond to her challenge, she ran full tilt through the cowslips.

Fifty guests sat round the rosewood tables. Each table was lit by pale yellow candles in Georgian candlesticks. The floral decorations were a mass of yellow petals, and wherever Roy looked in the dining room, shades of yellow greeted his eyes. Everything had a spring-like quality to it, and the curling candle flames added to the warmth.

Roy had been in a daze for most of the afternoon. But now that he was surrounded by chattering local dignitaries who were to make up the two teams for the Charity Cricket Match, he was once again back in his element. Though Helen was sitting beside him in her revealing emerald-green evening dress, he was determined to remain aloof but polite. To his relief, so far she was behaving herself and not flirting. He still hadn't fully recovered from their late-afternoon game of croquet. How suggestively she'd used the mallet!

At least I've resisted her so far, he thought, struggling with the leaves of an Israeli artichoke. Though why Nancy had to give me a room next to Helen's is beyond me. Whatever happens, I'm not going to sleep with her!

Briefly he flexed his buttery fingers in a silver finger bowl, but even that brought back dangerous memories. He remembered the first time he had ever seen a finger bowl, one December in the late fifties, when he took Helen to Scott's for dinner. It was she who suggested they had artichokes, and Roy, being at the time an ignorant working-class boy from the Fens, was immediately thrown when the officious waiter placed a finger bowl in front of him. Internally blushing at the memory, he saw himself again as a callow youth, unsuccessfully trying to eat the artichoke with his knife and fork. Again he heard Helen's throaty laugh as the hot butter and the slippery leaves shot over the table, and, worse, landed on the chiffon sleeve of her new dress.

Roy glanced briefly to his left to see if Helen was reading his embarrassing thoughts. She was engaged in heated conversation with Reverend Throgmorton on Marxism and Christianity, but Roy was certain the smile that was playing on Helen's lips was not intended for the Reverend.

He dabbled his fingertips in the appropriate bowl, and again he was back in Scott's Restaurant all those years ago. No sooner had the boy from the Fens mopped the grease from his mistress' dress and swallowed his fifth glass of wine than he felt dehydrated. So the youth picked up the finger bowl, with the inviting segment of lemon floating on its surface, and in one gulp drank the contents. This made Helen laugh till she cried. She laughed her way through the rest of the dinner. When he eventually got her home and ripped her clothes off, she went on laughing. She laughed so much she made his angry erection droop as he laboured between her thighs, trying to screw some sense into her hysterical body. Then, later, when she pulled herself together and stopped, the Great East Anglian Lover found he was reduced to twenty-four hours of impotence.

'Well, I'm sure Mr Hampton agrees with me, don't you, Roy?' Helen's modulated voice broke into his reverie.

'I'm sorry, I didn't quite catch what you said, Helen.'

'The Vicar was saying that pure Marxism and Christianity have a great deal in common. And I was saying they had little in common. To begin with, Christ preached the gospel of love. Oh, I know he slipped occasionally and said: "I bring the sword", but on the whole the gospel of love prevailed. Whereas Karl Marx was always preaching the gospel of hatred and war. And even, on occasions, the gospel of racism.'

There was a pause while the butler placed trout and almonds in front of the guests. Then the Reverend Throgmorton, an angular man with a cadaverous mouth, began to bone his trout. When eventually he responded to Helen's assault on Marx, he chuckled drily and said: 'Forgive me, Miss Reid, but what evidence have you to support such an assertion?'

Helen produced her most beguiling smile for the vicar, then glanced significantly in Roy's direction. Roy smiled back, sensing that Helen was preparing to dazzle the vicar with her prodigious memory. His grin broadened as he recalled those stimulating hours when he and Helen used to compete with each another at the LSE to see who could remember the widest range of quotations. Invariably Helen won. She possessed a photographic memory, whereas Roy had only a competent actor's memory. She could not only quote accurately from dozens of plays, poems and novels, but she also had total recall of the most complicated political prose.

Still smiling, Roy returned to his trout, only to catch Helen regaling the vicar with the fruits of her research.

'You see, Vicar, Marx was always advocating the use of war and violence as his way of revolutionising the world. As you probably remember in *Marx's Collected Works*, volume 14, page 516, he wrote: "Such is the redeeming feature of war; it puts a nation to the test. As exposure to the atmosphere reduces all mummies to instant dissolution, so war passes supreme judgement upon social organisations that have outlived their vitality." And his friend Engels agreed with him, when he wrote in *Die Neue Rheinische Zeitung*: "The next world war will result in the disappearance from the face of the earth, not only all reactionary classes and dynasties, but also entire reactionary peoples like the Slav barbarians. It will wipe out these petty, hidebound nations to their very names. And that is a definite step forward. For hatred of Russia was and still is the primary revolutionary passion among Germans, to which hatred of

Czechs and Croats has now been added. So only by the use of terror against these Slav peoples, can we safeguard the Revolution!"'

Helen paused, then added sweetly: 'That can be found in Engels' *Democratic Pan-Slavism*, which I think is in volume 8 of his *Collected Works*, page 378. I'm sorry, Vicar, if I seem to be pulling dialectical-materialist rank on you, but recently I have been studying some of Marx's and Engels' lesser-known writings. I think the quotations make it obvious as to *why* they're lesser known.'

The vicar was appalled by the amazing erudition of the attractive woman at his elbow, and also profoundly disturbed. Cataclysmic thoughts whizzed round in his head like catherine wheels. He knew only too well that the writing was on the wall: one day in the not-too-distant future, self-confident women like Miss Reid would be allowed to take Holy Orders. He could well imagine what kind of sermons such a vixen would preach! The vicar hooded his eyes. He was determined to put her in her place.

'Yes, I must admit, Miss Reid, that some of Marx's and Engels' Hitlerian sentiments would not have appealed to Our Lord. But in your enthusiastic denunciation of Marx, I believe you also accused him of propagating racism.' He smiled acidly, trying to hide his feeling of imminent triumph. 'Perhaps you'll be good enough to humour me, Miss Reid, by substantiating that?'

Helen took another sip of the 1971 Grand Crus Chablis, then, fondling the cut-crystal stem of the glass between her slim fingers, she murmured: 'I think a few choice quotations from the Great Atheist's own Bible will put your mind at ease, Vicar.'

Helen flicked a saucy glance at her ex-lover. Roy began to feel sorry for the beleaguered cleric, especially as an elderly couple opposite them were now listening as well.

'For instance,' Helen said, indicating to the butler that she had enough in her glass. 'For instance, Marx wrote an article called *On The Jewish Question*, which reminds me of another "great" German's credo. For in this particular article Marx affirmed: "What is the secular basis of Judaism? Self-interest. What is the worldly religion of the Jew? Huckstering. What is his worldly God? Money. We recognise in Judaism, therefore, a general anti-social element of the present time." And the Great Man ended his particular tirade with a sentiment which would have done credit to Hitler and Stalin, who as you know, Vicar, were both dedicated anti-Semites. For Marx proclaimed: "Once society has succeeded in abolishing the empirical essence of Judaism – huckstering and its preconditions – the Jew will have become impossible!" '

Helen was about to continue when the vicar waved his hand.

'I'm sorry, Miss Reid, I don't see how that makes Marx a racist. After all, he was Jewish himself.'

'Yes, but Marx never practised Judaism. In fact he was baptised into the Christian faith at an Evangelical Church in 1816. Then he abandoned Christianity while he was at university, but he was always far more abusive about Jews and Judaism than he ever was about Christians and Christianity. Mind, he was even more of a racialist about the blacks. In a letter to Engels, July 30th 1862, Marx wrote: "The Jewish Nigger Lasalle fortunately departs at the end of this week. It is now completely clear to me that he, as is proved by his cranial formation and curly hair, descends from the Negroes who joined Moses' exodus from Egypt. Assuming of course that his mother or grandmother on the paternal side had not interbred with a nigger in the interim! Now this Judaism and Germanism combined with a basic Negro substance must produce a peculiar product. The obtrusiveness of the fellow is also nigger-like".'

Helen stopped, her eyes stern and her mouth set in a hard line.

'I trust I don't have to say any more, Vicar. If you still don't believe me, you need only peruse Marx's and Engels' copious correspondence to find that they often used the English term "nigger" to refer to blacks and to any others whom they held in contempt.'

The vicar had stopped eating. Tentatively he wiped the corner of his mouth with his napkin. Then he looked round him and saw that the elderly couple on the other side of the table and several other guests were waiting for him to reply.

'Yes, well, I am forced to agree with you, Miss Reid, that when Marx and Engels wrote those obscene things, they inhabited a very different philosophical world to that illumined by Our Lord Jesus Christ. What I don't understand, however, is why such a beautiful woman as yourself should be so obsessed by the more unsavoury aspects of Marx's character?'

Before Helen could reply, Roy laid his cutlery on the side of his plate.

'Yes, Helen, I think the vicar has a point. When you were quoting from Marx just now, your eyes almost glazed over. It was as if Marx was some kind of demon inside you that you were desperately trying to exorcise.'

'God in heaven, Roy, grow up, will you?' Helen snapped back. Then, noting the distraught look in the vicar's eyes, she softened her tone.

'I'm sorry, Vicar, but here I am trying to help this besieged MP to fight the Marxists in his constituency, and yet he has the gall to accuse me of being "possessed' by Karl Marx!'

She swallowed the last of her Chablis, then banged her glass onto the table. The elderly couple opposite gasped. The other guests looked puzzled and stopped eating.

'I trust I haven't spoiled your dinner, Vicar, but there are certain facts about false gurus like Marx that should be trumpeted to the four corners of the earth. For too long there has been a deliberate conspiracy of silence shrouding the despotic and racist side of Marx's philosophy.'

Helen's knuckles blanched as she twisted the napkin on her lap. Roy wished he could calm her down, but she was oblivious to his concerned looks.

'Roy, d'you remember the Dostoevsky quotation that Solzhenitsyn used in his proposed Nobel Prize acceptance speech? Dostoevsky wrote: "One word of Truth can outweigh the whole world." Yet "the words" of so-called "truth" that Marx's disciples are always quoting are very carefully selected. According to his disciples, Marx only ever had love in his heart! So every time his guardians re-edit his works in Moscow, they cut out everything that could be "misunderstood" by the masses and the Party faithful. This includes, of course, all Marx's racism and war-mongering! Indeed, his disciples have done their best to remove everything from Marx's works that reminds them of those other two great "socialists". I'm referring, of course, to Adolf Hitler with his *National* Socialism and Joseph Stalin with his Union of *Soviet* Socialist Republics. If anyone wants to be a "socialist" after those two guys, then I would prefer not to know him! That includes non-Marxist socialists like Tony

Benn, who nevertheless believe that Marxism is a legitimate strand of socialism. Though it should be noted that Mr Benn, like many others, only quotes the "more enlightened" aspects of Marx's philosophy. Maybe Mr Benn doesn't know about Marx's war-mongering and his National Front tendencies. Well, Mr Benn obviously can't know, can he? Or he wouldn't have written in *Aspects of Socialism* that Marx was "a towering socialist philosopher whom we certainly rank with the greatest minds in history, along with Copernicus, Darwin, Freud and Einstein." Then Mr Benn goes on to say: "It would be wrong to blame Marx for Stalin's tyranny as it would be to lay blame for the Spanish Inquisition on the teachings of Jesus." Yet even Marx's greatest disciple, Lenin, would be the first to refute that! As Lenin told his own secret police; "When we are reproached with cruelty, Comrades, we wonder how people can forget their most elementary Marxism." If that isn't a Stalinist sentiment, I don't know what is!'

Helen paused, unaware that the bewildered guests were waiting breathlessly for the stunned clergyman's reply. At the head of the table Nancy and Freddy looked anxiously at one another. Nancy was about to say something when Helen hurled another missile at the vicar.

'And whether you or Mr Hampton like it or not, Vicar, Stalin was the perfect heir to Lenin. As Lenin was the perfect heir to Marx. Because it was Lenin, not Stalin, who said: "If for the work of Communism we must wipe out nine-tenths of the population, we must not recoil before these sacrifices!" In case either of you want to look it up, you'll find it in Lenin's *Selected Works*, volume 2.'

Everyone was now looking at Helen nervously, but she no longer cared whether or not she was making a fool of herself. Her only aim was to provoke the man she loved into standing up for himself in the political arena, so that he could again become the daring soul he was in his youth. Knowing she would never have another opportunity like the present, she felt that to go crazy at a dinner party could only do some good.

'Well, it's true, Roy. It's because people like Wedgwood Benn flirt with Marxism that they give credence to Marx's extremist philosophy. And it is the extremism, on *both* sides of the political divide, that threatens our democracy. As the result of the lunatic polarisation of both major parties, England could well lose her historic freedom in the not-too-distant future!'

At the end of the table, Nancy cleared her throat. Before she could pour oil on the troubled waters, Helen surged on.

'Yet although I would be the first to admit that Thatcher's authoritarian right-wing Toryism is potentially dangerous, it's the totalitarian left wing of the Labour Party which is the greater threat to the continuance of our democracy. If the hard left ever come to power in this country, which they may well do in the next ten years or so, they will be much harder to remove from office than Mrs Thatcher's present administration. You only have to look at twentieth-century history to see that the communist regimes are always much harder to dismantle than fascist regimes. Oh, I'm not accusing Mrs Thatcher of being a fascist, but there are racist supporters of hers who blatantly are!'

The Reverand Throgmorton could bear it no longer.

'Miss Reid, how can you possibly assert that it's "easier to dismantle a fascist regime than a communist regime"?'

'Take Hitler, for example, Vicar. Within weeks of Hitler's death, most of the horrors of the Third Reich were swept away and democracy was established. The same is true of fascist leaders like Mussolini, Franco and Salazar. This is because Naziism and fascism depend for the continuance of their success on the charisma of Der Fuhrer or the "Great Leader". So once the "Great Leader" is dead, the fascist regime can be dismantled and replaced with a more democratic administration. But communism is quite a different kettle of fish! Communism is self-perpetuating and doesn't depend on the charisma of a "Great Leader". Even when Stalin the God died – and he was the greatest murderer in all history, with at least sixty-five million deaths on his conscience! – his death made no difference to the communist regime in Russia, which has continued unabated in his absence. The same is true of China. Though Mao had only a mere thirty-three million deaths on his conscience!'

Pointing an accusing finger at the cleric's dog collar, Helen thundered on: 'And you know the reason why communism is self-perpetuating, Vicar? It's because communism is the first godless religion in the history of the world. That's why it's so difficult to defeat. Communism seems to offer its believers the perfect political panacea, with all men being equal before all men. But the great irony is that under applied Marxism everyone is equal, all right – in that they equally have no freedom!'

As her voice rose and the assembled guests looked on in embarrassed dismay, Helen knew she was not just shouting because she believed Marxism was evil and inevitable. No, her anger was for her lost youth and happiness. She had put a lifetime into researching the lives of men who had tried to make history in their own contorted images, and what had she got to show for it?

Impatiently she turned on her ex-lover. Roy realised that everyone in the room was staring at them both and wondering: 'Are they lovers having a row? Or husband and wife? Has the woman gone mad?'

The audience's fascination grew as Helen rose and brandished her arm above her head, like some ancient prophetess pronouncing a nation's doom.

'I can see it's hopeless trying to give you political courage, Roy,' Helen whispered hoarsely, with her outstretched hand pointing towards the ceiling. 'I'll just give you Heinrich Heine's prophecy about Marxism, then I'll leave you alone for ever!'

The audience now found the spectacle so bizarre and the woman's intensity so electric that no one moved. Even the host and hostess were hypnotised by Helen's staring eyes. The situation was profoundly un-English and therefore unstoppable.

'Heinrich Heine prophesied: "When you godless, self-appointed gods come into your own, there will be one free shepherd with an iron staff, plus a flock of human sheep which will be shorn to look alike and bleat alike. For the future smells to me of Russian leather, blood, godlessness, and many whippings. So I advise our grandchildren to be born with very thick skins on their backs!" '

When she finished, there was silence. Then several local dignitaries, thinking it was some sort of poem or a between-the-course speech, began to applaud. Others started laughing, especially the wives. Then Freddy and Nancy, as the perfect hosts, took the initiative and began applauding and laughing simultaneously. Immediately the guests joined in the laughing applause. Then the High Sheriff at the far end of the room jocularly banged his hand on the table, demanding: 'More, madam, more!'

Helen's vision swam. To be mocked on top of everything was too much for her. Roy stood up abruptly. He wanted to shout at the circle of laughing faces but knew it would only make things more embarrassing. He offered to escort Helen out of the lion's den, but she jerked away from him and waved her arms to silence the laughter and applause.

'I'm terribly sorry, everyone! Please try and forgive me . . . I don't know what came over me . . . I. . . .'

Helplessly she trailed off. Then, with a last despairing look at Roy, she fled out of the room.

Helen lay huddled up under the rose-pink coverlet in the moonlit bedroom. She was no longer crying but was still exhausted. There was a tap on the door. She peered at the ormolu clock on the Adam fireplace. It was three minutes to midnight.

'Come in, Roy,' she said hoarsely.

The door opened and Roy moved stealthily into the room.

'Well, close the door, darling.'

Helen lay back on the bed as the door clicked shut. Tentatively she touched her throbbing eyelids. Her face was swollen with crying. To her surprise, Roy sat on the bed beside her. Then he took her hand between his and began to stroke it like a newborn kitten. There was no sexuality in his touch, only friendship and unspoken sympathy.

'Aren't you cold, darling, just sitting there?' Helen said, allowing the coverlet to slide off her bare shoulders so that her breasts were revealed. Roy turned his head away but continued to hold her hand.

'Don't, Helen. Please, don't,' he whispered. 'I only came to say how much I admired you.'

She tightened her grip on his fingers. Without looking, Roy knew she was smiling.

'I know that sounds a bit pompous, Helen, but your strength of character is something I've always admired. In the old days I used to think I had it, too. But, as Albee said in *Who's Afraid of Virginia Woolf?* "There's been a lot of blood under the bridge" since then. No, please let me finish.'

Helen glared at his moonlit profile. She was becoming impatient with him. She knew he was going to give her a complimentary appraisal of her disastrous outburst in the dining room, but having already cried the humiliation out of her system, she didn't want to talk about it any more.

'Helen, for Christ's sake, stop looking at me like that.'

Helen smiled, knowing he was staring at her breasts.

'I'll stop accusing you, darling, if you'll stop fighting yourself.'

Then, before he could resist, she pulled his head down until she felt his lips part and his tongue probe her nipple.

As he fastened his eager mouth on her breast, a stifled shudder went through him. He clung to her and forced his mouth open wider. He wanted to swallow her breast, and at the same time be swallowed by her. His urgent need was only partially sexual desire, for he was like a deprived infant. Yet it was more than milk he wanted from Helen. He wanted to drink her essential courage. Like a loving vampire, he wanted to suck her belief in him into the depths of his being.

'Yes, I know, darling, I know,' she murmured, as she stroked his tousled hair. 'You want to make love to me but you can't. Don't worry, I won't seduce you. You're safe with me.'

He knew he was, so he clung to her, burrowing his head between her breasts. He felt ashamed, for he was aware he was exciting her but not fulfilling the promise. Within seconds he was consumed by guilt. He sat up abruptly and covered her breasts with the coverlet.

'I'm a real shit, aren't I?'

'You're no more of a shit than I am, darling.'

'Oh, Helen!'

'I'm being perfectly serious. What right have I to try and seduce a happily married man simply because I have the misfortune to still be in love with him? So why don't we both give our recriminations a miss?'

Roy nodded, then stood up and moved to the window. Without warning, he turned back to face the smiling woman in the bed.

'All right, I won't apologise for my boring puritan guilt. I won't even apologise for letting you behave as you did. And I won't talk about the past, which, as you've guessed, has become one of my favourite subjects. Yes, you might well grin, because you're right. Over the years I have changed, and not for the better. What I'm trying to say, Helen, is that I agree with everything you've thrown at me today. Well, nearly everything. And that Marx and Engels stuff you hurled at the Vicar was quite a revelation. Even when we were at the LSE I never came across those incredible quotations.'

'I'll send you all that stuff and anything else I come across, darling, if you think you can make use of it in your fight with the Trots.'

Helen paused. Then, keeping her breasts covered, she leant forward.

'That is, assuming you're actually going to fight the Trots.'

Roy half-smiled.

'The day after tomorrow I hope to speak in the Commons on the big security debate.'

Helen nodded and waited. Roy rubbed the corners of his eyes with his knuckles.

'What I'm getting at, Helen, is I could use the occasion to stir up the hornets' nest. By hornets I mean the hard left. Though, to be honest with you, until we met today I had no intention of stirring up anything. But now I think you could give me some ammo that would really make those bastards buzz.'

'I'm sure I could, darling. But you do realise that once you've stirred the bastards up, it's more than likely they'll then want to stir you up? And from that point on. . . .'

'I know, but what have I got to lose?'

'Knowing you, darling, probably your nerve.'

Roy frowned. Helen laughed and extended her hand.

'Now, now! Don't go sulky on me. I was only joking. Seriously.'

Roy crossed the room towards her, then paused at the foot of the bed.

'Well, climb in beside me, darling. I won't touch you any more than you want me to. Or anywhere.'

'I think it's safer if I sit here.'

He perched himself on the corner of the bed next to her protruding feet. Helen smiled, then moistened her lips:

'If I give you enough "ammo", as you call it, to drive your hornets crazy, what will I get as a reward?'

Roy thought for a moment. Being a professional politician, he came up with a professional politician's rejoinder.

'When you've given me the "ammo", Helen, I'll come up with an appropriate reward. In the meantime, you must promise to keep your breasts, and everything else, under wraps. OK?'
'OK.'
But the glint in her green eyes disturbed him, and though, according to the ormolu clock, it was only twenty past twelve, the night was young, and so was he – well, fairly young. . . .

MAY

It rained for the third time that afternoon but eventually the watery sun emerged from behind a bank of purplish clouds. As the last raindrops slanted across the cricket pitch, Roy turned at the end of his bowler's run. Then he paused to gaze at the double rainbow above the pavilion. He didn't hear his fellow players urging him to get on with it. With the cricket ball in his hand, he stood open-mouthed and marvelled at the iridescent arc in the heavens.

Two of the closer fielders shouted at him again. Roy nodded, cradled the cricket ball between his hands and started his long, rocking run up to the wicket. In his youth he had modelled himself on Freddy Truman and he still had a tolerably good bowling action. As he pounded over the shaved turf, he caught a glimpse of Helen in her deckchair by the pavilion steps. She was wrapped in his raincoat and obviously enjoying the match. With a final gasp, Roy swung his arm over as fast as he could and hurled the ball at the opposing batsman.

To his delight, the ball beat the batsman for sheer pace and cartwheeled the middle stump out of the ground into the surprised wicketkeeper's gloves. Instantly Helen was on her feet applauding, while the rest of Roy's team rushed forward to hug him and clap him on the back. Only the retreating batsman was less than enthusiastic. And that was just the beginning. By the end of the match, the wicketkeeper and the captain were carrying Roy shoulder-high back to the pavilion, as a reward for his taking five wickets for eleven runs and smashing the middle stump as his finale.

Two hours later Roy was downing his second pint of lager in the pavilion, surrounded by his hosts and his triumphant teammates. Wherever he turned, he was greeted with beery praise, and though Roy tried to prevent her, Helen insisted on hugging and kissing the hero of the hour in front of everyone. Every time she touched him he was reminded of the previous evening, which he desperately wanted to forget.

'Why don't we slip up to my bedroom, darling?' Helen whispered, surreptitiously nipping his earlobe with her sharp teeth. 'Then we can go on from where we left off.'

Roy shook his head emphatically. He was about to order another round of drinks when a small, athletic-looking man, with prematurely grey, curly hair, pressured Roy's elbow with his suntanned finger and thumb.

'Excuse me, Mr Hampton, but I wonder if you could spare me a moment of your time?'

Roy hesitated.

'It could be to our mutual advantage, Mr Hampton,' the man insisted, turning to Helen. 'Oh, I promise I'll only borrow him for five minutes, Miss Reid.'

Outside the pavilion, the late-afternoon sun threw long, cool shadows across the green. Roy followed the man down the steps. As they padded over the worn grass, the man said: 'I can't tell you how impressed I was by your fiery bowling performance this afternoon. Very reminiscent of Frank Tyson, if I may say so.'

'It was meant to be more like Freddy Truman.'

The man's bronzed features wrinkled with laughter, then he extended his hand.

'I'm Jack Winner, a close friend of Nancy and Freddy. It was Freddy who suggested I should have a word with you.'

'What about?'

'I'm the chairman of the JYC Management Consultants Corporation. We help firms with their relationships with governments, both here in the UK and overseas.'

'So?'

'So – we need an extra pair of hands to help us with our governmental relations. And your name's been mentioned to me several times by our mutual friend.'

Roy laughed, then absently brushed a greenfly off the sleeve of his white sweater.

'I'm glad you find that amusing, Mr Hampton.'

'Sorry, Mr Winner. It's just your enquiry has come as a bit of a surprise. You see, I wasn't thinking of leaving politics. At least, not yet.'

Winner grinned, revealing his recently crowned teeth. Then he undid the top button of his blazer to get at his wallet.

'There's no need to make up your mind now, Roy. Let's have lunch at my club next week. Here's my card. I'll give you a ring at the Commons.'

Roy studied Winner's card, then pocketed it.

'Mr Winner, may I ask why you are interested in me in particular?'

'Freddy recommended you. Said you were a live wire when you were both at the LSE together. And your bowling speaks for itself. Not to mention . . .'

'Not to mention what?'

'Well, I gathered from Miss Reid's entertaining little outburst at dinner last night that you've got the odd problem in your constituency. And with that kind of problem, it wouldn't surprise me if you found yourself looking for further employment in the very near future. But, as I say, why don't we have lunch and discuss the way the world wags?'

As Roy completed his car journey home, his mind was whirling.

What an incredible, unexpected weekend! Not only did I bowl better than I ever have in my life and was offered a potentially lucrative job on the strength of it, but there was also Helen.

The moment he thought of her, his elation subsided and he prickled with guilt. As he glanced in the driving mirror to check whether he could overtake a van safely, he saw that he had a smudge of lipstick on the left side of his mouth. Shaking his head in disbelief, he fished out his handkerchief and rubbed his lips fiercely. He was angry with Helen because she had insisted on kissing him 'properly and for the last time' on the steps of the house.

Well, he thought, as he wound through the back streets of Hackney and crumpled his lipstick-stained handkerchief into his glove compartment. Well, I certainly won't ever kiss her again, or touch her or . . . I may see her – occasionally. But last night is history and never to be repeated. Thank goodness no one need ever know. Within minutes I'll be back home, regaling the family with my cricketing exploits. Yes, the family comes before everything. Liz is still the centre of my life.

Smiling ruefully, he switched on the car radio to listen to the News. At first he couldn't catch what the reporter was saying because of radio static and the background rumbling of what could only be hundreds of tanks.

Christ, he thought, turning up the volume. Don't say we're being invaded by the Russians already!

As he drove down Hackney High Street, he was able to make out what the reporter was saying: 'So once again the Soviet leadership take the salute. The Politburo view their impressive military might as it passes below them through Red Square. What is merely another Bank Holiday for everyone in England is May Day with a vengeance here in Moscow. Again and again the President salutes the troops, in tank upon tank, as they thunder past him. On the shoulders of the tank commanders there are young, fair-haired boys, waving up at the President and his aged comrades. Now come the SS20 missiles on their cumbersome trailers. Everywhere red flags are flapping in the bitter wind. The gigantic banners of Karl Marx and Vladimir Illyich Lenin seem to have a life of their own as gusts of hail bombard the cheering spectators. And still the tanks and missiles come on, grinding last night's snow into brown slush under their caterpillar tracks. I'm now looking up at the onion domes of the Kremlin, which cannot fail to remind us of the Tsars and ancient Muscovy. Though recently of course it is the modern Tsars who are interred in the Kremlin's walls, including Stalin, Brezhnev and Andropov. Though there are rumours here in Moscow that Stalin, once his inevitable rehabilitation has been completed, will again take his original place beside Lenin in the Mausoleum in Red Square. . . .'

God forbid, Roy thought, switching over to Radio Three, where he was instantly assaulted by Shostakovitch's Tenth Symphony. Then he realised he had tuned in to the scherzo and started to laugh; he had read somewhere that Shostakovitch had depicted Stalin in the scherzo.

Yes, there's no doubt about it, he thought. Though Stalin is dead and buried, as long as there are KGB men in top positions in the Kremlin, Stalin might as well still be alive. For though the Soviets periodically whitter on about human rights, they only do this as a sop to the peace movement and to every wishy-washy liberal who wants to be taken in.

Roy snorted, then turned the radio off.

Helen has really got me steamed up, he thought. Not just sexually, but politically as well. But have I the nerve to go berserk in the House tomorrow? What purpose will it serve to put my head on the chopping block, anyway? I should never have gone to her room last night. . . .

It was still light when Roy let himself into the house but there was no sign of Liz or the children. He opened the back door quietly and peered into the twilit garden. Then his eyes grew accustomed to the dusky strangeness of the light. There, half-hidden in the long shadows on the lawn, was his wife, tending the border of their garden. For a full minute he watched her weeding the rose bed. Then he glanced to his left to see Alexa, sitting on the swing suspended from the apple tree.

How beautiful my daughter looks, he thought, in that cloud of apple blossom.

Roy was so taken by the vision that he didn't notice his daughter peering at him quizzically. As he crossed the lawn and tenderly kissed the top of her flaxen head, he became aware of her hostility.

'What's the matter, Alexa?'

'Nothing, Dad, except you've got lipstick on your ear lobe and you stink of Madame Rochas.'

'That's impossible, darling! I don't even know Madame Rochas.'

'I'm sure you don't, Dad. But your fancy-woman sure as hell does. See, Madame Rochas is the name of an expensive perfume and your floozie must cover herself in it.'

Roy gulped and backed away from the swing. Then Alexa started laughing.

'Now don't look all guilty, Dad, or Mum and I will believe you are. We know you have to kiss the odd lady in your travels. Anyway, Mum trusts you. She told me. Didn't you, Mum?'

Roy turned to see Liz watching him. Her mouth was smiling but her eyes were sad.

'Of course I trust your father, Alexa. Without trust, marriage is hopeless.'

'That's why I'm never going to get married, Mum!' Alexa shouted, winking as she ran into the house.

Roy followed his daughter with his eyes, then jerked his head round to see Liz standing by his shoulder. The sadness in her eyes was replaced by desolation. Before he could stop her, she pulled off her gardening gloves and touched his offending earlobe. In the fading light she saw that her fingertip was faintly smudged with lipstick.

'Yes,' she said, staring at her fingertip. 'Marriage is a hopeless institution without trust. But what happens if the trust is misplaced, Roy? What happens then?'

Alexa reappeared in the kitchen doorway.

'Mr Warrington's here, Dad, from round the corner. He says he's got some bad news that he needs to talk to you about urgently.'

Roy closed his eyes. It wasn't the first time he didn't know which way to turn, nor would it be the last, but he knew this was a pivotal moment in his marriage. Yet, as so often in the past, now the moment of decision was upon him he decided to deal with the easier of the two problems confronting him. He would postpone the potential crisis in his marriage and become the dutiful public servant by listening to the complaints of his constituent. He dragged his eyes away from his wife's accusing stare. With an assumed air of calm, he addressed the man framed in the kitchen doorway.

'Ah, Mr Warrington. I'm sorry you've got bad news. Why don't we go into my study and see what we can do about it?'

Then he smiled awkwardly at his wife and escorted his stoop-shouldered constituent back into the house. When the two men had gone, Alexa turned to her mother.

'There's nothing wrong between you and Dad, is there, Mum?'

Liz laughed as she picked up the trowel from the rose bed, then said, 'There's nothing wrong that a divorce won't cure, dear.'

For a moment Alexa was uncertain how to take this, but being by nature one of life's eternal optimists, she decided it was another of her mother's world-weary jokes. So she gave a cursory laugh and went off to raid the fridge, unaware that her mother was smiling hopelessly at the setting sun.

Roy's office-cum-study was in its habitual state of disarray. Sighing, the MP removed copies of Crosland's *Biography* and Tony Benn's *Arguments for Democracy* from the armchair by the window so his constituent could sit down. As Mr Warrington slumped into the chair, Roy shovelled more books from a swivel-stool onto the floor.

'I'm sorry about the mess, Mr Warrington, but I've too many books and far too few shelves.'

Roy turned on the angle-lamp on his desk. The man blinked as the study was doused abruptly in cold electric light.

It's like everything today, Roy thought. We switch from the soft afterglow of the sunset to an ultra-bright, neon-lit world. No wonder life appears to have such hard edges to it. Science and technology continually take our breath away. Twentieth-century man is instantly transformed from this, to that, before he can blink. Everything changes too fast. . . .

Roy dragged himself out of his reverie, only to see Mr Warrington wringing his hands and sobbing helplessly.

'Whatever's the matter, Mr Warrington?'

'I've been telling you, Mr Hampton, but you ain't been listening!' Mr Warrington rasped, rubbing his reddened eyes. 'I got this letter, see, on Saturday, saying my area manager wanted to see me on Tuesday. At first I didn't think nothing of it. Then a workmate of mine gave me a bell just now, and he told me the reason the area manager wants to see me.'

Mr Warrington paused for breath, unaware of the teardrops hanging from his nose.

'Yeah, there I was, Mr Hampton, watching fucking John Wayne in the fucking *War Waggon*, and me mate rings me up and ruins me fucking Bank Holiday movie! "Be prepared, Rog," he says: "They're going to give you yer cards tomorrow because the sales for jiffy cloths, cleaning stuffs and all that other kitchen rubbish you sell, have gone right down in your area. So they're going to have to make you redundant!" '

Roy tried to concentrate on Mr Warrington's words but was distracted by the vision of his wife's hurt eyes in the darkening windowpane. With difficulty he refocussed on the man's outpourings of despair.

'Every day more and more of us lose our fucking jobs under these arsehole Tories! It's all right Thatcher and her stinking cronies visiting the north-east, Wales and Scotland. But what fucking good does that do? That don't give us back our jobs. Look how they've carved up the steel industry. And the coal industry's next! So what chance do we salesmen have when no one can afford to buy anyfink? Thatcher ought to be bloody shot! Well, if she has her way, we'll have no National Health Service. Nor no proper schooling for our kids. The whole fucking country will end up like Lamberton! England'll just be a privatized rubbish tip full of poor out-of-work sods like me! In the end no one will dare to go on strike because that bitch in Number 10 will starve us back to work. Well, can't you hear that phoney voice of hers?'

To Roy's surprise, Mr Warrington uncoiled in the armchair and gave an outrageous imitation of the Prime Minister's unfortunate voice.

' "Now I want all you workers to stop being silly and selfish. I want you to ignore the advice of your horrible trade unions and put your backs to the wheel. We want the Falklands spirit again on your shop floors, we want. . . ." '

Mr Warrington trailed off in disgust, then he brushed another tear away from his chin.

'Well, that hard-faced, soft-spoken old cow thinks she's the fucking Queen, don't she? Mind, the rotten Royals are as bad, always swanning all over the world in their fucking royal yachts and in their special fucking planes! They don't give a shit about us, do they? All they're interested in is holding on to their land! She's the richest fucking Queen in the world, ain't she? Tony Benn's right. The Royals have got to go! And the fucking House of Lords and all the privileges have got to go with 'em. Not that I agree with everything Benn says. He used to be just as privileged as they are. Oh, I know he's been converted to the Cause, but converts are always dangerous. I mean, my niece became a Catholic recently, and now she's as nutty as a fruitcake. In fact, she's a religious maniac!'

Mr Warrington was now on his feet, rampaging round the study. Roy was so stunned by his passionate outburst and so unsure how to calm him down that he did nothing but play with the empty matchbox in his pocket.

Everything's out of control again, he thought. My wife is outside, brooding with jealousy and spoiling for a fight. MacMaster is bound to be in his grotty bed-sit, making love to that delicious girlfriend of his while plotting my downfall. Helen is probably home by now, wondering whether she should phone me to rev me up for the big debate tomorrow. And this poor fellow is rightly going crazy because the system is flushing him down the pan. To top it all, I don't know what to do about my wife, MacMaster, Helen or this poor devil! I'm like a priest, but a priest without powers, for all I can do is listen and nod my head sympathetically.

'Mind you,' roared Mr Warrington, 'I wouldn't trust Tony Benn as far as I could kick him! Well, he's never going to be out of a job like I am, is he? I mean, he and his wife are so fucking rich he could probably retire tomorrow. Not that he will, of course, because he's too ambitious. Mind, anyone could be the king of the socialists like Benn is with all that money behind 'em! Still, at least he and the Labour Party will get rid of this unemployment when they get into power, won't they?'

Roy nodded as he stood up to face his tear-stained constituent. For a moment he considered being bluntly honest with Mr Warrington. Roy thought of explaining to him about his worries concerning a future Labour Administration, but he knew it wouldn't help, so he simply said: 'Is there anything I can do to . . . Well, to make things easier for you, Mr Warrington?'

'Forgive me, Mr Hampton, but that's a fucking stupid question! I didn't come round here because I thought you could get me my fucking job back.' Mr Warrington spread both his knobbly hands over the littered top of Roy's desk and spat his words into the MP's bewildered face. 'Y'see, I know you can't get me my job back. And I know you can't persuade my wife not to leave me for her fancy-man. Any more than you can help me with my mortgage repayments.'

'Then why exactly have you come to me tonight, Mr Warrington?'

'Because you're the only MP I've ever spoken to! And though we ain't spoken often, you've always been polite. To be honest, I didn't know who else to turn to.'

The thin man blew his nose to stop himself crying.

'Don't get me wrong, Mr Hampton. I don't fink you're the world's greatest MP, but at least you try hard. I disagree wiv a lot of the fings you say, but I still believe you're a pretty good bloke – as politicians go.'

Mr Warrington blew his nose again, only harder. Then he rubbed the other side of his handkerchief over his damp cheeks.

'I'm sorry for making a fool of myself in front of you. Won't happen again. You just make sure you give that Thatcher cow hell whenever you can. And let's hope to Christ that things'll change, and quick enough. Or, before you know where you are, you'll be slung out on the shit-heap beside me! No, don't see me out. In the state I'm in . . . I'd prefer to find my own way, thanks.'

Roy leant across the desk and touched the sleeve of the thin man's maroon cardigan.

'Will you at least let me know if you . . . well, if you find another job?'

Mr Warrington grinned bleakly.

'Of course I will. Well, I'm bound to find a job sooner or later, ain't I? I mean, according to the fucking Tories I only need to get onto my daughter's fucking bike and ride round the fucking corner and there'll be hundreds of fucking jobs just waiting for me!'

'Yes, I must say that Thatcher and most of her Cabinet are pretty callous. They simply have no understanding of us in the working class, do they?'

Mr Warrington raised a quizzical eyebrow, then shoved his handkerchief into his cardigan pocket.

'Yes, I know what you're thinking, Mr Warrington. How can I, living in what's known as Nobs' Row and speaking with my middle-class accent, have the cheek to talk of "us in the working class"?'

'Well, it does sound a bit odd, Mr Hampton, coming from you, like.'

'I suppose there's no point in me telling you that I was born into the working class. My father was a meter reader for the gas board. The house in which I was brought up was practically a bunny-hutch. My mother still lives in that house – all alone since my father died of cancer – and the lavatory is still outside. As for my middle-class vowels, I picked those up at grammar school when I was in the school plays.'

Disgusted with himself, Roy stopped abruptly and shook his head.

'I'm sorry, Mr Warrington. All that working-class sob story about my childhood, although it's true, was completely uncalled for. What I'm trying to say is, I had no right to justify myself to you after ... well, after the ordeal you've been through. Let's face it, though I still *feel* working-class inside, I no longer *sound* working-class. And my lifestyle is certainly middle-class. Though my daughter, God bless her, is doing everything she can to rebel against it.'

Roy shook the thin man's hand and opened the study door. They exchanged brief goodbyes.

After he had gone, Roy emitted a long, audible sigh. Feeling thirsty, he left his study and went along the darkening passageway into the bathroom. He was pouring himself a glass of water when he saw the fleeting figure of his wife reflected in the medicine cabinet mirror. Before he could say anything, Liz disappeared into their bedroom. Roy sighed again, then drank the water and headed after her.

He paused outside the bedroom door which was ajar. He dreaded how he would find his wife. He expected her to be crying, or silent with rage. If she was in one of her silent moods she could sustain it all night. Once she had refused to speak to him for thirty-six hours, except indirectly through the children. He could cope with anything but her silence.

If only Helen hadn't insisted on kissing me like that before leaving, none of this would be happening. Still, I can't hover here all night.

Coughing to announce his presence, he pushed the door open but didn't go in. Instead he crouched in the doorway to pick up a carpet tack. It was the third he'd found loose that week.

Not only do we need new guttering and the outside of the house repainting, we also ought to have the whole place recarpeted. Not that we can afford it. Everything's so bloody expensive. By the time the pittance I earn as an MP has been taxed, I might as well be paid in toy-town money.

He started yawning compulsively. He knew this was a sign that he wanted to fall into bed and go to sleep, and preferably without having to face his wife's accusing eyes.

Yes, Eliot was right. 'Humankind cannot bear very much

reality'. And my problem is I find I can bear less and less with every day that passes. Though I'm probably not alone in feeling this. Take poor Mr Warrington. He's had enough 'reality' slopped over him tonight to last him for the rest of his life. Tomorrow will be even worse for him as he trudges to the Labour Exchange and round the Job Centres. Christ, what kind of civilisation is this where hard-working men are discarded like sweet-wrappers? Once you syphon off a man's dignity, what is he left with? Bitterness, despair and the ultimate 'reality' of self-loathing and desolation.

He found Liz sitting motionless at the dressing table, staring into the mirror. At first he thought she had been crying, but as he moved closer he realised he was mistaken. What he had taken to be tears were merely pinpricks of light from the table lamp. He was about to speak to her when Liz's forefinger began to probe the blueish shadow under her left eye. Fascinated, he wondered what she would do next. Her fingertip paused under her chin as if it had a life of its own. Her eyes remained expressionless as a smile hardened the upturned corners of her mouth.

'Alexa was right just now, wasn't she?' Liz said, still smiling.

'Right about what, dear?'

'Don't be obtuse, Roy. You're not in the House of Commons now. This mess you've got yourself into is real.'

'Darling, the lipstick on my ear was not what you think.'

'Wasn't it?' Liz snapped.

At that moment they both became aware of the bowl of carnations on the windowsill. The perfume was so potent that for several seconds husband and wife were spiritually at one as they savoured the fragrance. Then Roy broke the bond by moving closer to the dressing table.

'I didn't sleep with her, darling. I wanted to but I didn't.'

Liz swung round on her stool to face him. He leant forward to put a restraining finger on her lips. She jerked her head away but he was insistent.

'I'm telling you the truth about me and Helen, Liz.'

'Helen?'

Liz was now on her feet with her fists clenched.

'Yes, Helen Reid. We were at the LSE together and she always used to carry a torch for me. Can't think why.'

'Nor can I!' blurted Liz, fast losing control.

Then suddenly she understood everything. For years she had wondered whether Roy had been faithful to her during their engagement. Especially as most of the time they were apart.

'You and this Helen Reid were lovers while you were at the LSE, weren't you? Yes, while I was stuck in Peterborough at the training college, you were having it off with her down here. Don't try and lie! You're not very good at it. No, don't touch me. Don't you dare touch me!'

Her face was a mask of fury, so Roy withdrew his hand from her elbow.

'Christ, I've a good mind to kick you in the balls, you lecherous bastard! You knew damn well that whore of yours would be at Freddy and Nancy's, didn't you? That's why you were only too glad to pack me and the kids off to Peterborough. While I was listening to my father whittering on about the great days of steam engines, you were getting your leg over your old flame. Well, don't deny it. You probably screwed the bitch rigid. Then she told you what a mind-blowing lover you were. Just like your LSE days when you were deceiving your stupid fiancée! Oh, don't worry, I'm not going to cry. I'm too livid to cry!'

As Liz's voice became shriller, Roy grabbed hold of his wife's forearms and began to shake her like he shook Helen among the silver birches. He knew they were both out of control but there was nothing he could do but go on shaking her. He would have hit her, but she hit him first, flailing her fists into his face and chest. As the first bruise formed on his cheek and his ribcage started to ache, he found to his consternation he was enjoying the pain. Then she hit him in the throat so hard he had to gag for breath. In her jealous frenzy, she kicked his shins. Yelping, he fell back onto the bed, instinctively drawing himself into a foetal position because he thought she was going to kick him in the groin. Then, as suddenly as Liz's frenzy had flared into violence, it suddenly subsided.

For several seconds the alarm clock on the bedside table ticked to itself. Roy lay motionless and listened to the ticking. He forgot his throbbing cheek and the dull ache in his left ankle. Gradually the ticking gave way to the sound of Liz panting for breath. He turned over to look up at her. She was still standing over him with her arms clasped defensively over her heaving breasts, but there was no longer hatred in her face.

'I deserve to know the truth, Roy, about what happened this weekend.'

Roy closed his eyes.

'I'm sorry if I hurt you just now,' she said, slumping down on the bed beside him. 'But I hate you when you lie.'

Tentatively Roy reached out to touch her wrist, but she withdrew her hand and stared at the carnations in the window.

'I'd prefer you not to touch me, Roy. All I want from you now is the truth.'

He stood up to engage her eyes.

'All right, darling, I'll give you the truth,' he said slowly. 'Everything you accused me of doing all those years ago is true. The only excuse I can offer is that I was so lonely, stuck up here in London while you were in Peterborough, that I went a bit crazy, I suppose. My . . . affair with Helen was my last fling before marriage. Until I met her again on Saturday, I've hardly thought about her since. And I've never slept with anyone but you since.'

He paused, then whispered gruffly: 'That is . . . until last night.'

Liz stiffened, then started to shake.

'I tried not to make love to her, Liz, but she was so desperately insistent, so . . .' He broke off, aching to pull her into his arms to comfort her. But knowing she would rebuff him, he muttered: 'I know I was despicably weak, and stupid and . . . that I betrayed you. Look at me, darling, for Christ's sake look at me! Please! I promise you – on my knees – I promise you. I'll never do it again. With her, or anyone. Ever.'

Slowly Liz turned her head until her desolate brown eyes were peering into his. Her breasts and shoulders were still shaking and her fists were clenched. Thinking she was going to physically attack him again, he stumbled on with his confession.

'Listen, darling! You demanded to know the truth, otherwise I wouldn't have told you. I didn't want to hurt you. Though that's not strictly true. Sooner or later I would have told you, because you're right. Only the truth can bring us back together again. That's of course if . . . you're willing to give me another chance?'

He waited, but she turned away and tried to lose herself in the heady scent of the carnations. Dazed, he stumbled on.

'Believe me, darling, it was just one crazy night. She's not as attractive as you, anyway. I only did it because she was so screwed up and she'd made such a fool of herself in front of the guests. You see, despite her being a top-notch political historian, her private life's a wasteland. All her learning and her passion for endless research are substitutes for living. They're substitutes for what you and I have together. That is . . . if and when . . . you forgive me. . . .'

He trailed off. Then he knelt in front of her again, but still she wouldn't respond. He enveloped her clenched fists between the supplicating palms of his hands.

'Liz, darling, I'm not expecting you to forgive me immediately. But you must admit, until this came up, we've always had a pretty good marriage. Though I've occasionally betrayed you in my thoughts, I've never physically betrayed you. Until yesterday I've never even touched a woman with . . . carnal intentions. But last night she literally begged me to take her – and, Christ help me, I did.'

Liz snatched her hands away, then crossed to the open door, but Roy was too quick for her and barred her way.

'No, darling, you can't run away from it. If you now refuse to listen to what you demanded to hear, things will go on festering between us! You'll never trust me again. You'll always think I'm lying.'

'Please get out of my way.'

'You asked for the truth, darling!'

She looked him in the eyes. Then scarcely moving her lips, she said: 'No one wants to hear that kind of truth. Ever.'

She reached for the door handle, then turned back to see the raw desolation on his face.

'Even if in time I am able to forgive you, Roy, what guarantee have I that you won't go off with her again?'

'I'll swear on anything you like! From the Bible to my father's grave. You name it and I'll swear on it. Our marriage is more important to me than anything else in the world.'

'Including your career?'

Roy laughed: 'Especially my career.'

He held out his hands, but she ignored him and opened the door.

'Do you think . . . you ever will forgive me?'

'God knows. But I won't leave you. At least I hope I won't.'

'I love you, Liz. You know that, don't you?'

'You didn't love me last night. And I won't love you tonight. And maybe for many nights to come.'

Then she went out of the room.

'Where . . . you going, Liz?'

'For a walk.'

'But . . .?'

'I need to think things through, Roy. And so do you.' Her eyes flickered with tiredness. 'Oh, I know you say you won't ever go off again, but you've got to be certain, because there'll be no next time. If you're unfaithful to me again, as God's my witness I'll leave you. Or maybe I'll go off with someone myself. Either way, what we used to have together, in the form of loving trust, will be destroyed. Perhaps it's destroyed already.'

'Darling, I swear I'll never. . . .!'

'Don't swear to anything now. Just think things through. On every level. Then we'll talk.'

Before Roy could prevent her, she ran down the stairs. Then he heard the front door bang so he sat down on the bed and started thinking.

He was still thinking the following morning as he drove to the House of Commons. When Liz came back from her nocturnal walk, she refused to discuss the matter any further, and though she agreed to share his bed, she wouldn't let him touch her. To make matters worse, over breakfast she laughed hysterically at Sebastian's unfunny jokes. Then, when Roy attempted to discuss their marriage as he was leaving the house, she simply handed him his briefcase, looked him in the eyes and said: 'Give me time. You must give me time.'

He turned into the House of Commons car park. He scarcely registered the policeman who checked his pass at the barrier. Then, as he parked his Ford between a highly-polished, fifteen-year-old Daimler and a new Ford Capri, the strict security procedures triggered off a horrifying memory. He remembered talking with a journalist from the *Observer* in Annie's Bar inside the Commons. The journalist was buying Roy a drink when they heard the explosion. Moments later they discovered that Airey Neave's car had been bombed in the entrance to the House of Commons car park.

For what seemed a lifetime, Roy stared at his clenched hands on the steering wheel. His mind was in turmoil. Contorted images zig-zagged inside his head. One moment his wife was flailing her fists into his guilty face, the next his mouth was searching for Helen's breasts. Then both images were obliterated by smoking, twisted metal and Airey Neave's brave face contorted with pain. Within seconds Roy's imagination was engulfed in flames. Wherever he turned, there were mutilated bodies, exploding buildings and screaming children. He knew his thoughts were out of control, yet he could do nothing but let the tragic Northern Irish inferno rage through his mind. What were his humdrum problems compared to the everyday living hell that those poor bastards endured in that benighted province?

Roy was still submerged in his Irish nightmare when he found himself in the courtyard leading up to the Speaker's tower, overlooking the Thames. He was so locked in his thoughts he failed to register several colleagues who said 'Good morning' in passing. Then Big Ben struck the half-hour and he realised he was clutching his briefcase across his chest, gazing up at the sunlit clouds drifting over the Gothic spires of the Commons. He lowered the briefcase. He was about to retrace his footsteps when he changed his mind.

No point in making my way to my office, he thought.

He shared a room with David de Quincey, a fellow MP. It was only two minutes away on the Embankment, but he decided he wasn't up to dictating letters to Isla, his secretary, or having a chat with de Quincey.

No, what I need now is some spiritual solace. If I had more time I could go to the Abbey.

Roy was not a Christian, but he enjoyed sitting in abbeys and cathedrals, where his being could be suffused with a sense of peace and comfort.

I suppose it's their age and beauty combined with centuries of prayer that have such a soothing effect on my spirit.

Then he remembered the debate was due to start in a few minutes, so he hurried instead to the most ancient part of the Palace, the Great Hall of Westminster.

Soon he was standing under the vast, echoing hammer beam roof, with row upon row of carved angels gazing down on him. He was so completely immersed in his dream world that he was able to ignore the early-morning visitors chatting around him.

Using his doubtful gift of cutting-off from his surroundings, he let his spirit ascend into the living history of England which spread its architectural glory above his head. Whenever he needed to clarify his thoughts on the state of the nation, he would spend several moments in Westminster Hall reliving the past and trying to relate it to the present.

We are prisoners of our history, he thought, which is why we English are so in love with our unique past. Every city we visit, every country village with its churchyard, every manor house we pass in our travels, reminds us continually of our historical and architectural creativity. Of course, there is a crippling drawback to this one-way love affair with history. We do not spend enough time in the present, for in comparison the present appears to be drab. Unfortunately we no longer have the energy or fortitude or piratical poetry of the Elizabethans, or the high-minded, if misplaced, morality of the Victorian empire-builders. Everyone and everything have tended to become smaller, greyer and spiritually barren. Most of us have turned into 'wee timorous beasties'. And if that is what we are in the present, what comfort will the future hold for us . . .?

Roy let his thoughts trail off before he drowned in depression Chuckling to himself, he refocussed on the great hammer beam roof and the towering, smoke-begrimed walls supporting it.

Yes, this is the cradle of kingly and, later, parliamentary, power here in England. This hall, one of the largest in the ancient world, is the first great stone jewel of English civilisation. It is more important than all the cathedrals and abbeys on our island. Within these walls the laws of England were made and broken, then remade and broken again, and remade again and again.

In a trance the MP moved slowly down the centre of the Great Hall, accompanied by his echoing footsteps. Then he paused and glanced at a faded bronze plaque set in the massive flagstones: 'Here was Sir Thomas More tried for High Treason'.

Roy shook his head. Not even the wit and subtlety of that great and complex chancellor could save him from the tyrant's axe. And whichever way you look at it, Henry VIII was a tyrant-and-a-half. In his own way, Henry was the Joseph Stalin of his age.

He grimaced, then quickly turned on his most dazzling smile, for two little ladies in black bonnets were looking at him strangely. For a dreadful moment he thought they were going to ask him if anything was wrong.

If they do ask me, he thought, wherever will I begin? – because at the moment I can't think of anything that isn't wrong!

Before the old ladies could summon up the courage to address him, he strode forward purposefully. At the third step, the image of Henry VIII as a Renaissance Stalin repossessed him.

Well, thank God, the absolute power of kings is now ancient history. And although, in a minor way, I'm beginning to find myself in Thomas More's unenviable shoes because of my so-called 'treasonous' relationship with my constituency Party, at least the very worst my enemies can do to me is to refuse to reselect me in December. Unlike Thomas More or the Soviet 'enemies of the people', I cannot be punished with either the extreme penalty or with a labour camp. Unless, of course, we become a People's Socialist Democratic Republic. And we will never become that. At least, I hope to God we won't. Mind, the way things are going, with the laws being continually undermined and the extremists on the left and right forever screaming for one another's blood, well, anything is possible. Even the unthinkable. For the laws of rapacious nature, whether we like them or not, still govern man at the gut-level. Those laws will not be suspended just because we happen to be English. Or because we believe that dreadful things like that can't possibly happen in England. On the contrary, it is because we believe they can't happen that so far we have taken no steps to prevent them from happening. So one day the extremists on both sides might start screaming for blood. Then the unthinkable not only becomes possible, it even becomes probable.

From Roy's point of view, the big Commons debate on security matters was not turning out well. The debate was already into its fifth interminable hour and Roy couldn't see himself being called to speak for at least another hour, so now he was in danger of nodding off to sleep in the last row but one of the Opposition back benches.

As he struggled to keep his eyes open, he tried to remember his first visit as an MP to this famous chamber fourteen years ago. Nothing had changed much in the interim. Although Mr Speaker was not the same person, he still sat in much the same way as his predecessor, in his canopied chair at the head of the chamber. Roy always found the Speaker's traditional knee-breeches, peeping out from under his long black gown, faintly amusing. As Roy studied him, the Speaker adopted the traditional posture of resting his weary head on his hand so that both were enveloped in the curls of his full-bottomed wig.

Perhaps he's as bored as I am and nodding off as well, Roy thought, rubbing his eyes as the Speaker called another right-wing Tory to his feet. Then the Tory proceeded to shrilly hector the Opposition on the perennial chestnut of Soviet spies in nuclear research establishments.

By a conscious act of will, Roy forced himself to see the parliamentary ritual anew. Then he registered the two dispatch boxes on opposite sides of the table of the House. At the end of the table, resting on two golden hooks, was the enormous glittering mace, the symbol of the Queen's authority.

Mind, if Tony Benn has his way, I wonder how long that mace will be there, Roy thought, smiling to himself.

Eventually the right-wing Tory sat down, to be replaced by a left-wing Labour MP from the Welsh Valleys who berated the Government for spending too much money on the Secret Service, rather than on the mining industry in Wales.

Roy was now so sleepy that he had to focus on the Sergeant-at-Arms at the far end of the Chamber in order to keep awake. The Sergeant always fascinated Roy as he sat in his black knee-breeches, with his left hand resting on the hilt of his sword. Roy supposed the Sergeant appeared so impressive because he was the only person in the Chamber who was allowed to carry a weapon. The sight of the Sergeant's sword always served to trigger off Roy's imagination. He often had undemocratic visions of the Sergeant going berserk with boredom and lopping off a few of the most tedious Members' heads with his trusty sword. As Roy pictured this, he had to bite his lips to stop himself laughing out loud. It took a great effort for him to turn his gaze elsewhere, especially as the green-leather-covered benches were filled with dozens of suitable candidates for the Sergeant's trusty weapon.

Jesus, Roy thought, coming to with a jolt, if I go on thinking like this I'll end up as demonic as Terry MacMaster! Though, to be fair to Terry, if he had his way he wouldn't bother with a sword. He'd have everyone in this place shot instead. Well, nearly everyone. Naturally he'd have to exclude those gentlemen on my left. Well, no one could accuse our Great Leader there, with his red hair and his red tie, of being boring and sleepy. Then there are those other stalwart live-wires of the Left, Ian Mikardo, Joan Maynard, Eric Heffer, Martin Flannery, Ron Brown and Michael Meacher. Oh, and we mustn't forget dear old Dennis Skinner. Mind, I rather admire the way that Dennis and his energetic chums in the Tribune Group all but indulge in fisticuffs with those poor old Social Democrat MPs, to see who is going to sit where on the second row. It's a bit like Saturday morning at the pictures. Except I remember when we were kids we behaved better.

Roy was nearly asleep and beginning to feel there was no point in launching a kamikaze attack onto the decks of his own left wing.

What will it accomplish? I know I promised Helen that I'd knock 'em for six. But in her own way Helen, with her hysterical anti-Marxist ammunition, is as paranoid as Terry MacMaster with his anti-capitalist propaganda. Anyway, I'm not sure I'm cut out for a political war. There must be something else I can do to hold back the Marxist tide besides hurling Helen's missiles at all and sundry. There must be something....

Then Roy understood why he had allowed himself to become so sleepy. It wasn't simply because the debate was tedious and circular. It wasn't even because he had hardly slept the night before, worrying about his marriage. No, the real reason I'm sleepy, he thought, is because I'm frightened of what might happen to me if I stand up and tell this Party of mine what I think about some of the Labour MPs in this Chamber. Not that I'm any more of a coward than the rest of the Labour right wingers.

Our mutual problem is that we're all too scared to say what we really believe. In that respect Helen is correct. Since the death of Gaitskell, Labour's right wing has been in continuous retreat. It's true that Jenkins, Shirley Williams, Anthony Crosland, John Mackintosh, Brian Walden and Reg Prentice occasionally tried to fight the left on various issues. But only Prentice had the stomach for a real fight when the left started punching holes in the law, *vis-à-vis* Clay Cross. And though Jenkins backed Prentice initially, Jenkins then deserted him for the Common Market. So Prentice was left beleaguered, went 'crazy' and joined the Tories. Yet though I disagreed with Prentice joining the Tories, I still can't help admiring his guts. It must be pretty lonely for him now, being always surrounded by those Hooray Henrys and those dreadful ladies with their blue rinses.

Still, I suppose if Jenkins had been tougher earlier and had set up the SDP instead of drinking claret in Brussels, then Prentice would have joined the SDP. That's the main trouble with the SDP. It's too wishy-washy. It desperately needs people like Prentice, Hattersley and Shore, and trade unionists like Chapple and Duffy, to give it proper ballast and transform it into a genuine party of the people. In fact, into the new right-wing Labour Party.

Roy pulled himself up short. Suddenly he was worried by the direction his thoughts were taking him, especially as he was surrounded by many of the people he was thinking about. There, sure enough, was David Owen, 'the handsomest man in politics', smiling grimly as he exchanged some philosophical profundity with a very world-weary Roy Jenkins, whose puffy cheeks were looking even purpler than usual.

Then Roy felt compelled to look at his companion on his right. David de Quincey, with whom Roy shared his office, was an elegant, impeccably dressed man in his late thirties, and he was staring at Roy in the most disconcerting way. Roy wrenched his concentration back to the arguments in the security debate, and specifically onto Fred Drummond, the Lancastrian left-wing backbencher, who was relishing the situation.

'... And, as has been said before, Mr Speaker, we on this side of the House asked for this debate because of these everlasting revelations about spying here in the UK. The truth of which in most cases is still unproven. In fact, all we have at the moment are numerous hysterical allegations, all of which we're expected to believe.'

Drummond waved his hand to take in most of the Chamber.

'So, in my opinion, Mr Speaker, it would be much more convincing for the House of Commons itself to oversee all matters concerning national security.'

Yes, thought Roy, that would really suit you closet-Stalinists, wouldn't it? Then the Soviets wouldn't even need the KGB, because you could report straight back to King Street yourselves. As you do, anyway.'

Drummond was enjoying the sound of his own voice: 'For it should be the right of the people of this country to know what's being done by the security forces in their name. Even in the United States – that fountain of capitalist duplicity – even there they don't have to put up with the daft nonsense we have to put up with here!'

Bloody right they don't, thought Roy, but then of course the Americans don't have anything like as many security risks in the Senate and the House of Representatives as we do here in the Commons. Communism isn't a problem in the United States. Whereas here we've got so many red wolves in pink sheep's clothing that the prospects are appalling.

'It's the United States that's showing the way on security matters by opening up the Government's files. Thus ending all this unnecessary secrecy.'

Drummond's right hand tightened to a threatening fist.

'Yet our present Government refuses to do this because it wishes to use these constant spying allegations to whip up a climate of mass hysteria against the Soviet Union. That's why so many harmless Soviet officials are always being kicked out of this country.'

Before Roy could react, the Government side of the House reacted for him. Instantly there were cries of 'Go back to the Kremlin where you belong!' 'Yes, why don't you join the Politburo?'

This barrage of heavy-handed wit prompted the Opposition to start booing, but Drummond waved them to silence.

'Well, everyone knows, Mr Speaker, that the Soviet Union only maintains strong military defences because of its devastating experiences during the Four Year War. And that, plus being surrounded by NATO on the one hand and China on t'other, has naturally made the Soviets wary. In my opinion, the only way we can ease these tensions is to open up the books and show the Soviets that we're not involved in dirty tricks and fascist-type covert operations. That's why I ask the Members of this House to support the Opposition motion, calling for more open government on matters of defence and internal security.'

Minutes later the Speaker called out Roy's name. Still unsure what he was going to say, he rose to his feet. He noted that several MPs looked bored and sleepy.

'Mr Speaker. Right Honourable and Honourable Members know that I have always taken a keen interest in defence and security matters during the time I've been a Member of this House. That is why I would now like to draw the attention of this House to certain aspects of our current security services.'

God, I sound boring, he thought, but he ploughed on regardless.

'First, I regard it as a matter of extreme concern that the financial control of the security services is at present not sufficiently monitored. Indeed, it is hardly monitored at all. Which is why it is almost impossible for any Member of this House, or even the relevant Select Committee on which I happen to sit, to discover the true cost of the security service's activities, or the numbers of personnel involved.'

There were grunts of agreement from both sides of the House. Roy developed his theme for several minutes, but his heart wasn't in it. Behind him he could hear Drummond and other left wingers pooh-poohing his speech. So he brought his fiscal analysis to a halt, then said in a challenging voice: 'So whilst I agree with the sentiments of my Honourable Friend concerning the desirability for less secrecy in government, I cannot agree that the time is yet right for the implementation of the measures he suggests.'

To his delight, Roy heard the Lancastrian growl, then mutter something obscene concerning Roy's mother. Smiling broadly, Roy continued: 'Well, Mr Speaker, everyone knows that ever since Lenin established his personal dictatorship in Russia in 1917, the Soviet Union has always been a country in which the role of the secret police has been pre-eminent. As Vladimir Bukovsky, the famous Russian dissident, once observed: "If you removed the secret police from the Soviet Union, communism would cease to exist in that country within the week!"

Roy was interrupted by impatient Opposition calls of 'Stop filibustering and get on with it!'

'And it is because the Soviet Union, Mr Speaker, has always been dominated by the secret police that we cannot "open our books" to the world, as my Honourable Friend would like us to do. He knows as well as I do that the KGB operates covertly throughout all the countries that are party to the Western Alliance. And since the thirties, the KGB, or its then counterpart, has operated very successfully in London – and above all in Cambridge. So don't be fooled by the Soviet Union's "peace" propaganda, because the people who rule the Soviet Union are still empire-building Stalinists at heart!'

Roy continued to smile as waves of hostility swept over the green-leather-covered benches occupied by the Tribune Group and the Stalinist left.

Now is the time, he thought, to use one of Helen's missiles.

'If you don't believe me, perhaps you can explain why Stalin is being rapidly rehabilitated in Moscow? What I say is true, Mr Speaker. Barely a year ago in the updated version of the Soviet *Encyclopaedia*, when it came to deal with Stalin's role in the history of the USSR, there was no mention of the Great Terror, or of the millions upon millions Stalin killed in the camps. But his crimes were certainly mentioned in the earlier version of the *Encyclopaedia*. Yet in this later version Stalin is instead applauded as being a great war leader. And if that isn't the fastest rehabilitation of the greatest murderer in history, I don't know what is.'

The hostility from his own back benches was now so vociferous, Roy had difficulty in making himself heard.

Well, as I'm in for a penny I might as well be in for a rouble, he thought, raising his voice above the growing clamour.

'So when we deal with the Politburo, we are not dealing with great "democrats" in the Western tradition. We are dealing with dedicated Stalinists who have no shortage of innocent blood on their hands. So it is our duty to be wary. As a famous Russian proverb instructs us: "Just because the wolf is baring his teeth, he's not necessarily laughing!" That is why I believe we must not lower our guard, simply because the Soviets are smothering us in artificial doves' feathers. So, unfortunately, at present we have no alternative but to protect ourselves against our "comrades" in the Warsaw Pact by resorting to equivalent secrecy in security matters.'

Without looking, Roy gestured to Drummond, who was shouting at him.

'And as my Honourable Friend knows, this view has also been held by every previous Labour administration.'

Left-wing hecklers jeered: 'Oh, here we go again! Defence of Wilson, defence of Callaghan!'

Before Roy could control his impulse, he experienced a Helen-like rush of blood to the head. He threw all caution to the east wind – and the east wind was howling from his own backbenches. In a resonant voice he uttered the fateful words: 'And it is also unfortunate, Mr Speaker – and I feel I have to draw the House's attention to this – that *some* Members of this House owe their primary allegiance to Moscow and the Kremlin!'

There was a moment of silence as his voice rang out, then the wrath of the left wing deafened him with cries of 'Rubbish!' 'McCarthy!' 'Witch-hunt!'

Now I'm committed to Helen's path-of-no-return, he thought, as the bellicose protestations grew in volume around him.

'What I am asserting is the truth, Mr Speaker. In my own Party we allow anyone, of whatever dubious left-wing persuasion, to join us! And the minute they've joined us, they immediately begin to subvert and undermine the commitment to democracy which we've had in the Labour Party since its foundation.'

This attack on the hard left brought many of its sympathisers to their feet. Within seconds Roy felt as if he was once again in the verbal inferno that engulfed him three weeks ago at his local GMC. Only this time the Speaker was calling hoarsely. 'Order, Order!', but he was immediately drowned by the repeated screams of 'Witch-hunt! Witch-hunt! Witch-hunt!' Then the Tories howled their defiance at the left, and the Commons sounded like London Zoo at feeding time, and Bedlam at any time.

Though no one was listening to him except his friend David de Quincey and the odd sharp-eared Tory, Roy shouted at the beleaguered Speaker.

'But despite this, Mr Speaker, there are still some of us who will stand vigilantly against these armchair Muscovites who seek to destroy our great Party!'

Then, with a final backhanded gesture of defiance, he sat down to enjoy the left's stereophonic contribution to Rimsky Korsakov's *Night on a Bare Mountain*.

Well, he thought, trying to restrain a suicidal smile, obviously the left think they are witches, holding their Sabbath on a Russian 'bare mountain', otherwise they wouldn't accuse me of being the Witch-Finder General.

The answer to Roy's rhetorical question echoed through the Chamber, as the 'witches' continued in a litany of hatred with their cries of 'Witch-hunt! Witch-hunt! Witch-hunt!' Only then did Roy realise that the hair on the nape of his neck was standing on end.

Looking steadfastly in front of him, Roy endured the final hours of the debate. As the endless minutes ticked by, he felt the hatred mounting around him, and the moment the debate was over, he left the Chamber.

Clutching a large Scotch on the rocks, he walked out onto the Terrace. The sun had set behind the Mother of Parliaments, but the sky was still suffused with pink in the far west. He shivered and sipped his Scotch.

What the hell am I doing with my life? I hope to Christ Liz will forgive me. My marriage is very important to me. Yet why do I still feel there should be something more? Why can't I make resolutions and be certain I'll keep them?

He placed his drink on the stone parapet and stared down at the swirling Thames. Then the emerald lights strung across the arc of Westminster Bridge caught his eye. He found their prettiness reassuring.

If only I had the vitality and the dreams I used to have, he thought, as he took another swig of his Scotch. Though he had promised never to see her again, he felt a sudden urge to call Helen.

At least she believes I've got potential. She might even have been proud of me today. My unrehearsed rocket-launch in the Commons was almost impressive. Trouble is, the only thing it has probably achieved is to ostracise me from the rest of the Party. The fact that I'm standing here alone, drowning my sorrows, shows that nobody else wants to talk to me. Mind, that's hardly surprising when I have the smell of political plague about me . . . .

He pulled an address book out of his pocket. He was flicking through it to find Helen's number when he remembered his promise to Liz, so he put the book away and lit a cigarette instead. As he took his fourth satisfying drag, the irony of his situation struck him. Here he was smoking like it was going out of style, yet barely a month ago he'd made a resolution not to smoke. In the same way he had sworn never to see Helen again, yet he was already contemplating breaking his promise.

Well, I only promised that I'd never go to bed with Helen again. That doesn't mean I can't see her. Anyway, like everything else in life, we only make resolutions so that we can later enjoy the guilty sensation of breaking them. At least, that's how a typical English puritan like me gets his vicarious kicks. Though, in my case, I only half-break my resolutions so that I only have to feel half guilty. Except on certain weekends, of course. And that was just inconsiderate lust. At least, I hope it was only lust.....

God, wherever I turn, whatever I do, my actions have a look of expedient compromise about them. If only I had the self-discipline and moral courage to sustain me in my fight against the emotional and political vacillation which so often permeates my character. For this is the age when, even if you are no longer young, you've still got to act young and think young merely to survive. However much your body creaks, your heart and mind must never be more than twenty-one. And my daughter would tell me that twenty-one was ancient. So someone who is in his mid-forties is older and more irrelevant than Methuselah, which I suppose is why the youth of today want to kick us oldies into the gutter. It's not only in politics that the Terry MacMasters of this world are trying to enforce the continuous reselection of MPs. It's happening in every walk of life. The young are not only booting out the senior citizens, they are now beginning to purge the early-middle-aged as well. In the old days, even fifteen years ago, if you were a professor in a university, or a mature executive, you were as safe as houses – but today not even houses are safe any more. Nothing is safe unless you are bright, ruthless and very young. Also it helps if you can bribe the gods to keep you that way.

Roy's reverie on middle-age was disturbed by the sound of ice tinkling in a glass. He looked up from the river. Leaning against the parapet was the epitome of Tory youthfulness, in the personage of the Honourable Charles Derwent, MP.

Oh my Christ, don't tell me I've now got to do battle with Derwent, Roy thought, groaning inwardly.

The slim Tory continued to stare at the floodlit image of Lambeth Palace on the far side of the river, while he sipped his iced vodka. Eventually Roy broke the uneasy silence.

'Is there something you want to say, Charles? Or can I simply assume that we share a fascination for rivers?'

Charles, who had only turned thirty last Wednesday and who had barely recovered from his triumphant birthday party at Annabel's, smiled broadly. Then he adjusted the pale-blue linen handkerchief in the breast pocket of his exquisite dark-blue suit. As Roy moved away to buy himself another drink, he murmured: 'No, let me get you a drink, Roy. You've certainly earned one.'

'Thanks for the offer, Charles, but I think it's safer if I buy my own.'

'I must say, Roy, I'm rather surprised you won't drink with me, considering your courageous activities in the Chamber a moment ago. Indeed, it's because I was so impressed by your guts, if somewhat bemused by your tactics, that I want to buy you a drink.'

Roy shrugged.

'Don't shrug me off, my dear fellow. I'm only here to applaud you for putting a bomb under those Stalinist bastards in there. Mind, someone in your Party should have done it long ago. Now it's almost too late, because those closet-coms control your Party's machinery. Oh, I don't object to them simply because they're evil-minded, totalitarian sons of bitches. What I really object to is that they're so bloody uncouth.'

'Look, do me a favour, Charles.'

'Such as?'

'Piss off before I throw you in the river!'

Charles tilted his head back and laughed: 'Now don't get all shirty, there's a dear fellow. I hate the coms as much as you do. Only difference being, I belong to a proper Party which hates the coms to a man.'

'That's why I told you to fuck off, "Mr" Honourable Charles Derwent!' Roy snapped back. 'Just because we both don't like the idea of communism here in the UK, don't ever presume that we have anything in common!'

Charles opened his mouth to interject but Roy stopped him with a dismissive shake of the head.

'Before you say anything to the contrary, my friend, I'll tell you why we don't have anything in common, and that even includes our attitude towards communism. You only hate the communists because you're afraid of what they'll do to you personally. For you know that if the communists ever come to power in this country, they'll not only run all over your lawns, they'll nationalise all your companies and snatch all your privileges away from you. Now don't interrupt, Charlie, I've not finished yet.'

Roy threw his cigarette butt into the Thames, then raged on.

'You see, Charles, your fear and loathing of communism stems from the same source as your superior attitude towards the working class. And by working class, I'm not talking of the traditional peasant Tory that works on your estates in the shires. I'm talking of the industrialised working class in the East End of London, the Midlands, the north and the north-east.'

'Now wait a minute, Hampton....'

But Roy steam-rollered on. His East Anglian grammar-school aggression towards Tories and Toryism gave his speech a new vigour.

'The point I'm trying to make, Charles, is that you think that *all* workers are bolshie, if not already pro-Bolshevik! What's more, you know that they hate you, and that given the chance they would dismantle your world of unearned privilege!'

Charles slammed his half-empty glass down on the parapet and glared at Roy.

'My family work to keep their privileges, Hampton. Estates don't run themselves on their own, you know.'

'Oh, come on, Charlie, you can't fool me. Your family is worth a fortune, so you've got a helluva lot to lose come the Revolution! Yet you have the cheek to ponce around here playing at politics. Christ, you don't even need to get up in the morning, with the price of land forever going through the roof. You landed gentry have had it made in the last fifteen years. You get richer every time you blink. And it's only because you feel your wealth is threatened that you make all this fuss about the communists.'

Charles, who had now recovered his hereditary cool, shook his head.

'Hampton, you're talking socialist bilge and you know it. I'm not denying that I'm privileged and quite rich....'

'Quite rich!'

'All right, very rich. But I'm not fighting communism simply to protect my wealth and privilege. I'm fighting the bastards because I don't want us to turn into Poland. I don't want secret police monitoring my every movement. Or your every movement for that matter. Like Mrs Thatcher, I'm fighting the communists because if they get their way we can say goodbye to our historical freedoms in this country.'

'Don't come all that historical freedom garbage, Charles! What kind of historical freedom do you think the *unemployed* working-class man enjoys? Well, there are plenty of them around that you and Maggie have chucked out on to the dole. So if you're feeling brave enough, you can ask them what they think of their newfound freedom. But I shouldn't bother. If they don't strangle you for your impertinence, they'll probably tell you they've only got the freedom to accept hand-outs! Oh yes, and of course they're free to weep for their families, and for their loss of dignity.'

Charles started to protest but Roy cut across him.

'And the poor sods really do weep, you know! One of 'em broke down in my study yesterday evening. With tears dripping off his chin, he told me what he thought of you and your Iron Lady. So don't you come prating to me about freedom until *everyone* in this class-ridden country is free to go to work every day to earn an honest crust. For that's the only way he can hold up his head in front of his wife and children!'

Roy was now in such a state, he didn't know what to do or say next. He felt Big Ben was striking over and over in his skull. He clenched his fists, half-wanting to smash this privileged shit on the bridge of his arrogant nose, and half-wanting to weep like a child and throw himself over the parapet.

'Oh, don't get me wrong, Derwent. Although I loathe everything you stand for, I'm still going to go on fighting the communists. As I'll fight *any* extremists, of *whatever* political persuasion, wherever I find 'em! But I'm not fighting the communists to protect my property or my privileges. I'm fighting them because I know that if the communists ever gain power in this country, they will enslave the very people whom they have sworn to protect.'

'Exactly,' purred Charles, amused that the Labour MP was undermining his own case. 'That's my point. If the communists get control of the UK, even clandestinely, they will immediately set up their own rigid class system, like they have in the Soviet Union. Only, their class system will be much more exclusive than the ramshackle affair we have here in the UK.'

Charles was now thoroughly enjoying himself and finding it difficult to disguise the fact.

'Well, you must admit, Roy, that our class system is being undermined every day. Whatever background you come from, if you have the money or your son is intellectually bright, you can get him a place at any of our public schools. Especially Eton. Whereas in the Soviet Union, the Politburo and the Party *apparatchiks* send their children to "special" schools, while their wives shop in "special" shops, and their chauffeurs drive them to work in their equivalent to Rolls-Royces. What's more, they're driven in "special" lanes on the highways which are closed to the rest of the population. They all have three or four *dachas*, built at the workers' expense, in the countryside and on the Black Sea. Indeed, the Communist Party élite are so *over*-privileged that in comparison the ordinary Soviet citizen is not much better off than the Russian serf was living under the Tsars and the *boyars*!'

Roy brandished his empty glass impatiently.

'Oh, I agree with you that the class system in the USSR is far worse than ours, Charles. But we can't do anything to change theirs, whereas we can and we must change ours! And one of the reasons for the growth of Marxist-Leninism and Trotskyism in this country is that we still have an appalling class system. No, no, please hear me out. And communism will continue growing, as long as we have private schools which breed peculiar accents and poncy habits; for these schools make the kids that go there feel superior to the rest of us. And it's because this "privilege" garbage is still encouraged and supported by you Tories that the coms go on advocating class warfare. No, don't interrupt; I haven't finished! Anyway, you should listen – you might learn something about communism. And you Tories need to learn about communism, because most of you are pig-ignorant on the subject. Oh, I know Maggie reads Solzhenitsyn every night before she goes to bed, and occasionally has a chin-wag with the odd upmarket dissident. But she doesn't have communists sitting next to her in the Commons every day, like I do; which is why I know them intimately. And, believe me, Charles, when you're surrounded by them, you get to understand why they think the way they do; and that's important to know if you're ever going to beat them. And it's because you Tories haven't taken the trouble to find out *why* they think the way they do that you'll never beat them. You see, none of you have suffered socially like a lot of them have. Most of them have had deprived childhoods, exhausted parents, rotten schooling, and were brought up in slums and run-down council estates. But they soon discovered that there was another England. *Your* England, Charles, filled with private schools, vast estates and fast cars. As a result, these working-class boys developed great chips on their shoulders. They became so envious of your lifestyle, so full of hatred for your class and everything it stands for, that they started to read Marx, Engels, Lenin, Trotsky and Mao. And these very persuasive gentlemen told them how to make war on your class, how to destroy your class, how to destroy you!'

Roy paused, and for the first time Charles remained silent. Despite himself he was impressed by the older man's passionate outburst. He found Roy's analysis disturbing, so he nodded in encouragement. Roy smiled wryly, then pointed an index finger at himself.

'And the reason I know all this, Charles, is that I come from the same kind of background as these closet-coms myself. When I was in the sixth form at school, I too was filled with hatred and envy. In those days I also believed that we needed an extreme solution. I used to stand up in class and quote great chunks of Marx and Lenin at the history master. I can still remember one of my favourite Lenin quotes: "Wholesale terror should be unleashed against the bourgeoisie. All our class enemies should be put in concentration camps. We should find out what class a man belongs to. If it's the wrong class, we should instantly apply Red Terror. For if we do not cause Terror by on-the-spot executions, we shall achieve nothing. It is better to wipe out a hundred innocent people than to miss one guilty one"!'

This time it was Roy's turn to be amused, for Charles was unable to hide the fact that the Lenin quotation appalled him.

'Yes, pretty hair-raising stuff, isn't it, Charlie? But, God, how I used to relish chanting it when I was at school. There was one whole term when I was the next best thing to a Stalinist. I think I was in the fourth form at the time – round about 1953, the year Stalin died. Mind, I was pig-ignorant about what Stalin was really doing. It just seemed to me as a schoolboy that we could do with a leader "that really got things done in a hurry, no matter the cost". But it's embarrassing to go on about it now. Oh, and in case you're wondering – unlike Dennis Healey, I never joined the Communist Party. In fact, by the time I went to the LSE, I was merely left-wing Labour and a devoted supporter of Nye Bevan. But the point I'm trying to make, Charles, is that I only flirted with Marx, whereas a lot of my contemporaries went to bed with him. But communism only gains control over the minds of the young if the society they live in is diseased – as our society is. For wherever there is inequality, people will search for extreme solutions. So all these budding Trots and Marxist-Leninists are only the symptoms of the disease. The trouble with you Tories is you try to kid yourselves that the communists are the disease!'

Roy scratched his nose and glanced over Charles's shoulder at the endless traffic flooding over Westminster Bridge.

'You know, you're about the only Tory I've ever met who's genuinely interested, Charlie. So before I go, I'll make you a little prophecy on the subject; if Maggie and the rest of you right-wing Tories don't do something soon to start solving this mass unemployment, and if you don't put a stop to your mindless privatising and your more callous monetarist experiments, you might as well go out in the streets yourselves this very night and start recruiting new member for the *left* wing of the Labour Party! Because, believe me, every day Maggie takes us that bit farther on her Monetarist Mystery Tour – so even if she does manage to survive her second term – the legacy she will leave behind her will make the final establishment of extremist socialism in Britain inevitable.'

Then Roy smiled wearily and added: 'What was it Hamlet said to Horatio before his duel with Laertes? "Thou wouldst not think how ill all's here about my heart; but it is no matter".'

Charles smiled as Roy walked back with his empty glass into the Mother of Parliaments.

Two hours and several Scotches later, Roy found himself sitting alone in the Kremlin Bar, which was the Tories' affectionate name for the Labour Party's favourite drinking haunt in the

Palace of Westminster. He was amused that he was ostracised by the half-dozen hard-left topers lounging against the bar. Then one of them muttered uncomplimentary things about his disgusting McCarthyist performance in the House, but Roy still refused to budge. To his amazement the alcohol he was pouring into his system seemed to have little effect on him. Then he started giggling to himself and decided it was time he went home. He swigged back the dregs of his whisky, rose majestically to his feet, beamed at the barman, then walked unhurriedly across the bar.

He was about to open the door when the bleary-faced Member from North Yorks lurched off his bar-stool.

'D'know wot you are, Hampton?' said the broad-shouldered, drink-sodden Yorkshireman as he reeled against Roy. 'You're a fucking class-traitor! You've forgotten your fucking roots. Well, let me tell you, if you go in for any more of this witch-hunting, it's *you* who'll end up on the fucking rack!'

The drunken MP prodded his stubby finger into Roy's chest.

'Are you threatening me, Bert?' Roy said, squaring his shoulders.

'No, I'm not threatening you, Hampton. I'm warning you because this ain't the Tory Party, y'know. We don't fight by the Queensbury Fucking Rules here. So don't you square your shoulders up at me, laddie. I've had more backstreet scraps than you've had hot dinners. I'll wrap your bollocks round your head as soon as look at you!'

'Now, now, gentlemen,' intervened the barman. 'We don't need any of that, thank you.'

The other left wingers chorused their approval. So while two equally red-faced drunken MPs were busy calming the Yorkshireman down, Roy took the opportunity to beat a retreat.

As the chilly night wind buffeted his face, he realised he wasn't sober. For several moments he swayed on the steps to the Members' Entrance. Then he grinned owlishly at the policeman on duty at the door. The policeman didn't grin back.

'Hope for your sake, sir, you're not thinking of driving home tonight?'

Roy's instinct was to bluster, but another gust of wind slapped across his face, marginally sobering him.

'Don't worry, Officer. Just going to take a little night stroll along the river, then I'll call a cab.'

Roy glanced down at his left hand. Miraculously he was still clutching his briefcase, though somehow he had misplaced his raincoat. He couldn't face going back into the Commons, but knowing the policeman was watching him, he did up the buttons on his suit and set off in the direction of the Tate Gallery. He had barely walked a hundred yards when he heard someone shouting his name. Then he recognised the well-bred tones of his friend, David de Quincey. He turned and waved to him.

'Where the devil have you been, Roy? I've been looking for you everywhere.'

'Been in the Kremlin Bar, supping with the Politburo, haven't I?'

'Jesus! Talk about jumping out of the frying pan into the fire.'

Roy laughed, then David laughed. It took several moments for Roy to realise that they weren't laughing at the same thing, for David was pointing at something over his shoulder. Roy whirled round, then steadied himself against the railings. He was mystified, for no one was there. Unless, of course, his friend was pointing at the bronze statue of Oliver Cromwell, who was standing guard outside the House of Commons.

'What's so funny about Cromwell, David?'

'I was just thinking: at least Oliver would have applauded you in the House this afternoon. Your outburst was very much in his style. Didn't he once tell the Rump Parliament: "It is not fit that you should sit here any longer. You shall now give place to better men!"'

Roy laughed. 'You suggesting that old Olly was right-wing Labour?'

'Don't know about Labour, but John Lilburne and his Levellers found Cromwell pretty right-wing when he smashed 'em.'

'Yes, it's a shame we don't have the Lord Protector around now to smash the modern Levellers, like Tony Benn and his rancid pinkos.'

David nodded. Then both men stood in silence in front of Cromwell's statue. The Ironside General was dwarfed by the shadow of the Commons, but he created an imposing spectacle, with one hand forever on the hilt of his sword and the other forever on his Bible.

Roy broke the silence.

'This surely was one of England's greatest sons?'

De Quincey laughed, but in agreement.

'Well, it's true, isn't it, David? If Cromwell and his New Model Army hadn't brought Charles I to his knees when he did, there might have been a real revolution here in England 150 years later, as there was in France, and eventually in Russia and China. Whereas our English Revolution was little more than a limited religious skirmish. A typical middle-class revolution.'

'Don't you mean a typical businessman's revolution?' de Quincey interjected.

Roy pressed his eager face between the railings to see his hero better.

'You're right, David. Maybe it would have been better for this country if we'd had a full-blooded revolution way back in 1641? Then we wouldn't still be plagued with the class system and all its attendant ills today.'

Uncertain, de Quincey wrinkled his nose and joined his friend by the railings.

'Either way, David, it's a pity that the execution of "the Grand Delinquent" didn't finish off our ridiculous monarchy once and for all!'

Roy gestured at Cromwell through the railings.

'But, sadly, when the Lord Protector died, England as a republic died with him. And within months of Charles II's restoration, he was surrounded by courtiers and hangers-on, and so the class system has flourished unabated from the Restoration to the present day. And, God help us, as long as we have a monarchy, we'll always be held back by it. Well, there's no doubt about it, David, the unearned privilege, the poncy voices, the special schools, the Hooray Henrys, all stem directly from the Royals and their hangers-on.'

Roy was so involved with articulating the recurring problem of England, he wasn't aware he was swaying in the wind. De Quincey was becoming increasingly worried about his friend, but Roy was too oblivious to notice.

'Trouble is, we no longer have men like Oliver Cromwell who can ride out of the Fenland mist and save us from ourselves. Even when someone does appear with political conviction and an iron will, they generally espouse the wrong causes and end up fighting the wrong people.'

Roy shook his fist.

'Take Thatcher, for instance. She has political conviction of sorts, and she certainly has an iron will. But because she's so dogmatic and only moderately bright, not to mention lacking in foresight, usually she ends up championing the strong against the weak, the rich against the poor, and the privileged against the unemployed!'

Roy was now shaking his fists under David's nose.

'So though Thatcher has the undoubted potential to head a truly National Government, she never will. She's too busy listening to "Count Dracula" Tebbit and intellectual fruitcakes like Sir Keith, and they're encouraging her to become more extreme with every day that passes. The result is, instead of unifying and healing the nation, which she certainly could have done after her success in the Falklands, she has only succeeded in dividing the nation against itself. Well, it's true, isn't it? The gap that now exists in this country between the haves and the have-nots is nearly as great as it was in the thirties!'

Roy shouted his political fury at the moonlit statue of Cromwell. Then David grabbed his elbow and shook him.

'Hey, what the devil d'you think you're doing?' Roy snarled.

David released him, then stepped back under the street light to regard his friend closely.

'You're rambling like a crazy man, Roy, and it's not pleasant to watch. Especially as I've now asked you the same question twice and you haven't heard me at all!'

With difficulty Roy focused on his friend.

'I'm sorry, David. I didn't realise you'd said anything.' Roy trailed off. Then, after a swaying pause, he started again. 'You see, while I was talking to you just then, in my head I found myself involved in a battle between Cromwell and Maggie Thatcher.'

Roy laughed self-consciously. 'I'm sure I don't need to tell you who won.'

'Oh, I don't know. A battle between those two would be a pretty close-run thing.'

De Quincey, now very worried about Roy's mental state, rested a reassuring hand on his friend's shoulder.

'Look, I think I'd better drive you home, Roy.'

'I can drive myself, thank you!'

'No, you bloody can't.'

Roy tried to protest but David insisted. He guided his inebriated friend away from Cromwell's statue towards the Commons' car park.

'Hey, what was the question that you said you kept asking me, David, that I didn't answer?'

'I want to know why you went berserk in the Commons tonight.'

Roy laughed, then gave up leaning on David's arm and lurched off into the underground car park. Moments later he found himself sitting on the bonnet of a Rolls-Royce. David ran towards him.

'That's a Silver Ghost you're sitting on, for Christ's sake!'

'Oh, I thought it was the Holy Ghost,' Roy giggled.

David pulled him off the bonnet but Roy shrugged himself free.

'It's disgusting that an MP should have a car like this! That's one of the reasons why I went berserk in the House tonight, David. I'm sick to death of being a rotten hypocrite like the rest of our rotten Party!'

Roy gulped for breath, then said: 'Anyway, I didn't think what I said was particularly explosive.'

'Oh, come on, Roy! I've heard you say many things on the Floor of the House, and some of 'em vaguely outrageous, but to do a full-frontal *exposé* on all our closet-coms, well, that's just asking for the chop. Hey, don't go wandering off! My car's over here.'

David indicated a red 1976 Volvo estate. Roy, who was now clinging to one of the concrete pillars supporting the car park's roof, nodded sagely. Then he pushed himself away from the pillar and banged his fist on the hood of the Volvo.

'Why don't you buy British, you bastard?!'

David laughed, then climbed into his car and leant across to unlock the passenger door.

'Well, get in, you drunken bum, and I'll take you home.'

'I don't want to go home!'

'So I see, but you've got to.'

Roy thought a moment, then laboriously weaved his way round the car. After struggling with the handle, he clambered inside. David turned on the ignition and affectionately tapped his friend on the knee.

'You're under a lot of strain, aren't you?'

Roy shook his head, then rubbed his eyes with his handkerchief.

'I need some coffee. Daren't go home to Liz like this. After my weekend, she'll go crazy.'

Puzzled, David nodded as he backed the car out. He couldn't understand what Roy was talking about, but realised his friend needed to sober up and was determined to help him. Roy slapped his own face with the flats of his hands to knock some sense back into his head. He was relieved that David was going to look after him. He had grown very fond of de Quincey over the years, particularly since they had been required to share an office. Also, he respected David's political judgement, though in the last few months he had failed to tell David of his growing troubles with his constituency Party.

I shouldn't burden him with my problems, Roy thought, as they headed for the Embankment. He's got enough worries of his own, with his baby twins and difficulties in his own constituency.

'I think there's an all-night coffee-stand just along here, Roy.'

Then David indicated the briefcase Roy was clutching to his chest.

'Why don't you dump that on the back seat? That's if you can find any room in that garbage tip.'

Roy forced his reluctant head round to survey the back seat. He giggled when he saw it was taken up with two pink baby-chairs, a blue stuffed elephant, three rattles, a tattered golliwog and a half-empty packet of rusks. Still chuckling, he drunkenly strapped his briefcase into one of the baby-chairs.

As the first light rain of the evening began to fall, the Volvo glided to a halt by the kerb opposite Joe's All Night Booth. Moments later David returned with four coffees, three of which were for Roy.

'Now don't say anything till you've poured this lot down you. And be careful! It tastes foul, it's hot and these paper cups are flimsy. So if you don't watch out, you'll not only burn your tongue, but you'll spill it down your shirt.'

It took a quarter of an hour for Roy to drink all the coffee. By the time he'd gulped down the scalding liquid, he'd burnt the skin from the roof of his mouth and acquired a large coffee stain on his tie. He didn't care, because the caffeine had started to take effect.

'You know, David, what really gripes me is I never get any support from our Great Leader,' Roy said, as he finished off his third coffee. 'Or even from our Great Deputy Leader!'

De Quincey laughed ironically.

'Why should Kinnock and Hattersley back you, Roy? From their point of view, you're rocking the boat and making things unnecessarily difficult for them. You've got to remember they're two of the most flagrantly ambitious men in British politics, so you and your "ideals" are a pain up the arse.'

'Well, I could do with some support from someone, David!'

'Couldn't we all?'

'Oh, I know you've got your problems, too. But at least you've managed to make a deal with your Trot.'

David turned off the Embankment and headed towards the deserted, rain-swept City of London, with its crumbling eighteenth-century houses and its badly-lit, narrow streets.

'You *have* made a deal with your Trot, haven't you?' persisted Roy.

'Yes, but it's not going to hold for ever.'

'Why not?'

'Because once the Trots have got you on the run – like they have me – they like the smell of your sweat so much that they make sure you keep running.'

Roy was beginning to feel almost sober, so, after hesitating, he asked the question he'd been aching to ask for days.

'This deal you've made with your Trot, David ... what kind of deal is it, exactly?'

De Quincey was thrown. It was the one question he would have preferred not to have been asked. Unlike Roy, he wasn't a puritan moralist. He was a political *bon viveur* who understood the necessity to compromise when forced into a corner. But though he admitted this to certain of his right-wing Labour friends, he had never admitted it to Roy for fear of losing his respect.

'Don't you want to tell me about your deal with your Trot, then?' Roy asked again, keenly studying his friend's profile as they drove through the East End of London.

'In a way, I'd prefer not to,' replied de Quincey, slowing as the traffic lights turned red. 'But if you really want to know, I will tell you.'

Roy waited, then searched his pockets for his cigarettes. As the traffic lights blinked to orange, David said eventually: 'Well, part of the deal was . . . I agreed to go unilateralist.'

'Jesus!'

'I also promised I wouldn't make any more adverse comments about those two supremely democratic organisations, the IRA and the PLO.'

David's admission made Roy drop his cigarettes.

'My Christ! I didn't realise your Trot was a maniacal zealot!'

'He's not ex-Workers' Revolutionary Party for nothing.'

'Does that mean you have to openly support the PLO and the IRA?'

'No, but it does mean I must never take their names in vain.'

'They really are cunning bastards, aren't they?'

David nodded. Then, as they moved into the main stream of traffic, he narrowed his eyes against the blinding headlights of a huge Dutch container truck.

'Dip your lights, you moron, dip your sodding lights! If I'd known that going into the Common Market would fill the roads up with all this foreign garbage, I'd've voted the other way!'

The rain increased and both men were distracted by raindrops thudding relentlessly on the Volvo's roof. David slowed for another light and addressed Roy over his shoulder.

'Mind, from what you tell me about your Trot, Roy, it seems to me your local GMC will strike an even harder bargain with you than mine have with me. Especially if they hear about your shinnanikins when they tune into "Yesterday in Parliament" in the morning. Still, if it's possible to strike a bargain with your Trot you'll probably have to agree to it. Even if it does mean eating your own vomit.'

'Charming!'

'That's what we all say till we're on our knees.'

Roy coughed on his cigarette as some smoke went the wrong way.

'It's all so horribly depressing, isn't it?'

In disgust he made an expansive gesture with his glowing cigarette.

'Well, it's a fact: wherever you go, whether it's the Commons or your own constituency, you're surrounded by coms and Trots! It's hardly surprising that someone blew a gasket this evening. Though I'm beginning to think it was a shame it was me.'

Then, after a pause, he said: 'Mind, I suppose if I were truthful, David, I'd have to admit I've been dying to accuse those smug Stalinist bastards for years. But until tonight I've never been able to summon up the courage.'

Suddenly Roy jabbed his forefinger at the rain-streaked windscreen and shouted: 'Hey, look out!'

Hastily David jammed on his brakes and wound down his window, only to see an elderly woman barely a foot away from his front bumper. Before he could say anything, the woman banged her umbrella on the bonnet and screeched at him.

'Wot d'you fink you're doing, you madman?!'

'Forgive me, Madam, but you're not on a zebra crossing. If you step into the road like that without looking, one of these days you're going to get yourself killed.'

The woman, who was carrying two enormous plastic bags filled with old newspapers, battered her umbrella on the hood of his car again.

'Don't you get lippy wiv me, you young tike! One more word out of you and I'll have the filth on you!'

David tried to defend himself, but two articulated lorries slammed on their air-brakes directly behind him and started honking at him for obstructing the outside lane. Then the old lady crashed her umbrella down on the roof of the Volvo. As the blow reverberated on the protesting metal, both MPs put their arms over their heads. The old lady chortled and offered her last piece of advice before scuttling to safety.

'See where your frigging cheek's got you, you horrible little man? Now you're blocking up the whole frigging road. If I see you around these parts again, I'll get the frigging filth to arrest you and impound your frigging car!'

Two vans and a Mercedes joined in the honking, so de Quincey slammed his foot down on the accelerator. Then he crunched into fourth. As the Volvo shot forward, he muttered under his breath.

'Knowing our luck, Roy, the filth are bound to arrest us for something sooner or later anyway.'

They were now weaving round the outskirts of Hackney. With his free hand David beat a brief tattoo on the dashboard. Then he had a sudden thought and stopped drumming.

'You could always drop a line to the Labour Party National Executive, Roy, and demand that they set up a proper enquiry.'

'An enquiry into what?'

'Into your Trot and his Marxist-Leninist crew. You know, on the grounds you believe that at least half of them owe their primary allegiance to parties *other* than the Labour Party. I.e., they're either fully-paid-up members of the CP, or they're members of Militant or Socialist Action.'

Roy shook his head, spilling ash into his lap.

'What good will that do? Half of them on the National Executive are closet-CP themselves! So they're bound to protect my Trots.'

'Of course they're bound to protect them! But there are some on the NEC who are very anti the CP. So it'll be amusing to see how they try to come up with a half-arsed compromise. And you never know, there might be someone on the NEC who hasn't entirely sold out and could even unearth something on your Trot. It is possible. Very unlikely. But possible.'

Roy lit another cigarette with the smouldering stub of his old one, then made a face.

'I suppose it's worth a try. Though, as you say, it's very unlikely. Especially after my "Cromwellian" outburst tonight. But I'll draft a letter in the morning. Then perhaps you'll look it over for me?'

'Anything for a laugh.'

The Volvo squealed to a halt.

'Well, here we are, old matey. *Chez vous*. Or may I say *chez toi*?'

'God knows. Always been a duffer at languages. English through and through, that's me. That's why I suppose my particular case is congenitally hopeless.'

Grinning, Roy got out of the car. As the misty rainfall stippled his face, he breathed in deeply. 'Thanks for the lift and the advice, David. I deeply appreciate all the trouble you've taken with a maniacal sot. No, truly. For soon you may find it dangerous to talk to me. At least, in public.'

'Don't be ridiculous. It'll never come to that,' countered de Quincey, leaning out of his car window and enjoying the drizzle on his forehead. Though privately he was not so sure. He admired the political foolhardiness displayed by Hampton, but he was too wary a politician to contemplate taking such 'crazy' risks himself. Besides, he had a wife and two young children to worry about, so if push came to shove . . . who knows what he would do? To cover his indecision, he produced a small plastic container from the glove compartment and rattled it under Roy's nose.

'If I were you, I'd take a couple of these before you go barging in to face Liz.'

'What are they?'

'Double-strength Amplex.'

'I'd better crunch half a dozen or she'll complain I reek of Scotch.'

David poured six yellow spheres into Roy's hand, then winked.

'Once you've chomped your way through that lot, she might even agree to share the same bed with you.'

Roy laughed and thrust all the breath-sweeteners into his mouth at once.

'By the time I've finished with Liz,' he said, chomping the Amplex, 'she'll simply beg to share the same bed with me!' Then, returning de Quincey's lecherous wink, Roy spun on his heel and marched up the path to his front door.

As Roy entered the house, he swallowed the remains of the Amplex and prayed it had done the trick. Automatically he checked his wrist watch; seventeen minutes to twelve. Then he went into the living room, but there was no sign of anybody. The dining room was also empty, as was the kitchen, so he switched off the lights and crept upstairs.

Noting a faint glow under his bedroom door, he paused on the first-floor landing to remove his shoes. Then he took his shoes and briefcase into the study, where he wrenched off his tie. He wrinkled his nose when he observed the whisky stain on the stripes. Shaking his head, he discarded his tie and headed for the bathroom.

Ten minutes later he emerged smelling wholesomely of scented soap and Aramis. His teeth were sparkling and his tongue alive. He was naked but for his dressing gown, which he had tied at the waist with an elaborate bow. Tiptoeing, he climbed the stairs to the second floor. He was relieved there was no light under his daughter's bedroom door. As it was ajar, he stole into the darkened room. He smiled when he saw his daughter's sleeping face propped up on two enormous pillows.

Her long eyelashes made her look like a kewpie-doll. Then she stirred in her sleep. A plumpish white arm flopped out from under the duvet. Smiling, Roy covered her exposed shoulder, then kissed her on the nose. Still in a deep sleep, she responded with a purring sound as her romantic dream possessed her again. For a long while, Roy peered into the warm darkness and savoured his daughter's loveliness. He was aware that she provoked disturbing feelings in him, so he backed out of the room, quietly closing the door behind him.

On the opposite side of the darkened landing there was a thin strip of light under his son's bedroom door. He was about to knock, to suggest that Sebastian was working too late and would hurt his eyes, when he heard Liz moving about in their bedroom below. Grinning, he loosened the bow on his dressing gown. Then, squaring his shoulders, he ran lightly down the stairs into their bedroom.

He discovered Liz had only that moment got into bed and was switching off her bedside lamp. She intended to plunge the room in darkness before his arrival, but he was too quick for her. Even as she was pressing the switch, his urgent hands were squeezing her breasts. She was so taken aback by his sexual immediacy that at first she didn't resist his advances.

Before she could stop him, he kissed the nape of her neck and his fingers were prising her thighs open. Struggling, she protested, but he fastened his mouth onto hers and guided her reluctant hands down. She tried to squirm free, but his lips and groin demanded she explore them. As she was becoming moist herself, she probed her tongue deep into his throat and began to stroke the crown of his swollen phallus. Fiercely he thrust his knees between hers, desperate to sheath himself inside her. Then she grasped his penis, guided it into its proper home and gave herself up to the sensual joust.

Luxuriantly she curled her legs round his labouring back. Laughing, she urged him to penetrate her even more deeply. Despite his sordid moment of infidelity, she now felt certain he was hers again, and hers alone. As for Roy, he was making love to her with all his senses. He too was aware that she was his woman, and his alone. Then, before he could stop himself, he felt himself coming. He arched his spine, shuddered and spurted his sperm into the opening and closing neck of her womb. Liz's soft moaning turned to a sobbing cry as she climaxed beneath him, her teeth and nails gouging his neck and shoulders.

Then for an age they clung together like spent swimmers, and breathed in the rich sexual aroma permeating the midnight room. For once Roy didn't feel the need to ask her if it had been as good for her as it had for him, because he knew now, despite everything, they understood each other, body and soul. As they lay there, their limbs wrapped round each other like tendrils of ivy, Roy experienced a deeper sense of calm and peace than he'd known for years.

'Why are you grinning like a jackass, darling?' Liz murmured, slowly extricating herself from his embrace.

'Well, my darling, tonight I went a little crazy in the Commons, and tomorrow MacMaster'll know all about it.'

'What's amusing about that?'

'Nothing, really. I just love you so much that I want you to know. . . .'

Liz shook her head and placed a finger over his lips.

'Please, Roy, I don't want to talk about *that*. At least, not now.'

'But . . .?'

'What I'm trying to say, darling, is I . . . well, I forgive you,' she whispered. 'And I believe you'll keep your promise. But tonight is ours and I don't want her intruding.'

Roy laughed, then said quietly, 'I wasn't going to talk about that anyway.'

'You weren't?'

'No, I simply wanted you to know that I love being inside you so much that if you give me a couple more minutes, I think we'll be able to celebrate my craziness in the Commons all over again. And maybe if Apollo's on my side for once, I might even come up trumps a couple more times!'

'You've not been able to do that since our weekend in Venice four years ago! Well, not three times on the trot in one night! Anyway, isn't excessive virility very un-English once a body reaches early middle age?'

Then she squealed with girlish delight as she fastened her fist round his rising member.

'Ooh, now this is what I call a real "member" of Parliament.'

'Yeah, but you just wait till he takes his seat in the Ladies' Gallery.'

Then, before she could giggle again, it was 'once more into the breach, dear friends, once more!'

Sebastian noticed the difference the following morning when he heard his father whistling *Jerusalem* in the bathroom. Immediately he knew something momentous had happened, but he only guessed what it was when his father lustily started singing 'Bring me my arrows of desire' at the top of his voice. When Sebastian came down for his breakfast, he found his mother acting strangely as well. She had propped a battered paperback copy of *Anthony and Cleopatra* against her teacup, and was reading aloud in a mellifluous voice:

> 'His legs bestrid the ocean: his rear'd arm
> Crested the world: his voice was propertied
> As all the tunèd spheres, and that to friends:
> But when he meant to quail and shake the orb,
> He was as rattling thunder.'

Only when Sebastian heard his father's outburst on Radio Four's 'Yesterday in Parliament' did he realise how apt his mother's quotation had been. He looked up questioningly at his father who was now wading through his second Shredded Wheat. To Sebastian's surprise, his father only nodded and laughed. Then his mother, who was late for school but cheerful about it, winked at his father and joined in the laughter. Embarrassed, Sebastian glanced at his sister, but Alexa was too busy giving her eyelashes their final coat of mascara to notice their parents' strange behaviour.

Why am I worried? Sebastian thought, as he strapped his satchel on to his ancient racing bike. If they're happy and they've still got a sex life after twenty-two years of marriage, bully for them. At least it's better than the usual internecine warfare we have to endure during breakfast. Come to think of it, I've not seen them so full of *joi de vivre* since they came back from their weekend in Venice four years ago.

Sebastian climbed on his bike. It was going to be another grey day, but at least family life had the potential of a silver lining. After checking he hadn't forgotten his pen, pencil and pocket calculator, he rode off to school, whistling:

'And did those feet in ancient times
Walk upon England's mountains green?'

Liz drove her Mini to school in the same spirit. For the first time for weeks she felt optimistic about life. She deliberately suppressed any feelings of jealousy about Helen, and the vociferous cries of 'Witch-hunt!' which she had heard aimed at her husband on 'Yesterday in Parliament' as yet had no meaning for her.

Well, she thought, as she braked outside St Bede's Primary School, while the lollipop man escorted some children over the busy road. Well, I have to believe that he will never be unfaithful again, or I'll go crazy. And what happened to him yesterday in the House is always happening to some MP. Most of that crowd in the Commons are little better than overgrown schoolboys anyway. The kids crossing this road are better behaved than most Members of Parliament, so the sooner they start televising the activities of these middle-aged monkeys in that Westminster zoo, the better! Maybe when they see themselves on the 'Ten O'Clock News', they'll be so appalled by their antics that they might even reform themselves. The trouble is, for many of them, being an MP is simply a continuation of dormitory life in a prep school. No wonder we're in a mess in this country when we're being ruled by a bunch of whisky-swigging, loud-mouthed, self-opinionated schoolboys, with the world's most officious chemistry mistress egging them on.

The idea of Maggie Thatcher as a chemistry mistress made Liz laugh out loud. Then she wound down her window to wave at three kids in her class, two of whom waved back, while the third, a huge lad with a thatch of carrot-coloured hair, gave her a prolonged wolf-whistle.

Yes, she thought, sometimes life can be really worth living.

Since Roy had been forced to leave his car at the Commons because of his drinking exploits, he joined the other commuters on the local tube. The compartment was overcrowded but he was too happy to notice this. He didn't realise he was irritating the other passengers by whistling *Jerusalem* to himself all the way to Westminster Station. All he could think about was how lucky he was to have found such a remarkably well-balanced and understanding wife as Liz. He knew many women would never have forgiven him. It was reassuring that they had so much in common. Neither of them had mentioned their sexual exploits of the night before, yet they were still aglow from the experience.

Yes, that's one of the great joys of being happily married, Roy thought, still whistling. You don't have to discuss and analyse your emotions all the time. If the love between you is profound enough, you can forgive each other everything.

To Roy's amazement, this sense of euphoria held as he stepped in to the Palace of Westminster. He even found himself grinning inanely at the three policemen he passed in the Lower Waiting Room. Then he saw the red-faced, pugilistic, left-wing Member for North Yorks who had attacked him the night before. The huge Yorkshireman was standing by the statue of Keir Hardie and still looked half-seas-over. He was buttering up two Indian constituents with the promise of improved race relations and better housing.

'Hope you've got as little of a hangover as I have, Bert,' Roy said in passing. Then he gave the burly Northener a discreet wink and took the lift to the Committee Rooms on the second floor, where he was sitting on a tedious Committee for the new Consumer Protection Bill. Though he was fed up with being continually lobbied by bossy ladies from the Consumers' Association, he was able to remain high-spirited until lunchtime.

Then, to Roy's surprise, several right-wing Labour colleagues insisted on joining him for lunch in the Members' Cafeteria, which was over-heated and smelt of hot fat and mushy greens.

Still, Roy thought, even if it is verging on the nasty, it's subsidised by the taxpayers and therefore cheap, and yer common-or-garden MP can't be choosy. Besides, a canteen like this, in the bowels of the Mother of Parliaments, is the perfect meeting place for a cabal of unreconstructed Ernest Bevinites. For old Ernie – bless his trades-union socks! – would certainly have relished the sticky-shirt-sleeves atmosphere in here. The story about him at the Potsdam Conference in '45, when he went there as Foreign Secretary, may well be apocryphal but it's certainly typical of the great man. Apparently Bevin didn't care much for 'some o' the bloody rich grub at banquet', so he pulled some ham sandwiches out of his briefcase and ate them in front of Stalin! Yes, it's men like Bevin and Cromwell we need now. I can imagine Ernie sitting here at this moment, with his mouth full of steak-and-kidney pie and his vast gut propped up against the edge of the table. I can hear him berating us: "You're all lily-livered, daft brushes who deserve every bloody thing that's comin' to you!'

'And of course he's bloody right!' Roy said, involuntarily uttering his thoughts out loud.

'Who is bloody right?' de Quincey asked, raising an eyebrow, again concerned about his friend's mental condition.

'Sorry, David, I was thinking aloud.'

'So we noted,' observed Wriggley, a thin-faced, grey-haired right winger from the Midlands.

Roy laughed, then tried to explain himself: 'You see, I was just wondering what Ernie Bevin would have made of our present situation with the hard left.'

'Not a lot,' interjected Tom Harris. Harris, one of Roy's closer associates, was a North London MP who was well liked because of his sense of humour.

'No, Roy's right,' continued Harris, 'If Bevin was alive today, there would be no coms in the unions, for a kick-off. When Bevin was a union leader, he was the scourge of the communists! Then later, when he became Foreign Secretary, he used to read the riot act to Stalin and Molotov. Yes, those were the days all right. Well, let's face it, there's no one in the *present* Shadow Cabinet who is capable of reading the riot act to anybody. Least of all to the Soviets!'

'No one's arguing with that, Tom, but the reason we're having lunch with Roy today is, well, to show him that even if we don't necessarily approve of his suicidal tactics, nevertheless we give him quite a lot of marks for courage.'

This particular contribution was made by Rob Camber, a Home Counties 'Wet' right winger, who had a marked tendency to wring his hands as if they were sponges whenever he spoke.

Roy felt his good humour evaporating, so he interrupted Camber: 'Look, don't get me wrong, Rob. Naturally I'm very grateful the four of you have had the guts to lunch with me after my little outburst in the House yesterday. But, unfortunately, clapping me on the back for being outspoken isn't going to solve any of our problems. And we basically all have the same problems.'

Camber was now so desperate to diffuse the charged atmosphere that he started wringing his hands like a dervish. Roy waved his fork impatiently.

'Yes, I can see you disagree, Rob, but let me finish, please! Why don't we be honest with each other for once and admit that the real question that's facing us is what are we going to do to hang on to our seats come our reselection?'

Before Camber could wring his way into the conversation, Roy rapped his knife on the side of his half-finished plate of bacon and eggs.

'Oh, I know there's always the Manifesto Group, but what's it really accomplishing? I mean, God Almighty, take a heavyweight like Denis Healey, for instance. Not that he's in the Manifesto Group, of course. But during the last election, even a roughneck like Healey fudged the issue of unilateralism, and he's supposed to be one of the toughest men we've got! But his bullying has softened recently, and now he puts his own survival before the needs of his country. Mind, Roy Hattersley's just as bad, if not worse!'

Roy was about to launch into an analysis of Healey and Hattersley's pragmatic careers, when suddenly the two great men themselves appeared with their lunch trays and strode through the cafeteria. Though no longer in his original glory, Healey was the first to pass them. His world-famous eyebrows and purplish-mottled face attempted to smile. But the now more powerful Hattersley was not far behind, and as befitted so eminent a pragmatist, the Deputy Leader was doing most of the talking.

Before Roy could continue, his right-wing colleagues started jabbering about something else. It was as if the two statesmen were manipulating Roy's companions by remote control. Even de Quincey found himself muttering something about the chips being overdone. As for Rob Camber, he was wringing his hands with such fervour that Roy felt sure they would drop off.

Amused but marginally disgusted, Roy watched the famous eyebrows and the professional Yorkshireman as they seated themselves ostentatiously in the far corner of the cafeteria.

Wonder what they're plotting? he thought, addressing himself to his unappetising meal. One thing's certain, they are bound to be plotting something. Let's face it, they're simply the up-market version of the rest of us. And in this great country of ours, as long as politicians are plotting together, or against one another, they still foolishly believe they're doing something to help the country! No wonder the general public not only dislike us but actively mistrust us. Can you blame them?

Contemptuously Roy prodded his overdone fried egg until it popped. With growing fascination he watched the yolk coagulate. Revolted, he looked up from his plate to hear his companions indulging in parliamentary small talk. De Quincey caught his eye, implying that he should shut up about Hattersley and Healey. Roy grinned and excused himself from the table. The others were surprised he was leaving so soon but they didn't disguise their relief that he was going.

As he left the cafeteria, Roy realised how alone he was, and knowing in his heart that he wasn't good at being and acting alone, it quelled his spirit. By the time he returned to the Committee Room, he felt his nerve going and started to dread what was awaiting him in Pandora's box of political terrors.

At twenty-one minutes past seven the same evening, Roy escorted his wife and daughter to their hard seats in the local Red Cabin Cellar Theatre.

He was feeling depressed about his political future and was already wishing that Liz hadn't dragged him out to see yet another theatrical effort by her favourite left-wing youth group. Despite this, he was still doing his damndest to keep smiling. He thought it was the least he could do, considering Liz was looking radiant. His daughter, Alexa, was also up to standard, with a green streak in her punky blonde hair. Although it was a warm evening, she insisted on wearing her father's ancient herringbone overcoat, his old striped shirt with the collar cut off, a multi-coloured, flared skirt and a pair of winkle-picking, mauve pixie-boots.

As the girls took their seats, Roy scrutinised the growing audience. Most of them were scruffy-looking youngsters in cast-offs, sporting a plethora of badges, including CND, Greenpeace and Gay Lib.

Of course these kids have a right to protest about everything, he thought, stifling a yawn. But what the hell's going to happen to them all? The poor sods have only got a quarter of the job and social prospects that we were lucky enough to have when we were their age. To make things worse, most of them have only been half-educated as a result of being fucked up between secondary modern and grammar schools, which Shirl-the-Pearl then forced to go comprehensive. In fact, I wouldn't be surprised if twenty-five per cent of the kids in this cellar can't read properly, can't spell, and certainly can't write a grammatical sentence. And who's to blame? The state? Parents? Teachers . . .?

Alexa jiggled her father's elbow as she clambered over her peers, clutching a programme.

'Hey, Mum?'

'Yes, dear?'

'Hope this show ain't going to be as boring as the last show you dragged us to.'

'I second that,' murmured Roy as he looked round the cellar walls, but all he could see were two ten-feet-high posters of Lenin and Che Guevara. Oh yes, and there was an even bigger one of Mao Tse-Tung, slung under the theatre lights at the back of the cellar.

'What the hell are we doing here, Liz?'

'How many times do I have to tell you, darling? If we don't support theatre locally, especially Youth Theatre, it'll die, as it has done in Lamberton East.'

'Of course it'll die! No one but the crazy-converted wants to see all this half-baked Marxist slop.'

Liz sniffed, then turned to face the stage, presenting only her profile.

'Stop being so critical, Roy. The actors are only teenagers, doing their best. They deserve to be supported for the time and effort they put into these plays, if for nothing else.'

Roy rubbed his eyes and, as he stifled another yawn, registered the full extent of his daughter's make-up.

'What the blazes have you done to yourself, Alexa?'

'Just clocked me emerald eye-shadder, have you, Pops?'

'Please don't call me "Pops"! And it's not your eye-shadow that's thrown me, it's the yellow sequins on your lids and the pink glitter on your lashes!'

Liz laughed. 'Must say your father does have a point, dear. You do look a bit like a Kabuki actor in a No play.'

'Well, I wouldn't be seen dead in your gear, Mum,' retorted Alexa, as she turned back to her father. 'Oh, by the way, Dad, Granny rang from Peterborough this afternoon. Wants you to ring her when you get home.'

Roy looked puzzled.

'Did she say why she rang, dear?'

'Yeah. Said it's about Aunt Maureen. According to Granny, Aunt Maureen's gone all funny, like. She won't let Granny into her house any more. She'll only let her talk to Granny on her doorstep. Odd, isn't it?'

Now equally concerned, Liz squeezed her husband's wrist.

'Yes, I must say that does sound a bit odd, Roy.'

'I'll ring her as soon as I get home.'

Roy could see his mother. She was probably sitting beside the telephone at this moment, praying for it to ring. Even in this weather she'd have her frugal coal fire to warm her arthritic knees, as night after night she'd sit reading and sewing, occasionally moving into her cold kitchen to make herself a cup of tea. Then the moment it was dark she'd bolt and bar the doors, because Peterborough was no longer the harmless market town of Roy's youth.

Depressed by the thought of the infinite loneliness of his mother's life since the death of his father, Roy forced himself back to his immediate present. He would answer his mother's need the moment he returned home.

Liz nudged him fiercely in the ribs. 'Don't look now, Roy, but MacMaster and that pretty girlfriend of his have just plonked themselves at the end of the second row.'

Despite his wife's advice, Roy looked round at what he regarded as the incarnation of his political Nemesis. To his consternation, he caught Terry's eye immediately. The younger man responded by winking. Furious, Roy turned back to his wife.

'D'you realise that bastard is one of the prime movers behind this Marxist Theatre-in-Education crap? This is one of his biggest indoctrination centres in the borough. And as half these kids are out of work, this dangerous twaddle must seem to them to be manna from heaven!'

Roy was about to launch into one of his pet homilies on Marxism being pedalled in schools, but he noticed the lights in the cellar theatre were dimming. Seconds later the audience were in total darkness. Roy groaned.

'Shush, Roy! It's about to begin,' Liz reprimanded.

'What d'you bet the first line in the play has the word "revolution" in it?'

'Oh, come on, darling, they're not that crass. And do stop fidgeting. Both of you!'

Before she could finish, a spotlight illuminated a girl's white mask of a face in the dark acting area. The girl was no more than sixteen and had glowing eyes. Behind her they could hear the rhythmic tapping of a bongo drum as the girl started to declaim: 'I am the voice of Twentieth-Century History.'

A second spotlight snapped on, illuminating a boy's white mask of a face. Another drum throbbed in the darkness as the boy proclaimed: 'I am the voice of Pre-Twentieth-Century History!'

Alexa yawned: 'How borin'!'

Then the boy trumpeted: 'And I am proud of all the tyrants that have filled my years!'

Roy couldn't contain his laughter any longer. Liz nudged him in the ribcage.

'What's there to laugh at?' she hissed.

'Oh, don't worry about me, dear,' grinned Roy in the dark. 'I was merely applauding the author for not mentioning the word "revolution" yet. No, seriously, Liz, I think this is a very subtle piece.'

'Now don't you be a smart-ass with me, Roy Hampton. I know what you're thinking. But you keep forgetting the author's only sixteen and not yet as politically jaundiced as you are!'

The boy went on with his declamation:

'But Tyrannies come in many forms, Brothers and Sisters! Even here in Twentieth-Century Britain, we have our own "Democratic Tyrannies"!'

This was greeted by applause and cheers from the main body of the audience. Liz nodded her head in approval while Alexa indulged in a gargantuan yawn. Then, as the applause died down, the girl stepped forward and menacingly raised her arms above her head.

'But do not fear, Comrades! I, as the embodiment of the Progressive and Enlightened Forces of Twentieth-Century History, will help you smash the Tyrannies that control this country. I will bring down the Big Businesses, the Multi-Nationals, the City, and the Fascist Tories! But first and foremost I will topple Queen Maggie from her tin-pot Capitalist Throne. Then we'll have barricades in the streets and Revolution will sweep this country from one end to the other! Then you'll be free from your chains, Comrades! Free! Free!'

Before 'the embodiment of the Progressive Forces of Twentieth-Century History' could finish her battle cry, the cellar erupted. There was cheering and stamping, shouting and whistling. Then Roy turned to his right and laughed because, despite the din, Alexa was fast asleep.

What a brilliant idea, he thought, as he clamped his hands over his ears and started counting red sheep....

As usual the Theatre Bar was crowded with underaged youngsters buying alcoholic drinks. Roy carried two white wines and a tin of Coke over to his family. Before he could put the drinks on a paint-blistered ledge, Alexa snatched the Coke off him with a barely audible 'Ta'. He passed a glass of white wine to Liz, who was now looking round her with approval because the young audience was buzzing with excitement.

'Well, can you blame them liking it, Roy?' asked Liz as she watched the CND, Greenpeace and Thatcher Out badges jostling round her. 'It's their world that Thatcher's ruining. It's them she's depriving of jobs.'

'Yeah, we know, Mum, but we've heard it all before and it's too loud and it's boring.'

'How can you possibly say it's too loud, Alexa, when you always have your radio, gramophone and cassette player on full-blast at the same time?'

'Yeah, but that's great music, ain't it? I mean, that's interesting. Politics ain't interesting. Politics are boring. Ain't they, Dad?'

'Absolutely! Politics are nearly as boring as plays about politics.'

Liz shook her head.

'Darling, be fair! The show has some good points.'

'Such as?'

'Well ... Thatcher *is* a catastrophe as far as the kids are concerned. Sometimes I think we do need a revolution in this country to stir things up a bit.'

'I couldn't agree with you more, Mrs Hampton.'

Liz whirled round to see Terry MacMaster, with a grapefruit juice in one hand and a theatre programme in the other. Before she could respond, Terry flattered her with his most enchanting smile and murmured: 'Though we shouldn't keep meeting like this. People might start saying things.'

Roy was about to make a cutting retort, when Terry turned his dazzling smile onto the MP.

'Must say, Roy, I was most impressed by your little outburst in the Commons. Heard it on "Yesterday in Parliament" while I was having my morning bowl of Original Crunchy.'

'OK, Terry, OK. We've got the commercial. What are you really selling?'

'Very quick, your husband, Mrs Hampton. Sometimes I think it's a shame we're not on the same side.'

Liz smiled, then said quietly: 'Isn't there some kind of, well, creative compromise that you can both agree on so that you can be on the same side?'

Before Terry could reply, Roy cut in with a peremptory: 'Liz, please!'

Liz shrugged and returned to her wine, while Roy shoved his hands in his pockets and jingled some loose change.

'So what do you want, Terry? I know you never pay courtesy calls. It's against your Marxist principles.'

'Well, the real reason I'm here, Roy, is because I've written you a little note which should be waiting for you at the Commons tomorrow.'

'What's the note about?'

'This theatre.'

Roy registered surprise.

'You've written to me about the Red Cabin Theatre?'

Terry laughed.

'That's right, Roy. We want your support to help us stop the Council withdrawing their grant. You see, if they insist on withdrawing the grant, the theatre will be forced to close.'

Roy was so taken aback by MacMaster's gall that his mouth fell open, which made Terry laugh even more.

'Oh, I know asking a devoted right winger, like your good self, to assist us in such an enterprise is a bit like pissing in the wind,' Terry said, with a deprecatory glance at Liz and Alexa, 'if you'll forgive an old Bolshevik metaphor. But as you, Roy, are now in somewhat of a political bind, constituency-wise, I thought you might see your way to being vaguely radical for once. But don't say anything now that you may regret later. Do yourself a favour for once and *think*. All right?'

While Roy was trying to come to terms with Terry's proposition, the younger man bowed in Liz's direction, then sauntered back to his girlfriend, who was talking to several youngsters at the bar.

'God, he's a cheeky sonova...!' Roy said, trailing off as he noted his daughter's wry expression.

'You shouldn't knock MacMaster, darling,' interposed Liz.

'Why the hell not?!'

'Think about it.'

'What's there to think about?'

'Well, without knowing it, MacMaster may have just opened the door to that famous deal you and Harold are always talking about.'

Roy snorted and swigged back the last of his wine.

'Hm! I wouldn't dream of trying to make a deal with that little basket.'

He plonked his empty glass down and turned on his wife.

'I don't know about you – but I've had this place up to here.'

'And so have I, Dad,' Alexa chorused, discarding her Coke tin. 'Can I come home wiv you?'

'Of course.'

Roy was moving off with his daughter when he noticed that Liz was glancing at MacMaster.

'For Chrissake, stop staring at him, Liz! He's conceited enough as it is.'

Liz decided to tease Roy. She batted her eyelids, then caressed her upper lip with her tongue. 'I don't think Terry's conceited, darling. He's got the most provocative smile and oodles of charm. And at least he knows what he wants, and he's willing to fight tooth and claw for it.'

Roy realised she was trying to tell him something.

Does she really want me to make a deal with him? he thought, as he walked slowly away, unconscious that Alexa was by his side. Does she understand what a deal would mean? Oh yes, I'd probably keep my seat by being reselected. But at what cost to my pride and what's left of my dignity? Though maybe there is a way I could do a deal, and also get MacMaster out of my hair at the same time. Yes . . . I do believe there is a way. . . .

As Roy and his daughter left the bar, Terry watched them go. He stirred the ice-cube in his grapefruit juice with his forefinger, then turned back to his girlfriend, who also had her eyes fastened on the retreating MP.

Terry broke the silence between them.

'Hampton's always on the run, isn't he?'

'Is he?'

'Yeah. Mind, that lot only ever think straight when they're running. It's like Joan Maynard said at Conference – at least I think it was Joan – "The tide of history is with us, comrades." Of course, she's right. What's more, the tide is not only with us, but it's turned against Hampton and all the right wingers. So it won't be long before the tide sweeps away all that anti-socialist garbage.'

Angie pouted, then smeared more pink gloss over her luscious mouth.

'Well, Hampton may be anti-socialist, Terry, but he ain't exactly "garbage", is he? Oh, I know he ain't as lean and muscular and dishy as you, but. . . .'

'Of course he isn't!'

'That's wot I said. And I know he's got a bit of weight on him – but not too much.'

Impatiently, Terry swirled his melting ice-cube round his glass.

'What's your point, Angie?'

'Wot I'm saying is, for a middle-ager, Hampton is kinda sexy. In an uptight sorta way.'

Terry couldn't believe his ears.

'Sexy? He's about as sexy as "Woy" Jenkins!' Terry roared as he jabbed a thumb in Liz's direction. 'In fact, I can't think why a woman like her bothers with him! I bet he can't even get it up any more of a night!'

'I've known nights when *you* can't, Terry. Recently there's been more nights when you can't than when you can!'

For the first time that evening, Terry felt distinctly on the defensive.

'So I can't get it up sometimes? So bleeding what? I'm sure there were nights when even Trotsky couldn't! Or Lenin!'

'Wot about Stalin?' Angie asked innocently.

'Now that's not funny, Angie! Oh shit, that's the bell for the second half,' Terry barked, now completely out of sorts, as he propelled Angie towards the cellar theatre. His mood was not helped by Angie complaining: 'Just wish it weren't so boring, Terry,' as they disappeared into the darkening auditorium.

Roy opened his front door and registered the phone was ringing. Alexa ran down the hallway ahead of him to answer it. She picked up the receiver, muttered the number, then called over her shoulder.

'It's Granny, Dad!'

Moments later Roy was deep in conversation with his mother. From the tone of her voice, he sensed she was close to tears.

'Yes, of course I'll come to Peterborough, Mum. First thing Saturday morning. I'd come earlier but I'm up to my ears in the Commons. I'm afraid things are a bit difficult my end, too.'

There was a pause. Then his mother's tired voice, with its flat fenland vowels, said softly:

'I think my sister's going crazy, Roy. I really do. See, for the last three weeks or more, yer Aunt's refused to let me into her house.'

'Surely she's told you why she won't let you in, Mum?'

'Says she's got a guilty secret.'

'A guilty secret?'

'Ay, but she won't tell me what it is, see. And I can't work out what it can be. But then since yer Uncle Phil died, Mo's never been properly right. Though, as you know, son, many's the time I've asked her to come and live with me. I've even offered to go and live with her. But she won't have it! She says widders are best by 'emselves. Of course that's nonsense. Especially when there are so many widders. I mean, her whole street is full of widders! Mind, for that matter, so be ours. Well, all our men be dead, bain't they? Worn out in the factories and on the land. And all that's left behind is us old women.'

As his mother rambled on with her litany of desolation, Roy felt helpless. He knew he should visit her more often, but his hectic life at the Commons continually thwarted him. To make things worse, his mother never complained.

God help us, he thought, this country is full of old folk forced to live on their own. But what can we politicians do?

Then he heard himself say: 'But, Mum, are you sure you want us to meet in the cathedral? It's dreadfully cold in there.'

'Oh ay, I'm sure, son. See, I got a premonition, though it ent clear yet. And the cathedral's the only lovely place left in our godforsaken city. Besides, if yer train be late, I can always say a little prayer in one of them chapels, can't I? Praying's always a comfort to me. Oh, I knows you think I be foolish, but my belief is what keeps me together. And it keeps me in touch with yer Dad....'

His mother's voice went husky as she tried to prevent her tears from overwhelming her.

'Please, don't upset yourself, Mum. I'll meet you in the cathedral if that's what you want. In the meantime, try and talk some sense into Aunt Maureen. You can bring her and that mad dog of hers along with you if you like.'

'Now don't be a fibber, me duck. You know you don't care much for your Aunty, and you hate her dog. Mind, so do I. I'm always scared it'll bite me varicose.'

So the conversation went on until his mother remembered what Roy had said earlier.

'When you said things were difficult your end, son, what did you mean?'

Roy screwed up his eyes, then transferred the receiver to his left ear.

'It's nothing I can't deal with, Mum. Now look after yourself and keep warm. I'll see you midday on Saturday by the High Altar.'

Then he hung up. As he put the phone down, he remembered some lines from *Paradise Lost*. He closed his eyes to recall when he'd last heard them.

Of course, I was lying on that divan, with the Indian cloth on it, in Helen's bed-sit in Paddington when we were both at the LSE, and we'd been indulging in one of our quotation competitions – which as usual I'd lost. Suddenly Helen gazed at me and said: 'Darling, always remember Satan's words:

'The mind is its own place, and in itself
Can make a heav'n of hell, a hell of heav'n.'

Yes, he thought, how can I ever forget? But *is* it 'Better to reign in hell than serve in heav'n'?

The following morning Roy arrived early at his office. He had slept badly the previous night but had done his best not to disturb Liz, who appeared to be enjoying the dreamless sleep of the deeply-contented. His thoughts were jumbled as he sat down at his desk, so he was pleased de Quincey had not arrived yet and that he had the office to himself. One of the scourges of working at the Royal Palace of Westminster was that everyone except senior ministers had to share their offices with at least one other MP. But at least their office, in the Norman Shaw Building, was large and well-furnished, complete with a drinks cabinet, easy chairs for guests and a vase full of white carnations. Whereas most of the offices in the Palace of Westminster itself were cubbyholes, crammed with files, telephones and often three Members of Parliament.

Roy slit open another letter of complaint from an embittered constituent, then stopped to breathe in the scent of the carnations.

How the hell can I possibly help any of my constituents if I don't survive my reselection? His thoughts were disturbed by the telephone ringing.

'Hampton here.'

'There's a Mr Jack Winner on the line, Mr Hampton,' his secretary said.

'Oh, thanks, Isla, I'll speak to him.'

There was a pause, then Roy heard the confident tones of the chairman of JYC Management Consultants.

'Just calling you about that little lunch we discussed after the cricket match, Roy.'

'Yes, of course, Jack.'

'Is there any day next week that's convenient?'

'I suppose at a push I could manage Wednesday.'

'Fine – then let's say a quarter to one at my club.'

'Which club is that, Jack?'

'The Reform. So it won't offend too many of your socialist principles.'

Roy laughed.

'All right, Jack, but I feel you should know the chances of my leaving politics to join you are extremely remote.'

'Of course, old man, but we family men have to think of the future, y'know. As Harold Wilson always used to say: "A week's a long time in politics." So six months in politics must be a lifetime. See you Wednesday, then?'

Winner hung up. Roy stared at the receiver, then returned it to its cradle.

Perhaps Winner's right, he thought. Perhaps I should get out now while I've got a job on offer. It's bound to be worth getting on for twenty grand, which is a damn sight more than I get as an MP.

He sighed, then absently rearranged one of the carnations in the vase on his desk.

But somehow, he mused, being a consultant's not really my style. In fact, I'd hate to be a consultant. The whole country's full of bloody consultants, and what good are they doing us? I think I'd even prefer to make a deal with MacMaster. But either way you look at it, Wordsworth's right.

Instantly he began intoning to the carnations:

'Milton! thou shouldst be living at this hour:
England hath need of thee; she is a fen
Of stagnant waters; altar, sword and pen,
Fireside, the heroic wealth of hall and bower,
Have forfeited their ancient English dower
Of inward happiness. We are selfish men...'

Yes, he thought, it's true. We are still 'selfish', and England is still 'a fen of stagnant waters'.

Then, in a melodramatic voice, he went on with the sonnet. He realised he was hamming it up, but he also knew this ability to ham it up was an indispensable weapon for a politician. After all, Lloyd George and Churchill spent hours rehearsing their speeches and gestures. So with his right hand clutching his breast and his left outstretched, Roy became the actor of his dreams.

'Oh! raise us up, return to us again;
And give us manners, virtue, freedom, power.
Thy soul was like a star, and dwelt apart;

> Thou hadst a voice whose sound was like the sea;
> Pure as the naked heavens, majestic, free...'

Suddenly Roy realised he wasn't alone. Someone was framed in the doorway with his mouth understandably ajar. For a moment he thought it was Wordsworth's ghost. Then, to his relief, his actor's vision faded and he recognised the appalled face of de Quincey.

Before David could say anything, Roy muttered: 'I was merely giving myself a fillip before ringing up Terry MacMaster about the Red Cabin Theatre.'

Roy knew he sounded like a madman, but to his relief his friend simply said: 'Ah, I see,' and closed the door.

Hastily Roy picked up the telephone and dialled MacMaster's bed-sit.

'Oh, is that Terry MacMaster's residence?' he said, as he heard Angie's giggling voice answer the phone.

'Yeah, this is Terry's joint.'

'This is Roy Hampton speaking, and I'd like to have a word with him, please.'

As Roy spoke, de Quincey hung up his raincoat and slid his briefcase onto his desk. Although David was acting calmly, his thoughts were whirling.

I do believe Hampton is going off his head. Oh, I know MPs have been caught with their trousers down before. But no MP has ever been discovered declaiming Wordsworth to a bunch of carnations.

Still giggling, Angie handed the telephone to Terry, then flounced into the kitchen to finish making his health-food breakfast.

Knowing he had satisfied those delightful haunches during the night, the lithe revolutionary grinned, then picked up the telephone base and threw himself full length on the bent springs of his ancient sofa. This was a call he intended to enjoy, so he settled two cushions behind his head and purred into the receiver.

'You're up bright and early, aren't you, Roy?'

Terry extended his free hand towards the glass of chilled carrot juice on the coffee table.

'I'm sorry if I'm a bit premature, Terry.'

'What can I do for you, comrade?'

'Well, I've got your letter in front of me, Terry, and actually you're right.'

'I am?'

'Yes. I think perhaps we can ... do business.'

'You do?'

'Yes.'

Terry sipped the cool vegetable juice.

'Must say, comrade, I didn't think you'd be interested in "doing business" over something as contentious as the Red Cabin Theatre Company. You didn't even stay to the end of their play, did you? But then I suppose you found all that "red" meat a bit indigestible.'

'Oh no! I simply felt, well, a touch queasy,' Roy said, trying not to bluster. Then he switched the receiver over to his other ear, and cradled it in the crook of his arm so he could light up his first cigarette.

'Are you still there, comrade?' enquired Terry.

'Yes. And what's more, I've still got a bit of a gyp tummy. Mind, the wine at these theatre-club places leaves a lot to be desired, doesn't it?'

'I wouldn't know. Never drink the stuff. Though I'm sure you're right. Can't be up to House of Commons claret, can it?'

Roy heard himself laugh, but inside he was beginning to squirm.

And this is only the start of the slippery slope, he thought, as he took a long drag on his cigarette to calm his nerves.

'What I'm ringing you about, Terry, is, well, perhaps we should meet. You know, informally. So we can discuss the problems of the future funding of the Red Cabin Theatre Group.'

Terry toyed with his glass.

'You willing to put pressure on your right-wing friends on the Council, then, Roy?'

'Possibly.'

Terry smiled, took another sip of the juice, then said: 'And why would you want to do that, comrade?'

'I've always been a progressive in relation to the arts, Terry. And in a democracy like ours, I believe all sides of the arts should be allowed to have their say. So as this is an area we agree on, I thought ....'

Roy trailed off, embarrassed by his own heartiness. Then he

caught sight of de Quincey's eyebrow, which was now almost in de Quincey's hairline.

'Are you still there, Terry?'

'Yeah. And I always will be.'

Roy laughed again, but his laugh was hollow. He knew he was degrading himself but couldn't think of anything else to do but become a consultant. And as he couldn't bear that idea, he had no choice but to mumble:

'Look, Terry, why don't you come up to the House of Commons for a drink?'

'How many times do I have to tell you, comrade; I don't drink. Anyway, I've got an aversion to that place. So you come and see me instead.'

Roy shook his head, then stubbed out the remains of his cigarette.

'No, I've a better idea. As it happens I've got a surgery tomorrow evening in the constituency. Why don't you come to the surgery. . .?'

'I don't need to come to your surgery, comrade. There's nothing wrong with *me*. You come to my place. For a cuppa tea. Next Monday.'

'I thought we could meet earlier than that. . . .'

'Afraid I'm very busy till then, comrade.'

I bet you are! Roy thought, biting his lip.

'So if you want us to talk, Comrade Hampton, Monday's the earliest I can make. Unlike you MPs, we humble folk have to bustle about a lot. So see you Monday. Four-ish. I'll have the kettle on.'

'All right, if Monday's the only time you can. . . .'

Roy didn't finish his sentence because the phone went dead at the other end.

Roy tried to work on the train from Kings Cross to Peterborough, but for most of the journey he was unable to concentrate because of his mother's phone call the previous evening.

'What's happened to yer Aunty Mo, Roy, is terrible!' his mother said. 'Mind, I had a premonition something was wrong the moment I got to her place. See, I had to get a policeman to break into her house! I kept knocking and knocking on the front door, like, but she never answered. So the policeman and a neighbour had to break her door down. Yet to begin with we couldn't find her. We were just about to leave when I said we haven't tried the larder. So I went on ahead and pushed open the larder door – and there she were, dead as dead could be, poor soul. With a half-empty bottle of whisky beside her and sleeping pills scattered all round her.'

If only I could feel some genuine sorrow, Roy thought, as the train hurtled through Huntingdon. Trouble is, I never really liked Aunt Mo. She was always selfish and a dead weight on my mother's shoulders. But then I suppose my grandmother was responsible because she spoiled her and made her so useless. I can only pray that my mother won't regard Aunt Mo's suicide as a reflection on her. Because, God knows, my mother has been a good sister, and the best mother. The question is, will she be strong enough this time to bear being even more alone?

One thing's certain, I doubt whether I would have the resilience to be so alone and for so long. Christ in heaven, how long is it since my father died? Nearly a quarter of a century! My mother has been living with her memories all these years. This 'garden of England' is filled with folk who have nothing but memories, and nothing to cling to but personal histories. Wherever they turn, they are constantly reminded of their dead. Their photograph albums, which are their private shrines, are filled with yellowing snapshots of long-ago summer holidays, before Harry was killed in the trenches, or Bill didn't come home from Dunkirk, or Fred died with coaldust in his lungs, or Bert had that heart attack. Or Dad rotted away with cancer until he looked like he'd come straight out of Dachau.

He stared out of the window at the intensively cultivated fields, stretching to the low, grey Fenland skyline. Then unexpectedly a shaft of cold sunlight raced across the open fields, trying to outrun the train. Roy shivered. It was like an omen. Nature racing against machines. Then, as suddenly, the sun was extinguished, and the train rushed on.

Approaching the west front of Peterborough Cathedral, Roy again understood why it had been described as the finest Norman portico in Europe. Though he knew his mother was waiting for him inside, he couldn't help but pause and wonder how anyone could build so miraculous a structure. The three great ninety-foot arches towered above him, each surmounted by a gable and a cross. Then behind the northernmost gable stood the thirteenth-century belltower. At the south end of the great west front the spire probed the lowering sky, with its exquisite cluster of spirelets on flying buttresses.

Well, Roy thought, drunk on the godlike vision towering between him and the sky, we certainly can't build anything like this today – even if we could afford to. But how empty the Precinct is, guarded by those high walls. This cathedral no longer has any meaning for the majority of people who live in Peterborough. Nietzsche was right: 'God is dead.' At least, most of the time He seems and feels to us to be dead. We no longer have Him to hold us together. Today we have only ourselves. And according to the atheists, we should be strong enough to live without God. But since most of us who don't believe aren't atheists but merely agnostics, we find ourselves in the worst of all possible worlds.

He entered the cathedral by the great west door and hurried to comfort his mother. To his relief, she only clung to him a moment. Her eyes were red from weeping, but her face was calm and expressionless. She had suffered so much in her seventy-six years that she had finally purged herself of emotion. Roy took her hand in his. Her fingers were contorted with rheumatism and as cold as the cathedral itself.

'I knew we shouldn't have met in here, Mum.'

'Of course we should, son. This is the only part of the city that ent been ruined. There's real peace here. I been praying for her soul, see, though I dunno whether He were listening. Sometimes lately I think He's tired of listening to me. Tired of all my dead joining Him. Tired of me wanting to join my dead. Because this town's ruined. Everything here's been changed, and not for the best.'

How thoroughly English she is, he thought, as his mother rambled on. She refuses to show her grief in public, even to her son. She thinks it's undignified, so she keeps changing the subject to avoid bursting into tears. Yet if my mother was a Latin, Spaniard, Jew or Arab, she would be proud of her grief. She'd beat her breast and cover herself in sackcloth and ashes. How healthy that would be. Whereas we English bottle our grief up until it devours us from within. Yet if anyone has a reason to howl at the moon, it's my mother. This is the second sister she's lost in three years, not to mention the death of my brother when he was a teenager, with my father's death following soon after. Now all she has is me, my younger brother who lives in Australia and my sister who lives in Ireland. How does she bear it all? Like a true English lady. Yes, even though my Mum's working-class right down to the marrow of her old bones, she always keeps her infinite pain to herself. Then she cries herself to sleep when she can't bear to keep it to herself any longer.

'Where is Aunt Mo? I trust they've not just left her in the house.'

'No, she be taken to the mortuary.'

Then his mother gripped his wrist with her freezing hand and whispered: 'It be cold in here now, son.'

'Yes, let me take you home.'

'I don't want to go home. I'd like some coffee. Then I want to show you what I found in her house.'

Roy nodded. Then for a moment he allowed himself to be lost in the great Norman cathedral, arching above him. The building was so cold it took his breath away, but there was a remarkable lightness about it, for the windows, except in the spacious triforium, had little stained glass remaining in them. Roy knew who was responsible for that: his bigoted hero Cromwell, and his army of desecrating soldiers.

That's England for you, he thought. Even the best of them are still capable of doing the worst.

Then he turned and led his mother out of the echoing cathedral into the rebuilt centre of Peterborough.

Moments later, mother and son were walking across imitation honey-coloured marble floors. A hundred feet above them reared a vast roof of tubular steel and glittering glass, supported by immense, white stone pillars. To their left, a fountain splashed into a triangular, black marble basin. To their right, a glass lift slid sedately towards a restaurant high up in the dome, while all around them were the illuminated names of famous shops and stores; for Roy and his mother were now exploring the most up-to-date shopping centre in Europe.

Roy had visited his mother several times since the shopping centre had been built, but this was the first time he had been inside this modern wonder of the world. Already he was shaking his head.

In the old days, he thought, we built cathedrals to the greater glory of God and as monuments to our own artistic genius. Today we build glittering shopping centres that sell things that we don't really need to buy, in order to convince ourselves we're living life to the full.

Roy turned to see what his mother was thinking, but her eyes were hooded and her mouth a thin line.

'There's no denying it's a brilliant piece of modern design, Mum, but. . . .'

His mother silenced him by gripping his wrist between her cold finger and thumb.

'I brought you here for a purpose, son. Because, believe it or not, it's a hell-hole like this that's in some way responsible for what happened to yer Aunty.'

'Yes, but you still haven't told me why Aunt . . . ?'

'I know. Now we'll go to her house and you'll see only too clearly why!'

Without waiting for his reply, Mrs Hampton took her son by the arm and tottered forward. She was being driven by an inner force. Roy was relieved that her grief was rapidly turning to anger.

But how the hell can this cornucopia have anything to do with Aunty Mo's death?

His mother answered his thought.

'I'm sure Mo's not the only one these shopping centres have killed, son. I bet it's happening all over the country.'

As they came out of the shopping centre, Roy looked back at its impressive frontage. Then he glanced behind him at the cathedral's spires, which seemed to be holding up the heavy, iron-grey sky above them.

'Look, why don't we find a taxi, Mum? Then we can get to Aunt Mo's place quickly and I can make you a cup of tea.'

She shook her head.

'Taxis be a waste of money, son. If you had to live on my pension, you'd be more careful with yer foolish spending habits. Trouble with you young 'uns, you got no money sense. All me life I've scrimped and saved so me children could have a decent education. Sending you all to them grammar schools weren't cheap.'

Roy realised his mother was working herself up but hadn't the heart to stop her.

'Well, your Dad slogged hisself to death for you lot. Never saw ought for his labour either. What a terrible life he had: eldest of four brothers and four sisters. Had the brains to go to grammar school, but his Dad were a widower and down the mines being paid a pittance, so he couldn't afford to send your Dad to grammar school. Your Dad didn't have a chance. Out to work when he were thirteen. Imagine that! Being cuffed round the lughole in a butcher's shop all day, then hit by his Dad when he got home at night. For your Grandad were a violent man, drunk with beer and despair. God help 'em, but up north they had it real bad.'

Mrs Hampton stopped, then indicated all the empty shops that had been forced to close down because of the new shopping centre.

'Mind, it ent much different in Peterborough now than it was in Wigan then. This used to be a nice, thriving market town. That's why your Dad upped and left Wigan, because there were a lot of work here just afore the War. In fact, there were a lot of work here till they started to redevelop it and make it into one of them New Towns. But all the light industry they expected to come here, it never came, did it? So now we got double the population and God knows how many unemployed. It's hardly surprising the Social Services can't cope, when every day more 'n' more shops are forced to close and more factories have to lay off more 'n' more men! It's hopeless, I tell you, hopeless!'

She paused for breath while Roy escorted her over a zebra crossing. He saw that the centre of Peterborough was derelict. Everywhere he turned there were shops with metal grilles over their neglected frontages, padlocks and chains on their doors and 'For Sale' signs in their dusty windows. His home town reminded him of his own constituency, and of the derelict north and north-east. Much of Shakespeare's 'precious stone set in a silver sea' now consisted of empty shops and factories, and new shopping centres that only the moderately well-off could afford to shop in.

As if his mother was echoing his thoughts, she went on: 'And you know the only reason we are a horrible New Town, son? 'Tis because Peterborough happens to be the first major town atween London and the north. So all the people you don't want in London, all the coloured folk, the Indians, the out-of-work, the young who ent got no skills, well, you send 'em all down here, don't you? For you Londoners don't care about the rest of the country. You Londoners think the rest of England's a foreign country. That's why you send us all yer down-and-outs, like in the old days you sent all them convicts to Australia. Well, on me life, I can't see no difference!'

She continued in the same vein while they waited for a bus.

'Look at the bus service! All been cut back. Used to be a bus every eight minutes. Now you're lucky if you gets two an hour. Yet you have to get on a bus to go shopping, because since they put in all them new highways and motorways on the outskirts of Peterborough, there ent no shops left round locally no more. All been pulled down. Everything's been pulled down! Except this blasted shopping centre, which may be all right for young 'uns, but we pensioners can't afford to shop in it.'

Eventually the bus arrived. Immediately it was followed by another bus, both heading for the same destination. Roy offered to help his mother inside but she insisted on making her own way.

'Typical, see! Two buses, both going same place, both arrive same time. Whole town's gone to rack and ruin.'

His mother chattered on for the entire bus trip. Roy made no attempt to stop her, because he agreed with everything she said. As this was the first bus journey through Peterborough and its outskirts he'd made for many years, for he normally travelled from the station by taxi, he peered about him in an attempt to get his bearings. It was impossible. The town and its direct environs were so completely transformed that Roy was soon lost. It was as if someone had taken an axe to his childhood memories.

His mother let them into his aunt's soot-stained, red-brick, twenties house. Roy noticed that many of the neighbouring houses were owned by Pakistanis.

Aunt Mo wouldn't have cared for that a lot, he thought, as they moved into the shadowy hallway. Still, when you think of it, the influx of so many disparate races and the doubling of the population in a market town must have put an intolerable strain on the residents. Especially as the town has had to cope with so many strangers in so short a time, many of whom can't find jobs. It's not surprising there's resentment here. My mother's right. We Londoners forget what happens to our population overspill. Yes, and the only wealth London produces is through its banks and money markets. It's the rest of the country that creates the real wealth.

Roy followed his mother into his aunt's gloomy living room. Something was wrong with the room, but at first he couldn't make out what it was. His mother folded her bony arms across her chest as she waited for him to react. A shaft of pale sunlight lanced through the clouds and momentarily illuminated the room. Then Roy realised what was odd about his surroundings.

'Good grief!' he muttered, pointing to the mantelpiece. 'Why the hell's she got four brand-new clocks?'

His mother smiled grimly and waited.

'And whatever could she do with two television sets?'

His mother remained silent, so he went over to the Victorian table on which stood three portable radios, two of which were in their original packaging. Roy picked up one of the boxes in its cellophane wrapping.

'Aunt Mo didn't steal all this, did she?'

The old lady didn't reply but walked out of the room into the hallway. As she mounted the winding stairs, he hurried after her.

'Where did she get all this stuff, Mum?' he called, following her up the stairs.

His mother paused on the landing to massage her left knee, which was badly swollen with rheumatism.

'There's more, son. Much more.'

Then the old lady straightened up. Though her knee was still aching, she pushed open a bedroom door. Roy peered over her shoulder at an Aladdin's cave of brand-new consumer goods. At a quick glance he registered two new toasters, four boxes of wineglasses, three cutlery sets, a portable typewriter, yet another clock, and countless knickknacks. Most of them had not been opened.

'Mum, you still haven't answered my question. Did Aunt Mo steal all this?'

Slowly his mother moved into the room. Then, gasping, she subsided onto a high-backed chair by the window.

'Yes,' she said, scarcely moving her lips. 'In a way, I suppose you could say she did.'

She was close to tears again, not only because of her sister's death, but also for the twenty-six years of living and fighting alone. Roy could bear it no longer. He crossed the sunlit room and knelt by his mother's chair, taking her chilled hands between his. He was appalled to see how misshapen her fingers were. The single gold band on her wedding finger would never come off again, for the knuckle joint was swollen to double its original size.

'Please don't be too proud to cry in front of me, Mummy. I know I'm not the best of sons, but I still love you. But you know that....'

His mother nodded, then her tight-lipped mouth hardened. Her eyes were glistening with tears, but Roy knew she still wouldn't cry properly. She refused to give in. When at last she spoke, it was in a stifled whisper, as if she didn't want to hear what she was saying.

'When I said that yer Aunt, in a way, thieved all this, I didn't mean that she did it knowingly. She didn't. See, it all started round about the time that blasted shopping centre opened. Though her loneliness started long afore that, of course. If only Mo had come to live with me like I asked her to. Then none of this would've happened. Why did she have to get it into her silly head that widders should live alone?'

The old lady paused to brush an arthritic hand over her brimming eyes.

'But then I suppose she ent been in her right mind since yer Uncle Phil dropped down dead with that heart attack. Ever since then she's been acting strange and not been able to cope. Yet, though she couldn't cope, she still wouldn't let me help her. Trouble was, everything round here changed too fast for her. What with them Indians and Pakis moving in as neighbours, with their cooking smells and strange ways. And then everything she'd known from childhood being knocked down and rebuilt. Even them woods nearby were chopped down to build that horrible crematorium. Poor Mo just got so ... I don't know ... so....'

'Disorientated and alienated?'

'Well, if them words mean what they sound like they mean, then, yes. So she went more 'n' more into herself. In the end she'd hardly go out of this house at all. I know it were fanciful, but she became, well, afraid of her neighbours. Afraid of everything! Not that her neighbours had been anything other than polite to her, y'understand. But she got to such a point, she wouldn't go to her local shops at all, because they were taken over by Indians and Pakis. . . .'

'Are you saying that Aunt Mo was a racist, Mum?'

'What would you know, son?' his mother flared back. 'You don't have to live with 'em! Because you're middle-class now, ent you? Well, whatever you say, that's what you are. And the middle class are always telling the working class that the working class are racist! That's easy when you don't have to *live* with the coloured folks. And most of you middle-class people make sure you don't have to live with 'em. Oh, I know you live in an area where there be a lot of coloureds about. But there ent none in your posh row, are there? That's the trouble with you middle-class folk; you're always going on about "the evils of racism", but I notice none of you go rushing out to live with 'em. Anyroad, I don't want to get into this no more.'

Mrs Hampton hobbled to the other side of the room, then unconsciously ran her fingers over a box of sherry glasses.

'Oh, I'm not accusing you of being hypocritical, son. I'm just saying you got to try to be a bit more understanding about yer Aunt's point of view. You ent had to, well, adjust to living with all these people that suddenly come out of the blue. And let's face it, Roy, she were already in her late sixties, so it were hard for her to change and learn to deal with everything. That's what's happened to all us old 'uns in this town. And it ent right, is it? Because it were us and our husbands that made this town what it was afore it were spoiled! And no one asked us if we wanted our town changed. No one asked us if we wanted all these new young people. We were just another part of London's big experiment. That's what it is, a ruddy experiment!'

His mother was now sitting on the high-backed chair, and the words were pouring out of her like tears.

'And it ent just the coloured folks that's the problem. It's all them school-leavers who ent got no jobs, or even prospects of jobs. So what do they do? They vandalise us old 'uns' property, smash our windows and our greenhouses, pee in our gardens, knock down our fences. Or they knock us down when we come out of the post office with our pensions and thieve our purses.

God help us, some of the more godless of them steal the poor boxes in the churches, then bust the church winders and knock down the church walls.'

Again she paused with her head in her hands, rocking backwards and forwards on her chair.

'Tain't worth living round here no more, son. Just hopeless, hopeless. . . .'

Roy moved towards her. When he reached her, he put his arms round her. For a moment he thought she was going to resist him, then he felt her hot tears dripping onto his shirt front. He hugged her closer, but it was only when she had finished crying that she hugged him back. For what seemed a lifetime, the old woman and her middle-aged son clung to one another in Aunt Mo's treasure house. Then Mrs Hampton sniffed loudly and gently pushed Roy away from her. She fumbled with her black handbag, searching for the lace handkerchief which she always took with her whenever she went to town. Then she dabbed her red-rimmed eyes and blew her nose. Then, to Roy's amazement, she began to chuckle.

'What a silly old biddy you got for a mother, eh, son? Here am I crying about I dunno what, and I still ent told you how yer Aunt got all this stuff, have I?'

Still chuckling, his mother pointed at the consumer goods in the room.

'If she didn't exactly steal all this stuff, Mum, then. . .?'

'She got it on the never-never, son.'

'She did what?'

'Aunty Mo got everything in this room and all that junk downstairs – on the HP!'

'How do you know?'

'Well, after they took her to the mortuary yesterday, I started asking the neighbours how she managed to get hold of all these goods. It were them who told me that she'd, well, persuaded them to sign all these HP forms for her. Trouble was, each of 'em thought that they was the only ones signing. So she never told nobody that she was buying things that she didn't need and she certainly couldn't afford! Well, she didn't even tell *me*, her own sister. Come to that, I remember signing a couple of HP forms for her myself. And I never thought nothing of it, neither.'

His mother paused for breath, then went on in a rush: 'Not

only that, Roy. She also bought a lot of this stuff with mail-order forms. I mean, you only have to look round to see there are mail-order forms all over the place.'

Dazed, Roy shook his head.

'But, Mum, why did she want all this stuff in duplicate and triplicate when she obviously didn't need it and couldn't afford it?'

'She weren't in her right mind, son. Being alone all the time, plus all the changes round here – well, they must've driven her dotty. The policeman who found her with me, he said that lonely old folk do strange things. He said he wouldn't be surprised if the reason she ordered all this stuff was because it was her way of getting to see new people without ever having to go out. Well, stands to reason; a lot of this stuff had to be delivered. And as she ordered so much, she'd get a delivery every day. So every day she'd see either the postman or the delivery man. The policeman said she probably found it easier talking to them than to any of her new neighbours. Maybe she even fell in love with the postman or . . . Oh, I know it doesn't make sense, but I'm sure there are millions of folk like her rotting away with loneliness. All buying things they don't need, with money they ent got. And then when things get too much for them, and they realise how horribly in debt they are, well, one night they can't bear it any more, so they swallow handfuls of sleeping pills. . . .'

His mother broke off and stared out of the window.

'What Mo didn't realise, son, was that someone would have to find her. Someone'd have to clear the mess up after her. Someone'd be left wondering whether they did enough to help her when she were alive. God forgive me, but I do believe suicide's a selfish thing to do. And yet I can't blame her. No more than I can blame the man I read about in the paper yesterday, who three weeks after he were thrown out of his job cut his wrists in the bath. I suppose when you lose yer pride, and you lose hope, and nothing makes sense, then all you want is out. Mind, I sometimes feel like that meself. But I hope to God I'd never be that selfish, because I'd hate you or any of my children to find me – like I found her. Still, I hope the poor sweetheart has at last found some peace. No one should have to live on the rack like that.'

His mother started laughing through her tears again.

'Don't make much sense, do it, Roy? But then, so much that folk do nowadays don't make sense.'

She waved a dismissive hand at the consumer goods around her.

'Well, it serves all them shops and stores and mail-order-form places right, dunnit? They'll never get their money back now. They'll all have to come here, won't they, and fight among themselves to see who gets what. I won't be around to help 'em.'

She paused to look round the room, then crossed to the half-open door.

'No, I won't be around. I'll not come to this house again. Ever.'

As Roy guided his mother down the drab passageway leading to her back garden, he was again reminded of his childhood, and the hours when he and his brother played cricket with an old piece of wood and a tennis ball in the alleyway. His sister was only ever allowed to be the wicketkeeper. The times the neighbours had complained to his father about the ball bouncing off their windows, or knocking the petals off their prize roses. . . .

Still smiling, he pushed open the stiff garden gate for his mother and made a mental note to oil it. Then he stepped into the garden and gasped in delight. He had always known his mother had green fingers, but this year she had excelled herself. The garden was ablaze with flowers and flowering bushes. There were clusters of bluebells under the pink blossoming cherry tree, and round the base of the two Cox's Orange Pippins were grape hyacinths, late primroses and clumps of violets. As the wind keened through them, the petals of the redcurrant were torn from the branches to stipple the grass. A brief burst of sunshine highlighted the blood-red camellia bush, then the sky was grey again.

'What a magnificent display, Mum!' he explained as they walked down the centre of the narrow garden, pausing under the first white blossoms on the apple tree.

His mother, unimpressed, waved her arm at something over his shoulder. At first he thought she was showing him a greenfinch which had alighted on one of the upper branches.

Then he realised she was pointing at the huge pillars supporting the flyover at the bottom of her garden. The authorities had planted several fir trees at the base of the flyover in an attempt to hide its barbaric ugliness, but the trees were still too young to disguise anything. Then Roy became aware of the noise of the traffic on the flyover.

'That's why you can never hear the birds chirping in my garden, son, except at dawn or dusk. You only hear 'em then because there are so many of 'em. Rest of the time there's just that din on the flyover and the smell of diesel oil. Can't tell you how glad I am that yer Dad ent alive to see this. Not that our garden were ever private, with all them other gardens overlooking us, but it was never stuck in the middle of a highway like 'tis now.'

Roy nodded.

'Wouldn't you fancy a cup of tea, Mum? I know I would.'

The old lady smiled and fished her back-door key out of her purse to let them into the house. She put the kettle on, telling him to get the salad things out of the fridge for their lunch. He struggled with her ancient tin-opener as he tried to prise open a can of luncheon meat. When she saw he was making a mess of the tin she took it away from him, and within seconds had it open and the luncheon meat on a plate. Roy shivered, then pretended he was scratching himself, for his mother's kitchen was always cold, even in summer.

They sat down opposite each other at the old kitchen table. As they sipped their tea and cut up their tomatoes and cucumber, Roy remembered how when he was a schoolboy he had tried to do his homework on this very table, while his younger brother and sister chased one another round the kitchen.

Yes, he thought, it's a miracle I passed my exams. Mum's kitchen seems to shrink a little more every time I see it. God knows how we all lived in here. Mind, the front room isn't any bigger, and the bedrooms were obviously designed for dolls. How my mother managed to keep the place tidy and us fed and clothed on the pittance my father earned, and yet still remained sane, I'll never know.

'They're going to do the autopsy on yer Aunt on Monday, so the funeral's planned for Thursday. You going to be able to come, Roy?'

'I'll do my damndest. It all depends on a meeting I've got on Monday.'

'You are in a spot of trouble, ent you, boy? Now there's no use you shaking yer head. It's written all over yer face. Well, ent you going to tell yer old Mum what be troubling you?'

'Oh, come on, Mum, you've got more than enough on your plate without me bothering you with. . . .'

'Rubbish! What's a mother for if you can't tell her yer heartache? Anyways, I got a right to know. You came out of my body, remember. And you're my eldest son and I'm proud of you. Oh, I'm not saying I understand all this . . . political stuff you keep spouting, but I knows you're an honest boy. So you can only be in honest trouble. And if it's honest trouble you're in, why should you hesitate to tell yer old mother about it, eh?'

If only it were 'honest trouble', Roy thought, taking a prolonged sip of his tea to hide his expression.

He was saved from confessing his proposed deal with MacMaster by a loud knock on the door. Roy pushed back his chair to answer it, but the door opened and a stocky, bearded man wearing horn-rimmed spectacles came into the kitchen. For a moment he didn't recognise Bernie Stallybrass, his mother's seventy-three-year-old neighbour, especially as Bernie had mud on his big, smiling face, and was wearing an oversize pair of paint-stained overalls and wellington boots. He was carrying two wooden boxes filled with petunias, and several of the largest yellow-and-brown pansies that Roy had ever seen.

'My God, if it ent the political wanderer from the Big City!' Bernie said, his ruddy face creasing with laughter. 'Oh, I'm sorry, Madge. I got no right to come barging in on yer grief like that. It's just that when I saw Roy there, well, it were such a nice surprise I forgot me manners. Not that me manners have ever been much to write home about at the best of times. Right, Madge?'

'You bet you're right, Bernie Stallybrass. Well, don't stand there laughing like a jackass, put them petunias down on the side there and come and get yer cup of tea. Roy, fetch them homemade scones from the cake tin. Oh, and get Bernie a cup. No, no, Bernie, Roy'll get it. You know you're clumsy and you'll only break everything. Hey, and mind where you put them muddy boots! Keep 'em off that carpet.'

As Roy poured Bernie some tea, then collected a teaspoon from the drawer, he couldn't help smiling.

If only Mum had married Bernie years ago, he thought. But they're both too proud, too stubborn and too East Anglian to do anything as sensible as that. As a result, Bernie's been a widower nearly as long as my mother's been a widow. Yes, there's no doubt about it: people down here live in a different England. For one thing, they find it much harder to 'make deals' in this part of the country. Especially marriage deals. Though perhaps if my mother had land or wealth, things might be different. But I doubt it. Everyone round here is so maniacally independent. It's as if they live on tramlines that can never diverge. It's also something to do with their generation, because their youth was ruined by Hitler's ambition. Then those that did manage to survive the War had to live through ten years of ration books and austerity. So by the time they had brought their children up in the next-best-thing to poverty, they themselves were middle-aged and totally exhausted. Yes, Roy thought, my mother and Bernie belong to the Lost Generation. All they have left now is their loneliness, their bewilderment at the changing world around them, and their fierce pride.

As Roy finished his lunch and answered the questions that Bernie kept firing at him about his life in London, he began to feel more and more as if he were living on a different planet.

'Well, considering the way you say you live in London, lad, don't you think that you're betraying your class? I mean, how can you live in that nice house surrounded by all them shitty Tories? I beg pardon, Madge, but them Tories are enough to make a vicar swear. How can you live with them kind of people when you remember where you came from? No, I ent finished yet, Roy. Your Dad were a shop steward in his time, as I were shop steward at Rotherington's; and it were people who sounded like *you* who were always pushing us around. Well, don't that make you feel ashamed, lad! Joining the very class that's held down yer father 'n' me? If it don't make you feel guilty, it bloody should!'

Roy smiled wearily and shook his head.

'No, I don't feel guilty, Bernie. Oh, I used to. In fact, it's only recently that I've stopped feeling guilty. But don't get me wrong: underneath I'm still the same boy who was brought up in this house, with my parents' values and what I can only call a working-class approach to life. But I have now become middle-class. No, Bernie, I let you have your say, so please let me finish. Because, although I am middle-class, I'm still fighting *for* the *working* class. But I'm not fighting to *keep* the working class as working class. I'm fighting to try and get rid of *all* the lousy classes in this country. I want the working class to have a better standard of life, both for them and for their children. Because there's no merit in being poor or neglected, or in being riddled with envy. And there's certainly no merit in being looked down on by your so-called "betters".'

'Right, lad! That's why we've got to make the unions even stronger, so they can put an armlock on these filthy Tories! If necessary we should have a General Strike. Arthur Scargill's right; this is a battle to the death. Either the working people of this country are going to have the riches of this country, or there ent going to be any riches for anyone!'

Both men were so engrossed in their argument that they didn't notice Mrs Hampton move away from the table, laden with dishes. Unlike Liz or Helen, or any other woman that Roy came into contact with in London, his mother assumed that her opinion was not required. It was all right to talk about the house or cooking or the children, but because of her narrow upbringing and the insularity of her life, unless she was asked directly for her opinion, she would say nothing. After all, it was a man's world, and she no longer had a man to guide her thinking. Anyway, she never took what men said seriously. Oh, they were great authorities on how to run the world, but they weren't good at changing nappies or managing the household accounts. It was a well-known fact that men couldn't cope with real life.

Roy stood up and faced Bernie.

'Bernie, you don't really believe all that.'

'Why the hell shouldn't we have the riches? We earn the bugger!'

'I'm not saying you shouldn't have them. But nothing will be achieved for anybody if we reduce this country to the lowest common denominator. So if we say there'll be no more rich men in this country, it won't be long before the entrepreneurs and the big business men leave this country for pastures new. And what will you replace them with? State control of everything?'

'Why not? If the state is controlled by the Labour Party and the unions, then we won't need yer entrepreneurs and yer corrupt big business men, will we?'

Bernie banged his fist down on the table. Roy rubbed his eyes. The last thing he needed was a political scene with his mother's next-door neighbour.

'Believe me, Bernie, state control would only make things worse. I mean, look at the state of the nationalised industries now. In most cases there is no real incentive, so nobody wants to work hard. That's why it's important to have a mixed economy. Otherwise, if the state took over everything, like Tony Benn wants, we could easily end up with greater inefficiency than we've already got and have even more corrupt practices, like they have throughout the Eastern bloc. You see, Bernie, wherever there's state control, there's endless bureaucracy. So funds get ripped off, and no one can find out where the money has gone because there's been a bureaucratic conspiracy to fix the figures.'

Roy trailed off. He knew he wasn't at his best. There were times when he hated being a politician. He felt like a hard-drinking muscleman in a pub. In other words, he was always the target, and there was always somebody who wanted to knock him down to show that they were tougher than he was. He turned to his mother who was still washing up.

'Do you fancy a little walk, Mum?'

Then he turned back to Bernard. 'Sorry to spoil our fascinating talk, Bernie, but I'm afraid I need a rest from politics sometimes. Perhaps you'd care for a walk too?'

'No, lad, I've come round to help your Mum put these petunias out.'

'Ay, you take a walk on yer own, son,' agreed his mother. 'Can't beat a breath of Peterborough air to ruin yer lungs. No, I'm only joking, lad. Besides, you've earned a bit of peace and quiet, what with me bending yer lughole and now Bernie here having a go at you.'

Roy touched his mother's sleeve.

'Are you sure you don't mind me...?'

'Of course I'm sure, son. Anyroad, I'm feeling much better now I got that off me chest. Well, don't stand there gawping like an Aunt Sally. Off you go.'

'Yeah, you take a stroll, lad,' Bernie growled, 'and see what they done round here. But watch where you're going, because you can easily get lost. Even I got lost on the Hereward Estate t'other day!'

Roy laughed, kissed his mother on the cheek and left the house.

Within minutes of leaving his mother's house, Bernie's prophecy came true when Roy discovered he was lost. The green spaces and leafy trees of his childhood had gone. In their place were rows of identical red-brick houses, all built in the last fifteen years.

Yes, he thought, as he increased his pace and headed for a bus stop. It's during the last fifteen years that the battles between the trades unions and the elected governments have been at their height. But why couldn't I explain to Bernie why he is wrong about the trades unions? Probably because it would take too long and it's too complicated.

As he reached the bus stop, a green single-decker lurched round the corner. Without thinking, he got on it in the hope it would take him away from the sprawling council estate into the countryside. He needed to breathe in the fresh scent of wind-blown grass, and touch the bark of ancient oak trees that had been there long before he was born and would still be there long after he was dead. His anticipation increased when the bus conductor told him they were going as far as Helpstone, a little village some six miles away where his mother was born. But that was not the reason he wanted to return there. The village called him for quite a different reason. Whenever he went there, it was a pilgrimage to the heart of his own private England. He hadn't visited Helpstone for over fifteen years, so he feared it might have changed. To try to dispel his growing anxiety, he returned to the problem of trades union power.

Oh, it's true that the trades unions have a genuine grievance because they are now being squeezed by the Tories, but in many ways the unions have asked for the trouble they've now got. As far back as the summer of 1968, it was pressure from the unions that made Harold Wilson capitulate over his 'In Place of Strife' proposals. And Wilson's proposals were modest, because they only aimed to bring the trades unions within the framework of law.

Roy shook his head.

But Wilson's defeat by the unions was only the beginning of the slippery slope. For it was the passing of Heath's Industrial Relations Act – which again only sought to bring the unions within the law – that brought the battle between government and unions to fever pitch. Again the unions won hands-down. The result was a revolutionary shift of power from Parliament in favour of the unions. Perhaps the seminal moment was the release from jail of the famous five East London dockers who had been sentenced under the Tories' Industrial Relations Act. But Heath only released them because the General Council of the TUC threatened to call a General Strike if he didn't.

Yes, Roy thought, as the bus moved out of the suburbs into the countryside. Yes, that was the fateful moment: when a Conservative government lost its nerve in the face of extra-parliamentary blackmail. And the dangerous power of the unions was further strengthened by the National Union of Mineworkers when they routed Heath's government with their strike. Until that moment, the unions had always been unsure of the full extent of their power. But, unfortunately, afterwards the unions began to believe themselves to be all-powerful. They no longer saw the necessity to keep their bargains with management. As a result, their power and influence over the governing of the country grew to unacceptable proportions. That's why it's only natural that a right-wing Tory government, elected to power by the populace, is now trying to claw back its parliamentary privileges. The tragedy is, there is so much unthinking hatred between the governing Tories and the trades union movement that they can scarcely talk to each other; so the unions are now unable to carry out their legitimate functions.

Yet the alternative is to have a Labour administration, in which the unions will again have too much power and will again act irresponsibly. For it's obvious that the unions are only paying lip service to the Shadow Cabinet about pay restraint. The moment we form a government, the unions will turn their backs on any form of incomes policy. Once again we'll have galloping inflation and a perpetual run on the pound.

The bus pulled up in Helpstone. As Roy stepped into the

lane, the fenland wind slapped his face, dragging his hair across his eyes.

I really must get it cut, he thought, hunching forward into the wind on the short walk to the centre of the village. He had only covered a hundred yards when the wind gave way to a fine drizzle. Soon it stopped and a patch of pure blue sky formed above the steeple of the little Parish Church of Saint Botolph. The church front was washed in misty sunshine. Open-mouthed, Roy paused to stare at the magnolia tree in the vicarage garden. Although the season of blossom was nearly over and the nearby willow no longer had its first pale yellow fronds, the trees conveyed to the ex-grammar-school pupil the springs of his lost youth. He always regarded Helpstone as a special shrine, for it was the birthplace and resting place of England's greatest nature poet, and England's only peasant poet, John Clare.

Roy touched the wet, grey stone of Clare's memorial.

People consider Wordsworth to be the greatest nature poet, he thought, but really he was a mystic pantheist who evoked nature to refresh his soul. Whereas *you*, John, had genuine clay on your hands, brambles under your feet, and you observed nature with a keen, cold eye. You loved nature for itself and not as an escape. You worked most of your life as a labourer in these fields, tilling the soil, gathering the crops in a good year, going hungry in a bad. You and your family often starved. Yet, because you had the true gift of poetry, you had your moments of glory when the lords and ladies of London came to see you in your peasant's cottage, with your peasant's gaiters on, smoking your peasant's pipe and staring at them all with your peasant's vacant stare. You were the heart of the English countryside. You had no pretensions – just genius. So, in the end, to the 'great world outside' you became a pastoral oddity: a fellow with rustic speech and worse manners, who, strangely, could create beautiful rhymes.

Yes, it's no wonder you went mad and ended your days in Northampton Asylum, when the great lords and ladies looked upon you as a diverting freak in a circus. God in heaven, I wonder what you would have made of England now?

Roy turned away from the memorial and gazed at the television aerials on the vicarage and on the thatched roofs of nearby sixteenth-century cottages. Four cars zoomed past, leaving behind them the whiff of petrol. Then an RAF fighter screeched across the heavens and was gone, and silence resumed its reign in the village.

Roy smiled and re-read the verse carved into the wet stone.

> 'O let one wish go where I shall be mine,
> To turn me back and wonder home to die,
> 'Mong nearest friends my latest breath resign
> And in the churchyard with my kindred lie.'

Well, that certainly isn't your greatest poem, my friend, and I wonder whether you would still want to 'wander home and die' here. But why not? Helpstone is fairly unspoilt as most villages go.

Would you have gone mad if you'd had the advantages of our welfare state? Probably not, but then you wouldn't have written the greatest sonnet on loneliness in the language.

As Roy headed slowly for the churchyard, falling mist began to shroud the sun. He smiled, because the ever-changing weather was also part of the deep Englishness of the place. He pushed the gate open and scrunched over the gravel towards Clare's grave at the back of St Botolph's Church. He was unaware he was murmuring Clare's sonnet to himself.

> 'I am – yet what I am, none cares or knows;
> My friends forsake me like a memory lost;
> I am the self-consumer of my woes –
> They rise and vanish in oblivion's host,
> Like shadows in love frenzied stifled throes
> And yet I am, and live – like vapours tost
> Into the nothingness of scorn and noise,
> Into the living sea of waking dreams,
> Where there is neither sense of life or joys,
> But the vast shipwreck of my life's esteems.'

Roy paused. The next couplet always disturbed him so much that he could scarcely voice it. He paused to look down on the poet's simple grave. Without checking to see if anyone was watching him, he half-knelt in the rain-laden grass and placed his hand on the bevelled gravestone. Then he whispered to the poet's ghost:

> 'Even the dearest that I love the best
> Are strange – nay, rather stranger than the rest.'

As he uttered the words, he felt tears pricking his eyes. He didn't know what he was weeping for. Was he weeping for the long-dead poet who had been the constant inspiration of his later years at grammar school? Was he crying for his mother, who in her own way was as lonely as Clare had ever been. Was he shedding tears to commemorate a lost, romantic England that had only ever existed in his imagination? Or perhaps he was just exhausted, and had lost control because he knew he was fast running out of time in life and politics? Or was it perhaps a combination of all these?

He no longer had the pride to care. It didn't matter, because at last he felt he was communicating in some small, desperate way with the very essence of England and with the spirit of his favourite poet. So with ridiculous tears coursing down his cheeks, the boy who had never truly grown up murmured the last verse of the poem to its creator's gravestone.

> 'I long for scenes where man hath never trod,
> A place where woman never smiled or wept;
> There to abide with my Creator God,
> And sleep as I in childhood sweetly slept,
> Untroubled and untroubling where I lie;
> The grass below, above, the vaulted sky.'

Then Roy registered the simple words engraved on the base of Clare's grave:

A POET IS BORN NOT MADE

For some reason this made him look up. He discovered the weather had taken yet another turn, this time for the better. Though the sun could not fully penetrate the ever-massing clouds, it was slowly fringing the clouds with fire. Roy felt that at any moment the mist and drizzle would be burnt away and the sky would appear a bright spring blue. Then the England of his childhood, and the childhood of his friends, one of whom was buried in this very graveyard, would again become the incandescent reality that it was in his soul.

Suddenly all the birds in the trees started singing as if it was the very first evening of the world. Although he knew that the blackbirds, the thrushes, the skylarks, the swallows and the swifts were only singing because they always sang at this time of day, he chose to believe they were also singing in that English country churchyard to give him the courage to go on, and to bless him with a melody he could return to, when the dark night of the soul is abroad.

Roy drew up outside the decaying Victorian house in which MacMaster had his basement bedsit. He checked his watch: it was three minutes to four.

Better not to be too early or look too eager, he thought, winding up his window and staring into the run-down street. He tried to conjure up a certain English churchyard with the birds in full chorus, but the darkness and poverty of his immediate surroundings dispelled the remembered magic of the previous Saturday afternoon.

As he got out of the car, three West Indian kids grinned at him. They dribbled a football between his legs, before skidding round the corner. Then a Sikh, with a gorgeous black-and-scarlet turban, cycled by in his postman's uniform, having finished his rounds for the day. But the Sikh wasn't smiling. He was gazing inwardly, so obsessed with his own world that he almost hit a mangy marmalade cat slinking across the road.

Christ, he's about as with-it as I am! Roy thought, pulling himself together and locking his car. But having locked it once, he wasn't satisfied and checked it again, for he knew this was a prime area for theft and vandalism. Then he wondered if he was overdressed for the occasion. Momentarily he considered wrenching off his tie and undoing his top shirt button to appear more casual, then decided against it.

MacMaster's bound to sneer at me however I'm dressed, he thought.

He tried to push open the front gate which lead down the crumbling steps to MacMaster's basement, then discovered the gate had no hinges but was supported by an overflowing dustbin. He lifted the gate up, leant it against another dustbin, and jogged down the steps to MacMaster's front door.

Before ringing the bell, he glanced through the eye-level railings into the street at the dusty pairs of feet striding past. Someone dropped a smouldering cigarette butt which bounced through a gap in the railings and almost hit him in the eye. He was about to protest when he saw the size of the smoker, a six-foot-seven black giant.

Well, as my churchyard is English, he thought, so is everything and everyone in this street. Even if they're not English now, by the next generation they will be, so they have the same rights as I do, including the right to discard their cigarette butts without looking.

Roy rang the bell. Thirty seconds passed and no one answered. Then he heard Angie giggle. He pressed the bell again and the door was opened immediately. Angie greeted him with her most voluptuous smile. Despite himself he couldn't help ogling her, for her sweater emphasised her breasts. With a great effort he managed to drag his gaze away from her perky nipples.

Angie's smile broadened. Then she slid her tongue over her lower lip. For a time it seemed that neither of them would say anything. In her own way Angie rather fancied Roy, and if Terry hadn't been at home she might well have let the MP possess her. As she leaned nonchalantly against the warped doorpost, she tried to imagine how Roy's teeth would feel on her nipples. For a moment she thought Roy was going to lean forward and grab her breasts, but instead he scratched his forehead and said: 'I believe Terry's expecting me – for tea?'

'Yeah, he is,' Angie replied, tugging her sweater down snuggly over her hips. ''Fraid we've got to go through the kitchen to get into the living room.'

Still smiling, Angie encouraged him to follow her into her dark kitchenette, which smelt of boiled beetroot.

'Bit dark for you in here, isn't it?'

'It's wot Terry calls our crap-hole.'

'Yes, I suppose it is a bit of a strain starting a revolution on Social Security.'

Angie didn't laugh as she crossed the damp linoleum to attend to the kettle on the stove.

'I know you thought your remark was funny, Mr Hampton, but Terry and me are proud to be starting a revolution on the dole. Well, as Terry always says: you got to use the bourgeois capitalist system and rip it off for all it's worth. D'you like milk in your tea, or d'you like it straight like we have it?'

'I'd like some milk, please.'

MacMaster made his presence felt by shouting from the other room.

'Well, don't stand on ceremony, Comrade Hampton. Come in and see how the Workers live.'

After some aimless small talk, Roy leaned forward in the dilapidated armchair and gave his tea a significant stir. He was distracted by the thought of Angie in the kitchen. She was probably listening at the keyhole. He glanced at the bed near the window, then at MacMaster, who was lying full-length on the sofa sipping his glass of iced water.

Terry grinned, for he sensed what Roy was thinking: about Angie, the bed and himself. As this was a meeting he had long anticipated, he did nothing to ease the growing tension between them. He intended to enjoy the MP's discomfort to the full.

Yes, Terry thought, everything is turning out exactly as Fat Phil of County Hall said it would. I'm in charge now because I've got the majority on the GMC. For, as Phil said, and as Lenin would have agreed: 'We must use every weapon in the socialist armoury to achieve our historical aims.'

Roy was about to come to the point of his visit, but again he hesitated. His adversary, lounging on the uncomfortable forties sofa and surrounded by portraits of his political mentors, was confident and at his most charming. On Terry's right was a large poster of Trotsky looking self-satisfied behind his goatee beard and his pince-nez, and to Trotsky's left, a smaller photograph of Mao Tse-tung who appeared to be beaming directly at Roy. Then there was Lenin on Mao's left – only he wasn't smiling. The camera had caught him with an angry arm raised above his head as he hectored the masses on the joys of the Bolshevik one-party state, or, as Robert Mugabe was to say some sixty years later, 'a one-party democracy'.

'Tea all right, is it, Roy?' smiled his host, now lounging directly under Mao and emulating the chairman's good humour.

'It's fine, thanks. Well, I suppose I might as well come straight to the point, Terry.'

'No rush, Roy.'

'Yes, but we're both busy men, so why don't we get down to cases?'

'Sure, if that's what you want.'

'The fact is, Terry ... I've decided to support you over the Red Cabin Theatre.'

'That's nice.'

'I've looked into their finances and they've done a lot of, well, very interesting work over the last couple of years. My wife thinks that they're worth supporting, and she should know, being a teacher. So tomorrow I intend to put pressure on some of my associates on the Council to see if I can persuade them to renew the Theatre's grant.'

Roy stirred his tea vigorously to ensure the sugar had melted, then added: 'Well, we can't let the Theatre go to the wall when the funding required to maintain its existence is really so little, can we?'

'My very sentiments.'

The MP put his cup down on a badly-scratched side-table, then changed his mind and picked it up again.

'But what I've really come to talk to you about today is the little impasse . . . that's developed between us.'

MacMaster straightened up on the sofa. His mouth was still smiling but his grey eyes were expressionless.

'I'm always willing to talk about the building of socialism, comrade.'

Roy gave a half-laugh, then took a quick sip of his tea which was still too hot. 'I thought you might be interested. What I'm trying to say, Terry, is I think I've come up with a possibility that might appeal to you. You know, that would enable us to get out of each other's hair – as it were.'

'Nothing I like more than possibilities, comrade.'

Roy snatched a breath and put his cup on the table. Then he pulled an unopened packet of cigarettes out of his trouser pocket. He was about to rip off the cellophane when MacMaster shook his head.

'I'd prefer you not to smoke in here if you don't mind, comrade. Angie and I still value our lungs.'

Roy coughed and hastily shoved the cigarettes back into his pocket.

'Of course. Point taken.'

'So what is this possibility, comrade?'

'It's something that might really interest you.'

'Good.'

'And it wouldn't put too great a strain on your moral principles.'

'Do tell.'

Again Roy picked up his cup and held it between the fingers of both hands to steady his nerves. As he gripped the cup, he could feel his palms itching with sweat. He knew he was about to betray himself. He was angry because he was acting foolishly. He should have discussed the MacMaster deal with his wife, or at least with David de Quincey, but he hadn't discussed it with anyone.

'As you probably know, Terry, there is another parliamentary constituency near here that's going to have a by-election in the next couple of months.'

'You mean Croydley?'

'Quite. And I know the powers-that-be there pretty well. Although I haven't as yet made any noises in that direction ... all things being equal, well, I'd be more than willing to use my influence to get *you* short-listed for the seat.'

Terry grinned, then sniffed.

'Mmm ... that definitely does have possibilities. If you were able to persuade the Croydley Labour Party to short-list me, comrade, what would you want in return?'

'I'd have thought that was obvious,' Roy said quietly, now perspiring under the armpits as well as in the palms of his hands.

'Sometimes I'm a fraction slow when it comes to grasping the "obvious", comrade. So perhaps you'll be good enough to spell it out for me?'

'Well, as you know, Terry, in the reselection procedure coming up in December, as the resident MP here in Lamberton North I will automatically be on the short-list.'

'Indeed you will, comrade.'

'Yes, but because of your power base on the GMC, Terry, if you wanted to, you could make sure that I was the *only one* on that short-list. Well, it's perfectly possible within the rules, isn't it?'

'Perfectly.'

Terry was now gazing at the ceiling. Roy was in such a state of perspiring suspense, he thrust his hands into his trouser pockets to conceal his anxiety. After an effective pause, the revolutionary stroked his knuckles along his cheekbone, then smiled.

'I see what you're getting at Roy. If I scratch your back, you'll scratch mine?'

'Exactly! Do you mind passing me the sugar?'

'My pleasure.'

Roy dug his spoon into the sugar bowl, then poured a heaped-up spoonful into his tea. He didn't want any sugar but he was desperate to involve himself in some physical activity while he waited for MacMaster's answer. As Terry was now stroking his other cheekbone, Roy decided he had no choice but to push on.

'Then . . . you will think about it, Terry?'

'Sure. I've only got one problem, comrade.'

'Which is?'

'If I were to back you come your reselection – in fact if I were to take your advice and ensure that there was only you on the short-list. . . .'

'Yes?'

'Well, if I were to do that, comrade, I'd want to be absolutely certain that I was backing a genuine, full-blooded socialist, wouldn't I?'

This was the moment Roy had been dreading. Was it worth half-lying to this Trot in order to keep his seat in Parliament? Or should he tell the unvarnished truth? Or perhaps he should tell the truth but wrap it up in a socialist dressing to appease his interrogator?

Yes, that's what I'll do, he thought. It's perfectly legitimate. Most of my political peers do it all the time. Anyway, I won't exactly be lying, I'll merely be telling selective bits of the truth. . . .

'You can see my point, can't you, comrade?' Terry went on cheerfully. 'I mean, I'd look stupid with my record if I backed someone who wasn't a genuine, full-blooded socialist.'

'Oh, but I *am* a genuine socialist – on many issues. For instance. . . .'

'Yes?'

'I'm passionately in favour of banning all arms trading to South Africa.'

Christ, how limp and pathetic can you get? Roy thought, hastily swallowing the remains of his over-sweet tea.

Terry thought it was pathetic too: 'Yeah, but even the Liberals, SDP and the Tory Wets'll go along with that. What's your view on Europe?'

'In principle I believe we should come out of the Common

Market, but not too precipitately. And naturally I endorse Labour's Alternative Economic Strategy on unemployment and the creation of new jobs.'

'Naturally. What about us having an independent nuclear deterrent?'

Roy spread his arms expansively and nodded.

'On the whole I think we should scrap it. So long as we can remain under the US nuclear umbrella, of course.'

'I see. So you haven't changed your mind on the US bases here in the UK, then?'

The younger man looked suitably concerned about the older man's mental state. Then he crossed his arms over his chest, put his head enquiringly on one side and waited.

'Look, don't get me wrong, Terry. I'd prefer that we didn't have Cruise here. Well, it would be much better if we could negotiate a deal with the Russians whereby all nuclear weapons became unnecessary. Then everybody would be happy. The trouble is that's never going to happen. And I feel if we don't participate in helping the Americans to defend Europe, eventually the Americans will get so sick of their so-called European allies never backing them up, that they might decide to go isolationist. Then, before we know where we are, we'll end up as a Soviet satellite. And I've no wish to live as they have to in Eastern Europe, thank you very much.'

'Nor have I, comrade.'

Roy looked quizzically at the East End revolutionary.

'What's more, that's been my position ever since I joined the Party, comrade,' Terry added. 'And by "the Party" I mean, of course, the Labour Party.'

'Yes, but I don't want us to end up with a regime like Castro's Cuba, either.'

'Naturally. Cuba's at a different stage of social development.'

Terry contemplated his glass of water.

'So, all in all, you're saying that we only disagree about US bases on UK soil, comrade?'

Roy guffawed.

'Wouldn't go that far. But the Labour Party is a broad church, so I don't see why we can't. . . .'

'Thank you, Harold Wilson! Now don't get me wrong, Roy. I'm not saying there aren't possibilities which could make us both happy. But before we go any further, there is one other thing.'

'Thought there might be.'

Terry rubbed his eyelids and stifled a yawn. With his eyes half-closed, he said in a matter-of-fact tone: 'I dunno whether you know it, comrade, but I'm at the forefront of a local campaign which advocates that all Labour MPs should contribute twenty per cent of their salaries to Party funds. How's that grab you?'

The casualness of Terry's question took Roy off his guard. The MP had been expecting his Trotskyite companion to come up with something tricky, but not that tricky.

Terry opened his eyes and smiled innocently.

'Have I said anything to disturb you, comrade?'

'No. It's just. . . .'

'Just?'

'Well. . . .'

'So the idea of donating twenty per cent of your salary to Party funds, comrade, brings on a touch of your habitual queasiness, does it?'

'No!'

'So what's your problem, comrade?'

Roy was now sweating all over and so nervous he didn't know whether to play with his teacup or the cigarettes in his pocket, or wring his hands like the 'wet' right winger, Rob Camber. In the end he did nothing but mutter: 'Well, I suppose if everything else works out, I could see my way to. . . .'

Instantly MacMaster was on his feet, extending his hand.

'Congratulations, Roy. That is indeed an impressive fiscal gesture. Allow me to shake you by the hand.'

Terry seized the MP's hand and pumped it vigorously. Roy felt embarrassed because his palm was dripping with sweat. Eventually he slid his hand free.

'So we've got a deal then, Terry?'

'No.'

'But I thought. . . .?'

Macmaster cut him short by abruptly crossing over to the dusty window to watch the passing feet tramping by. Bereft of words, Roy stared at his adversary's lithe back. Before he could muster his thoughts, Terry turned away from the window. He smiled. It wasn't a cruel smile, for there was a hint of compassion.

'I'm not turning you down, Roy, because I disbelieve all your socialist protestations. On the contrary, I'm sure you're a comrade of great moral fibre. Witness your bravery in the House last Tuesday. And although I thought you were misguided on that occasion, nevertheless, I greatly admired your guts.'

'Then why are you turning me down?'

Terry flexed his right hand. The dusty sunlight made his fingers glow. Roy thought he could see the blood pumping through Terry's veins. Then a bluebottle distracted him by buzzing against the windowpane.

'You still haven't told me why you are turning me down.'

'I'm turning you down, "Mr" Hampton, because I don't like Nobs' Row where you live!'

'What?'

'I don't like the way you speak. Or the way you dress.'

'Now look here, MacMaster. . . .!'

'No, *you* look here, Hampton!' Terry snarled. 'If you were honest, you'd admit that you don't like where I live, or the way I speak, or the way I dress, either.'

Roy opened his mouth to utter a curt rejoinder, but the younger man thundered on.

'See, however hard you try not to show it, Hampton, it's obvious you hate my guts. Not only that, but you feel you're slumming here. And so you sodding well are. But, unlike you, *I* don't need to eat humble pie to hold on to my job. I haven't got a sodding job to hold on to! And because I admired you for sticking up for your principles in the Commons last week, so now I despise you for crawling to me, simply to hold on to your lousy Parliamentary seat!'

So shattered was Roy by this onslaught of truth that he could do nothing but bite his lip and shake his head. MacMaster used the moment to narrow the physical distance between them. Then, with both fists clenched, he thrust his face into Roy's.

'Anyway, Hampton, how you can have the nerve to come slinking round here to try and make a "sordid deal" with "Trotskyite scum" like me? It's just mind-boggling! It's not unlike . . . a great king coming to the lowest beggar in his kingdom in the hope that the beggar will kindly help the king to keep his throne. Then, as soon as the king is once more secure on his throne, the first thing the king does is to sneer at the beggar for being so stupid as to help him keep his throne. Don't try and work it out, Hampton; we Marxists are over-fond of parables. The great Bertolt Brecht taught us a thing or two in that respect. I'd give you an apposite quote, if I could remember one, but unfortunately I'm not blessed with your memory.'

Then, mockingly, Terry touched his forelock and bowed to the MP.

'Well, good afternoon – Sire. When you think about it later, you'll see I'm right. Oh, and do see yourself out – Your Majesty.'

The girl was riding the man hard in the moonlight. Her breasts rose and fell as she drove her pelvis violently against his. She loved the feel of him inside her. The urgent rhythm of her body was now so intense that when the first orgasm overwhelmed her, she let out a cry. Her back arched, the neck of her womb opened and closed on his swollen penis. She shuddered as another orgasm possessed her. But still her lover refused to spurt his semen. In desperation she started to gyrate her hips, sucking him to his limit inside her, but still he held back. It was like making love to a warm-blooded statue.

A cry of frustration escaped her lips. She wanted to give herself up to a succession of orgasms, but because her lover was immune to her considerable charms, she was no longer enjoying the experience.

I'll fix him, she thought. There's one thing he can never resist.

Without warning she pulled herself off him and ran her tongue over his nipples and down his rib-cage until her mouth was entangled in his pubic hair. She moistened her lips and her experienced fingers wound themselves round his penis. As she licked the petal-soft crown, she glanced up at his face. The left side of his mouth was smiling, but not at her.

This made her so angry, she almost bit his cock. At the last moment she decided that biting it would have limited returns. Instead she squeezed it as hard as she could. Then she laughed when he let out a stifled yelp.

'Steady on, Angie, for Chrissake. It's the only one I've got!'

'Well, you don't deserve to have one at all, Terry. I mean, Jesus, it's worse'n trying to make love to Trotsky and Lenin rolled into one!'

Terry laughed, then gave his penis a shake as it started to go into decline.

'Sorry, love. I'm so keyed up, I'm not with-it.'

'You're not still thinking about how you screwed Hampton this afternoon, are you?'

'Course I am.'

'That's a bit shitty, ain't it?'

'Is it?'

'Yeah! Well, it don't do much for a girl's confidence, does it? I mean, you seem more interested in screwing him than in screwing me!'

'It was really beautiful, Angie. Led him right up the garden path, I did. Then I cut off his goolies.'

'I've a good mind to cut yours off for all the good they're doing. Well, look at it!'

She pointed a withering finger at his groin.

'Wot use is it shrivelled up like that? I always thought a true Englishman stood to attention in the presence of a lady.'

Terry laughed and sat up on the bed.

'You should've seen Hampton's face, Angie. Christ Almighty, he looked even more miserable than Keith Joseph at a press conference, and nobody looks that miserable.'

Angie pouted, then stretched, allowing her breasts to swell in the moonlight.

'Still say you were a bit cruel to the poor bloke, Terry.'

'Cruel to Hampton?'

'Yeah.'

'Crap! He'd've treated me the same way if he could've got away with it. Anyway, this is a fight to the death. And now he's running scared, I'm certainly not going to let up on him.'

'Well, you're certainly not getting it up!'

Terry swung his legs off the bed, then launched himself full-length on the tattered carpet where he proceeded to do ten rhythmic press-ups.

'Well, you're not getting it up, are you?' his mistress insisted, with her white arms folded over her breasts.

The revolutionary didn't pause with his press-ups but barked back: 'Look, I like sex as much as the next man, love. Why else d'you think I keep so trim, if not to pleasure you nightly? Trouble is, there's nothing sexier than politics.'

'Ooh, you....!'

Before Angie could finish her remonstration, Terry leapt to his feet, then dived on top of her. As she protested, struggling underneath him, she felt his penis harden.

'In fact, politics are so sexy, Angie,' Terry whispered, with a grin, 'that when you start to win like I am, it's like having an everlasting climax. Talking of which....'

He was about to straddle her to make his point, when she pushed him away from her and jumped off the bed. Then she flounced round, her curls tumbling on her shoulders and her upper lip stretched in an uncompromising line.

'Sometimes I wonder about you, Terry.'

'What d'you mean?'

His mistress put her hands on her hips, then changed her mind and crossed her arms over her nipples.

'Well, recently you ain't said anything about your ... well, about your....'

Her voice trailed away. As usual she was having difficulty expressing her zig-zagging thoughts. So Terry prompted her.

'I haven't said anything about my what, darling?'

'Well ... about the wonderful future we're supposed to be fighting for. Well, you ain't, have you? Sometimes I dunno whether you believe in the future any more, Terry.'

'Course I do, luv.'

Angie moved closer to him, but there was nothing sexual in her movements. Her wide blue eyes gazed at him, demanding reassurance.

'If you believe that there is going to be a wonderful socialist future, Terry, tell me about it. You used to tell me about it all the time when we first met four years ago. And I need you to tell me about it now.'

She slumped down on the bed beside him, her hand seeking his and her need for solace glistening in her eyes.

'You got to give me something to hold on to, Terry. So I can put up wiv having to live in this shit-hole day in, day out. Christ, when we first met you had a job. Oh, I know you hated working in the building trade, but at least in them days we could afford to go out to the odd restaurant or the movies.'

'Don't let's go into all that again, Angie. You know perfectly well why I gave up the job. It didn't leave me enough time to work for the Party.'

'All right, I'm not arguing about that, Terry. Wot I'm saying is, I can put up with all this squalor and crap, but only if I can be sure that in the future things are gonna be different.'

Terry stroked her hand, then looked into her troubled eyes. Suddenly he felt weary.

Perhaps we both need reassurance, he thought, in order to keep going. And, God help me, I really love this girl.

Then he cleared his throat and drew his forefingers down the bridge of her nose.

'We have to suffer now, Angie, so that the glorious socialist future can become a reality.'

'Yeah, but I still don't see why you have to be so horrible to people like Hampton.'

'Believe me, Angie, if there was another way to win through, I'd take it. But there isn't. See, we can't start proper stateplanning, and implement a siege economy here in the UK to solve all the unemployment, until all the reactionary dross like Roy Hampton and his right-wing clique are swept away.'

Terry's eyes shone in the moonlight.

'The point is, love, we real socialists are still only in the early stages of destroying the capitalist system. And until it is destroyed we can't even think of building our New Society. That's why, at the moment, I only seem to have destruction on the brain, because there's still so much that's rotten that has to be destroyed. Well, there's the private schools, the City, the big corporations, the multinationals, for a kick-off!'

The thought of so much destruction fired Terry's imagination. He snatched his hand away from Angie and started pacing the room. He was in such an elated frenzy he didn't notice his testicles swinging against his thighs or that he had his fists clenched.

'And the destruction of all those corrupt institutions is only the beginning of our revolutionary task. We've also got to slam a draconian wealth tax on the aristocracy, the company chairmen and the landed gentry. We've got to slam it on anybody who earns a penny over twenty grand. Then we've got to nationalise the banks and the building societies, plus everything the Tories have denationalised. Then we've got to close down the right-wing gutter press and implement state control of TV, radio and the rest of the media. And we've got to do all this before we can start building our Perfect State, in which everyone will be equal in every way: education, health, housing, jobs, living standards – you name it.'

The revolutionary allowed his ringing tones to die away, then placed his hand on his heart.

'And believe me, Angie, if I'm one of the ones who have to be sacrificed in order that the class struggle may be won by the oppressed workers, then that's hard luck on me. For I'm more than willing to take all that's coming to me so long as the working class win through in the end. Christ Almighty, the people of this country have been shat on long enough! So I'll suffer anything to make our vision of a bright future for them come true. Absolutely anything!'

By now Angie was on her feet, her blue eyes full of adoration for her revolutionary lover. Shaking her head to hold back her tears, she flung her arms round her hero's neck and murmured over and over: 'Oh, that was beautiful, Terry, just beautiful. . . .'

Then the two stood with their arms round each other in the moonlight.

In another bedroom, a man contemplated riding his woman in the moonlight, but his desire to make love faded with the thought. To revive his shrinking member, the man stroked the woman's tousled hair, then nuzzled his mouth onto hers. But as her tongue tried to joust with him, he knew it was hopeless. So he rolled off the woman's body and switched on the bedside lamp.

'Now what's the matter, Roy?'

'Nothing.'

'You're thinking of Helen again, aren't you?'

'Of course not.'

'You sure?'

'Absolutely.'

Grim-lipped, Roy turned to his wife: 'It's got nothing to do with her at all. It's that bastard!'

'MacMaster?'

'Yes. He made me pull down my trousers this afternoon, then laughed in my face and sent me packing!'

Liz chuckled and trailed her cool fingertips down the curvature of his spine.

'Well, now you've got your trousers down, darling, why don't we make full use of the situation?'

'It's not bloody funny, Liz!' Roy snapped as he flounced out of bed in search of his dressing gown. His wife groaned, then shaded her eyes against the light from the bedside lamp.

'You're not going for another nocturnal stroll, are you?'

Roy tightened the sash on his dressing gown, then prowled over to the window. He was so preoccupied by his thoughts that he didn't react when Liz switched off the lamp. For a long moment he stared vacantly into the moonlit street. There were still several people about. He shook his head and lit a cigarette.

'The whole country's going to be taken over by animals like MacMaster,' he muttered 'And the tragedy is, no one believes it. I know there are a hell of a lot of Tories who are prize pigs too, but at least most of them aren't dangerous. The majority of 'em are far too stereophonically stupid to be dangerous, whereas "comrades" like MacMaster, though they may be smug, are certainly not stupid. But what the hell can I do to stop them?'

Liz didn't reply because she was unsure what to say. As she didn't know how to express her thoughts coherently, she decided to approach his 'problem' at a tangent. She rolled onto her side, drew the sheet round her shoulders and addressed the back of his head.

'Did I tell you I was doing the Russian Revolution with my kids in class today, darling?'

Bemused, Roy peered over his shoulder: 'What, *all* of it?'

Liz giggled.

'No, a potted version, silly.'

'What has you teaching the Russian Revolution got to do with my war with MacMaster?'

'Well, it seems to me that you're getting more like Lenin every day.'

'Like who?'

Liz silenced him with an imperious finger.

'It's true, Roy. You only want to smash MacMaster because he's got your neck in a noose. That makes you like Lenin.'

'Makes me like Lenin!' Roy screeched. 'I must be going stark, staring mad!'

Liz shook her head.

'According to this text book I'm using, apparently Lenin only started denouncing Stalin – who in *your* case is MacMaster – for Stalin's various terror campaigns, *after* Lenin had had his stroke.'

'But I haven't had a stroke.'

'Politically you have. And when Lenin had his stroke, suddenly he found he was being manipulated and gagged by Stalin. It was only then that Lenin acknowledged that Stalin was a potential monster, which he himself had created. No, I insist on finishing, Roy. In that respect, you're the same as Lenin. For years you've seen what's happening to the Party, along with the rest of your right-wing friends, and for years you've all closed your eyes and put your heads in the sand because at the time you weren't personally threatened. But now you *are* threatened, you're becoming hysterical. You see monsters everywhere!'

'You call this giving me moral support, Liz?'

'No, but it's why I quite admire someone like MacMaster. At least he doesn't keep changing his mind about his political objectives. And he consistently goes on fighting for what he believes in.'

'Rubbish! For every ounce of genuine belief in MacMaster, there's a stone of pure envy.'

Roy turned back to the window.

'What's more, knowing that sod, he's probably plotting against me at this very moment. Mind, they say Stalin did most of his creative thinking when everyone else was asleep.'

'Come on, darling, you can't simply shrug MacMaster off by calling him Stalin. He's nowhere near that ruthless.'

Roy lit another cigarette.

'I agree he's not that ruthless – yet. But you give him one whiff of real power and he'll start belching fire.'

'If he does "start belching fire", Roy, it'll be procrastinators like you and your right-wing friends, plus the injustice in this country, that'll make him belch fire. Smoking like a chimney won't save anything.'

'Can't you stop criticizing me for once, woman? Haven't I got enough on my plate without. . . .'

Roy broke off, no longer able to contain his bitterness. Husband and wife, overwhelmed by tiredness, were so furious at the other's intransigence that a controlled debate was no longer possible.

Roy wrenched open the door.

'Where you going?'

'My stomach's killing me. I think I'm getting an ulcer.'

'By the time you've finished, the whole family will have one!'

Roy's only response was to snort. Then he turned his back on his wife and strode down the stairs. Liz was too tired and too cross to stop him. She pulled the sheet over her head and prayed for some sleep.

The following morning, Roy still had an upset stomach, which two glasses of Enos did little to alleviate. For the first time, he seriously wondered if he had an ulcer, but as Liz was markedly silent over breakfast, he realised he'd get little sympathy, so he said nothing.

Three-quarters of an hour later, he was in his office wearily dictating his third letter to his secretary. But he lacked his usual fluency, and continually had to rephrase expressions. Isla recrossed her legs, then cleared her throat and murmured: 'Perhaps we would make more progress, Mr Hampton, if I paid you a little visit later this afternoon?'

Roy smiled and muttered an apology. Isla smiled back, closed her notebook with its highly legible shorthand, and left the room.

After she had gone, Roy sat motionless, staring at the motes of dust which seemed to be forever climbing a shaft of sunlight above his desk. To his relief, the ache in his stomach was passing, but he sensed his present lethargy was only the prelude to a new storm.

He had a presentiment that something disturbing was about to happen. He wasn't certain whether it was going to happen to him personally, or to someone close to him. Was it about to happen to his mother? She was also prone to premonitions. Or was it preparing to strike at his wife? Or his children?

'Why the hell are you so glum, Roy?'

Roy turned his head slowly. Then he realised that David de Quincey had been sitting quietly, working at his desk for the last half-hour. As Roy gazed at David, he wished to God he could shake off the dread in his mind.

'Are you all right, Roy?'
'Yes.'
'Let me guess what's worrying you.'

Roy smiled but said nothing. David leaned forward, his elbows on his desk and his narrow chin cupped in his hands.

'My guess is that you tried to make a deal with your Trot. And to your horror the bastard has actually accepted your deal.'

Roy went on smiling, then scratched the mole behind his ear.

'I'm afraid the opposite is true, David. Oh yes, I tried to make a deal all right, but the sonovabitch turned me down. And though I hate to admit it, I rather respect him for it. You see, he knew I was betraying myself simply to save my political hide. Mind, my wondrously supportive wive feels much the same about my quest for political longevity.'

'Are you saying she actually supports MacMaster's position?'
'Oh, she doesn't support him all the way.'
'Nevertheless you do seem to have a bit of a leftie wife.'
'Yes, I do, don't I? Trouble is, she believes what she says.'

De Quincey stood up, then crossed to the window to stretch his legs.

'Roy, did you write to the National Executive about MacMaster like I suggested?'
'Certainly.'
'You didn't show me the letter.'
'No, I'm sorry, but I did send it. Believe it or not, I got a reply this morning.'

Roy shuffled through the papers on his desk until he found the letter. De Quincey was unable to conceal his astonishment.

'Don't tell me the NEC are going to instigate an enquiry?'
'They didn't go that far. Though they hinted they might get round to thinking about thinking about it.'

De Quincey's cynical laugh was cut off by Roy's phone ringing. He let it ring four times before he answered it, for he had a renewed presentiment there would be anguish on the end of the line.

'Hello, Roy Hampton here? What was that? I'm sorry, I can't hear you.'

This was hardly surprising, for the caller was standing in an open phone booth at Waterloo Station.

'Roy, it's me, Harold Bunting. I want to meet you on the embankment outside the National Theatre.'

Roy scratched his head. He had been greeted with strange requests in his time, but the idea of meeting the councillor outside the National Theatre struck him as exceptionally bizarre.

'Surely it would be more pleasant to have a drink in the Commons, Harold?'

'Not saying it wouldn't, lad, but for my purposes outside the National's better. I got to talk to you urgently. And some fresh air might put it into some kind of perspective.'

Roy was now certain there was something wrong. He sensed his presentiment was about to come true.

Perhaps I've inherited some of my mother's Fenland witchery?

'OK, Harold, I'll get there as quickly as I can. Shouldn't be more than a quarter of an hour.'

As Roy hung up, de Quincey raised an enquiring eyebrow.

'Something wrong, Roy?'

'If the griping in my gut is anything to go by, yes.'

Roy hurried out of the office, but immediately whirled back.

'Will you tell Isla that if anyone wants me, I shouldn't be more than an hour? I'll definitely be back for my lunch appointment.'

Harold sat on a bench overlooking the Thames. His breathing was ragged. He felt as if the muscles of his heart were being squeezed in a vice. Protectively he clasped his hands over his swollen stomach. Then, wheezing with the effort, he glanced at the burnished watch which he kept on a fob chain in his worn, shiny-black waistcoat.

A river police launch droned by on the sunlit water. Though it was a sparkling spring day in the middle of May and tourists were buzzing round him, the councillor was too obsessed with his guilty thoughts to notice. The moment was approaching when he would have to confront his young friend with the truth. He was laboriously filling his pipe with tobacco when Roy's shadow intruded between him and the sun.

'Why did you want to meet down here, Harold?'

The councillor grunted. Then, without looking, he jabbed a calloused thumb behind him. Roy turned to see what he was pointing at. There, blocking out the skyline, was the concrete bunker known as the National Theatre. The councillor grinned.

'Well, you must admit, Roy, it is the ugliest building for miles, so it suits my present mood perfectly.'

Roy laughed as he watched theatre enthusiasts come and go through the glass swing doors. Then he turned back to his friend.

'Meeting like this makes me feel we're about to enact a scene from John Le Carré.'

'You're nearer to the mark than you think, lad.'

Roy chuckled, then joined the old man on the bench.

'Well, you'll be the first Labour councillor that's gone in for treason, Harold.'

'Oh, I dunno. I once visited Cambridge, so anything's possible.'

Roy chuckled again. Then Harold levered himself to his feet and waddled off under Waterloo Bridge. Roy caught him up. As they moved under the shadow of the bridge, the younger man was disturbed to notice the older man's dangerously florid complexion.

'Don't you think you ought to sit down, Harold? You don't look your best at all.'

'I'm all right, lad.'

'You sure? You look like a boiled beetroot!'

'Hardly surprising. Well, they are bound to arrest us any day now, aren't they?'

'Arrest us?' Roy said, laughing and involuntarily grasping his friend's elbow. The councillor didn't laugh back. As Roy peered at him closely, he experienced a sudden dryness in the mouth.

'Harold, you're not seriously saying . . . ?'

'They won't arrest you, lad. It's me and Taplow they're after.'

Roy, astonished at the casual way his friend had made this revelation, could only gasp: 'What the hell are they going to arrest you for?'

'Bribery. Fraud. Embezzlement. You name it.'

'Jesus Christ! Look . . . let's sit down and talk this through quietly.'

'If you don't mind, lad, I prefer to keep walking.'

'Listen, Harold,' Roy said, his fingers tugging at his friend's sleeve. 'When you say that you and Taplow are involved in bribery and fraud, how in God's name. . . ?'

Harold cut him short.

'Taplow and me were the chairman and the vice-chairman

of the Town Planning Committee, and we were given some presents from developers in return for planning permission. And I'm afraid, among other things, we were also fiddling the Party Tote.'

'Oh my God!'

'Couldn't have phrased it better myself.'

The councillor paused to get his breath, because the pain around his heart was spreading across his chest. He couldn't bear to look Roy in the eye, so he shambled on.

'Don't worry, lad. We're about to be shoved off the gravy train. See, for the whole of this last week the police have been investigating us. It's all been very discreet, but it won't be long before their accountants've been through the books. Then they'll put two and two together, and I'll be lucky to get away with four years inside.'

The old man paused to lean heavily on the embankment wall. The sun was hot and he was perspiring. Roy stood a yard away from the councillor.

'Harold, what made you accept all those presents and fiddle the Tote?'

The councillor glanced up as a seagull swooped between the two men. Together they watched the white wings glide down and settle on the brown water below them.

'Well, Harold?'

'To begin with it was an act of necessity, lad.'

'Necessity?'

'Yeah. Remember when they put that pacemaker in me ticker couple of years back, then they did that job on the varicose in me legs?'

'Of course I remember.'

'What you probably don't remember was my impatience.'

The old man continued to peer at the swirling river. Sodden driftwood hurried by on the incoming tide.

'Y'see, lad, I just got so sick of being on that NHS waiting list month after month that I decided to have both me operations done private. Trouble was, I was broke at the time. And as I didn't belong to BUPA, the operations cost a bleeding fortune. So I started ripping off Party funds to pay the hospital bills.'

Harold chuckled drily.

'Then I was so shaken by what I'd done, I decided to have

a holiday. So I ripped off some more and went to Trinidad for six weeks!'

'Yes, I remember wondering at the time how you could afford six weeks in the Caribbean.'

'Why the blazes shouldn't I have six weeks of bleeding sunshine for once in my rotten life?! I've worked for our lousy Party for nearly fifty-five years. Since I were a lad on the docks. What have I got out of it, eh?'

The pain in Harold's chest was excruciating, but he snatched another wheezing breath and went on.

'I tell you what I've got out of it, lad. For a kick-off, I've got a son who can't bear the sight of me, and a wife who hardly ever sees me because I'm always "too busy" out on Party business. And, of course, I got this clapped-out old ticker that makes my life an absolute bloody misery! You see, the pacemaker in here ....' Angrily the councillor jabbed a dirty thumbnail against his breastbone. '... Although it keeps me going, it's only by a whisker. Wouldn't be surprised if I had a stroke any day now.'

Harold waved a dismissive hand under Roy's nose.

'Don't look at me in that . . . compassionately condescending way, Roy. You know very well when we first met, I used to be like you. Twenty years ago I, too, used to have dreams of helping my class to get out of the shit. I were so bloody starry-eyed in them days, I refused to believe that a lot of "comrades" in this great Party of ours were really just using the Party as a stinking gravy train.'

The councillor's voice was hoarse and his body was awash with sweat.

'Then, about the time I needed my operations, I started to realise that all my ideals were slowly being . . . well, eroded away. That's what comes of devoting your life to local politics, ain't it? That's why, I suppose, I woke up one fine morning, and for the first time in my rotten life I knew myself for what I was.'

Roy stared intently at the councillor.

'You don't have to say anything, lad. I'm well aware that other people have known only too well what I am for years. What's more, I bet they've been whispering it behind my back. And they're right: I am just a loud-mouthed old-fashioned Party hack!'

The councillor prodded his stubby forefinger fiercely into Roy's rib-cage.

'Fact I'm just like *you*, Roy!'

Then he lurched round and shook his fist at the black spires of the Mother of Parliaments on the north side of the Thames.

'But then we're not alone, are we, lad? That dump upriver is filled to bursting with time-serving rip-off artists like us.'

Furiously Roy held up both hands to ward off the councillor's accusations.

'Now, Harold, that's quite enough of this nonsense. Just because you're a self-confessed embezzler and you've got yourself involved in bribery, fraud and God knows what else, it doesn't mean you've any right to call me a loud-mouthed Party hack. There are many things I may be, but I'm not a hack!'

Harold wheezed, then tugged a handkerchief out of his trouser pocket to wipe his burning, damp face.

'You can glower as much as you like, Harold, but I'm still not a hack.'

'Aren't you?'

'I'm sorry, but I've got better things to do than burn myself to a crisp on the embankment listening to your rotten confession.'

Roy snatched a packet of Rothmans out of his pocket.

'Jesus, to think I went out of my way and used my influence to make you the chairman of the Town Planning Committee! I only did that because I thought you were a good, reliable, honest man. Yet now you not only turn out to be a thief but you also have the gall to insult me.'

Laughing in disbelief, Roy broke off to light his cigarette.

'Your behaviour's unbelievable, Harold, it's just unbelievable!'

'Glad you find it funny, lad.'

'I don't! If the whole thing wasn't so blatantly crazy, I'd probably scream.'

Roy took a fierce drag on his cigarette. Then, laughing bitterly, he turned towards the Royal Festival Hall, which was now directly behind them.

'The more I think about it, the crazier it gets. It was only a week ago I wrote to the NEC to ask them to investigate MacMaster and his Trots. Now it seems I should've asked them to investigate you and Taplow!'

Harold nodded his head contritely in agreement.

'Of course you're absolutely right, Roy. But at least *I* know what's happened to me – which is more'n you do, friend.'

'I never put my hand in the till, Harold.'

'Been taken out to a lot of "business" lunches in your time though, ain't you? And in return for them lunches, you've given some very helpful, off-the-record, "professional" advice, ain't you? And you've never said "no" to the odd "thank you" case of claret that's been delivered by post after, have you?'

'I only ever had one case, Harold, five Christmasses ago. And it was Burgundy. I felt pretty guilty about it, too.'

'Still drank it though, didn't you? Hey, where are you going?'

'Back to the Commons.'

'Afraid some of my dirt'll rub off on you, are you?'

Roy turned back and stared steadily at his wheezing friend.

'There's no way you can associate me with your lousy crime, Harold.'

Harold chortled, but his heavy eyes were dimmed with sadness.

'Don't worry, lad, even if there was a way to incriminate you, I never would.'

Then the old man tottered forward and grasped Roy's sleeve.

'Why the hell d'you think I brought you out here, lad?'

'God knows.'

'I brought you out here because I wanted to tell you the horrible truth about me face to face. Didn't want you to read about it in the local rag, then wonder why your old friend hadn't told you the truth before.'

Harold tightened his grip on Roy's sleeve and thrust his desperate face into Roy's. The younger man recoiled from the old man's sour breath, but the councillor wouldn't let him go.

'I'm finished, boy. I can't take any more. So now it's up to you to blow these hard-left thugs out of the water before they sink you good 'n' proper. Yes, I know – who needs advice from an old crook like me? Well, I may be corrupt, greedy and past it, but some of the Stalinist scum we're up against are just plain bloody evil.'

Abruptly Harold let go of Roy's sleeve. Then he swayed in the hot sunshine before staggering against the embankment wall.

'But you ain't got the guts to fight 'em to the death, have

you, lad? You're like the rest of the right wing. Full of sound and fury, signifying sod all!'

The councillor steadied himself and held out an imploring hand.

'No, don't turn away from me, Roy. I know you're a good bloke. Your problem is you're weak. Like the rest of us. And with the rough stuff that's now smashing its way out of the woodwork, it's the "good" an' the "weak" that'll be the first to go to the wall.'

Without warning, the old man clutched his chest as a searing pain knifed through the valves of his heart.

'Oh, my fucking Christ!'

Roy was so taken aback by the sudden contortions convulsing his friend's face that he simply gaped as the councillor buckled to his knees, then keeled over against the embankment wall. But when he saw that the concrete was speckled with Harold's blood, he leaped forward and propped the councillor's lolling head against his knee. Harold's cheek was bleeding profusely. Clumsily Roy staunched the wound with a handkerchief. Then he realised Harold was trying to tell him something. At first he couldn't make out what it was because the old man's blueish lips refused to respond to his demands.

'What are you trying to say, Harold?'

With a great effort of will, the councillor forced his lips to whisper: 'Can't breathe. Call a bloody ambulance, for Godsake!'

Desperately Roy craned his neck round to catch the attention of a passer-by, but no one seemed to notice that a man was down on his knees, cradling another man who was bleeding onto the flagstones. So Roy shouted at a girl who was passing them and averting her eyes.

'Call an ambulance! There's a man here having a heart attack!'

The girl stopped, then ran towards him.

'Where's the nearest phone?'

'The Festival Hall. And hurry, for Christ's sake!'

Nine-and-a-half minutes later an ambulance wailed towards St Thomas' Hospital Casualty Department. The councillor lay corpse-like inside, his greyish-blue face covered by an oxygen mask. Opposite him an ambulance attendant was monitoring the old man's intake. As the ambulance approached the hospital, the attendant turned to the anxious MP who was sitting beside him.

'You don't mean he's going to die?'

'Well. . . .'

'He can't die! He's one of my oldest friends. He can't die!'

As the attendant averted his eyes, Roy realised how unthinkingly inhuman he had been to Harold on the embankment.

How could I possibly have said those hurtful things to him? Christ Almighty, but for Harold I wouldn't be an MP today. Without his unstinting support all these years, God knows what would have happened to me. I know I helped to make him the chairman of the Town Planning Committee, but how could I possibly call him a crook and a liar . . .?

Roy covered his face with his hands. Then he peered through his fingers at the old man on the stretcher. Hesitantly, he reached out and touched his friend's inert chest. Then the ambulance rocked to a standstill. The attendant leaped to his feet, pushed open the doors and jumped out into the courtyard. Dazed, Roy climbed out after him.

Outside, Roy struggled to find the appropriate words to express his guilt. Before he could speak, the attendant trundled the stretcher past him into the casualty department. Distraught, Roy leaned against the ambulance. In an effort to stop his tears, he glanced across the river to the Palace of Westminster, brooding against the clear sky. The dark, fretted spires beckoned to him ironically. Then Big Ben struck twelve times. As the resonance died away, Roy trudged into the hospital.

I hope to Christ that wasn't poor Harold's death-knell, he thought, as he numbly followed the stretcher through the echoing vestibule.

But Roy knew his friend was dying.

What's worse, you may die without me having a chance to tell you how deeply sorry I am for what I said. Because you're right, Harold. In my own way I've been a fraudulant hack, too. Only I haven't been as honest as you. But from now on, I promise I will be both honest and resolute.

Roy was drinking his second cup of tea when the young Indian doctor came over and told him that the worst had happened.

The old man had died as the attendants were lifting him out of the ambulance.

Yes, Roy thought, shivering and weeping, you died as Big Ben struck twelve. Though I'm sure you didn't hear it. Any more than you heard my internal confession of guilt.

His mind was now drifting in a timeless zone. So much so that he couldn't remember asking the doctor whether he might pay his friend a last visit. The doctor advised against it because of the old man's livid face, but Roy insisted.

Seconds later, he was standing alone with Harold's corpse, surrounded by screens. As always with hospitals, the lighting was harsh and cold. Tentatively, Roy touched the claw-like hand of his dead friend. He could not help noticing the dirt in the fingernails and the frayed shirt cuff. Then, stiffening his resolve, he focused on Harold's face, propped up on the pillow.

Where's the dignity, he thought, where's the rotten dignity in this?

As the tears dripped off his chin, he shook his head.

Forgive me, old friend, for being so selfish as to hurt you at the last. Though probably you'd be the first to agree that under the circumstances, death was the best solution. If you had lived, they would have hounded you into the grave.

As Roy stared at him, he began to laugh. Then his laughter grew.

Jesus Christ, he thought, now laughing and crying simultaneously. I'm sure if you could see yourself, Harold, you'd laugh too. To live the whole of your life sporting the Labour Party's red rosette in your buttonhole, and then to die having turned bright blue! It's so ludicrously ironic that it's enough to make the dead sit up and howl with laughter.

Still chuckling, Roy scraped his knuckles across his eyes to wipe the tears away. He didn't realise the Indian doctor was standing beside him and asking him if everything was all right. Being the true Englishman he was, Roy replied: 'Yes, everything's all right, thank you, Doctor.' But inside himself, he knew that nothing was right.

From that moment, the rest of the afternoon blurred past him. He could barely recall waiting for Olive, Harold's wife, who was on her way to the hospital. He didn't remember staying on while she paid her last respects to her husband's contorted body. As he drove her home in his car and listened to her sobbing beside him, the self-induced trance remained with him. For he was aware that though he was making sympathetic noises of condolence, nothing could console her.

What's going to happen to Olive? he thought. If she doesn't know about his embezzlement now, she will very soon. How will she live with that? God Almighty, the things politics drive us to do. Again, Harold's right; my dithering and my abrupt changes of mind and purpose are equivalent to putting my hand in the till. Yes, his words on the Embankment were a dying man's challenge to the living, like John of Gaunt warning Richard II:

> 'Methinks I am a prophet new inspired
> And thus expiring do fortell...
> This land of such dear souls, this dear, dear land,
> Dear for her reputation through the world,
> Is now leased out, I die pronouncing it,
> Like to a tenement or pelting farm;
> England, bound in with the triumphant sea,
> Whose rocky shore beats back the envious siege
> Of watery Neptune, is now bound in with shame,
> With inky blots and rotten parchment bonds;
> That England, that was wont to conquer others,
> Hath made a shameful conquest of itself.'

As Roy escorted the desolate widow into the arms of her son, Gaunt's words continued to haunt him. In his own insignificant way, he felt a cheapened Richard II himself.

Well, it's true. For years I've watched the hard left taking over the Party and for years I've done nothing but pretend it wasn't happening. Oh, stop it, Hampton. There must be a limit to masochism – even for an Englishman.

On returning home, Roy was greeted with the hissing of steam and the clattering of copper-based pans. Liz was boiling spaghetti, bought that afternoon from Antonio's on the High Street, and also brewing an enormous panful of chile for the deepfreeze. She had started cooking in a cheerful frame of mind, but since hearing Roy's news her culinary enthusiasm had diminished.

In silence Roy watched her adjust the flame on their Cannon

gas cooker. Then, as he poured himself another glass of Scotch, Sebastian came into the kitchen. His son's untidy mop of hair covered his eyes, but his face seemed longer and sadder than usual. Simultaneously his parents registered how physically uncoordinated their son was. When he leaned against the kitchen table he seemed like an ungainly stork. Most of the time his parents didn't notice his lack of physical grace because he exuded such genuine warmth and was always so considerate of others. Despite this social handicap, Sebastian was a fine athlete. Generally he won the annual school cross-country run and he was an exceptional hurdler. But as he came into the kitchen, he had other things than running on his mind.

'Lexi's just told me about Councillor Bunting, Dad. It's terrible!'

'Yes, I can't get it out of my head,' assented his father, swirling the whisky round in his glass.

'I'm glad I wasn't there to see him.'

'It was so bloody undignified. Whatever else you say about Harold, he was a stickler for old-fashioned English dignity. Not just his own, either, but everyone's.'

Liz wrinkled her nose over the simmering pan of spaghetti sauce. 'Well, now the poor man's dead, darling, they won't be able to bring all that embezzlement stuff out in the press. At least Olive will be saved the scandal.'

'Rubbish!'

Startled, Liz turned away from her cooking.

'What do you mean, "rubbish"?'

'Just because Harold's dead, it doesn't mean it's the end of it. Quite the contrary.'

'But surely. . . .?'

'You're forgetting that Taplow's still alive. The police are bound to charge him. And that's not the worst of it.'

Roy drained his glass and barged past his son, who was leaning on the table. As he tugged an ice-tray out of the deep-freeze, Liz went back to stirring the sauce.

'How can Harold's death not be the worst of it, dear?'

'Now that Harold's not around to defend himself, MacMaster will use the ensuing scandal to really stir things up.'

'You can't blame him for that. After all, it is only a smaller version of all that early-seventies corruption in the north-east.'

'You don't have to tell me!' Her husband clonked three ice-cubes into his empty tumbler. 'As things stand at present, I daren't even prod the National Executive Council to investigate MacMaster and his crew. There's nothing the hard left'd love more than to humiliate me now that Harold and Taplow have been shown up as rotten apples. You don't have to look at me like that, son!'

'Didn't realise I was, Dad. Sorry.'

'I know what you're both thinking. How can I possibly rant on about MacMaster when one of my oldest political chums has snuffed it? What you're forgetting is that I've had the poor sod's death on my mind for most of the day now. Oh, I know he helped me to become an MP, but equally I helped him to an important chairmanship on the Council. And now, unfortunately, as a result of him putting his hand into the till, it's *me* who's got to pick up all the pieces.'

Roy wrenched the cap off the whisky and slurped a triple measure into his glass. The ice-cubes cracked as the alcohol splashed over them.

Sebastian glanced at his mother, who nodded and said: 'Do you think all that Scotch will help matters, dear?'

'Christ knows!'

Roy tipped a third of the whisky down his throat.

'What are you going to do, Dad?'

'About what?'

'About MacMaster and everything?'

'I'll have to wait for his next move, I suppose.'

Liz tapped her son on the shoulder.

'Open the back door, there's a love.'

'Why?'

'To let out some of this steam, silly. Then make yourself useful and lay the table.'

Sebastian groaned but opened the back door.

'D'you want some of this spaghetti, Roy?'

'No, thanks.'

'You're not going to drink all night, are you?'

'Maybe.'

Armed with knives and forks, Sebastian hustled round the table. He was deliberately noisy in setting out the cutlery, hoping it would distract his parents and stop them rowing. He could see they were spoiling for a fight and that if his father drank too much the sparks would really fly, because nothing made his mother more furious than Roy being drunk.

Surprisingly, it was Liz who defused the growing tension.

'When you've finished laying the table, Sebastian, perhaps you'll be good enough to ask Lexi if she wants any dinner?'

Sebastian cleared his throat hesitantly.

'What's the matter, dear?' his mother enquired, straining the steaming spaghetti into a plastic colander.

'I'm afraid Lexi's like Dad, Mum.'

'In what way?'

'She won't want any spaghetti, either. She's just started another of her crazy bread-and-banana diets.'

His mother flared back at him. 'D'you mean I've cooked all this bloody pasta and nobody wants any?'

'Don't worry, Mum, I'll have three helpings.'

Liz laughed, then drained the pasta over the sink. Eagerly Sebastian sat at the table, but he looked concerned when he saw his father contemplating pouring himself a fourth Scotch.

'Dad, you say you've got to wait for MacMaster to make the next move. Why can't you beat him to the post and make your move first?'

Roy screwed up his eyes, then, sighing, pushed the bottle of Teachers away from him.

'The truth is, son, I don't know what move to make. At the moment MacMaster's taken the initiative away from me. I'm sure your mother's told you what happened to me yesterday. I've never been so humiliated in my life.'

'Dad, please don't upset yourself. . . .'

Sebastian leaned across the table and seized his father's hand. Roy, embarrassed by his son's loving impulse, instinctively wanted to withdraw his hand, but Sebastian tightened his grip. Still at the sink, Liz saw what was happening and turned away smiling.

The last thing they need now, she thought, is to have me throwing my arms round them both and flooding them with silly tears. Yet they do look so sweet. I'm sure if only Roy'd let himself be loved more openly by the kids, and more often, he'd find they'd give him such support. Unfortunately he's like his mother: uptight and too English.

When she turned back to them, father and son were no

longer holding hands but grinning sheepishly at each other. Then Roy banged the table.

'Where's the bloody grub, then, woman?'

'I thought. . . ?'

'It's not just women who change their minds, you know.' Roy winked at Sebastian, then drummed the table with his knife and fork. 'Is it, son?'

'Dead right, it's not, Dad!' Sebastian laughed as he imitated his father's drumming with the cutlery. Liz joined in their laughter and began heaping their plates.

'Damn! I should've warmed these plates up,' she cried.

'As long as the grub's good – and it always is, dear – we don't care whether you serve the stuff on a pack of ice or on the tablecloth. Do we, son?'

Still laughing, Sebastian nodded enthusiastically. He didn't even mind his father calling him 'son' every other sentence, for he knew this was his father's way of showing how much he loved him. Then to both mother and son's amazement, Roy cheerfully returned to the ominous subject of MacMaster.

'You know you asked me just now, son, what was going to happen between MacMaster and me?'

'Yes. . .'

'It's suddenly occurred to me what might happen.'

Liz paused with the pan of tomato sauce.

'Yes, dear?'

'As a result of poor Harold's death, there's bound to be a Council by-election in his ward before long. And once Taplow's been arrested – which will probably be any day now – there'll be immediate pressure on Taplow to resign from the Council. So within a couple of weeks at the most, there'll be a great deal of in-fighting to decide who is going to stand at the by-election as the candidates for Harold and Taplow's seats on the Council. Well, don't just hover there, dear, with that delicious-smelling sauce. Let's be having some of it.'

Taken off-guard by Roy's sudden reference to the food, Liz almost jumped. Smiling, Sebastian stood up, relieved her of the pan and dolloped the sauce over everyone's spaghetti.

'So there'll be in-fighting to decide who's going to be the candidates for the councillors' seats, Dad. But how does MacMaster fit into all this?'

'Who would make better councillors than "Maestro" MacMaster himself and one of his hand-picked cronies?'

'Yes, but why would MacMaster want to do that?' interrupted Liz as she sat down at the head of the table. 'I thought he hated places like Parliament, County Hall and. . . .'

'He hates Parliament all right. At least, at the moment, he says he does. But I think he's got a sneaking desire to end up in County Hall. That's where his favourite pin-up boy works.'

'Ken Livingtstone?'

'Absolutely. You see, I believe our Terry has modelled himself on "conquering" Ken. So he may well try to get himself selected to run for office locally, as his first step up the greasy pole.'

'Yes, but what's the point of him following in Ken's footsteps when Mrs Thatcher is going to abolish County Hall?'

'People like Ken and MacMaster don't worry about minor political hiccups like that. Ken only uses County Hall as his base for publicity purposes. Once County Hall's gone, he will either manoeuvre his way into Parliament or start extra-parliamentary ructions out on the streets. MacMaster's the same. He may well decide to stand for the local Council simply to make himself look politically "respectable". And also to rub my nose in the dirt.'

'Mum, this spaghetti sauce's fantastic!'

'Thank you. If MacMaster does get himself selected, dear, what will you do then?'

Her husband twirled a wodge of pasta round his fork and brandished it like a bloodstained club.

'Ah, then it will be War in Heaven – which only one of us will survive.'

'And in the meantime?'

Roy considered a moment, then mumbled, with his mouth full of spaghetti: 'I might even take to prayer.'

'It's not that bad, Dad, surely?' his son interjected, then waved at his mother. 'Can I have a bit more parmesan?'

As Liz slid the cheese towards Sebastian, she had a sudden comic vision of Roy on his knees praying. Then she glanced up at her husband's worried profile and realised he wasn't joking.

The sun beat down on the plain wooden coffin and the vicar droned on: 'Man that is born of woman hath but a short time to live, and is full of misery.'

You can say that again, Roy thought, as he clutched his mother's black-gloved hand more tightly. She responded by pressuring his knuckles with her rheumatic thumb.

'He cometh up and is cut down, like a flower; he fleeth as it were a shadow, and never continueth in one stay.'

Roy glanced to his left at his mother's shrunken frame, clad from head to toe in stifling black. Through her veil, her red-rimmed eyes stared dully at the raw earth which had been shovelled out of the grave. Then she peered into the grave itself in which lay the box containing her sister. She scarcely noticed one of her sister's neighbours picking up a handful of soil. It was only as the neighbour cast the earth onto the coffin lid that Mrs Hampton realised she must do the same. Suddenly she realised she hadn't the strength to stoop and thrust her hand into the soil. Her eyes and mind were swimming as the sun grew even hotter. God was hammering her into the grave with the terrific heat of His noonday fire.

As she swayed against him, Roy felt she was about to faint. Swiftly he encircled her bony waist with his arm while his free hand supported her elbow.

'It won't be long now, darling, ' he whispered as the vicar intoned: 'Earth to earth, ashes to ashes, dust to dust; in sure and certain hope of the Resurrection to eternal life, through our Lord Jesus Christ, who shall change our vile body, that it may be like unto His glorious body, according to the mighty working, whereby He is able to subdue all things to Himself.'

Roy heard his mother mutter something. Then as he bent closer to her lips, he understood she was reassuring him: 'S'all right, son. I'm not going to faint.'

How strange it is, he thought. My aunt being buried in sanctified ground and probably going to heaven, all because she was adjudged by the coroner to 'have taken her life while being of unsound mind'. On that basis we can all be saved, thank God. Recently I feel my mind has been 'unsound' a damn sight more times than it has been 'sound'. So if, one midnight when I'm in that parlous condition, I should impulsively add twenty or thirty sleeping pills to my daily consumption of whisky . . . with a little luck, if this vicar knows what he's rambling about,

I shall shoot straight up to heaven to collect my angel's wings before you can say 'Jack Robinson'. Or do I mean 'Jesus Christ'?

Roy shook his head, then gathered some earth for his mother so she could pay her final respects to her sister. As the soil made a crumpling sound on the coffin lid, two jackdaws in a blossoming hawthorn bush croaked their approval. Despite himself Roy smiled.

It was a quarter past five that evening when Roy made his way to a telephone booth on Kings Cross Station. As he dialled, he tried to forget the last impression he had of his mother sitting stiffly on an upright chair in her cool kitchen. When he kissed her goodbye, she clung to him a moment, then gently pushed him away.

Why did she push me away?

He was jerked back into the present by the mellifluous voice on the other end of the phone.

'Yes?'

'It's me – Roy.'

'Who?'

'Roy Hampton.'

'Ah.'

'I need to see you, Helen.'

'I was wondering when you'd ring.'

Roy waited, then brushed away the beads of perspiration forming along his hairline. The weather was freakishly hot for the middle of May and the telephone booth was stifling.

'Why don't you come straight over to my flat, darling? I'm more than happy to give up researching Harold Wilson's "middle" period for the evening.'

'Can't we meet somewhere in the open? I need some air.'

'Well, to my knowledge there aren't any bluebell woods around here, darling.'

'Helen! You promised you wouldn't. . . .'

He heard her inviting chuckle at the other end of the line.

'Helen, please!'

'I'm sorry, darling, but you're so deliciously teasable.' Then her tone became more off-hand. 'Where would you like to meet?'

'Kensington Gardens are only five minutes away from you. Why don't we meet there?'

'Yes, but surely you don't. . . .'

'I'll meet you by the bandstand. You never know, they might even be playing.'

'God forbid!'

When he arrived at the bandstand, Roy discovered to his great amusement that they were playing. But as he had never been partial to military marches, and the bandsmen looked hot and sweaty in their uniforms, so the moment he spotted Helen he guided her away from the glittering brass and rhythmic noise.

Besides, he thought, it was bandsmen like these who were blown to bits by the IRA. What with my aunt's funeral, and next week having to go to Harold's, the thought of death chokes me so much that all I want to do now is run back to life.

'It's good of you to meet me here, Helen, after . . . well, after what happened at Ufferton.'

'Which presumably you don't want to happen again?' Helen said, smiling wryly. 'Otherwise you would have agreed to come to my house, wouldn't you?'

'You're right,' Roy nodded. 'I shouldn't have asked you to come here. I promised Liz I'd never, well, never. . . .'

Helen's eyes widened, waiting. Roy felt his face prickle with guilt. He knew he was acting foolishly, but he also knew Helen loved him enough to indulge him, and at the moment he craved to be indulged. Or at least listened to.

If only she didn't have such eyes, he thought, and if only I didn't always act on impulse. I should never have rung her up.

'Helen, I wouldn't blame you if you turned your back on me and left me to stew in my own juice.'

'You know I'd never do that,' she said. 'Anyway, who'd want an overdone MP?'

Still smiling, she placed her fingertips lightly on his shoulder. For a worrying moment he thought she was going to kiss him. Seeing the anxious bewilderment in his eyes, she withdrew her hand.

'You were a marvellous lover that night, darling,' she murmured. 'But you already know that, don't you?'

'Helen, please, don't let's torment ourselves. I'm not saying

I don't want to make love to you now. I do! But for the sake of Liz, who I love very much, and my children, and, above all, my own sanity, I beg you not to dwell on the past. For it *is* the past. At least, for me it is. I can never return to it. Most of the time I daren't even think about it, let alone . . . Jesus Christ, what the hell am I doing here?'

'Yes, what *are* you doing here, darling?'

His only response was to move away from her and trudge through the grass towards the Round Pond. She caught him up. She wanted to touch him again, but when she realised he was trembling she controlled her impulse.

'Well,' she said, 'if you don't want my body, I can only assume you're lusting after my mind.'

Roy didn't reply. He watched his feet swishing through scores of beheaded daisies. Then he told her of his funereal day in his home town. Before she could return to the subject of their aborted affair, he went on, as if in explanation, to recount his recent political activities.

'So you've come to me for political advice, Roy, and nothing more?'

Ashamed, he walked on.

Well, she thought, if advice is all I can give him, I suppose it's better than nothing.

She admitted that she'd heard the recorded extracts of his outburst in the Commons on 'Yesterday in Parliament', but made it clear she wasn't over-impressed by his delivery or even by the intellectual content of his attack. Yet she implied she was more sympathetic about his 'on the belly' performance with MacMaster earlier that week.

They were now standing by the Round Pond in Kensington Gardens. It reminded them of their sunlit Saturday by the lake at Ufferton, with the four black swans and a skylark singing above them. At Ufferton they were alone, whereas here by the pond they were surrounded by people of all ages and nationalities. On the scummy water there were some ducks, one white swan and numerous sweet-papers, matchsticks, cigarette butts, a Coca-Cola can, plus page three of the *Sun*.

Disgusted, Roy and Helen watched a miniature, remote-controlled motorboat, manipulated by a bearded enthusiast, as it zoomed across the pond and scared three ducks into flight. The swan paddled to one side to let the boat pass. The boat's only accomplishment was to sink page three of the *Sun*. As the photographed nipples slid into the depths, Roy glanced at Helen. They were both thinking the same thing: this was also part of the England they loved. Yet they wished they could protect the pond and the wildlife from the mindless carelessness and casual violence which always seemed to intrude on London's beautiful parks.

For several moments they observed the bustling crowd encompassing the pond. Then they exchanged ironic smiles, for most of the crowd were tourists speaking in every language but English. The few that were speaking English had American, Canadian or Australian accents. Then Roy turned away from the pond and wrenched off his black tie.

'I know what you're thinking, Roy, and believe me, there's only one thing you can do now. At least, politically there's only one thing you can do.'

'What's that?'

'Join the SDP while there's still time.'

'Impossible! We'll never defeat the hard left except from *within* the Labour Party.'

'Tosh!'

'Anyway, the SDP isn't a serious party, Helen. Before the decade is over, it'll be relegated to MacMaster's dustbin of history.'

'Well, if you're not going to join the SDP, darling,' Helen murmured, 'and I'm sure you're not going to join the Liberals, what *are* you going to do?'

'Now Harold Bunting's seat on the Council has fallen vacant, I'm waiting for MacMaster to make his next move. If he decides to stand for the Council in Harold's place, I'm going to blast the smug bastard out of the water!'

'How?'

Roy leaned forward and whispered something in her ear. Irritably she closed her mouth and raised her eyebrow.

'You're going to do what?'

Roy smiled, then whispered again. Momentarily Helen was so taken aback that she didn't respond. Then she shook her head and smoothed a crease in her dress.

'If you do that, Roy, they'll crucify you.'

'Probably.'

'What's the purpose of it, then?'

'If I keep my nerve and go through with it, Helen, I'll be the first Labour MP with the guts to be nailed up in public for what he believes. And who knows? In the process I might even succeed in warning the Great British Public of the danger they're in.'

'Have you told your wife you're planning this?'

'No. I wasn't sure whether I had the stamina to go through with it until this afternoon.'

'Why, did something earth-shattering happen to you this afternoon?'

'My mother hugged me, then ... gently pushed me away from her.'

'So?'

'So – I believe that in her own strange way she was telling me something. Of course, I may be wrong. But when she pushed me away, I think she was telling me it's time I stopped clinging to her. And to my wife and children. And also to you. Instead I must now stand at my full height – and fight to the end.'

For the first time, Roy looked Helen full in the face. She gazed back at him with her luminous light-green eyes. Normally he would have turned away because her intensity quelled his spirit. This evening, however, was different. Roy suddenly felt stronger than the bright, sensual creature opposite him. This time he was determined to withstand the political tempest that, like Prospero, he was about to raise.

'Well, my dear,' Helen said, turning away, 'if you think that is your way to salvation, then that's the thorny path you must take. I still believe in the end you'll join us in the SDP. You see, no one can bear to be politically alone for very long. Even Churchill, in his "wilderness years", was often so overwhelmed by despair that he didn't know what to do with himself. And his crusade against the Nazis was relatively simple for the populace to understand. At least Churchill was pointing at an external enemy. Whereas you are about to go crazy about the enemy *within*. And although *we* know that MacMaster and Co. are spiritually communists ... because none of them are actually card-carrying members of the British Communist Party, you're going to find it almost impossible to convince the moderate-minded mass of the British people that MacMaster and Co. *are* communists.'

'What you say is true, Helen, but I can still do more to expose them from within the Party than from outside. Although I wouldn't dream of comparing myself to Solzhenitsyn, I'm sure you'll agree that he was a far greater threat to the Soviet hierarchy while he remained a Soviet citizen than he is now, when he's forced to live in exile in the United States. So even if I wanted to join the SDP – which I don't, because as a party it's still far too middle-class – now is not the right time. This is the time to save the Labour Party from itself, because it is still the only genuine party of the people. And if I have to fight alone, I'll fight alone.'

He broke off as he remembered the final stanza of his favourite Browning poem:

> 'There they stood, ranged along the hillsides, met
> To view the last of me, a living frame
> For one more picture!'

To his delight Helen continued with: ' "In a sheet of flame I saw them and I knew them all".'

Then, together, the two ex-lovers proclaimed the final line to three Kensington sparrows twittering above their heads:

> 'And yet
> Dauntless the slug-horn to my lips I set,
> And blew; "Childe Roland to the Dark Tower came."'

JUNE

Inside the low-ceilinged Labour Party hut, with its corrugated roof and damp, green walls, seventeen Labour supporters sat on the obligatory hard, folding chairs. The Eden Ward Labour Party meeting had been in progress now for seventy-three minutes. The chairman, Charlie Northover, sat behind the table coughing into his handkerchief. The Ward Secretary, Josephine Risworth, doodled on a piece of blotting paper.

Northover peered into the smoke-filled room as another coughing fit possessed him, then he recovered and addressed the Ward Secretary.

'Ask Comrades MacMaster and Keithley to come back in, will you, Josephine?'

'Certainly, Comrade Chairman.'

The secretary went out through a side door. She had only been gone a moment when Northover was again seized by his barking cough.

'If only I could shake this godawful stuff of my chest!'

'Have you tried Zubes, comrade?' volunteered a woman in a plaid headscarf from the front row.

Before the chairman could reply, Josephine returned with 'Comrades MacMaster and Keithley'.

'Take a seat, comrades,' the chairman muttered between coughs.

Terry glanced at Joan, who was looking disconcertingly attractive in a beige jump suit. Her hair was carefully dishevelled. As she crossed her long legs, Terry decided the time was fast approaching when he'd have to do something 'positive' about her. He was disturbed in his libidinous reverie by the chairman rubbing his hands together.

'Well, we're very pleased to announce that you, Comrade MacMaster, and you, Comrade Keithley, have both been selected to be the Labour Party candidates for Eden Ward in the forthcoming Council by-election.'

This was greeted by hearty if sporadic applause from the body of the hall. Terry turned to Joan, winked with his upstage eye, then got to his feet to address his clapping supporters.

'Comrade Chairman, comrades all. On behalf of the working class, I want to thank the Party for putting its trust in Comrade Keithley and myself – because it is the working class that we represent, unlike some MPs and local councillors I could name!'

There was another sustained burst of applause.

'And believe me, comrades, if we are elected on June 22nd, we promise we will continue the great struggle for the implementation of *real* socialism here in Lamberton North, because real socialism is the only hope left for this country. Everything else, from Keynesianism, Liberalism, Labourism, Fascist monetarism and every other "ism", have all been tried – and they've all failed! So now this poor country of ours is so bereft and helpless, it's literally crying out for socialism. Socialism is the only way there can be a decisive shift in the balance of power towards the working people and their sorely oppressed families.'

Terry waved an ominous finger.

'We cannot countenance any more corruption and thieving, as was recently perpetrated by Messrs Bunting and Taplow. I call 'em "Messrs", comrades, because they are traitors to their class, and have spent a lifetime trying to witch-hunt all the real progressive socialists in our great Party. No wonder they call themselves "unreconstructed Gaitskellites"! If we find any more around, we'll "unreconstruct" them, won't we, comrades?'

More laughter and cheers from the hall. Although Terry's throat was now extremely dry because of the layers of sluggish cigarette smoke, he felt like Moses bringing the Tablets of the Law down from Sinai.

'I'm glad you all agree with me, comrades; because we can't afford to tolerate any more McCarthy witch-hunts of our left-wing comrades. I'm with Tony Benn on this! As I'm with him on many things. Tony's correct when he says that the Labour Party must be open to all ideas, including those of the great Karl Marx himself, who, as you know, was the true progenitor of the class war!'

Terry's sea-grey eyes had now darkened to stormy pinpricks.

'Because one thing is certain, comrades: there has to be a

class war. For until that war is won, the rank and file will never inherit the earth!'

Then, as suddenly, Terry smiled, and the cultivated rasp in his voice gave way to a husky softness.

'So all I'm saying, comrades, is you can rely on me, if I'm elected, to be a full-time councillor for this ward. Because my one desire is to be at the service of our supporters and at the forefront of socialism, fighting to uphold the rights and dignity of the working class. Thank you, comrades.'

Still smiling radiantly, Terry sat down next to Joan. The chairman cleared his throat and smiled back.

'Couldn't put it better meself, comrade. And now, perhaps Comrade Keithley would like to say a few words. . . .'

The following lunchtime, the Members' Dining Room in the House of Commons was only three-quarters full. Roy and David paused in the doorway. To their right were various Labour MPs with their jackets off and their shirt sleeves rolled ostentatiously above their burly elbows. To their left, Tory MPs sported immaculate ties and perfectly cut suits, and did their best to appear cool in the sweltering heat. In the no-man's-land in the centre of the dining room were stray Liberals and the occasional beleaguered Social Democrat.

As a waiter escorted David and Roy to their table under the portrait of Disraeli, they could not help being amused by the antics of their peers. It seemed to them droll that Labour and Tory MPs never dreamed of sitting together. Both sides of the political divide even went so far as to pretend that such personages as David Owen, David Steel and Cyril Smith, who were sitting in the middle of the room, didn't exist at all.

Roy pulled back his heavy chair, covered in green leather with the Royal Palace of Westminster's crest on its back. As he sat down, he stroked the dark wooden panelling on the wall, then sheepishly smiled up at Disraeli's amused portrait directly above him. He turned and looked across the room to where Eric Heffer and Ian Mikardo were finishing their lunch. Heffer was wearing a pale-grey suit and a casually knotted, blood-red tie, while Mikardo, in shirtsleeves, was lighting a huge cigar.

'Doesn't Mikardo remind you of a Soviet Party boss?' David whispered to Roy.

'Absolutely! That's why he's such a fantastic operator in the House,' Roy rejoined. 'Yes, if ever a man could be a covert Stalinist, it's probably Mikardo. Not of course that anyone would believe it. As far as the general public is concerned, Mikardo's gruff, hoarse whisper and those honest-looking bloodhound eyes ensure that he comes over as a genuine man of the people.'

David leaned forward.

'Don't look now, Roy, but I think Heffer's looking at us, and if looks were laser beams. . . .'

Roy smiled, then studied the menu.

'D'you think people like Heffer, Benn and Michael Meacher realise they're riding the tiger?'

'What d'you mean, Roy?'

'Well, they think they're in control of the hard left, but "comrades" like Mikardo, Scargill and McGahey will tear them to pieces if ever they get into power. You see, in their own fanatical way, Heffer, Wedgie and Meacher are still vaguely parliamentarians. Though they're often espousing "Trottish" causes, they're not really full-blown Trots. I'm not saying they wouldn't like to be. They just don't have the guts.'

'I still don't see what you're driving at.'

'My point's simple: if the hard left, i.e. the Mikardos of this world ever get real power, the first people they'll purge are pseudo-Trots like Benn and Heffer. Though Benn and Heffer aren't smart enough to realise this. I don't suppose they've studied Robert Conquest's *The Great Terror*. If they had, they'd realise the Stalinists hate the Trots more than they hate the capitalists. So if the latter-day Stalinists ever get the chance, they'll follow the example of their great mentor, Uncle Joe, and purge every Trot, Militant and Workers' Revolutionary Party member they can get their claws on.'

David was so taken aback by Roy's analysis that he ordered two carafes of white Burgundy. Roy chuckled as he informed David that MacMaster had been selected as the Labour Party candidate for the forthcoming Council by-election. Still grinning, he then told David what he was proposing to do about it. David was so appalled by Roy's proposal he asked him to repeat it. Which Roy did. They both looked up as Mikardo and Heffer left the dining room.

'But that's madness, Roy, absolute madness!'

'What have I got to lose?'

'Your seat, for a start!'

'Way things are at the moment, I'll probably lose my seat anyway.'

'Yes, but they can take your membership of the Party away from you. D'you want to be thrown out of the Party?'

'Not particularly.'

'Look, this isn't funny, Roy!'

'Never said it was. How's your pork?'

'Tough! But you're having me on, aren't you? You're not really going to make that announcement.'

' 'Fraid so. Already set the wheels in motion.'

David waved a fork at their elegant surroundings.

'You'll miss all this, y'know.'

Amused, Roy toyed with his glass of wine, then decided against drinking any.

'In some ways, perhaps. But I'm beginning to believe that MacMaster's right. This whole edifice is a facade. Well, what relevance does it have to modern Britain? Who needs the ritual and filibustering?'

'Oh, in some respects the Mother of Parliaments is a bit old-fashioned, but. . . .'

'Yes, it's an old-fashioned drain-cover that's barely holding back the stench of what's about to crawl out of the drain. I hope I'm not putting you off your crackling.'

David laughed, but inside he wished that Roy wasn't so loud and demonstrative. Especially as the Right Honourable Peter Shore was passing their table. Momentarily Shore glanced at them, then brushed his curtain of hair away from his nose and left the dining room. As Shore passed their table, Roy inclined an eyebrow in his direction.

'Mind, I do have time for him. At least he was consistent on the need for a rigorous defence policy, which is more than you can say for the rest of them. In my opinion Shore's the best of the bunch. Shame he did so badly in the election for the leadership.'

Impatiently David waved the decanter.

'For Christ sake, have some more wine. You're going to need it or you'll blow a fuse.'

'No more wine for me.'

'What's the matter? You feeling ill or something?'

'No, but from now on I'd like to make my decisions without the aid of alcohol. Or nicotine.'

'What's the point of kidding yourself, Roy? Your so-called plan of attack against MacMaster will only turn out to be another inconsequential gesture.'

Roy was about to shrug but thought better of it. Instead he allowed himself a wistful smile as he pulled a letter out of his pocket.

'This is the press release I intend to give the Street of Shame after lunch.'

'D'you want me to read it?'

'Why not? Everyone else will before the day's out.'

David took the press release and pressed its edge against his cheek, unsure whether he wanted to read it.

'Go on, risk it, David. It won't bite.'

David laughed, then read the press release.

'Certainly unequivocal.'

'Isn't it?'

'See you on the bonfire, then.'

Roy looked puzzled.

'What bonfire?'

'Oh, didn't you know? That's how they deal with heretics. And right-wing witches.'

'Then you'd better watch the "London Programme" tonight, hadn't you?'

'Why?'

'That's when I go up in flames.'

In the bathroom, the man and the woman were both naked. The man was lying in the bath, which brimmed over with richly scented bubbles; the woman was staring in the mirror and wondering whether she should pluck her eyebrows.

'I'm sorry, darling, but I still don't understand how you could agree to go on the "London Programme" tonight. Especially after your inflammatory statement to the press.'

Roy chuckled and scooped a handful of bubbles off his forearm.

'Don't suppose I could persuade you to give my back a scrub?'

'No!'

Still chuckling, Roy flicked some foam onto his wife's bare

shoulders. She whirled round and was about to clonk him with her hairbrush when he blew her a kiss.

'Please give my back a scrub, darling,' he pouted, luxuriantly sploshing his feet in the soapy water.

'Oh, all right.'

Pretending to be cross, Liz roughly applied the sponge to the back of his shoulders.

'You really are the most infuriating man.'

'Ouch!'

'You still haven't told me why you wanted them to print it?'

'Because I know the electorate agree with me.'

Liz snorted, gave his back a final fierce rub, then threw the sopping sponge at him. Roy ducked, laughing.

'If nothing else, darling, that rub-down was certainly abrasive.'

Scraping the remaining bubbles off his chest and groin, he stood up in the bath.

'Can you pass me that towel?'

Without looking, Liz tossed a candy-striped bath towel at him, then returned to her struggle with her eyebrows.

'I still say you could have discussed the whole thing with me before going berserk in the press! Why didn't you discuss it with me, anyway?'

'I'm not up to another row.'

Liz turned to face him as he finished towelling himself.

'You used to talk everything over with me.'

'Yes, but in the last few months you have sided more and more with the left against me, haven't you?'

'I've only done that because in the last few months you've moved farther and farther to the right!'

Roy was now standing on the bath mat and frantically searching in the wall cabinet.

'Jesus, there's no talc left!'

'Don't blame me; blame that "cosmetic expert", your daughter.'

Roy ignored her jibe and peered through the rivulets of condensation running down the mirror at the puffy bags under his eyes. Despite the bath, he still felt tired and nervous. Then Liz's image materialised in the mirror beside him. Gently she placed her cool fingertips on his bare shoulder.

'What's happening to us, darling?' she whispered.

225

'I'm afraid politics have worn us down, love, and we're fast running out of resilience.'

Her mouth smiled but her eyes were sad.

'That bath hasn't done much for your colouring. You still look grey round the gills.'

'I've got what is known in Politburo circles as the "Kremlin Complexion".'

Impatiently Liz draped a towel round her waist and flounced through the open doorway into their bedroom. She was about to slam the door in irritation when she called out over her shoulder.

'Why the devil do you keep making allusions to Russia all the time? We're in Britain, for Godsake!'

'Are we?'

'Oh, do stop being an old wanker, Roy.'

'You may think this is Britain, but it's not the Britain I grew up in.'

'For pity's sake, don't start all that Golden Age grammar school twaddle again!'

Before he could reply, she slammed the door. Roy refused to be beaten. Forgetting he was naked, he charged down the corridor after her. He didn't notice Alexa giggling at him on her way downstairs. Once inside the bedroom, he put his hands on his hips and bellowed at his wife.

'I'm not talking Golden Age grammar school twaddle! This isn't the Britain I grew up in! There used to be a genuine sense of hope in this country in the fifties and early sixties. Oh, I know the oil crisis, loss of Empire and failure of the welfare state all helped to undermine the national morale. But in those days I was proud I was British. Not in any jingoistic sense, either. I didn't need a ridiculous Falklands War to rally my spirits.'

Liz ignored him and continued to put on her bra and pants. She had heard it so many times before. Roy snatched his shirt off the bedspread.

'Yes, I know you've heard it all before, but there's still so much of England that's extremely beautiful. Oh, I know it's absurd, but sometimes just thinking about our cathedrals, our country pubs and churches, well, it makes me want to cry. In fact, in Helpstone I did cry – over John Clare's grave. You should've heard those birds singing. Incredible. Oh, sod it!'

'Now what's the matter?'

'Button's come off my cuff. I don't suppose you'd...?'

'You can sew it on yourself! There's a needle and cotton in the Wedgwood pot.'

Grimacing, Roy took the sewing equipment out. After three attempts at licking the strands of cotton together, he threaded it through the eye of the needle while Liz vigorously brushed her hair in the mirror.

As he sewed, he said: 'You think I'm a sentimental old fart, don't you? Well, whether you do or not, I believe that Clare's churchyard and everything it represents is worth fighting for. Trouble is, however hard I fight, I know it's probably a losing rearguard action. A vain attempt to hold back the Visigoths – if only for a few more years.'

Liz threw her brush down on the ornate porcelain tray.

'Look, why don't you stop bellyaching, Roy, and piss off to the States? They love your sort of sentimental patriotism there!'

'What's the point of me going to the States? No one could be more English than I am. Besides, what would the Yanks make of an unreconstructed Gaitskellite with a penchant for cricket?'

Liz was not amused. She scowled at him in the mirror.

'I still say if you repeat all that stuff on TV tonight you'll be ostracised by the Party, and before the week's out you'll wish to God that you could go to the States!'

Deftly Roy flicked his black-and-red striped tie into a Windsor knot. Then he caught the hostile look in his wife's eyes.

'Are you implying *you're* going to ostracise me as well, Liz?'

'I'm not implying anything. I just don't know how much of this hatred and bitterness I can take.'

Liz's reply was muffled, since she was slipping a sleeveless dress over her head. Roy offered to help her but she shrugged him away.

'Listen, darling, if the worst comes to the worst, I can always leave politics.'

'To do what?'

Roy dabbed some Aramis aftershave on his chin.

'Yesterday I was offered a job. Over lunch at the Reform.'

With a final yank, Liz pulled up the zip on the back of her dress.

'Who offered you the job?'

'A fellow called Winner. Friend of Freddy and Nancy's.'

'What kind of job is it?'

'It's in an international consultancy firm.'

Liz looked hurt.

'What's the matter, darling?' Roy asked, checking his tie in the mirror.

'Why didn't you tell me about this job before?'

'Didn't think it was important.'

'You didn't think. . . .' She cut herself short. 'How much is Winner offering you?'

'Eighteen grand. With an increase every six months.'

'Are you going to take it?'

'Depends.'

'On what?'

'On what happens in the next few months.'

For the first time she caught his eye in the mirror.

'Surely you'd hate being a consultant?'

'Mm. That's why I didn't mention it.'

Roy crossed to the open door. He was leaving the bedroom when he glimpsed Liz waving at him in the mirror.

'Don't forget to take your key with you. I may not be up when you get back.'

'Aren't you going to watch me on telly, then?'

'Sure. What else can I do but watch you? You never ask my advice – and you rarely tell me anything until you've made your decision.'

Roy made a placating gesture.

'Don't let's row now, darling. We'll discuss the job and its implications later, all right?'

'Anything you say – sahib.'

The walls of the Hampton living room were painted in what was known as 'apricot white' while the doors, window frames and skirting boards were stripped pine. A comfortable chocolate-coloured sofa, with white cushions, was being occupied by Alexa, who was lying full length on it in her rumpled school uniform. As she painted the talons on her left hand with a second coat of purple nail varnish, she grunted and thrust her feet in the air to dry her purple toenails. Opposite her was a twenty-four-inch colour television on which a popular American cops and robbers series was in full swing. Although the San Francisco car chase was hair-raising, mercifully everything was happening in technicoloured silence, for the sound was switched off. That, at least, was how Liz felt as she brooded on her favourite rocking chair and thumbed through the TV Times.

'Mum?' sulked Alexa, brandishing her nail varnish brush. 'Can't we at least have the sound up till 'e's on?'

'No, you watch far too much TV as it is.'

'Then why have we got to watch *'im* then?'

'Your father is not " 'im" he's "him"!'

'Well, in the mood "he" went out in, "he's" bound to make a fool of 'imself.'

'Can't you try to be a little understanding for once, Lexi? Your father is under a lot of pressure at the moment. From all quarters.'

Sebastian, who had been sitting quietly at the Georgian desk by the window, looked up from his calculus homework.

'If he is under such pressure, Mum, why do you keep bitching him?'

Alexa fanned her damp fingernails in front of her face.

'Yeah, Basty's got a good point, Mum. Why *do* you keep bitching Dad?'

'Because I believe what he's doing is wrong. Both for himself and . . . for the family.'

Liz jabbed her finger at the television screen.

'That's him! Turn the sound up.'

'Do we have to?'

Sebastian swivelled his chair round as a close-up of his father dominated the screen.

'Yes, why don't you shut up, Lexi, and play with your nail varnish?'

'Wot d'you fink I'm doing, crud face?'

Dismissively, her brother strode across the room and turned the sound up.

'That loud enough, Mum?'

'Yes. Now both of you, shush! – please.'

At that moment Nancy Harper, the popular West Indian interviewer for the 'London Programme', appeared on the left of the screen. Her glamorous dusky face beamed at the hypnotised viewers.

'So in the "London Programme" tonight, we conclude with an interview with Mr Roy Hampton, the Labour MP for Lamberton North.'

There was a two-shot of Nancy and Roy. Liz couldn't help noticing that her husband's hands were twitching as Nancy gestured at him.

'Mr Hampton – as you probably heard in the News – has just announced to the electors of Eden Ward in Lamberton North that under no circumstances should they vote for Mr Terry MacMaster and Miss Joan Keithley in the forthcoming Council by-election. Mr Hampton has taken this precipitate step despite the fact that both Mr MacMaster and Miss Keithley have been selected as the new Labour Party candidates by the local Labour Party.'

Nancy turned back to Roy with her most alluring smile.

'Those I think are the facts, are they not, Mr Hampton?'

'Yes, but before we go any further, Nancy, I feel I must make it clear that I have not advised the electors in my constituency to vote for any *other* candidate.'

Nancy continued smiling.

'What you say of course is true, Mr Hampton, but I'm sure you will be the first to admit that if the Labour voters act on your advice and stay at home, it will be the Tories and the SDP/Liberal Alliance that will benefit from their absence.'

Liz could bear the tension no longer and shouted at the screen.

'Of course they'll bloody benefit!'

She was so cross with Roy that she scarcely registered his reply.

'Yes, I suppose they will benefit, Nancy, but I cannot be held responsible for that.'

'Then who is bloody responsible?' Liz snarled at the screen. 'King Kong?'

Nancy had stopped smiling and briefly glanced down at her notes. Then in her most mellifluous tone she murmured: 'Well, leaving that aside for the moment, Mr Hampton, nevertheless doesn't your advice to your constituents go against the basic rules of the Labour Party?'

Before Roy could answer, she held up a small yellow booklet, entitled *The Labour Party; Party Constitution and Standing Orders*. Deftly turning to page three, she read aloud: ' "Conditions of

Membership, clause III, section 3; Each Individual Member must; (a) Accept and conform to the Constitution, Programme, Principles and Policy of the Party".'

She placed the yellow booklet on the table in front of her, then with a sympathetic smile continued: 'I believe I'm right in saying that that particular section of clause 3 of the Party Rules means that every member of the Labour Party must support all duly nominated Labour candidates, whether at parliamentary or local level, once they have been officially endorsed by the Party Membership. Therefore under no circumstances can a member of the Party, like yourself, Mr Hampton, ask the electorate to vote against a duly nominated candidate.'

'Yes, that's right, Nancy – technically.'

'Only "technically", Mr Hampton?'

Liz was now on her feet, waving her fist at the televised image of her seven-inch husband.

'Roy, for Godsake, stop playing stupid games!'

'Mum!'

'Your father's trying to be a smart-ass, Sebastian, but he's only succeeding in being stupid!'

Sebastian shook his head and refocused on his father, who was now explaining what he meant by 'technically'.

'The point I'm trying to make, Nancy', insisted the MP, expansively tapping the booklet on the table, 'is that although this particular clause does apply to what I've done, it shouldn't. You see, both MacMaster and Keithley are avowed Marxist-Leninists who shouldn't be in the Labour Party in the first place!'

'They've got as much right as you have!' Liz hissed as she grabbed the *TV Times* and unconsciously began to rip strips off the innocent hurdler on the cover.

Oblivious to his wife's reaction, Roy's hairline started to sweat because of the throbbing heat emanating from the studio lights. It required a great effort of will to maintain his cool demeanour.

'As I'm sure you are aware, Nancy, the Marxist-Leninist tradition is totally undemocratic. You know what Lenin himself said about democracy, don't you?'

'Well, er. . . .'

'He said "I spit on Democracy. We Marxists believe in Marx's revolutionary dictatorship of the proletariat, and that justifies the use of unlimited power based on violence and bound by no laws. There are no morals in politics, only expediency. That is why I want Terror written into the Criminal Code".'

Nancy interrupted with a strained smile.

'Yes, I'm sure Lenin said all that, but what exactly does it have to do with . . .?'

'Everything! Because Mr MacMaster and Miss Keithley believe in Lenin's interpretation of Marxism. Therefore they obviously cannot believe in democracy or liberty, can they? Of course, Lenin was equally forthcoming about liberty.'

'Naturally, but. . . .'

'Indeed Lenin once went as far as to proclaim: "The people have no need for liberty! Liberty is one of the forms of the bourgeois dictatorship. In a state worthy of the name, there is no liberty. The people want to exercise power, but what on earth would they do if it were given to them?" '

Liz was so put out by what she believed to be Roy's smugness that she punctuated his every sentence with a derisive wave of her shredded *TV Times*.

'So I'm sure you and the viewers can see, Nancy, that it is my duty as a Labour Member of Parliament to warn the electors not to vote for people who avowedly revere Lenin. Like Messrs MacMaster and Keithley.'

Now completely out of control, Liz struck her husband's face on the screen with her magazine.

'How the hell do you know that MacMaster believes all that guff?'

Sebastian leaped to his feet.

'For Pete's sake, Mum! Let's have either you or Dad! I can't stand both of you together.'

At that moment his father smiled at him; at least, that was how it appeared to Sebastian.

'That is why I have written to the electors, Nancy, to warn them of the insidious, totalitarian intentions of these two Marxist-Leninists.'

'God, your father's so bloody pompous sometimes. Switch him off before I kick the screen in!'

Her son folded his arms.

'If you want him off, Mum, you switch him off.'

Before it could turn into a genuine battle of wills, Alexa yawned, lurched off the sofa and switched off the set.

'Will you two stop it? Now you've made me spill varnish on me uniform!'

In the television studio, suddenly Roy felt tired. He was no longer sure what impression his words were having on the viewers. As Nancy began her next question, he started worrying whether he was doing the right thing. Perhaps he shouldn't have used the Lenin quotations that Helen had provided him with in Kensington Gardens. Perhaps the quotations would only succeed in blurring the issue with the electorate. Perhaps. . . .

Biting his lower lip and resisting the compulsion to mop the perspiration from his brow, Roy forced himself to listen to what Nancy was saying. Simultaneously he noted the red light blink on over camera two as the camera crabbed across the studio floor to shoot him in a revealing close-up.

'But surely, Mr Hampton, there are those in the Labour Party, specifically on the radical left, who would argue that Marxist-Leninism is *philosophically* a relevant strand of Democratic Socialism? Mr Tony Benn, for instance, has argued that it is perfectly legitimate for a socialist to believe in various tenets of Karl Marx.'

Roy knew this was a unique opportunity to have a legitimate 'go' at Wedgwood Benn. Momentarily he considered launching into Helen's plethora of quotations on Marx as a racist and warmonger, but the second before he spoke he checked himself.

I mustn't overplay my hand at this point. There's still a long way to go.

Instead he smiled at the beautiful interviewer and said: 'You are quite right, Nancy. Mr Benn does believe it is legitimate for a socialist to involve himself with various aspects of Marxism. But I'd like to quote the words of an even greater man than the formidable Mr Benn. I am of course referring to Alexander Solzhenitsyn, who said that if we are foolish enough to try and combine democracy with Marxism, all we will achieve is "boiling ice". And at present, in my opinion, the Labour Party is tragically attempting to force this "boiling ice" down the throats of the electorate. If it continues, it will be parliamentary democracy that will be the ultimate loser.'

As the MP's words rippled into thousands of homes throughout the south of England, in one particular room he was being accompanied by an incessant typewriter. The typist's lean features were seen in sharp silhouette in the basement window. The early evening sun slanted between the rusty railings but the typist was oblivious as he composed his election address.

On the other side of the room, his mistress lounged in her fluffy bathrobe on their small double bed. She yawned as she tossed her curls away from her ears. Then she propped herself on her elbows and gazed vaguely at their eight-inch portable Hitachi television set. The MP was still in full flight. By the window the typist listened to his adversary's pronouncement, then threw his head back and laughed.

'For Chrissake, turn that fool off, luv, before I split a gut.'

The Marilyn Monroe of Lamberton North yawned again, then padded over the threadbare carpet. She considered changing the channel but then decided simply to switch the sound off. The result made her giggle, for now Roy looked like a mouthing goldfish in an aquarium. The girl turned back to the typist who, though he was only able to use two fingers on each hand, still succeeded in rattling the keys at great speed.

'I don't see how you can be so casual about it all, Terry.'

'Don't you?'

'No! I mean ... well, ain't Hampton screwing fings up for you, saying all that stuff on the telly?'

Terry laughed, then wrenched the page out of his typewriter. He reread the contents quickly, corrected two spelling mistakes and made an indentation for a new paragraph. Her lover's casual approach to the broadcast niggled Angie, so she lolled on the corner of his battered desk and swung her exposed long legs provocatively under his nose.

'Terry, I'm trying to get your attention.'

Terry sniggered, then stroked her upper thigh.

'So I see.'

'No, not in that way!'

'Then cover 'em up or I'll have to shove it up.'

Angie pouted, then gestured at the political goldfish on the screen.

'Wot I'm getting at, Terry, is surely he's doing you a lot of damage wiv all that "communist" smearing?'

'Now don't you worry your pretty little muff, darling.'

'Terry!'

Stretching elaborately, the revolutionary grinned.

'Believe you me, Angie, the only person Hampton is doing any harm to is himself.'

'But. . . .'

'There's no "buts" about it, luv. Hampton is simply indulging in scare-mongering, and there's nothing the Great British Public hate more than scare-mongering. Can you blame 'em? Let's face it: not even Kinnock and Co. are stupid enough to actually suggest that *philosophically* Marxist-Leninism has no place in the Party. Oh, sure, sometimes they get pushed into a corner and have to make a bit of a hoo-hah about organisations like the Militant Tendency and Socialist Action. Then they chuck a few Militants out and make the rest swear their allegiance to the Party.'

Terry paused, then grinned wolfishly as he inserted a new piece of carbon between two sheets of paper.

'But the beauty of it is that Kinnock, Hattersley and Co. can do nothing about Militant or Socialist Action except periodically chastise them. That doesn't change any of Militant's or Socialist Action's beliefs, does it? Or their intentions. So the Labour leadership can only ever win empty victories. You know what Lenin said, don't you?'

'Which – er . . . particular fing that Lenin said did you have in mind, Terry?'

'The pertinent thing, of course! And I quote, if somewhat loosely: "Britain will never go communist by direct revolution. So it is the duty of all comrades to use subterfuge, guile, lying and cheating. In fact you must use everything and anything; just so long as you infiltrate the Labour Party and the trades union movement, and support them both as the rope supports the hanged man!" What a great prophet Lenin turned out to be, eh?'

Angie's eyes were now as round as blue Wedgwood saucers.

'Yeah, when you come to fink about it, it's just wot's happened, ain't it?'

Terry nodded, then simultaneously went on typing and talking.

'That's the beauty of it, Angie, for now we're starting to gain genuine power through the parliamentary system. See,

"Democratic Socialism" is a word that can embrace anything you want it to.'

The revolutionary turned back to face her.

'And by "anything" I also mean revolution. So long as the revolution's done by stealth, of course. The British people won't buy anything that's too sudden or too violent.'

To Angie's surprise, Terry lifted her in his arms and swung her round.

'Sometimes I think it's a great pity I'm not a drinking man, Angie.'

'Why do you say that?'

Laughing, Terry gave Angie an extra spin, then propelled her over to the bed.

'Well, if I was a drinking man I'd toast that clown on the telly for being so stupid as to crucify himself in public.'

Dismissively, Terry turned off the television. Roy's goldfish features disappeared in a blink of light.

'That's exactly what Hampton's done – at least, as far as the Labour Party's concerned. By denouncing me and Joan like that, he has broken the cardinal rule of Party solidarity. Not even his friends can save him now.'

Terry launched himself on the bed beside Angie.

'Especially if I lose the by-election.'

Casually he loosened the sash of Angie's bathrobe.

'And I want to lose it.'

Taken aback by her lover's latest revelation, Angie sat bolt upright on the bed, unaware that her large breasts were now bobbing on a level with Terry's lower lip.

'You saying that you don't want to be a councillor, Terry?'

'Of course I don't. Being a councillor is about as bourgeois and reactionary as you can get.'

Terry was now nuzzling Angie's left breast, but she was so bewildered she scarcely noticed.

'If you don't want to be a councillor, why the hell are you standing at the by-election?'

Amused, the revolutionary pushed his acolyte back against the pillow and ran his tongue round her pale brown nipples.

'There's two reasons why I'm standing, oh love of my life.'

He bit her nipple, but still she didn't respond.

'The first reason I'm standing at the by-election is because it makes me look respectable and democratic – in the bourgeois meaning of those words, of course.'

'Of course.'

Terry thrust his tongue into her ear, which made her giggle, then blithely continued with his explanation.

'And, secondly, I know that if I stand, Hampton won't be able to resist challenging me in public. He'll want to get his revenge for me humiliating him in private.' He chuckled as he contemplated probing her hot spot with his tongue. 'Can't tell you what a pleasure it is doing business with an MP once you've got his trousers down. Well, if they're not bending over backwards, they're just begging to be kicked in the goolies.'

'Hey, where are you going?'

'To put the kettle on. Fancy some herb tea.'

Angie lay back on the pillows, her fluffy mind in a whirl of feathers.

'Terry?'

'Yeah.'

'What happens if you win the election?'

Terry put his head round the door, grinning like a marmalade cat.

'Whether I win or lose we'll still have to throw Hampton out of the Party. We can't have every "Woy", Dick an' Harry flouting Party Rules, can we? You know what Lenin said about that, of course?'

'No, but I'm sure you're going to tell me.'

'Lenin said: "Party discipline is imperative at all times. So it is our duty to throw the old shirt of Social Democracy, which is rotten and unsavoury, into the dustbin of history".'

'Oh, I didn't realise the phrase "dustbin of history" was Lenin's. Always thought it was yours, Terry.'

Terry was disconcerted by Angie's remark and muttered: 'A lot of what Lenin and I say is interchangeable.'

'You mean, great minds think alike?'

'You could say that!' said Terry, kissing her to shut her up.

'Hey, Terry, whose tongue's that? Yours or Lenin's?'

Terry began his election campaign the next morning. As he tramped the streets and pushed leaflets through the doors and smiled until his face ached, only occasionally did he think about his adversary. Then he couldn't help feeling a sense of pity. He knew Hampton was like a shark stripped of its teeth, thrashing about in a steel net. So he dismissed the MP from his mind and pressed the bell of yet another door in yet another high-rise block of flats. The door opened and three little black faces grinned up at him.

Simultaneously, barely a mile away in a gloomy chapel hall, Roy Hampton was addressing members of the Lamberton Branch of the General Municipal Boiler Makers and Associated Trades Unions. Unfortunately Roy's audience only consisted of six middle-aged men in tired, blue suits. Five of them were smoking, four were prematurely grey, three had dandruff on their shoulders, two were yawning and one was shaking his head in disagreement.

As Roy came to the end of his prepared speech, he found he was compelled to gaze at the dissenting trades unionist who was sitting by himself at the back of the hall. He couldn't understand why the fellow was disagreeing with him, for usually the members of the GMBATU were uniformly right-wing Labour – especially in Lamberton. As Roy ploughed on, the man continued to shake his head. Roy became obsessed by his silent critic, perhaps because the man had a gaunt face and haunted eyes. He felt the man was trying to tell him something but was unsure how to go about it. Then Roy glanced back at old Bill Sodger, the Branch Chairman, who was nearly asleep, as he poured more words over his tame audience:

'And it's because we've been so slack over the last ten years, comrades, that the Marxist-Leninists and the Trotskyites are beginning to manipulate our Party. If they continue to get themselves elected as MPs and councillors, then it will not be long before we have some kind of totalitarian rule here in the UK.'

Roy punctuated his words with an expansive gesture.

'Oh, I know that the communists are always denying this will happen. They say applied Marxism in Britain will turn out differently to the so-called applied Marxism of the Soviet Empire and Red China. But there is no historical evidence to show that a Marxist Britain will be any different. That is why it is our duty to fight these extremists now before it's too late....!'

Moments later Roy was walking towards his car on the far side of the derelict car park. As his feet scrunched over the bed of cinders that someone had thoughtfully strewn on the remains of the tarmac, he felt overwhelmed with tiredness. The warm evening breeze fluttered some chicken feathers against his ankle. He paused to pick up a particularly long brown feather, wondering who had plucked the poor bird. When he reached his car, he discarded it. He was searching for his keys when he realised someone had stolen his petrol cap.

Jesus, I hope they haven't siphoned off the petrol as well!

He fished his keys out of his pocket, then noticed the same 'someone' had snapped the aerial off his radio. He was about to examine the rest of his car when he became aware that he wasn't alone.

Tensing his muscles, he turned slowly to face what he sensed was a malignant force behind him. For a moment he couldn't believe his eyes, because the only other person in the car park was the gaunt trades unionist who had shaken his head throughout Roy's speech. There was something about the man's yellowish eyes and his slightly jaundiced skin that made Roy wary. Then the man moved towards him, his skinny arms swinging loosely by his side. As he approached, Roy could see that he was in his late fifties, and that his narrow eyes, screwed up against the evening sunshine, had a disconcertingly tigerish look to them. Roy felt that whatever the man's body did during the midnight hours, the eyes themselves never slept. He didn't speak until he was close to Roy. When he did, Roy noticed with distaste that even his ground-down teeth had yellow stains on them.

'Admirin' the workers, are you, Mr Hampton?'

'I beg your pardon?'

The man pointed beyond Roy's shoulder to the allotment, which stretched either side of the derelict car park. On the allotment were a dozen men, close on retirement age, in shabby shirts with sleeves rolled up above their bony elbows. They were all hard at work.

As the men laboured lovingly between the rows of their healthy green vegetables, occasionally discarding their forks for hoes and rakes, suddenly Roy was reminded of his own youth. He remembered his halcyon teenage years, before his father died, when he too would weed and water the lettuces while his father was sowing winter cabbage or supporting the top-heavy runner-beans with extra canes. Father and son would savour the hot sunshine on their backs and fondle the freshly-dug earth between their fingers. They worked silently together through the long Sunday afternoons under the immense white Fenland skies. They were so close to each other that they had no need of words. Sometimes his father would lean on his fork and point to a chaffinch in the nearby hawthorn hedge. Or he would encourage a bold robin to hop onto his clay-stained boot. Then he would mutter something about the robin being the gardener's second-best friend: 'See, lad, the worm's our very best friend, because the worm's constant burrowin' through the earth enables the soil to breathe. . . .'

'Well, it's men like them tilling the earth, that *we're* fighting for, ain't it, Mr Hampton?'

Roy, startled by the trades unionist's perception, could only nod in agreement.

'Yes, an Englishman's right to have his own strip of ground on an allotment is certainly worth fighting for, Mr – er . . .?'

'Oh, you don't have to call me "Mr", bruvver. My name's Geoff. Geoff Nightingale. So why don't I call you "Roy" and you can call me "Geoff"?'

Roy laughed, then glanced back at the men on the allotment. They were really working now that they were labouring for themselves rather than for their bosses.

'You've obviously got something on your mind, Geoff. What is it?'

Geoff scratched the inflamed boil on his protruding cheek-bone. The boil burst and a trickle of pus oozed down his cheek. Geoff noted the distaste in Roy's eyes and, realising what had happened, clawed a crumpled handkerchief out of his pocket and dabbed the pus away.

'Sorry about that, Roy. Afraid I'm always bursting out in boils. Tried everyfink I know to stop 'em, but they keep erupting. A bit like the coms, who also keep popping out in the most unexpected places.'

'Oh, you mean *you're* not a com, Geoff! What I mean is – I thought you *were* a com because . . . well, because you seemed to disagree with everything I was saying in there tonight.'

'The last fing I am is a com! And actually I agreed wiv everyfink you said tonight.'

'You did, Geoff?'

'Absolutely. What I *don't* agree with is your tactics.'

'Have you a better idea how to deal with MacMaster, then?'

'Sure.'

'Which is?'

Geoff grinned. 'You've got to smear the bastard, of course! And the Keithley bitch. And you've got to smear 'em good and proper so that they're finished round here for ever. Now don't look so shocked, bruvver. It's a very naughty world we live in. So we've got to be naughty if we're going to survive. And if *we* don't survive, what chance have those poor sods on that allotment?'

Then, before Roy could challenge the Serpent in the Garden, he flickered his thin tongue across his thin lips and slid away.

'Hey, just a minute, Geoff!'

Nervously Roy called after him. For a moment he thought Geoff was going to ignore him. Then the trades unionist paused on the edge of the kerb, turned abruptly and walked back towards him.

'Do I detect a spark of interest in my proposition, then, Roy?'

'Yes. I mean, no! I mean. . . .'

'What *do* you mean, Roy?'

'How the hell can I smear MacMaster and Keithley when there's nothing to smear them with?'

'Oh, I'm sure there's lots about Keithley and MacMaster that'd make pretty lurid reading once all the facts were known. For a kick-off: maybe that Keithley bitch is into leather and chains, and MacMaster's a transvestite? Anything's posible.'

Roy shook his head emphatically and moved away.

'Now, now, Roy, there's no need to run for cover. I was only flying a kite to see if you were interested.'

'I'm not!'

'Stop being so fucking squeamish, friend. I mean, Christ Almighty, we are dealing wiv filthy Marxists. One of whom is an acknowledged scrounger who is plotting revolution on social security. At the same time he's living in sin wiv a blonde tart wiv big tits. I've also discovered that while MacMaster was at the LSE, he not only nicked most of his books from Foyles but he also cheated in one of his exams. Not to mention putting a girl who worked at the Baker Street Classic in the pudding club, and then forcing her to have an abortion.'

'He did what?'

'Oh, yeah. There are even rumours that suggest that MacMaster was also screwing a New Zealand fairy who he shared a room with. Apparently MacMaster did the buggering as his contribution to the rent.'

'That's libellous crap!'

Geoff grinned mirthlessly.

'Is it?'

'Of course it's crap. MacMaster's no more of a poof than I am!'

'Maybe he ain't *now*, but he was certainly ambidextrous then.'

Stunned and uncertain, Roy could only gape into the man's yellow eyes.

'As for the red-headed whore called Keithley,' Nightingale continued, 'she had an abortion while she was up at Oxford. And it's rumoured she's had another one since. Also I know a bloke who says he can lay his hands on some porno photos that Miss Keithley had done soon after she came down from Oxford. She only had 'em done for kicks, of course. Though these Oxbridge types are always doing everything for kicks, ain't they?'

'Now that's enough of that!'

'If you don't believe me, I can always produce people to corroborate my evidence. Or you can hire a private dick who'll probably come up wiv even juicier titbits. I mean, for all we know, Keithley's a lesbo-tart and MacMaster's her closet-queen ponce.'

Clenching and unclenching his fists, Roy shook his head.

'I'm not saying it isn't true. It's just. . . .'

Geoff cut across him impatiently.

'Look, Roy, you've got to destroy them before they destroy you! But if you start to leak some of the shit in their pasts to the press, within days both of 'em'll be only too happy to flush themselves down the pan. Then with them in the sewer where they belong, you'll find that all your dithering right-wing friends'll start getting brave again. And once the right wingers recover their courage, they'll help you kick all those commie friends of MacMaster and Keithley off the GMC. So once again you'll have a secure base here in Lamberton, and your seat in the House will be – well, safe as houses. Now, Roy, before you shake yer head again – fink it through. If we don't create a fucking scandal round those two Trot bastards, we're never going to make up the lost ground here in Lamberton. Especially since your pals Bunting and Taplow were so fucking stupid as to get caught with their hands in the fucking till!'

The trades unionist paused to let his message sink in. The evening breeze stiffened and an empty Coca-Cola bottle rolled leisurely across the car park. In desperation Roy glanced back at the shadowy figures of the men toiling in the allotment. His thoughts were muddled.

If I smear MacMaster with that filth, will it do anything to preserve democracy and the English way of life for those poor sods on their vegetable patches? Oh, I'm sure with half a bottle of Scotch inside me, I could probably convince myself it would. But now I'm stone-cold sober, I know that by smearing MacMaster in his own dirt I'll be even more despicable than he was when he recruited those old-age pensioners and the unemployed simply to kick me out of Parliament. . . .

'You don't care much for the idea of a smear campaign, do you, Roy? But it's been done before. And not too long ago. And very successfully.'

Nightingale moved a pace closer.

'And if you recall that *other* occasion, Roy – as I'm sure you do – you'll see that some of the smearing you've got to play with is almost identical. Especially the rumours relating to MacMaster buggering that Kiwi fairy while he was at the LSE. Well, there's nothing the average Labour punter hates more than buggery. So you see, my friend, whether you like it or not, a full-blooded smear campaign is the only way you're going to save your political hide.'

Roy tried to interrupt, but Nightingale cut across him.

'Let me finish and I'll leave you be, Roy. The other advantage you'll gain by smearing 'em both is that it'll force the NEC to agree with you when you say that neither MacMaster nor Keithley should be the official candidates of the Labour Party. Then, once the NEC start to back you, it means that even if your local GMC try to move against you for breaking Party Rules, the NEC will be forced to protect you. Because, as you know, the NEC can always overturn decisions made by the local GMC if they feel the GMC in question is being unconstitutional. Then you'll be able to claim you only broke the rules because MacMaster and Keithley were not fit to be Labour candidates. And once you've turned the searchlights on the MacMaster-Keithley homo-porno shit, there's going to be no one round here who will dare to disagree wiv you.'

'But what happens if you suddenly decided to turn one of your famous searchlights on to *my* past, Mr Nightingale?'

The yellow-stained teeth beamed at the MP.

'I wouldn't dream of smearing you, Roy. You're on our side.'

'Am I?'

The sallow face looked puzzled.

'What do you mean?'

'I sometimes wonder if I'm on anybody's side. Except England's.'

Geoff laughed.

'We're *all* on England's side.'

'Are we?'

'Are you suggesting that even if I wanted to, Roy, I could dig up stuff about you that could be used in a smear campaign against you?'

'I'd hate to put it to the test.'

The gaunt man crossed his arms. Roy could scarcely make out his features, for it was rapidly growing darker.

'All right, Roy, I'll put it fair and square to you. Unlike MacMaster, you ain't spent half your life living on welfare while you were plotting to bring down the state, have you?'

'No, but. . . .'

'You ain't got a mistress, either? And you're certainly not a screaming poofter!'

Roy hesitated a moment, and in that moment he conjured up Helen's mocking smile. But the past was the past and he was determined to exorcize it, so he said: 'No, I'm not a screaming poofter, Mr Nightingale, and I haven't got a mistress. Nor am I going to answer any more of your questions!'

'Why, d'you have somefink in your past that won't bear looking into, then, Roy?'

Why am I standing here talking to this disgusting creature? Roy thought, as his sense of guilt began to dry up the roof of his mouth.

'Oh, come on, Roy. I don't believe a man like you has ever done anyfink that you've really been ashamed of. Christ, you didn't even send your kids to private school like a lot of your

PLP playmates, and you're not the type to take bribes. So you've got a record as clean as a whistle.'

Still refusing to be drawn, Roy fished out his keys and jiggled the appropriate one in the lock. Then he remember the case of 1968 Burgundy on his front doormat which had been given to him for 'services rendered to industry'. Guiltily, he swung the car door open and found he could almost savour the deep-fruited aroma of the Burgundy as the cork came out of the first bottle. Then an acrid smell twitched him back into the present. Nightingale was urinating against the fence and the night breeze was wafting the smell into Roy's nostrils.

Christ, the sonovabitch is so confident I'll fall in with him, he even has the gall to piss in front of me!

Furious, Roy climbed into his car and banged the door. Geoff zipped up his flies and strolled towards the parked car.

'OK, Roy, OK. If you want to be crucified upside down, that's your look-out. If you change your mind, you can always leave a note for me in the Red Cockerel.'

Roy switched on the engine, then backed out of the car park.

Politics is such a shabby profession, he thought. But am I that shabby? On the other hand, would I really be to blame if I exposed MacMaster?

Scarcely aware he was driving, he accelerated down the shadowy street.

What would MacMaster do in my place? He'd probably follow Lenin: 'When we are reproached with cruelty, we wonder how people can forget their most elementary Marxism. The important thing is not to defeat an enemy but to finish him off!'

If only I wasn't so tired. . . . But if I fight cancer with cancer, won't I end up as bad as them? Christ, I can't remember when I've felt so clapped out . . . !

With a sudden jerk, his head slumped forward. To his horror he realised he'd fallen asleep at the wheel. Instinctively he slammed on the brakes. The metal hubs of the wheels squealed against the lip of the kerb and the car mounted the pavement. Blinking desperately, Roy wrenched the steering wheel round as the car skidded towards a low brick wall on his left. There was the piercing sound of tin scraping brick. Then the car screeched to a halt.

Panting, he switched off the engine and climbed out of the car. He examined the scratched paintwork and saw how close he had been to smashing his car into a lampost. To rid himself of his sleepiness, he wetted his fingertips with spittle and rubbed the cool moisture over his eyelids. It brought him a little relief. He glanced up and down the street, deserted but for a grey-and-white scrawny cat rubbing its arched back against a lampost. He decided it was safer for him to leave the car for the night and walk home.

Two-and-a-half minutes later, approaching Nobs Row, he was distracted by the faint sound of boys' voices singing 'The Lord Is My Shepherd, I Shall Not Want'. He wondered where the singing was coming from. Then he noticed a faint glowing in the stained-glass windows of St Thomas', on his left. The small fourteenth-century church, with its stocky Saxon tower, was set back from the road in a narrow, triangular churchyard, shrouded by yew trees. Roy pushed open the gate, which complained on its hinges. Then he walked up the path, savouring the night scents of mint and honeysuckle. The choirboys' voices lifted his spirit above the oppressive yew trees and the surrounding rooftops. He felt he had wings and was flying beyond the cross on the spire, into the arc of the moon in its last quarter.

Quietly he clicked open the latch on the church door. Holding his breath, he stepped inside. The choirmaster was conducting enthusiastically. Roy glanced round the nearby pews. They were empty, so he shuffled forward over the cold flagstones and slipped into the nearest pew. Without being fully aware what he was doing, he knelt on the faded crimson cushion. It was so long since he'd prayed that for a moment he didn't know how to start. Or even whom to pray to. The choir was singing an anthem of Thomas Tallis. He knew he'd heard it somewhere before but couldn't place where. The purity of the boys' unbroken voices, their shining faces and the swelling of the notes in the flickering candlelight combined to wash his mind free of filth and doubt. It was as if the boys, with their ravishing anthem, were praying for him. As he was unable to create the words of a prayer, he allowed the singers and the music to be his prayer; for himself, and for his family, and for England.

Even as the prayer possessed him, he knew that if he did defeat MacMaster he would do it without resorting to Satan's weapons. For it was better to 'Serve in Heav'n than reign in Hell'. Far, far better.

One afternoon in the second week of June, Terry found himself on the eighth floor of the Wilberforce tower block on the outskirts of the Eden Council Estate. Angie, carrying two plastic bags filled with leaflets, stood a little behind him. In front of him was a pink door in need of a new coat of paint. Barely managing to stifle a yawn, he rang the bell for the umpteenth time. He had never campaigned publicly for himself before and he was not finding it to his liking. He couldn't control the public as he was able to control his local GMC. The electors asked him unanswerable questions. Or, more precisely, they kept asking him questions which he preferred not to answer.

'I don't fink Mrs Wheeler's in, Terry,' Angie observed, in an attempt to stop him yawning for the third time.

But the door opened and an overweight woman's pasty face framed itself in the darkness between the door and the doorpost.

'What d'you want?' the woman whispered, opening the door another six inches.

'Hello, Mrs Wheeler. I'm Terry MacMaster, the Labour Party candidate for the Council election.'

'So?'

Before Terry could reply, a fat tabby cat muscled its way between the woman's slippered feet, then stroked its furry tail against her calves.

'So you've come about the voting, have you?'

'That's right, Mrs Wheeler. As you probably read in the local paper, Councillor Bunting died just recently, so now we have to have a by-election.'

'We put a couple of leaflets through your door about Terry that you might've seen, Mrs Wheeler,' chipped in Angie brightly.

With a mocking grimace, Terry controlled his irritation. He hated to be interrupted – especially by Angie, who could be unreliable.

As the fat woman bent down to pick up her portly cat, Terry turned up the corners of his mouth until it settled into a radiant smile.

'We know you voted Labour in the past, Mrs Wheeler, so we'd like you to vote for us again.'

The woman edged back into her gloomy hallway and encouraged her tabby to lick her neck.

'Yes, of course,' Mrs Wheeler whispered. 'Now I know who you are.'

Terry nodded enthusiastically and went on smiling.

'Yes, you're the communist that our MP was talking about on the telly, ain't you?'

Hesitantly Angie glanced at her lover, but if anything his smile broadened. Then it faded, to be replaced by a look that was so brimming with candour and compassion that it almost moved Angie to tears.

'I'm afraid, Mrs Wheeler, our MP is mistaken in his assertion,' said Terry gravely. 'I've only ever been a member of the *Labour* Party. My views are the same as those that were passed at the Labour Party Conference.'

Mrs Wheeler opened her mouth to interject but Terry pressed home his advantage. He reached out and probed his fingertips deep into her cat's furry neck. The tabby responded by stretching in his mistress' arms, so Terry stroked its wispy ears.

'It's because I am a passionate member of the Labour Party, Mrs Wheeler, that I'm so active in the local Party. I'm pushing like crazy for better housing here in Eden Ward. Not to mention more jobs. I'm also doing everything within my power to try and save the hospital and improve the pensions. And I'm against all the Tory cuts, Mrs Wheeler, absolutely!'

Terry gave the woman his searingly-honest look. She looked troubled. Then she peered down at his sinuous hands as they delved into the rolls of fat round her beloved pussy's neck.

'You're sure you're not a communist?'

Terry laughed.

'Oh, come on, Mrs Wheeler, I don't think you think I look like a communist.'

He brushed his free hand through his closely cropped curls.

'I haven't got any horns, have I?'

The woman shook her head, partly in agreement and partly because she found the radiant young man in his black leather jacket so beguiling.

Terry saw he was progressing. 'I'm sure you've seen me on

the street several times, Mrs Wheeler. I'm not one of those who go skulking around in holes.'

'Yes, I must say you don't *look* like a communist. But there's a lot of 'em about these days, ain't there?'

'I don't fink there are, Mrs Wheeler,' interjected Angie, now bored with the conversation and beginning to fancy a large nut cutlet with a sesame-seed salad.

The fat woman was still not convinced. Instinctively she manoeuvred her cat away from the young magician's hands.

'I don't care what you say, young lady, they're always talking about the Reds. I mean, every time you turn on the TV or read the papers, there's another one of 'em's been discovered. An' some of 'em have been working for the Reds for thirty years or more!'

Terry knew it was time to laugh again, so did.

'Well, *I'm* no communist, Mrs Wheeler. I'm just an ordinary member of the Labour Party. So please vote for me on Thursday and we'll really get something done about your pension – OK?'

'Well, I'll have to fink about that, Mr MacMaster. You've got to be careful these days. Well, you have, ain't you?'

'You can trust me, Mrs Wheeler. I'm from around these parts!'

'Oh dear!'

'Now what's the matter, Mrs Wheeler?'

'I wouldn't trust no one from around *these* parts!'

The woman scowled, then took a tentative step towards the young campaigner. Whispering, she indicated the pink doors of the three other occupants on the eighth floor.

'I certainly wouldn't trust anyone on this floor!'

Suddenly concerned, she pointed an accusing fat finger at Terry's leather jacket.

'*You* don't live on another floor in this horrible tower block, do you?'

'Oh no, Mrs Wheeler,' Angie answered for her lover. 'We live on the other side of the estate. So you can trust our Terry because he does nothing but work for the Party from morning till night. And often from night till morning.'

Clenching his teeth to hide his growing fury, Terry shot Angie a withering glance. But she was oblivious.

'And you don't need to worry about us living together, Mrs

Wheeler. As soon as my Terry's won the election, we're going to make it legitimate and get married. Ain't we, Terry?'

For the first time since he left the LSE in his early twenties, Terry found himself at a loss for words. Before he could prevent it, his mouth jerked open and remained ajar. He was so horror-stricken that for several seconds he couldn't control the muscles of his jaw. For her part, Angie was so enthusiastic about their forthcoming marriage that she stepped in front of her goggle-eyed lover to stroke the fat woman's cat. To Terry's consternation, Mrs Wheeler beamed at Angie.

'I'm so glad you're getting married, luv. Was beginning to wonder whether it'd gone out of fashion with you young 'uns. Congratulations to you both.'

Without thinking, the fat woman offered Terry her cat's paw for him to shake. Terry was so flustered he shook it.

'Well, all I can say, Mr MacMaster, is I hope that you and the young lady'll be happy together, because me and Joe had a terrible time of it. Though I do miss Joe in the winter.'

The woman nodded towards her bunioned toes, snugly encased in a pair of old fur-lined slippers.

'I mainly miss Joe because of my feet. Never can get 'em warm. He said I'd got the coldest feet this side of Siberia. And he should know, because when he were young, he were at sea on a trawler in them parts. During the war he took supplies to the Ruskies in Murmansk. Are you *sure* you're not a communist?'

Terry stuttered. He had barely recovered from being 'maritally' devastated and here he was again being accused of being a communist. But he managed to close his mouth, then had to open it again to say: 'Absolutely! I mean I'm absolutely certain that I'm *not* a communist, Mrs Wheeler!'

He started to back away.

'Well, er ... we look forward to you voting for us, Mrs Wheeler.'

'Have to fink about that, won't I? Still, as I said, it's nice you're getting married. And I hope you'll be happier than me and Joe.'

Mrs Wheeler was closing the door when she voiced an afterthought.

'Don't suppose yours'll be a white wedding, though, will it? Never mind.'

Angie was about to protest, but the fat woman shut the door in her face.

'Wot a cheek!'

Terry growled.

'Wot's the matter, luv?'

'All that marriage shit! Why'd you come out with it?'

Angie looked nonplussed. She pouted.

'Well . . . I thought it was about time we did get married.'

This was more than the revolutionary could bear. In rapid succession he cracked his double-jointed thumbs.

'You thought it was almost time we . . .?' he trailed off in speechless apoplexy. 'Can you tell me any other self-respecting Marxist-Leninist who's been stupid enough to get himself spliced?'

Angie scratched her head, then produced a stick of pink lipstick from her raffia bag. Furiously Terry waved his fist.

'You just name one Marxist-Leninist that's been dumb enough to get himself trapped in wedlock!'

'Well . . . there's Marx and Lenin, for a kick-off. Not to mention Arthur Scargill, Mick McGahey, Lord Scanlon and. . . .'

Terry grabbed Angie's wrist and shook her, and most of the leaflets, with his photograph on them, flew out of Angie's hand and fell like heavy confetti into the passageway.

'Look, I'm not in the mood for those kinds of jokes, Angie,' Terry snarled as he went down on his knees to collect the scattered leaflets.

Angie joined him.

'I weren't joking, Terry.'

'I'll pretend I didn't hear that. Now you pick up the rest of the leaflets, then go and chat up old Robinson at 115 while I deal with the Umgabis next door.'

Angie smiled mischievously and thrust some leaflets into her bag.

'I'll bet the Umgabis are married!'

If steam could have come out of Terry's ears . . . Angie bit her lip as tears of laughter formed in her baby-blue eyes.

God, she thought, when he gets all snotty like that, he's so sexy I could jump on him and gobble him whole!

She rang old Robinson's bell and simpered to herself: still, if you don't understand politics – and I don't – a few sexy looks is the next best thing.

As the door opened, she thrust out her lower lip and her breasts. Immediately old Robinson's rheumy eyes came out on stalks, and Angie was sure that he at least was going to vote for her husband-to-be.

Roy knew he was drowning. The billows tumbled over him for the last time. He was still amazed at their extraordinary colour, for they were red as blood. Even the featherdown foam was crimson. As the surge of the waves pulled him down, he had a final glimpse of a church spire with St George's flag flapping on its pinnacle. Then the sound of a boys' choir drifted to him over the relentless sea. No sooner had the country churchyard and the banner of England's patron saint been overwhelmed by the red waves than the vision of a dappled wood, decked with yellowy-green spring leaves and carpeted in bluebells, violets and primroses, took the place of the flapping flag on the spire. Then, faster than the speed of thought, the countryside was washed over with bloody foam – as was the country pub, and the locals in the pub garden who were sipping the froth off their real ale and listening to the nightingale in the nearby copse. . . .

Image after English image materialised before Roy's drowning eyes: lovers walking hand in hand down leafy lanes, the Oxford and Cambridge boat race, the resounding 'thock' as the batsman struck another four through the covers, the scent of new-mown hay and freshly cut grass, butterflies, lupins, apples thudding on last year's leaves, his mother gardening, his father digging, his brother fighting, his sister crying, his son running, his daughter yawning, his wife smiling, Helen kissing, Harold dying . . . himself drowning . . . and his beloved England weeping . . . weeping. . . .

Anguished, he let out a final cry as the blood-red water rushed into his lungs. But in the act of choking to death, he willed himself to live. With the last of his ebbing strength, he swam upwards through the nightmare, with MacMaster's octopus streaking after him. As the vermilion tentacles clawed at his throat and groin, he thrust out both arms and grappled his hands into the mass of carnivorous seaweed which was the octopus's heart. Then, still screaming his fear and defiance, he woke up . . . to find he was pulling his sleeping wife's hair.

'What the hell do you think you're doing, Roy?'

He was too horrified and dazed to answer. His eyes couldn't focus in the early morning darkness. He began to shiver as the cool air washed over his perspiring body.

'I'm sorry, darling. Last thing I meant to do was wake you up.'

'Wake me up? You nearly pulled all my hair out!'

Feverishly, Roy wiped his pyjama sleeve across his damp forehead.

'I had another of those nightmares.'

Liz switched on the light, then poured herself some water from the glass jug beside her bed.

'I'm getting sick of this happening night after night, Roy.'

'Join the club. When you've finished, can I have a sip?'

Without looking, Liz passed him the glass, then switched off the light.

'Had another union meeting tonight. This time with a big audience of eleven!'

'What else can you expect? No one's interested in your fight.'

'I know. Mind, they said they'd back me, of course – though they're already converted. But it seems to me that's all I ever do.'

'Sorry, Roy, but you've lost me.'

'Well, either I'm preaching to the converted or I'm shouting myself hoarse in a vain attempt to be heard above the enemy baying for my blood.'

'God, you sound more and more like a Social Democrat with every day that passes!'

Roy slumped back against his pillow.

'Be fair, darling. There are insults and insults.'

'If you're not a Social Democrat, why don't you stop making a fool of yourself? Ever since you came back the other night with that bloody boys' choir singing in your ears, you've either been on cloud nine or sweating your way through some nightmare about England. Well, I'm right, aren't I? Your bad dream just now was all about your 'Golden Age' England being destroyed by Machiavellian monsters like Terry MacMaster, wasn't it?'

'Yes, but. . . .'

'No "buts", Roy! If you go on like this, you could easily have some kind of minor nervous breakdown.'

Roy laughed indignantly in the darkness.

'Why only minor?'

'Look, your present mental state doesn't strike me as funny. Especially as you have developed this habit of assaulting me in my sleep. I wouldn't mind if it was a sexual assault. . . .'

Liz sighed, then turned over to face him. She could make out his silhouette by the light of the street lamp.

'Why don't you resign your seat, darling, and be done with it?'

'How the hell would we live?'

'You could take that job that Freddy's friend offered you.'

'I don't want to be a business consultant.'

'Why not? Eighteen thousand a year's more than you get as an MP, and the hours are bound to be better.'

'I'd only take a job like that as a last resort. Anyway, he's given me until the New Year to make up my mind.'

'I suppose you could always go back to teaching drama at the Poly.'

'Not a chance!'

'Oh, I'm aware they're cutting back on staff all the time, but. . . .'

'It's not just that, Liz. Since I left the Poly, it's acquired a new head with very leftist sympathies. And the last person she'd want on her staff would be me! Well, the Trots have gnawed their way into a lot of these further education institutions now. Not that I blame 'em.'

'You don't?'

'No. Mind, it's taken long enough for me to get the message. More and more, I believe that communism only rears its ugly head where there is a political vacuum.'

'Don't start on all that again, for Christ's sake!'

Groaning, Liz buried her head in the pillow and clamped her hands over her ears, but there was no stopping him.

'I'm only agreeing with what you've been telling me, Liz. We right wingers in the Party have asked for the trouble we're having now. What's more, it's entirely as a result of right-wing Labour's complacency that we've now got an extreme right-wing Tory government! The reason that Thatcher and Keith Joseph were able to move the Tory Party so far to the right in the late seventies was because *we* didn't stop the Labour Party moving so far to the left in the previous decade. So Thatcher has used the opportunity to what's known as "balance things up". That's why we've now got four million unemployed, rotten housing, no job prospects, and basic spiritual and mental depression throughout most of the country. Let's face it, Thatcher isn't in power because people like her! She's in power because they think she is a good leader, and they also feel she's less dangerous than the hard left. Unfortunately, the top people in the centre ground of politics, i.e. right-wing Labour, the Tory 'Wets', and, God help us, the squabbling Alliance, still refuse to join forces to make a strong, radical Centre Party. Instead, they spend their time being petty-minded and slanging each other, so they are unable to present a moderate alternative to the electorate. But if they *did* join together, then. . . .'

Roy trailed off as he realised he was speaking his subconscious dream out loud. Then he peered down at his wife and chortled. She was asleep and fortunately hadn't heard any of his 'blasphemous' utterances. As no one was listening but himself, he brushed a strand of hair away from Liz's forehead and murmured: ' "The pity of it, Iago, the pity of it".'

Then he remembered Helen, in one of their quotation sessions, answering his Othello line: 'Roy darling, you mustn't wallow in self-pity. Instead you must:

> . . . fight to recover what has been lost
> And found and lost again and again: and now, under
> conditions
> That seem unpropitious. But perhaps neither gain nor
> loss.
> For us, there is only the trying. The rest is not our
> business.'

It was half past eight in the morning on the day of the Council election. The sun was already hot and the Spring Street Market was bustling with customers. As Roy parked his car on the single yellow line, the bright June morning made him want to whistle. He locked his car, checked to see if there were any officious traffic wardens about, and then headed into the market. Within moments he was part of the bustle, breathing in the appetising smells of the fruit and the vegetables, intermingled with the scent of roses, carnations and bunches of mimosa. He bought half a dozen pale-yellow roses to put in the vase on his desk, and selected three large peaches and some strawberries.

'Wot about the bananas, guv, or the pears, or. . .?'

'No, thanks. These are perfect.'

Roy paid the laughing little Cockney woman. This was the heart of the real London. Everywhere he turned he was greeted by Cockney sparrers, shouting for custom and selling their wares. What did it matter that some of it had fallen off the backs of lorries, when it was all being sold with such humour and enthusiasm?

Though it was MacMaster's 'big' day, Roy still felt irrepressibly cheerful as he headed back for his car. He wished he could stay and talk with the vendors, for he knew they were wise about the way 'the world wags'. In fact he did stop and chat to several friendly stall-keepers. He asked them who they were voting for, and discovered that only one of them was going to vote at all. And she had voted already – for MacMaster.

Moments later he was stuck in the morning traffic jam on the High Street. Winding down the window, he poked his head out to see what was causing the trouble. The traffic lights had frozen on orange. He glanced at his watch impatiently. It was eight minutes to nine and there was no sign of the traffic moving in either direction.

Roy rubbed his eyes. The nightmares were beginning to take their toll. Yet he felt strangely elated. Perhaps it was the sudden aroma of freshly-baked bread, or the long-legged girls in their skimpy summer dresses, crossing directly in front of him. . . .

He was prevented from savouring other smells and sights by an alien thumb and forefinger pressuring his elbow. Controlling his irritation, he turned to see who was making free with his jacket.

'Oh, hello, Terry.'

Roy noticed the younger man was seated on a woman's bicycle. The spectacle was made more bizarre because the wicker basket attached to the handlebars was filled with leaflets showing Terry's handsome features.

'I see you're doing your rounds on your bike, Terry.'

'We unemployed have it very hard. And it's not my bike; it's Angie's.'

'Naturally.'

Terry, who had done nothing but smile since the beginning of this chance encounter, continued to flash his perfect teeth at the MP. Then he pointed to a policeman who was trying to encourage the traffic to move.

'Strange how the filth are always around whenever there's a hold-up, isn't it?'

Roy smiled back and nodded.

'So how's it going, Terry?'

Terry went on grinning, but his eyes darkened.

'You've been very helpful, Roy.'

'Really?'

'Oh yeah. And after the result tomorrow, you can rely on me being just as helpful to you. Well, give my regards to the PLP – while you still can.'

Without waiting for Roy's response, he pedalled off. At that moment the policeman managed to induce some movement in the cars nearest to the lights. Seconds later the Capri in front of Roy's estate jerked forward. Roy twisted the key in the ignition but the engine refused to turn over. He pulled out the choke. Still nothing.

It's the bloody new starter motor they've put in! he fumed.

Before he could fiddle with the choke again, the motorists behind him started honking. Sweating with frustration, he stuck his head out of the window and shouted: 'No point in bloody honking! Can't you see the bloody thing's gone dead on me?'

MacMaster, who was now by the traffic lights, turned to wave cheerily at the MP. In a fury, Roy opened the car door and clambered out into the honking street, only to come face to face with another policeman. He ignored the policeman, thrust his arm through the open driving-seat window and released the handbrake. He was about to push his car up onto the kerb when the white-helmeted officer stepped in front of him and peeled off his black leather gloves.

'You'd better push her onto the pavement, sir.'

'What the hell d'you think I'm trying to do, officer?'

The two Members of Parliament leaned on the warm stone

parapet, nursing their glasses of chilled white Burgundy. The slimmer of the two was laughing heartily at the other's discomfort. Eventually Roy snapped back at de Quincey.

'It's all right you laughing, David. It didn't happen to you!'

'I'm sorry, but the thought of you pushing your pile of tin onto the pavement while MacMaster rode off into the sunrise, well, you must admit, it's pretty funny.'

Roy nodded, then turned away from the Thames, which sparkled below them. The sun was beating down on the back of his neck. He loosened his tie, then stripped off his jacket. Fifty yards away along the House of Commons Terrace, other MPs of various political persuasions were jostling into the enormous green-and-white striped drinks tent which billowed slightly as the beginnings of a breeze whispered over the river. Then the Home Secretary and the Foreign Secretary sauntered past Roy towards the drinks tent.

'Do you know what today is?' David murmured, in an attempt to regain his friend's attention.

'Yes, it's the day that MacMaster and Keithley become revolutionary councillors in my constituency.'

David sipped his white wine, then shook his head.

'That's not what I meant. Today's the twenty-first of June, right?'

'So?'

'So it's Midsummer's Day, the longest day of the year.'

Instantly Roy conjured up a scene from the most magical English play ever written. There, in his imaginary midsummer wood, was the lissome half-naked figure of Titania, Queen of the Fairies. To Roy's amazement, she had Titian-coloured hair, and her ultra-white skin was stippled with freckles. Good Christ, he thought, it's Joan Keithley! Then the satanic figure of King Oberon stepped into a shaft of moonlight, wearing the smiling face of Terry MacMaster.

'There's no doubt about it, David.'

'No doubt about what?'

'I'm sure those bastards are going to win!'

'If your Trot doesn't win tonight, he'll win next time. With those boys it's simply a question of when.'

'So what are you going to do, David, when *your* Trot levels a loaded pistol at your head?'

David finished his wine and placed the empty glass on the

parapet. He studied eight bronzed oarsmen, who were labouring against the incoming tide under the shadow of Westminster Bridge. A pleasure launch, crammed with tourists, followed in their wake.

'Don't say you're developing my habit, David?'

'Which habit's that?'

'Daydreaming!'

'Sorry, Roy. I was thinking about what you said.'

'You mean your Trot is now putting unbearable pressure on you?'

'Yup. Especially the last couple of weeks.'

'Why didn't you tell me before?'

'Like you, Roy, I try not to burden my friends unnecessarily.'

The sun was now at its hottest. Roy placed the chilled wine-glass against his burning cheek.

'What are you going to do about your Trot?'

David thought a moment, then frowned.

'Probably nothing.'

'You mean you're going to lie back and let the sod cut your throat?'

'No.'

'If you're not going to fight him,' Roy asked, mystified, 'what the hell are you going to do?'

'Well . . . between you, me and what's left of our democracy, I'm seriously thinking of crossing the picket lines,' David said, scarcely moving his lips, with his hand shading his eyes against the intense midsummer glare.

For several seconds Roy peered at his friend in disbelief.

'You're not planning to join the Tories, are you?'

'No.'

'Surely not the Liberals?'

'Not exactly.'

'Oh Jesus, you're not going to do a Roy Jenkins on us, are you?'

David couldn't resist a sly smile. For at that moment Roy Jenkins in person was striding purposefully onto the Terrace, in animated conversation with David Owen.

In unabashed horror Roy jiggled his friend's elbow and whispered: 'You're not really going to do a "Woy" on us, are you?'

'No, but I might do a David Owen. Where are you going?'

Roy turned in the open doorway that led to the Commons.

'Back to the Committee Room, where else?'

'Hey, Roy, d'you still want Wendy and me to come over to dinner tonight for the result?'

'Of course. Oh, and thanks for the vino.'

Roy was about to leave when he remembered something.

'Did I mention that Olive Bunting will be joining us tonight?'

'Olive Bunting?'

'My old mate Harold's widow. She's taken his death badly. Feels personally responsible for what he did. Of course she's quite blameless, but she's been so upset by the ensuing scandal that she's now got a drinking problem.'

David shrugged and held his empty wineglass against the sun.

'Do you know anyone who's got anything to do with politics who *hasn't* got a drinking problem?'

'Yes. Terry MacMaster.'

With his shoulders hunched in self-mockery, Roy retrieved his jacket from the parapet and plodded back into the Commons. David watched him go. Then, checking no one was looking, he ambled across to the drinks tent. Within seconds he was chatting to David Owen and Roy Jenkins.

Well, he thought, as he ordered the SDP luminaries another round of drinks, I've got to begin somewhere. . . .

The last rose streaks of sunset were fading. Night was conquering the longest day, but the six of them still remained round the white garden table, listening to the birds' chorus.

Yes, Roy thought, uncorking a bottle of brandy – when it's as warm as this, we should always hold our dinner parties out here on the lawn. Especially on Midsummer Night, when the scents of the honeysuckle by the garden wall and the night phlox under the apple tree can ravish the senses.

Then to everyone else's amusement, Roy let out a startled bleat as a great bomber moth bounced off his nose before zig-zagging between the beckoning candle flames. Because he had drunk too much he tried to swat the moth and missed, making his guests laugh even more.

'What an absolutely idyllic evening we're having,' laughed David as he extended his brandy balloon for a refill.

Roy recovered his good humour and sloshed some more Cognac into his friend's glass.

'Yes, on a night like this you wouldn't want to be anywhere else in the world.'

Wendy, David's wife, took off her enormous spectacles and wiped them with her napkin.

'Magical, isn't it?' she said in her ineffective whispery voice. 'If you close your eyes and breathe in the night scents, you could almost believe that the fairies will come tripping out of the shrubbery.'

'And they'll be lead by Puck!' chimed in Liz, 'with Oberon not far behind.'

Taking this as his cue, Roy declaimed:

> 'I know a bank where on the wild thyme blows,
> Where oxlips and the nodding violet grows;
> Quite over-canopied with luscious woodbine,
> With sweet musk-roses and with eglantine;
> There sleeps Titania sometimes of a night,
> Lull'd in these flowers with dances and delight;
> And there the snake throws his enamell'd skin,
> Weed wide enough ... to wrap ... a fairy in.'

With a flourish, he plucked an evening primrose and wafted it in front of Wendy's laughing face:

> 'And with the juice of this I'll streak her eyes,
> And make her full of hateful fantasies.'

He was about to continue when he was distracted by his son.

'Hey, Sebastian, don't sit there stuffing your face with all those After Eights! Maybe our guests'd like some.'

Wendy giggled and waved her slim hand.

'Not for me, thanks. Got to watch the old waistline, you know.'

This was too much for Liz.

'Jesus, Wendy, if you get any slimmer, you'll disappear.'

Then Liz turned to Olive Bunting, who was already on her second brandy and was not making much sense because she had consumed a bottle of wine earlier.

'Perhaps Olive would care for a chocolate, Sebastian?' Liz suggested in the hope that this would slow her guest up, but Olive shook her head emphatically.

'No . . . thanks. Chockies'd only shpoil the effect of thish . . . lovely brandy . . so can I have some more, pleashe, Roy?'

'Of course, Olive.'

With a curt shake of the head, Liz indicated it would be unwise to give Olive any more, but Roy ignored her. Then to try and gain her husband's attention, she changed the subject.

'Shouldn't Lexi be back from the cinema by now?'

Their son swallowed the last After Eight. 'Oh, don't worry about Sis, Mum. She's got enough slap on to deter the most diligent rapist.'

Wendy gave one of her breathless laughs.

'You get worse, Sebastian!'

Then she picked up the jug of cream and turned to Olive, who was now having difficulty directing her glass to her mouth.

'Cream, Mrs Bunting?'

'No thanksh. Nor coffee, neither.'

Roy offered David a Havana cigar.

'What time's your daughter supposed to be home then, Liz?' David said, rustling a cigar against his ear.

'We don't like her coming home much after eleven. Mind, she's generally good and comes in on time.'

Sebastian discarded the empty After Eights box, then pointedly studied his watch.

'In that case Sis has only got two minutes and fourteen seconds to "be good in".'

David laughed and sniffed his Havana.

'Mm, these are excellent cigars, Roy.'

This brought Olive temporarily out of her alcoholic haze. She scratched a hairy mole to the left of her nose, then held out a podgy hand.

'Could *I* have a chigarr . . . pleashe?'

'Certainly.'

Olive rummaged round in the box of Havanas. Then, in a wavering imitation of David, she held the cigar under her reddening nose and made snuffling noises at it.

'Always wanted to try a chigarr . . . but Harold would never let me. He said it wasn't . . . feminine. Though shoving yer hand in the till, of course, is very . . . mashculine!'

'Why don't you let me cut the end of your cigar off for you?' Roy said in an attempt to avert an emotional outburst.

Tearfully Olive shook her head. Then without warning she

bit off the end of her cigar with her false teeth. Grimacing in disgust, she spat several strands of tobacco into the grass. Before she could mutilate the cigar any further, David leaped to his feet and helped her light it. After a flurry of puffing and coughing and with huge tears rolling down her cheeks, she got it going.

'Please, don't upset yourself, Olive love,' Liz pleaded, hovering round her weeping guest. 'What Harold did wasn't your fault....'

Roy held up his hand for silence, for he thought he heard the telephone ring. After listening intently he realised it was his imagination – the third time in the last half-hour he'd been mistaken. He was now very jittery, waiting for the results of the by-election. Brandy bottle in hand, he stood poised under the moonlit apple tree, listening to his heart beating furiously. He was distracted by Olive sobbing by his elbow.

'It's no use you trying to comfort me, Liz,' wailed the distraught widow. 'Nothing'll change the fact that I lived off the ... prosheedings of Harold's thieving for two whole yearshh! In my heart of hearts, I knew he were doing something wrong. I just pretended I didn't!'

Olive lurched to her feet. Before anyone could steady her, she reeled over to the apple tree and wrapped her stubby arms round it.

'It's true! Never once did I arshk where the extra money came from!'

Gasping for breath she pushed herself away from the tree and precariously reeled back to the table.

'If there were any real justice, *I* should be in prison,' she blubbered. 'Like Fred Taplow's soon going to be in prison.'

Liz tried to make her sit down, but Olive was so entrenched in her drunken misery that she brushed Liz aside and sobbed to the midsummer moon.

'That's what's wrong with Britain today. Everyone's like my Harold – trying to rip everyfink off all the time. And we're all of us guilty. Guilty as hell. But we're all such ... hyppercrits that we pretend we're innocent and look the other way. Well, ishthetruth! We're always accusing everyone else of ripping off everything, but we never accuse ourselves!'

To Roy's dismay, she threw her clammy arms round his neck and splashed his cheek with hot tears.

'Yesh, everyone's guilty but you, Roy. I really admire you.'

As Roy tried unsuccessfully to disentangle himself from Olive's dripping embrace, he heard Liz challenge the widow, behind him.

'Why do you admire my husband, Olive?'

'Because he's one of the few in the Party with the guts to stand up against the communists and the Trots. Your husband's put his seat on the line, Liz. And he ain't put his hand in the till like my Harold!'

Another embarrassed pause. Then Roy removed Olive's arms from around his neck and gently but firmly sat her down in her chair. Before she could protest he relit her mangled cigar.

'You shouldn't keep saying these things about him, Olive,' he murmured.

'Why not?'

'Harold only did what he did because he lost his faith in the Party. He was sick of seeing everyone else lining their pockets.'

'That's just what I mean, Roy!' protested Olive, with the cigar clenched between her teeth. 'What kind of a man can become even more corrupt than the Party he belongs to, just to make a protest *against* the Party he belongs to?'

Liz snatched the brandy bottle away from Roy and poured herself a large slug.

'Yes, Olive, but at least your husband was behaving more honestly than people who savage the Party because they know they're not going to reselected!'

Sebastian surged to his feet.

'It's been a nice dinner party, Mum, so for God's sake, don't start in on Dad.'

Roy waved his hand angrily at Sebastian.

'No, son, let her finish!'

Liz started to speak, but Olive knocked her chair over and staggered past her towards the house.

'This cigar's making me feel very . . . queasy.'

David and Wendy rushed forward to help the drunken old lady, but she would have none of it.

'I'm all right, thank you. I know where the bathroom ishh. No, no, I wanna go by meself.'

David opened the door for her as she barged past him into the house. When he returned to the table, he realised the atmosphere was charged, and that Roy and Liz were spoiling for a fight.

'Hey, you two, why are you glaring at each other like that?' Wendy asked, seating herself between the strained husband and wife.

'Doesn't matter,' Liz muttered, her eyes still fixed on Roy's candlelit face. 'It was rude of me to bring it up in front of guests.'

'You can say that again!' Sebastian said, putting his arms behind his head and peering up at the Great Bear in the heavens.

Liz ignored him and went on.

'It's just I'm against witch-hunts, Wendy.'

'Yet you don't seem to mind MacMaster witch-hunting me!' countered Roy.

'Yet, he's right, Liz,' interposed David. 'If there's any witch-hunting in the offing, it's being initiated by MacMaster – and your husband'll be the one that's burnt at the stake.'

'You're just as bad as him, David!'

Smiling, de Quincey savoured his cigar.

'Maybe I'm worse, Liz.'

'What's that supposed to mean?'

'Well, my reselection's coming up the beginning of next year and I don't intend to lose my seat.'

'Don't tell me you're going to be a "real" hero, David, and keep your seat by switching parties?'

There was a pause as the last blackbird stopped singing. David stared steadily into Liz's waiting eyes.

'There's no crime in thinking about changing parties, Liz, is there?'

Liz started to reply, but Wendy thrust her face directly between Liz and her husband.

'You didn't tell *me* you were thinking of switching parties, darling!'

'There's a lot I don't tell you, darling.'

Wendy sulked, then blinked.

'I know. But *why* don't you tell me?'

In the distance a hunting owl hooted. Before answering his wife's soulful accusation, David glanced significantly at his hostess's taut mouth.

'The reason I don't tell you, darling, is because I don't think *I* could cope with a full-time politicized wife.'

Roy was about to intervene on his wife's behalf, but Liz was already on her feet, her brown eyes blazing and her right hand clenched.

'Now you listen to me, David de Quincey. When Roy and I first got married, I wasn't at all "politicized", as you call it! Quite the opposite: I was just an ordinary, unthinking member of the Labour Party. And whatever Roy told me to believe, I believed. But after a while I started thinking for myself.'

She paused for effect, then smiled at her husband.

'Of course, Roy approved of my "thinking" in the beginning, when we were both on the left of the Party. But recently he's started to object to my "thinking" because he's moved farther and farther to the right of the Party . . .!'

To everyone's surprise, Sebastian's voice rang out from the darkness.

'Dad may have moved farther and farther to the right, Mum, but you've also moved farther and farther to the left!'

Disconcerted, Liz swivelled round to face her agitated son.

'And it's because you and Dad have both become extreme, Mum, that recently our house has been like a battleground. And Lexy and I are sick to death of you wrangling all the time!'

'You can say that again!'

Liz and Roy whirled round to confront the shadowy figure of their daughter who was only six feet away from them. Before Roy could stop himself he berated Alexa.

'D'you realise you're late, Alexa?' he shouted. 'It's ten past eleven now!'

'So wot?'

'Now don't you speak to me like that, young lady, or I'll . . .!'

'Oh, don't come all that pompous rubbish, Dad. Be honest for once!'

'I beg your pardon?'

'Yeah, be honest. Well, let's face it – you and Mum were so busy slanging each other, you couldn't've cared less how late I was! Or where I was!'

Alexa had her hands on her hips, with her young breasts thrust forward.

'Anyroad, I wasn't late, Dad. I've been standing there behind that bush of honeysuckle, listening to all you "grown-ups" for at least five minutes. And now if it's all right wiv you, I'm going to bed. Because I'm fed up to the back teeth of hearing that left is right, or right is left, or left is bloody wrong, and right is bloody right!'

The fourteen-year-old girl turned abruptly on her heel and marched across the lawn into the house. Roy was the first to recover.

'Hey, you come back here, my girl! No one uses language like that in front of my guests. Where the devil do you think you're going, Basty?'

Sebastian strode past his father, then snapped back over his shoulder.

'I'm going to bloody bed, Dad!'

'Now you wait one minute, boy . . .!'

Impatiently Liz snatched at her husband's shirtsleeve.

'For Godsake, leave them be! You're enough to make anyone swear.'

Roy yanked his arm away from Liz's clutching fingers.

'Now don't you use them as ammunition, Liz!'

David stood up and cleared his throat hesitantly.

'Yes, well, folks . . . I think Wendy and I had better be going.'

'Yes, I think we had, darling,' breathed his wife. 'You see, we promised our baby-sitter we'd be back by midnight.'

Holding up his arms to make peace, Roy shook his head.

'Now hang on, Wendy, hang on. I don't like the evening ending like this . . .'

Abruptly he trailed off. This time he was certain he could hear the telephone ringing in the living room. Without waiting for his guests' reaction, he ran over the lawn, wrenched open the conservatory door and picked up the receiver.

'Hello?'

For a moment he listened to the voice at the other end, then put his hand over the mouthpiece and called out into the garden.

'David, it's the results!'

'In that case Wendy and I'll hold on.'

'Yes, why don't you all come in and bring the brandy with you?'

Moments later everyone was crowded around the telephone.

'Sorry about that, George, but I've got some guests here. No, no, I'm very glad you rang, George.'

Roy snapped his fingers under David's nose.

'Pen!'

De Quincey handed him his ballpoint.

'Right, fire away, George.'

Roy listened, then turned to his friend triumphantly.

'The Alliance has beaten MacMaster in a surprise result!'

'That's fantastic! Calls for another brandy.'

This was too much for Liz, who flounced out of the room trumpeting: 'You make me heave! You both make me heave!'

Roy waved his wife away, then covered his spare ear with his hand.

'I'm sorry, George, I missed that. Would you repeat it . . .? My God, that really is good news.' Then he turned to de Quincey: 'George said that the Tory pipped Keithley at the post as well!'

'Better and better. Allow me to freshen your glass.'

'Thanks. So what are the details, George?'

Lodging the phone between his shoulder and ear, Roy scribbled rapidly on a small pad.

'Only a forty per cent poll, eh? Arnold (SDP/Liberal Alliance) 543, Royce (Tory) 536, MacMaster (Labour) 511, Sibberton (Tory) 501, Keithley (Labour) 495 . . . Christ, George, it was pretty close, though, wasn't it . . .? Yes, well, perhaps you can give me the full breakdown in the morning . . . What was that?'

Roy paused to register his delight.

'Did MacMaster really say that publicly, George? Well, no one can say your sitting MP is just a "wet, waffling flannel" any more, can they? Yes, well, thanks for calling, George – and you watch out for yourself, too.'

Roy grinned at his guests, then pointedly said into the phone: 'No, I'm being serious, George, watch out for yourself. You know what Robespierre said on the subject? "Once a guillotine starts its good work, no one should ever feel safe. For one head in the basket is never enough!" So if they chop me, George, eventually they'll get round to chopping you, too. Well, thanks again for letting me know. Good night.'

Roy hung up, then swirled the brandy round in his glass, savouring its bouquet.

'Good old George! He's one of the few inside-leg-men I've got left, David. I don't see him very often, but he's always reliable and he's got guts.'

Roy paused, noticing Wendy was puzzled.

'What's the matter, Wendy? The cause has just struck a resounding blow for democracy.'

'Yes, well, I read some French history in the Sixth Form, Roy, and I don't remember Robespierre saying all that stuff about "one head in the basket is never enough".'

Roy swigged back his brandy, then winked.

'Of course you don't remember Robespierre saying it, because he didn't. But I bet he sure as hell wished he had!'

Laughing, Roy clapped de Quincey heartily on the back.

'D'you know what else George told me? He said that MacMaster went crazy when he heard the result announced, and then he publicly put all the blame on me for his losing the election. Seems a lot of people actually accused him of being a communist on their doorsteps!'

De Quincey adopted a deadpan expression and murmured: 'What a dreadful thing to say to a Marxist.'

Then both men sagged at the knees with laughter, clapped each other on the back and danced together round the sofa. Bemused, Wendy watched them, praying their masculine silliness would soon subside so she could drive David home to their children and sanity. Then she put her hand to her mouth nervously, for there in the doorway, arms crossed, stood Liz, with scorn and anger etched on her face. For a grim moment Liz observed the elated antics of the two men until she could contain her contempt no longer.

'How can you two dance around like roosters when all you are celebrating is a blood bath? It's people like you who are tearing the Party to shreds!'

'*We're* tearing the Party to shreds?' laughed Roy derisively.

'Yes!'

'Well, that's certainly original, darling, when it's *me* who's in danger of being chucked out of the Party by the *coms*. And the coms shouldn't be *in* the Party in the first place!'

Furiously shaking her head, Liz was about to launch into an abusive tirade. Then the pale, blotchy figure of Olive Bunting lurched into the doorway.

'I'm terribly sorry, everyone, but I've just been terribly ill ... so I think I'd better go home.'

The clock in the ancient church tower struck the twelve strokes of midnight. Overarched by heavy-leafed yew trees, the crumbling graveyard was swathed in darkness.

Nothing moved between the gravestones save a church mouse which scuttled under a bush as it heard the sly footfalls of humans approaching. As the feet crept closer over the uneven flagstone path, an owl came to rest on the northernmost tip of the belltower. But the humans were too busy to notice the unblinking eyes of the predator, or the fur stiffening on the mouse's neck.

The church clock ticked on imperviously as the couple, shadowed by two giant rowan trees, made their way to the east end of the church. The heavy foliage blotted out the half-moon. A breeze sprang up and there was a sudden whispering through the grass. Then the owl clamped its talons into the mouse's squealing throat.

The girl opened her startled lips to shriek, but before she could utter a sound the man clamped his hand over her mouth. With his free hand he ripped off her panties, pushed her forward onto the tomb and thrust his weapon into her from behind.

'God, that was like being fucked by a whirlwind, Terry!' the girl giggled as she pulled on what was left of her underwear.

'Keep your voice down, for Chrissakes.'

The girl laughed again. Then, clasping Terry's hand, she led him from under the rowan trees into the starlight. The moon came out from behind the first cloud of the evening. As its silvery-white light struck the girl's face, Terry started to count the freckles on her exposed throat. Then his eyes fastened on her Titian-coloured hair, now greenish-coppery in the moonlight. The girl returned his measured gaze. Her strong yet over-wide mouth was still smiling.

'I don't know why, Terry, but I always imagined that you'd be a gentle lover.'

Terry sat down on an adjacent tomb, which he assumed was a pirate's because of the skull and crossbones chiselled into the stone. For a long moment he let his finger tips explore the lichen on the tomb. Then he said: 'According to Angie, I am a gentle lover. Most of the time.'

Joan sat down beside him. She pressured her knee against his thigh but he didn't respond.

'I suppose the reason you were so violent, and are now so withdrawn, is because we got beaten tonight, isn't it?'

Terry laughed, then leaned forward and squeezed her breasts. Instantly she slid her hand towards his groin, but he shook his head and stood up.

'What's the matter now?'

'You may find this hard to believe, Joan, but I feel guilty.'

'You're not married to Angie, for Pete's sake.'

'True, but she is my common-law wife, so I've a moral obligation to her.'

Joan sniggered: ' "There are no morals in politics, only expediency." '

'Who the hell said that?'

'You mean there are quotations of Lenin that you *don't* know?'

Laughing, Terry pulled a sticky pine cone off an overhanging tree. He sniffed at the cone, breathing in its fragrance. Joan crossed the short distance between them.

'You actually love that silly girl, don't you?'

'She isn't "silly". And yes, I do.'

'Then why did you hump me over that tomb just now?'

Terry thought for a moment. Then, noting that the hunting owl was whooping again, he discarded the cone and fixed his storm-grey eyes on the girl's face.

'I screwed you over that tomb because I wanted to, and also because you wanted me to. You see, underneath, you and I are two of a kind. No, don't lower your eyes, woman. You know it's the truth. When it comes down to it, you and I are dangerous intellectual animals who are not frightened of being ruthless.'

He placed his slim fingers either side of her throat.

'In fact, my sweet, we are the new English breed who know what we want. What's more, we intend to get it.'

Without warning, he kissed her hard on the mouth. Responding, she thrust her tongue between his teeth, but he jerked his head away.

'You really are a sensuous bitch, aren't you? Nothing turns you on more than a combination of politics and sex. In fact, I'm sure if I invited you to suck my cock in the middle of one of Mrs Thatcher's Victorian cabinet meetings, you'd jump at it.'

'Damn right I would. But as we haven't got Mrs T. to hand at the moment, I'm just as willing to do it in front of this angel on Jeremiah Thudwacker's gravestone.'

Terry grinned wolfishly, thought about whipping his prick out again, then decided against it.

'Seriously, Terry. What are we going to do now we've been beaten?'

'I always find the scent of blood in the air makes the hackles on my neck rise. Don't you?'

'Scent of whose blood?'

'Hampton's, of course.'

'What exactly are you planning to do to him?'

'Shove a Cruise and two Pershing missiles up his arse and blow the scum right out of the Party!'

'How?'

Terry stroked the roughening stubble on his chin.

'Simple. All I need to do now is to give our Party's "great and impartial" National Executive a little prod.'

'What kind of prod?'

'I'll remind them that Hampton's broken the Rules. Then they'll have no alternative but to throw him out of the Party.'

Joan was unimpressed and drifted round the corner of the church. After a moment's hesitation, Terry followed her.

'Don't you think the NEC will rule in our favour, then, Joan?'

'No, they're bound to procrastinate.'

'I know.'

'So?'

'I'll give them till Parliament's recalled at the beginning of October.'

'And if they dodge the issue in order to maintain good, old-fashioned Party unity? What will you do then?'

'Well, according to the Rules, as Hampton is a *resident* in this constituency, we in the *local* Executive can throw him out of the Party ourselves.'

They were now standing by the churchyard gate, so Terry looked both ways before stepping out into the lamplit street. He was pleased to find the road deserted but for two policemen who already were heading away from the graveyard. The sight of the vanishing Law made them laugh.

'Are you saying, Terry, that whatever the NEC do, we're still going to be able to fry Hampton?'

'To a crisp.'

There was now a mocking gleam in Joan's eyes.

'You think of everything, don't you – darling?'

Terry's mouth tightened. He clenched his fingers round her wrist.

'If you're trying to create a Brave New World, comrade, you've got to do a helluva lot more than just "think". Make sure you remember that when the flak starts to fly in October.'

Joan winced as he increased the pressure on her wrist.

'Don't do that, Terry – it's painful!'

'So is what we're about to do, comrade – and never forget it! This isn't an Oxbridge fun-club. And though you may get some vicarious kicks out of it, you may also get yourself kicked – in the tits. Especially if you lose your nerve when Hampton finds himself in a corner – as he will. And when he's in that corner, he's going to forget all his puritan grammar-school rules, and he's going to start a dirty-tricks campaign. At the moment he believes he'll never stoop that low, because he regards himself as a moral sonovabitch. But when the chips are down and he's facing expulsion from the Party, he won't be able to resist smearing us.'

'There's nothing he can dig up on *me* for his smear campaign,' protested Joan, wrenching her wrist free.

'Isn't there?'

She backed away from his cold gaze.

'There's nothing in my past, Terry, that . . .'

'Stop lying, comrade!'

'I'm not lying!'

Terry smiled with the left side of his mouth, but his eyes were like chips of hail.

'Don't play the innocent with me, sweetheart. I've had you looked into. I know all about your two abortions and your sex-play up at Oxford. I've even seen some of your centrefold snapshots.'

'You bastard!'

Terry encouraged the other side of his mouth to complete the smile.

'I told you we were two of a kind, comrade.'

Before she could interject again, he held up a warning finger under the streetlight.

'We'll talk about it all at Zorba's Café at nine o'clock tomorrow. And don't be late like you were last time.'

She was about to protest when he placed his raised finger over her lips.

'Don't say anything now that you'll regret in the morning. And don't say anything to anybody about tonight. Especially to Angie. Remember, I'm not a middle-class jerk like you're used to dealing with. Tonight you've been slumming with a streetfighter, Miss Keithley. But you'll find if you keep your nose clean and back me to the hilt I'll save your skin – but I'm real mean if I'm double-crossed,' Terry whispered. Then the metallic shimmer in his eyes faded and he was his charming self again.

'By the way, I enjoyed tonight.'

Joan refused to be charmed.

'If you "enjoyed it", comrade, why did you go berserk when the results came through, and then accuse Hampton of smearing you as a communist in front of everyone?'

The revolutionary continued to smile, but without malevolence.

'That was just for public consumption. If I hadn't accused Hampton of slander, I wouldn't have the grounds to write to the NEC, would I? Well, don't just stand there thinking what to say, comrade. Let's just put this evening down to experience. You can always console yourself with the thought that our humping session among the angels would at least have met with Lenin's approval.'

Grinning from ear to ear, he propelled her along the pavement as the church clock struck one.

'And the reason Lenin would've approved of our little blasphemous act on holy ground was because he was always saying: "Religion is the vodka of the people so we must fight religion any way we can. For it's in the interest of the struggle of the classes that we reduce our morals."'

Then he escorted her round the corner and winked: 'We really must do it all again sometime, mustn't we, comrade?'

The church clock struck two.

'You asleep, darling?'

A long pause.

'You're not, are you?'
'I was!'
'Well, I was just thinking . . .'
'Can't you do it with your mouth closed?'
'I'm being serious, Liz.'
'Recently, you've been nothing else.'
Liz opened her eyes and stared at the moonlit ceiling.
'What were you thinking?' she asked wearily.
'Only that we spend over a third of our lives sleeping. Or trying to. Seems such a waste, doesn't it?'
'That's not what you're really thinking.'
'True.'
Roy ached to touch her but didn't.
'What I was really thinking was, well, recently you're . . . so hard to talk to.'
Without moving her tired body, Liz turned her head away from him.
'After your "triumphant" display tonight, what is there to talk about?'
'Don't I at least deserve a cuddle?'
'Oh, I suppose now you're going to accuse me of being frigid!'
'Of course I'm not, darling. It's just . . .'
'Just what?'
'I just want you to understand that as far as MacMaster and Keithley are concerned, well, I had to do what I've done.'
'There was no need to be so cock-a-hoop about it.'
Roy grinned wryly in the dark.
'Now be charitable, darling. It's not often Good wins – anything!'
'I presume by that you're inferring that MacMaster is Evil?'
'No. But he is dangerously misguided and malicious.'
'Rubbish!'
'All right, maybe he's only malicious, but the people who are manipulating him are very dangerous. You see, whether MacMaster knows it or not, he is being manipulated by the Communist Party. So come the revolution, he'll be the first to get the chop because he's still got the odd ideal intact. And there's nothing the CP hates more than ideals.'
Snatching up her pillow, Liz got out of bed.
'Where you going, darling?'

'To the spare room.'

'Why?'

She clutched her pillow against her breasts and glared at him.

'I don't know about you – but I've got to teach in the morning!'

Overtaken by panic, Roy seized his wife's hand.

'Please don't leave me tonight, sweetheart. My mind's whirling.'

For a moment he thought she wouldn't respond. Then with a lifeless sigh she sat down on the bed.

'All right, I'll stay. But stop lecturing me. I've had politics up to here!'

Roy slumped down beside her and tentatively put his arm round her exposed shoulder.

'I know, darling, I know.'

'There's no point in us sitting here like Noddy and Big Ears, is there?'

Roy chortled and climbed over the rumpled coverlet to his side of the bed. Too tired to laugh, Liz crawled in between the sheets. Roy snuggled up behind her and casually stroked his foot against hers.

'Jesus, your feet are like icebergs, Liz.'

'If that's anyone's fault, it's yours!'

Roy nodded and slipped his arm round her waist. She stiffened and he immediately withdrew it.

'Just think of it, darling,' he whispered. 'In less than six weeks we'll be on holiday in Devon. That'll give us time to make peace with each other and ... be loving to each other again. And six weeks is not long to wait.'

'It'll probably be too late nevertheless.'

For a moment he didn't understand her remark. Then slowly he began to realise its implications.

'Are you saying ... you don't love me any more?'

'No. But like you, Roy, I'm also very close to breaking.'

She paused, then said in a flat voice.

'Sometimes I feel I could cry for a week.'

Roy was heartstricken.

'My darling!'

With her head buried in the pillow, Liz allowed herself the luxury of an ironic smile.

'Don't worry, Roy, I won't cry.'

Then she turned to him and sadly stroked her fingertips across his furrowed brow.

'We used to be so close, didn't we?'

'Yes.'

'But unfortunately now, most of the time, you are just – my husband. And the trouble is, Roy, in my opinion, "my husband" is betraying his background and his youth. Our youth – and all our ideals. Well, it's true. When we first met we both used to agree that nearly everything should be nationalised, so that the working man could at last work for himself and for the nation, and not for the bosses. Yet now you seem to be against anything being nationalised.'

'Only because the things that *are* nationalised should be made to work properly before we nationalise anything else.'

Liz sat bolt upright in the bed.

'But even on the unions you've changed! You used to be pro them, and now . . .'

'I still am pro them, Liz. I only ever attack them when I think they're blatantly abusing their power. And by "them" I am of course referring to their leaders. People like Arthur Scargill, Mick McGahey, Ken Gill and Ray Buckton, who all use their unions as power bases to further the communist cause. That's why I believe that maybe it's necessary to legislate, so that the members of a union can vote by secret ballot to determine whether they want to go on strike or not.'

Liz made a scoffing noise and aggressively folded her arms.

'Talk about a Wilsonian U-turn, Roy! Well, when Barbara Castle put forward *In Place of Strife* in the early seventies, I distinctly remember *you* backing Callaghan against her. I remember you saying that *In Place of Strife* was a piece of *anti-*union legislation.'

Roy rubbed his eyes: 'I know I did, darling, but I was naive in those days. Christ, I even thought Wilson was right in those days. Mind, I did say that Shirley Williams and her comprehensive system was going to be a disaster.'

'Oh, I agree Shirl the Pearl's a disaster, but the comprehensive system could be marvellous. It's just dying on its feet because the Tories are starving it of funds.'

'Balls! It was the destruction of the grammar schools that's ruined education!'

Something in Liz snapped. Suddenly she pummelled her fists into his chest. Shocked, Roy reeled back. Then he remembered that the last time she had struck him was after his weekend with Helen. He tried to restrain her, but she went on pounding his rib-cage, whimpering: 'Stop it, Roy, stop it, for Godsake, stop it!'

Then as abruptly as she had started to assault him, she stopped. Roy was so dazed that he could only murmur: 'Well, you started this round off, sweetheart, not me.'

Liz was still panting from her frenzied exertion. Slowly she recovered and wiped her tear-stained face with her forearm. As the harshness of her breathing subsided, she nodded: 'I know, love, I know.'

Then she threw her arms round his neck and sobbed.

'Why are politics always so vicious, Roy? They destroy friendship. Love. Everything.'

She clung to him and rocked to and fro. Then gently she disengaged herself.

'This is getting us nowhere, is it?'

She pressed a corner of the sheet against her moist eyes, then retreated into her pillow, murmuring: 'Well, neither of us are making much sense, are we?'

Roy smiled wistfully as he stroked her tousled hair.

'No, I suppose we're not. There's nothing for it but to try and get some sleep.'

Still smiling, he kissed her lightly on the nose.

'Tomorrow'll be better, love. You'll see.'

Liz continued to stare sightlessly into the darkness.

'Tomorrow has to be better, Roy. It has to be.'

So they lay together, yet apart, with their eyes open. Occasionally their bodies brushed against each other as they turned over and over in their vain quest for sleep. For they knew that only a miracle would make 'tomorrow better'. And they were both certain that there were no such things as miracles in twentieth-century England. At least, not for people like them.

Then, as the church clock struck four, exhaustion overcame them and they were blessed with sleep –

> '. . . that knits up the ravell'd sleeve of care,
> The death of each day's life, sore labour's bath
> Balm of hurt minds. . . .'

AUGUST

Gingerly, Roy's bare feet picked their way over the hot pebbles which stretched out a mile in either direction. As another sharp stone bruised his heel, he couldn't help wondering why this expanse of Devon beach was called Skipton Sands. He paused to mop the salty sweat from his brow, switched the picnic hamper to his other hand, threw the two bathing towels over his left shoulder, then continued his painful descent to the sea. He had been clambering over the shingle now for more than ten minutes.

If only I'd had the sense to bring my tennis shoes, he thought – like the rest of the family, who were bringing up the rear. He paused again so they could catch him up. Then he gazed round him at the half-naked pink and brown bodies soaking up the sun; most of them overweight, too skinny or out of proportion.

Just like my body, he thought, as Liz and his two grumbling, bored children crunched past him over the endless shingle.

In the third week of August the Hamptons were halfway through their annual three-week summer holiday. So it was hardly surprising that the unreliable English weather and unappetising English food were making everyone tetchy.

With his shoulders slouched forward, Roy trudged on. Alexa stopped to wait for him, but she was only waiting to complain.

'God, this is borin', Dad. Summer holidays are a drag at the best of times, so why d'you always make us walk so far before we can strip off and get into the sea? This is only the third hot day we've had since we've been here and all we've done this morning is lumber for miles over this rotten beach!'

'The reason we're walking so far is to get away from these people. I simply can't bear plonking myself down in the middle of all this suntan oil and steaming humanity. It's worse than being in the Commons!'

'You know your problem, Dad? You're a snob.'

'I'm not a snob. Ouch!'

'Those delicate little tootsies've trod on another rock, have they?'

Alexa laughed. Then, to make her point, she ran nimbly over the cascading pebbles, protected by her sneakers.

God, I hate summer holidays in England, Roy thought. Trouble is, on an MP's salary I can't afford to take the whole family to Spain or Italy.

The picnic hamper was now becoming very heavy. Roy called his troops to a halt.

'We can sit here, Liz,' he shouted, dumping the hamper and towels on a patch of coarse sand.

Liz furiously sprinted back to him. With a contemptuous flick of her thumb, she indicated the sun worshippers dotted around them.

'You mean we've walked nearly a bloody mile to find an empty stretch of beach, and now you want us to park ourselves right in the middle of all these roasting sardines?'

Roy nodded hopelessly.

'I thought we'd walked far enough, dear, and there doesn't seem to be an empty stretch of beach anywhere.'

Liz was about to lecture him when they noticed a naked two-year-old happily peeing on the beach in front of his besotted parents. Four yards to the boy's left, an eighteen-stone woman struggled under a minute towel to prise her enormous breasts out of her bra. The struggle ended with one of her blotched udders lobbing itself over the top of the towel into general view. The two-year-old, having finished peeing, pointed his podgy fist at the woman's teat, shouting: 'Look, Mummy, look!'

Roy threw his eyes to heaven, but Liz was quick to comment: 'No use looking up there for help. This is a disastrous holiday and we might as well face it.'

Roy grunted, then nodded as he slumped to his knees and unzipped their picnic bag. Immediately his children joined him, demanding food. As they bickered about who was going to eat what, Roy unpacked the chilled container and spread the slices of ham, cold roast pork and corned beef onto four paper plates. Next he pulled out the Devon baps, tomatoes and cucumber. While Alexa and Sebastian fought over who was going to cut up the pork pie, he produced a bottle of cold Alsace Sylvaner and a corkscrew. He glanced up to watch Liz climbing into her black swimsuit, with the aid of two judiciously-wrapped bathing towels. Dismayed, he registered the lines of tension round his wife's eyes. Then he wrenched the stubborn cork out of the wine bottle.

But his mind was elsewhere. While he sloshed wine into Liz's paper cup and tried to control his irritation with his argumentative children, he couldn't help thinking: I wonder what MacMaster's doing now? I'm sure he's having a better time than I am. That's the trouble with being an MP. You work such ridiculously unsocial hours that when you eventually get a break for a holiday, you're so tense, neurotic and anxious that you're incapable of enjoying yourself. Yet there's no point in my staying in London during the Summer Recess, because there's nothing I can do.

Roy emptied his paper cupful of wine in one swig. Then he stood up and made his way over the shingle down to the sea's edge. Ice-cold foam swirled round his aching feet. Even the speedboats screaming in the middle distance and the huge oil tanker on the horizon faded to insignificance in the awesome presence of the sea. For though the sun was beating down onto Shakespeare's 'wild and wasteful ocean', the sea remained hungrily grey-green below its frothing surface and infinitely forbidding – reminding him that he was a proud member of an island race.

Yes, these cold miles of heartless water are the reason we've been conquered so rarely. Yet now we are in danger of being conquered from *within*. Although the summer folk around me, drinking in the sunlight, don't realise it.

Perhaps that's for the best. They have enough to concern them as it is. Some of them are bound to be unemployed or worried about their jobs; or perhaps their parents are dying, or their children are being badly schooled, or their marriages are in tatters. And apart from this brief lull in their humdrum existences, they have nothing to recharge their batteries. Most of them have to endure their tedious factory lives for forty-eight weeks of the year, saving up their crumpled pound notes for a measly three-week summer holiday. Christ Almighty, to save up a whole lousy year for three weeks of this!

Then his thoughts drifted to MacMaster again. Although over the last few weeks he had rehearsed seemingly every permutation of what he could do to MacMaster, or what MacMaster could do to him, he still found his mind was always drawn back to his adversary.

Well, he thought, gazing out at the glittering sea, I suppose we've reached a kind of stalemate. I've written to the NEC to ask them to investigate Macmaster and his 'Trottish' friends, and he's also written to the NEC demanding that I be expelled. But other than an ambiguous acknowledgement from the NEC, so far I've had no response. Maybe MacMaster's fared better with his request. Though I doubt it. Most of the NEC are on holiday at the moment – either at Blackpool or on the Black Sea! In any case, they're bound to want to postpone their decision on such a contentious matter as my expulsion from the Party. Especially as the right wingers on the NEC will naturally want to support me, whereas left wingers like Meacher and Heffer will be only too pleased if I am consigned to political oblivion.

Roy rubbed his scalp because of the intense heat, wishing he'd brought his cricketing sunhat with him.

Yet what the hell can I do to protect myself?

Unless the NEC comes out in my favour, MacMaster's still got me by the short and curlies. As I'm a resident in my own constituency, he can persuade our GMC to expel me from the Party themselves. And as long as the GMC adheres to the rules, there is no way that the NEC can prevent MacMaster expelling me.

Sebastian and Alexa came jogging down the beach in their swimming costumes. They waved to their father cheerily as they ran into the waves. Seconds later, Liz, in her sleek one-piece bathing suit, crunched past him over the pebbles. But she neither waved nor glanced at him. As she hesitantly submerged herself in the cold water, he couldn't help admiring her slim shoulders and girlish, Botticelli neck. True, she had a little weight on her bottom, but her waist and bust were still firm and youthful. Then she ducked her head under the foam. When she emerged, dripping with spray, she waved to him. He waved back and wished to God he'd learned to swim when he was at grammar school.

Perhaps I *should* smear MacMaster and Keithley, he thought. But instead of leaking it directly to the press, maybe it would be safer, and more subtle, if I got that Nightingale creature to send all his filth to the NEC direct. Yes ... then the NEC would realise that if they didn't take action against MacMaster and Keithley, I would eventually make all the defamatory material public myself, with very damaging results to the Party as a whole. In fact, the more I think about the idea, the more attractive it becomes. . . .

He was unable to develop this dubious line of thinking any further, for someone tapped him on the shoulder. It took a moment to gather his thoughts and focus on the intruder.

'Don't stand there goggle-eyed, Roy. Let's go for a drink.'
'What are you doing here, David?'
'We're visiting Wendy's parents in Dartmouth.'
'Incredible!'
'What's so incredible about it?'
'We're staying in Dartmouth too.'
De Quincey tipped back his head and gave a staccato laugh.
'Are your family on the beach then, David?'
'Yes, Wendy and the kids are over in that cove. The twins are so fair-skinned we always have to find some shade. So what about us having a jar?'
'Won't Wendy mind if we slope off?'

Twenty minutes later, the two MPs were sitting in the sweet-smelling garden of the Green Dragon, which was perched on the brow of a hill overlooking the sea. For several minutes there was an appreciative silence between the two men as they sipped the local Hackawton brew. They were already on their second halves and intended to have more, for the Green Dragon sold thirteen different kinds of real ale.

'It's wonderful to have the opportunity of sampling so many different breweries. It's a bit like wine-tasting – except that you don't have to spit any of it out.'
'Yes, you can't beat English hops, can you, David?'
'No. German beer and Danish lager are all very well, but this is the real taste of England.'
Yes, Roy thought as they watched a bee drone onto the stamen of a wild rose, an English pub garden is unique.
De Quincey finished his beer. He was about to speak his mind to Roy when Roy swept up their empty glasses.
'It's my round, isn't it?' he said as he hurried back into the

Green Dragon. While he was gone, David studied a storm cloud which was passing over the sun.

Then, glancing downwards, he realised the cloud was casting a mottled shadow on the pub's white plastered walls. He smiled as a house martin swooped out of the eaves before zig-zagging over the orchard. Then the sun burst out from behind the cloud, and once more the garden was washed in shimmering light.

If only life could always be as bright and expectant as this, David thought, as he watched his friend with a glass of beer in either hand striding through the buttercups on the uncut lawn.

Roy set the glasses down on the wrought-iron table. As they savoured their beer, he said: 'On our way here, David, you implied you had a definite reason for our having a drink together. What is it?'

David wiped a trickle of ale from his lip, then screwed up his eyes and grinned: 'I think I can do something to alleviate your current *Weltschmerz*.'

'My what?'

De Quincey laughed.

'*Weltschmerz*. It's German for "world-hurt" or "world-weariness".'

'Why, have you discovered a panacea for my problems, then?'

'Well, if you do what I have just done, Roy, you'll immediately get a new political lease of life,' murmured David, putting on his sunglasses.

'I don't believe it!' Roy protested, suddenly realising what his friend had been hinting at from the moment they left the beach. 'You haven't, David. You can't have!'

'Yes, it was announced last night on the Nine O'Clock News.'

'How the hell could you get on the Nine O'Clock News stuck down here in Devon?'

'Drove over to the BBC studios in Plymouth, didn't I?'

'And you just . . .?'

'. . . Announced that I was joining the Liberal Party – yes.'

'Holy shit!'

David guffawed, then addressed himself to his half-pint of Directors with renewed relish.

'Now, don't get your knickers in a twist, Roy. I'm not suggesting you become a Liberal.'

'Glad to hear it!'

'I think you're more suited to the SDP.'

'But I can't bear Shirley, and Owen's an ambitious Flash Harry, and Roy's worn-out.'

'Yes, but there are younger people who are now joining the SDP, who would have joined the Labour Party in the good old days. Which is why the SDP is your natural home, Roy.'

'Now wait a minute . . .?'

'Oh, come on, Roy, you know perfectly well the SDP has got much the same policies as the old Labour Party had before Harold Wilson muddied the waters. If you were honest with yourself, you'd admit that they are the politics you're fighting for now. Well, you believe we need a prices-and-incomes policy, don't you?'

'Yes, but. . . .'

'There are no "buts", Roy. Either we control inflation Maggie's way, which means high unemployment and a lot of suffering. Or you try to control it Kinnock's way, which means you hold down prices and pray the unions will control wages. Either way, the result is a mess. Whereas with the SDP's statutory prices-and-incomes policy . . .'

'Yes, of course I agree with a prices-and-incomes policy,' Roy interrupted, waving his glass. 'But I wouldn't dream of joining the SDP until someone in the SDP can explain to me how a prices-and-incomes policy can be *enforced* on the unions. Oh, I know you all say you'll take "tough action to control private monopolies and stop unnecessary price rises in the nationalised industries". But you'll be resisted so fiercely by both the private and the public sectors that your prices-and-incomes policy will be on the scrapheap within months of the Alliance taking office. That's if they ever do take office, which seems to be highly unlikely!'

'Yes, but if more people like you and me leave the Party, Roy, then the electorate will eventually come to trust us. That's why it's our job to recruit as many of the disillusioned right wingers as we can.'

'You mean as many as *you* can?'

'OK, OK. But you just think it over, and you'll find that you agree with far more of the SDP's policies than you do with the present Labour Party's policies.'

'I don't know about that. . .'

'Yes, you do, Roy. You're a multilateralist who believes we

need American bases in the UK – like the SDP. Also you believe in the importance of contributing to NATO – as do the SDP. And you think we should have more decentralisation. You're a great advocate of a mixed economy. You don't want anything else nationalised. You also want the trades unions reformed. All of which the SDP want as well.'

Roy pushed his chair back into a cluster of buttercups. A sky-blue butterfly flitted past. To his horror it was snapped up by a thrush's beak. Upset, Roy turned away. Sometimes he found nature so predatory that he was almost glad he was a human being.

'Don't let the fate of a butterfly distract you, Roy. You know you have far more in common with the SDP than you do with Kinnock's Labour Party.'

Roy shook his head.

'Oh, I know there are several policies which I have in common with the SDP, David, but. . . .'

'Only several?'

'All right, quite a few! But there are also some I disagree with passionately.'

'Such as?'

'Well . . . the SDP's middle-class support for the public schools and for private beds in the National Health.'

'So you're against freedom of choice?'

'You bet I am, when only the rich can afford to have this so-called freedom of choice! Also, I'm not at all pro-Europe. Oh, I'm not saying that we can get out of it now, but I blame the Tories, the Liberals and some of my own right-wing Labour friends for getting us into the Common Market in the first place.'

'You're splitting hairs, Roy.'

Roy stood up, his head swimming because of the heat and the fermented hops.

'All right, David, let me put it in a nutshell. The SDP's leadership structure is blatantly undemocratic, and its entire support is middle-class. Also it has no real base in the unions, so therefore it has no genuine working-class support. I'm not saying it needed to have turned out like this. On the contrary, it's a great shame that someone like Callaghan didn't take the initiative in the seventies to denounce the hard left as potential totalitarians. Then, as the leader, he could have broken away from the Marxist part of the Labour Party and taken with him all the right wingers and moderates. Then together Callaghan and the moderates could have formed a new Democratic Labour Party. That way, the hard left would have been seen for the Marxists they are, so no one would have voted for them. Unfortunately this didn't happen. Only the self-seeking, middle-class right wingers went over to form the new party, which is why the SDP has such a soft centre. . . .'

David's barking laugh stopped Roy in mid-flow.

'What's so bloody funny?'

'You are, Roy.'

'Why?'

'You've fallen for my story, hook, line, and sinker, haven't you?'

'Story?'

'Of course.'

'You mean . . . you haven't joined the Liberals?'

'Not yet. But I am thinking about it.'

'You . . . Byzantine bastard!'

De Quincey threw his head back and another machine-gun burst of laughter chattered from his throat. Furious, Roy surged to his feet.

'Why, in God's name, did you go through all that pretence about announcing it on Radio Plymouth when. . .?'

'I wanted to see how you'd react.'

'You mean if *I'd* been willing to join the SDP, then *you'd* follow suit and join the Liberals?'

'Something like that.'

David stopped laughing. His blue eyes and tanned, lean features had a strained look to them.

'What I'm trying to say, Roy, is I haven't your guts. Or even your convictions. But if and when you decide to, well, move over, there's a fair chance you'll find me at your elbow.'

David paused to remove his sunglasses, because there were speckles of pollen on the left lens. He breathed onto the smoky glass, then polished the lens on his trouser leg.

'Though if you don't decide to move soon, Roy,' he went on, not looking at his friend, 'I may have to find some guts of my own – and move by myself. Because unless I agree to eat huge wodges of humble pie, which will be kindly provided by my Trot on my return from this holiday, then I'm certain to lose my seat come my reselection next year.' He paused again to put on his glasses. 'So if I want to stay in politics, I may have no choice but to join the Liberals.'

Roy's mouth snapped open to reply, but he was distracted by the approach of Liz, Sebastian, Alexa, Wendy and the twins, walking towards them over the lawn.

'I think we'd better discuss this another time, David, don't you?'

David smiled, then stood up to greet Liz. But before their wives converged on them, he couldn't resist a final barb.

'Whether you like it or not, old friend, the Alliance is the only home we've got left – and if we don't join – and very soon – we might have to walk the streets and find some *real* work.'

Roy didn't reply, for he heard Helen whispering to his subconscious: 'In the end you'll join us in the Alliance, darling, because you've nowhere else to go – except into my bed. . . .'

SEPTEMBER

The early September moon was at its full, the dome of the Dartmouth sky fretted with stars. At a quarter to two in the morning on the last day of the Hamptons' holiday, Roy was sitting by himself in a deckchair on the moonlit lawn. He glanced at the clock tower to his right as the single stroke for the quarter-hour resounded across Dartmouth's silent estuary. Smiling, he stared intently at the shapes of the sailing boats, bobbing their fairy lights on the black water below. For the last four years the Hamptons had rented this fisherman's cottage because it was high on Jawbones Hill, with a small garden overlooking the whole of the estuary.

The wind whipped the bottoms of Roy's cotton trousers against his ankles. Shivering, he crossed his legs and zipped up his anorak. He wondered if he was going crazy. He knew his family, who were sensibly tucked up in their beds, regarded his plan as perverse. And when he announced he needed to be alone under the stars before setting off on his pilgrimage, they told him he was growing more eccentric by the hour. He could still hear Liz saying: 'Well, if you want to go on this nonstop driving antic, more fool you. Frankly, I've had enough of your strangeness over this holiday. So why don't you take my Mini and tootle off by yourself. I'm only too happy to drive the kids back in the estate.'

Roy continued to smile in the darkness, knowing his forthcoming pilgrimage was eccentric, which was why it was so attractive to him. He stood up and stretched his arms towards the moon. His midnight vigil was almost over. He felt like one of Chaucer's pilgrims, so to get himself into the right mood he intoned to the stars:

> 'Befelle, that, in that seson on a day,
> In Southwark at the Tabard as I lay,

>   Redy to wenden on my pilgrimage
>   To Canterbury with devoute corage....'

But he couldn't remember any more, so he glanced back at the boats in the estuary, recalling that Chaucer's pilgrim, the Shipman, actually came from 'Dertemouth'. Then he fastened his eyes on the shadowy towers of Dartmouth Castle which lowered down over the mouth of the estuary.

Yes, this is as good a place as any to start a whirlwind pilgrimage. For it was here that Richard Coeur de Lion assembled a hundred ships and two thousand men for his crusade against Saladin, and here that seven-hundred-and-fifty men sailed in thirty-one ships to the Siege of Calais.

The church clock struck two. It was time for him to begin his journey into the past. With a parting glance at the historic estuary as a night fishing boat chugged out towards the open sea, he climbed the steep hill to Liz's Mini.

He drove for an hour and twenty-two minutes through swirling mist. Around him stretched the forbidding wastes of Dartmoor. Already he had been forced to stop several times because of the fog. Each time he had thought he was lost, but he dared not step outside to ascertain his bearings, for the fog's malevolence made his skin crawl. Eventually he nerved himself to drive onto a muddy verge. According to his map he had arrived at the first stage of his pilgrimage. Then, bracing himself, he climbed out of the car.

Tendrils of mist groped at him out of the darkness. The fine hairs on his neck prickled as the adrenalin pumped through him. It was now three in the morning, and he was standing barely half a mile away from Princetown, in the centre of Dartmoor. On his left were the high, spiked walls of Dartmoor Prison. On his right lay nothing but thirty square miles of sodden moorland. The infamous Princetown drizzle streamed out of the darkness. Although the only sound he could hear was the rain falling on the quagmires and the hammering of his own heart, he thought he heard the howl of the Hound of the Baskervilles. He was sure the slithering noise to his left was an escaped convict scaling the prison walls....

Stifling the scream in his throat, he wrenched open the car

door. He knew he had been foolish to come to one of the eeriest spots of England, but he felt he should experience at first hand what it was like to be imprisoned in the Devil's own landscape. He needed to savour the metallic taste of fear on his tongue.

How can I appreciate the light if I do not peer into the darkness?

As he drove away from the mist-shrouded prison, he thought it no wonder that the prison exuded cruelty and despair. It was still as grim and oppressive as when it was first built. And, like so much of England, it was still being used long after it should have been destroyed.

After navigating across twenty miles of sinister moorland, Roy passed with a sense of relief through the deserted town of Tavistock. As dawn approached, he motored through Camelford on the second stage of his pilgrimage. Checking the rumpled map of Cornwall on his knee, he turned sharp right. Five miles to go now. The eastern sky, touching the Cornish hills, was pale primrose.

Moments later Roy had arrived and was clambering up the lichened rocks. As he reached the summit, the dawn sun rose out of the hills and illuminated Tintagel, King Arthur's castle. The impact of history and myth was magnified because the crag, crowned with the ruined castle, was only joined to the mainland by a narrow isthmus. Wherever Roy looked there were precipitate coal-black cliffs pounded by ocean.

The sun rose higher. In Roy's imagination – and it was to fuel his imagination he had come – Arthur Pendragon's castle seemed to be rebuilding itself to its original glory, in a sheet of flame. Allowing the vision to expand and possess him, for one moment of suspended time he was in the world of living legend. He saw Uther Pendragon seduce the beautiful Igerna . . . and she, during a triumphant dawn such as this, gave birth to the Once and Future King. . . .

Then he covered his eyes as a sword of light, like Excalibur, seared through his sockets and stunned his mind. For a full minute he stood with his eyes closed, the dawn sun in his face. Then he realised it was the sun that had blinded him, not Arthur's sword. When he opened his eyes he started laughing at himself, for he knew King Arthur had never lived – except, of course, in every English heart.

And that's all that matters, he thought. Because Arthur is one of England's sacred myths, and myths are the spiritual lifeblood of the nation. For I know the cavern below the castle is not Merlin's cave, but I still need to believe that Merlin's spectre haunts its recesses. And one day I hope to see the rare Cornish chough which the locals say is Arthur himself, reincarnated as a bird.

As Roy climbed into his car to set off on the next stage of his romantic pilgrimage, he thanked his stars he was born an Englishman, who could, with a little effort and a little travelling, renew the spirit of his heritage so swiftly, yet so deeply.

While Roy was winding his way to Exeter, Terry MacMaster was asleep in his Victorian basement, dreaming of bright, new council houses, surrounded by the fresh green of young trees. And behind the trees, there were towering, highly-productive factories with gleaming murals, in which no worker laboured for more than twenty hours a week. Then, as Terry's dream continued to blossom, he turned over and snuggled up against Angie's delicious bottom. He now found himself high on the steps of Windsor Castle, with a blood-red flag cracking in the wind from the turret above. Below him were sixty million people, all chanting his name. As the entire nation sent up a paean of praise, he extended his arms to them – and his arms stretched out to infinity.

This is what Lenin must have felt like, he thought, when he took Russia by storm.

Then, as Winston Churchill, Attlee, Macmillan and Margaret Thatcher were crawling up the steps of Windsor Castle to offer him Caesar's laurel crown – which he was planning to refuse – Terry suddenly saw the lone figure of Roy Hampton, wielding a great broadsword which flashed like blue lightning in the dazzling sunlight. To Terry's dismay, the MP sprouted angel's wings and flew over the adoring multitude of the revolutionary's subjects, with the sword held high above him. And, as the sword descended on the Socialist Saviour's head, Terry read the fiery lettering on its blade: 'I am the sword of your misspent youth, MacMaster, and when the truth is revealed I will fall upon you and your career!'

'You bastard, Hampton!'

Angie jerked awake and saw her lover, sitting bolt-upright, shaking his fist at the dawn. Terry's forehead was awash with sweat and he was trembling. Tentatively Angie put her arm round his shoulder and pulled him closer to her.

'It's all right, baby. You've just had a bad dream.'

'Yes, but if Hampton's got any dirt on me, Angie – that is, any real dirt! – where do you think he keeps it? In a safe in his house? Or at the Commons?'

Momentarily Angie looked puzzled. Then she realised Terry was voicing his latest obsession about the MP. Only yesterday he had told her that he had heard from one of his legmen that Hampton had discovered about his cheating at the LSE, his thieving from Foyles, and the Baker Street Classic usherette's abortion. But Angie still didn't know about his brief homosexual student affair with his New Zealand roommate. At the last moment Terry had lost his nerve and failed to tell her about it. Yet it was that affair that was now revolving in his mind. For he was certain that if Hampton had acquired the dirt on the affair and decided to spill it to the press, Terry's political credibility would be destroyed.

'Just think what a mess Hampton could create, Angie, if he's actually been smart enough to dig up some eyewitnesses and got some statements from them.'

'You mean about the abortion you made that poor girl have?'

'Yes! And if he has got statements about the abortion, the question is: does he keep the stuff in his house?'

'Well, if he does, Terry, wot can you do about it?' sighed Angie, stifling a yawn.

'I could get a friend to have a look, couldn't I?'

'You mean ... you'll get him to break into Hampton's house?'

'I wouldn't call it "breaking in", exactly.'

'Wot *would* you call it, then?'

'Well, more of a little look-round. Now don't you start getting all moral, Angie. Remember he's having a good time at the moment on holiday. He's not having to rot away like we are in this shit-hole!'

Angie shook her amber curls vigorously and wagged a finger at him.

'Now come on, Terry. Just because he's having a smashing

time on some rotten beach, it don't mean you've got to behave like a louse.'

'It's Hampton that's the louse, not me. Well, he's the one who's planning to smear me!'

'How do you *know* he's planning to smear you?'

For a moment Terry was nonplussed, so Angie pressed home her rare advantage.

'Terry, face facts. If Hampton was planning to smear you, why hasn't he done it already?' Fact, why didn't he do it during the by-election campaign when it would've hurt you most? No, don't try and wriggle out of it! You know damn well that whatever else Hampton is, he's basically a decent bloke. Like you are. And as he hasn't smeared you, I hope to God you won't break into his house while he's on holiday.'

Terry was distracted by a bluebottle buzzing against the windowpane. The fly reminded him of something. Then he remembered. He had been sitting in the dining room at County Hall, with Fat Phil stuffing himself on profiteroles and telling him how to recruit the long-term unemployed and the OAPs, and there had been a bluebottle tapping at the window.

Yes, he thought, I wonder what Fat Phil would do if he was about to be smeared by someone like Hampton?

Terry closed his eyes in disgust, because he knew perfectly well that Fat Phil 'would take whatever action was necessary'.

Angie watched her lover as he struggled with his conscience.

'Now don't do somefink you'll regret, Terry.'

'I've got to think about it, luv. And I've got to think about it quick, because I've heard from my sources that Hampton gets home from his holiday tonight.'

'There's nothing to fink about, Terry. You mustn't do it!'

'Don't worry, luv.'

The revolutionary leaped out of bed.

'Where you going, Terry?'

'Thought I'd take a jog round the council estate. It's so depressing that it might help me to see things clearer. Then, who knows . . .?'

For the third time since beginning the ascent, Roy paused for breath. He was a hundred yards from the top of the ancient tor which was crowned with the fourteenth-century Tower of St

Michael. Breathing deeply, he unfurled his shirtsleeve and mopped his damp neck with it. It was now three o'clock on a very hot September afternoon and Roy was feeling his age. The car journey had taken him longer than he expected.

Five more steps and he was on the summit of the 'Rendezvous of the Dead'. He had climbed Glastonbury Tor because, according to Arthurian legend, Glastonbury was the mysterious Isle of Avalon. Perspiring but elated, he subsided on the worn grass beside the tower and gazed down over the ancient town. Tourists wandered past him, but he saw only a black barge drifting on the twilit waters, with the dying Once and Future King trailing his hand among the water lilies.

As he conjured up the vision of his childhood, when for hours he had devoured books on King Arthur, Tennyson's words came back to him. He heard Sir Bedivere's plaintive cry to the wounded king, after the Battle of Camlann had destroyed the Fellowship of the Round Table:

> ' "Ah! my Lord Arthur, whither shall I go?
> For now I see the true old times are dead;
> But now the whole ROUND TABLE is dissolved
> Which was an image of the mighty world;
> And I, the last, go forth companionless,
> And the days darken round me, and the years,
> Among new men, strange faces, other minds." '

He found the poem so apposite to his own life that his eyes started to smart, as they had in Clare's churchyard. He rubbed his eyelids fiercely. The last thing he wanted to do was blubber like a child. As he stared sightlessly at the sun-etched ruins of Glastonbury, he remembered fragments of Arthur's words to the desolate Bedivere:

> ' "The old order changeth, yielding place to new,
> And God fulfils himself in many ways,
> Lest one good custom should corrupt the world . . .
> But now farewell. I am going a long way . . .
> To the island valley of Avilon;
> Where falls not hail, or rain, or any snow. . . ."
> So said he and the barge with oar and sail
> Moved from the brink, like some full-breasted swan
> That, fluting a wild carol ere her death,

Ruffles her pure cold plume and takes the flood
With swarthy webs. Long stood Sir Bedivere
Revolving many memories, till the hull
Look'd one black dot against the verge of dawn. . . .'

As the words faded, Roy found he was also standing and 'revolving many memories'. But below him there was not 'one black dot against the verge of dawn' but dozens of multi-coloured, two-legged dots, patrolling the roofless ruins of the abbey. He was tempted to run down the green flanks of the tor and find the bronze inscription among the ruins: 'Here lie the bodies of King Arthur and Queen Guinevere.' But he knew that the nourishment the Arthurian myth was giving him would be shortlived once inside the abbey gates. The sight of the children looking bored with the abbey, and their parents looking bored with their children, would be enough to destroy any fantasy. As he was desperate to hold on to his Golden-Age image of England, if only for one day, his instinct told him to drive out of Glastonbury while the myth was still resounding in his head.

After an elaborate cream tea in the village of Milton Cleveland, Roy whistled along the road. It was still hot, so he had both windows open. Late-afternoon blackbirds carolled in the sun-dappled hedgerows. His spirits were high, for he was now on the last stage of his eccentric pilgrimage. Within the hour it would be over and life would return to normal. Then within twenty-four hours MacMaster would be on his heels. He smiled as he sped between two juggernauts. He felt like Orestes, pursued by the Eumenides.

Why do the myths have such a hold on us? he thought. When we're confronted with the mythical soul of England, it gives us false courage. Places like Tintagel and Glastonbury, with their heroic legends, make us feel that we too are capable of heroic acts. Because, deep in the well of our being, there is still the essence of an England that now seems lost. The desire still exists to ring the cathedral bells inside ourselves. But, sadly, we have to steep ourselves in our legendary past in order to hear the faint reverberations of those bells.

Roy turned off towards the village of Hanging Longford. The

name suited his mood. He had not slept for thirty-six hours, and felt it would be wise to find some woodland copse and take a nap before completing his pilgrimage. He wanted to prolong the dying moments of his perfect day.

More people should try going on a pilgrimage, he thought, as he parked on the outskirts of the village. And if some people find the Arthurian legend isn't to their taste, there must be other well-springs of England they can go in quest of. There must be other places, in other landscapes, that will refresh their spirits and once more awaken their love and belief in their own secret England. For everyone has their own secret England.

He was now strolling in Grovely Wood. The twilit sun filtered through the moss-stained trunks as the first leaves drifted down in the warm air. He selected a sunlit grove, surrounded by giant copper beeches, and threw himself down on a bed of leaves. As he closed his eyes, he remembered making love to Liz, when they were first engaged, in a similar beech grove. Then there were those happy days when he and Sebastian played frisbee among the beech trees in Epping Forest....

Yes, he thought, growing sleepy ... yes ... that was when Lexi lost her Snoopy-dog and we spent hours searching for it, and Liz did nothing but laugh, and Sebastian did nothing but complain that his horrid little sister was ruining the game. Perhaps I should have brought them with me on my pilgrimage. Perhaps I don't share my secret self enough with them. Or with anyone. But then, who does? Who is brave enough to? Christ, we all love this wonderful, maddening, absurdly green, mythical, anachronistic island of ours. But we're so inhibited, so frightened of being patriotic, even in the best sense, that we pretend we don't need to love our country. We pretend it's chauvinistic to be romantically patriotic. Maybe that's why, as a race, we have so little confidence in ourselves. We don't dare to believe that the nation that had the greatest empire in the history of the world should be allowed to have a second bite of the cherry.

The fast-fading sunlight played across his bewildered features as his sleepy mind ticked from thought to thought.

... But then we are the first nation to have had a parliamentary democracy, a constitutional monarchy, an industrial revolution and a trades union movement. And you have to pay for being first! The penalty is that our parliamentary democracy has to function without a written constitution, and so is open to continual abuse. Our constitutional monarchy is the source of our class system, with its accompanying snobbery. And the results of our industrial revolution are Victorian factories and antiquated trades unions. So I believe we can only make our national dreams into a vibrant reality if we regain confidence in ourselves as a nation. No other nation on earth – and especially, God help us, the French! – is bashful when it comes to proclaiming their national genius. Who's ever heard of a Frenchman that's modest about being French?

Thinking about the French brought on an attack of heartburn. Roy jerked awake and thought he had gone blind in his sleep. Wherever he peered there was darkness. Shaking, he held his right hand in front of him. He was relieved to make out its silhouette against the rising moon. Then he remembered he had fallen asleep in Grovely Wood, without completing his pilgrimage.

Once inside the car, he hurtled off into the night.

He had been driving for half an hour when a distant church clock struck eleven. He glanced out of the window. There, grey and forbidding under the lowering night sky, stood the vast Celtic shrine. He flicked out his indicator and bumped on to the deserted path. Then he climbed out of the Mini and crossed to the fence overlooking Salisbury Plain. Below him was the awesome spectacle of Stonehenge in the moonlight, but he made no attempt to move away from the intruding traffic noises behind him. He needed to see whether the pagan cathedral of stones could transcend the oil fumes and the rattling exhausts. Slowly the belching petrol was superseded by a greater reality, which emanated from the towering bluestones in the moon-washed field.

As Roy gazed at this wonder of the world, built in the dawn of history, he completed his Arthurian journey and watched Merlin building Stonehenge, with the help of the Devil. . . .

Then he was distracted, for several people were moving among the stones. They must have broken through the barbed-wire fence, he thought, to daub graffiti on the Slaughter Stone. Or, worse, to chip their initials into one of the lintels.

Roy headed for the car. If he hadn't been so tired, he would have called the police or chased away the vandals himself. Then he remembered the old lady who had her bag snatched on the Eden Council Estate.

I wasn't able to catch the thieves then, and they were much nearer. Imagine what a fool I'd make of myself, chasing some fleet-footed hippie round the Slaughter Stone.

He was easing the Mini into the inside lane when he felt the warning vibrations. For a moment he thought he was suffering a psychic reaction to Stonehenge, but as he increased speed he knew that something had happened at home – to his family! His children's distraught faces were blotted out by the oncoming headlights.

For the next two-and-a-half hours Roy drove like a dervish. As he swung into Nobs' Row, he knew something was very wrong. It was almost two in the morning and his house was ablaze with light. Before he could get out of the car, the front door swung open and Sebastian charged down the steps.

'What the hell's going on, son?'

'We've been burgled, Dad!'

'Oh, no!'

'The place has been ransacked. Anything worth anything's been taken. And all Mum's jewellery!'

At that moment the church clock struck two.

Roy raced up the steps into the house. As he came into the living room, the raw smell of Dettol hit his nostrils. At first he could not understand what was happening. Liz was on her knees in the middle of their beige carpet, with a policeman standing over her.

For a long moment Roy wavered in the doorway, taking in the devastation. At a glance he saw that the cushions on the sofa were split open. There were feathers everywhere. The contents of Liz's desk were strewn in the fireplace.

'Where's Lexi, darling?'

'She's upstairs, trying to put her room back together.'

Roy shook his head.

'What the hell are you doing on your knees?'

'I'm cleaning up after the filthy swine!'

As Liz looked up, he could see she had been crying. In her right hand she clenched a dripping sponge which she thrust back into the bucket of disinfectant.

'You mean, the thieves actually . . .?'

The uniformed policeman, a red-faced veteran in his late fifties, nodded.

'Yeah, I'm afraid so, sir. They also excreted in the kitchen.'

'Jesus Christ!'

Roy touched his wife's shoulder.

'Are you ... all right, darling?'

'Never felt better. Well, there's nothing like coming home from a disastrous holiday only to find every piece of jewellery stolen. Then to make things really dandy, you have to go down on your hands and knees to clean up the bastards' shit.'

'I'll clean it up, darling.'

'Too late! I've done it.'

Biting her lip, Liz picked up the bucket and left the room. The policeman cleared his throat.

'I understand from your wife, sir, that this is the first time you've been done over?'

'Yes, officer.'

'Well, all I can say, sir – and it's no consolation – is you've been bloody lucky, living in Nobs' Row as you do.'

Roy smiled bleakly.

'If I were you, sir, I'd have a large Scotch. It'll help your blood pressure.'

'Can I get you one, officer?'

'No, thank you, sir. Got a long night ahead of me.'

Roy poured himself a Scotch from the decanter.

'Why did the thieves ... do it on the carpet? Was it contempt, or fear?'

'Both, I'm afraid, sir. Mind, you could've had it worse. Before the War they were quite fond of doing it in the beds.'

Revolted by the thought, Roy set the Scotch down without drinking it.

'Don't suppose you'll catch whoever did it, will you?'

'We'll try to, sir. But this looks like an amateur job to me. Probably some black kids or young tearaways.'

The policeman shook his finger and pointed to the mantlepiece.

'I'd rather you didn't touch them glasses, sir. As you can see, them are the ones the thieves drank out of. Might be worth calling in the fingerprint boys in the morning to give them a brush-over. Though I'm afraid I can't hold out much hope. What's so funny, sir?'

Roy stopped laughing and sipped his Scotch.

'Nothing, officer. It's just that I've been promising my neighbours for months that I'd have a burglar alarm put in.'

The stocky policeman guffawed, then stopped abruptly.

'Sorry, sir. No offence. But burglar alarms are all very well as window-dressing. And it's true an alarm might've stopped the laddies who've done your place over, but not even Fort-bleeding-Knox can deter a real professional. Still, that's modern Britain for you, ent it? Gets worse every day. Even when we do catch the scum, the judges go soft on 'em. So what can we do?'

'Surely Mrs Thatcher and her hit-boys are always coming up with new, inspiring, draconian ideas on law and order?'

'They help a bit, I suppose. But until we start locking up some of the rough stuff and throwing away the key, there'll always be steaming turds on someone's carpets. Well, 'night, sir. I'll come back for the details first thing in the morning. That is, unless you want me to . . .?'

'No, no. I think we're too tired to make any sense tonight.'

'That's how I feel most of the time, sir.'

Still smiling wryly, the policeman trudged towards the door.

The following evening, Angie was shredding a dozen giant carrots with her ancient grater. Behind her Terry paced the length of their dilapidated kitchen.

'Look, will you please stop accusing me, Angie?'

'It's not that I don't want to believe you, Terry. I do, but . . .'

Terry grabbed Angie's wrist and prised the carrot-grater away from her.

'Will you stop playing with them fucking carrots and listen to me?'

'You're hurting me, Terry! And I've told you before, if you hurt me I'll leave you.'

Terry stared at her balefully, then shrugged and released her.

'I'm sorry, luv, but the strain is getting to me a bit. And if *you* don't believe I'm innocent, who else will?'

Angie pouted, then swung out of the kitchen. Nonplussed, Terry followed her into their living area, which was in its usual disarray. His dressing gown was strewn over the fender, and Angie had discarded her panties, two pairs of rainbow-coloured tights and her pink denim skirt onto the threadbare rug. But the Marilyn Monroe of Lamberton North was oblivious as she picked her way through the debris, to the bookshelf which was strategically situated under the portrait of Leon Trotsky. She snaked her hand behind Mao's *Little Red Book*, flanked by the Penguin biography of Tito and Lenin's *Left-Wing Communism, an Infantile Disorder*. After a struggle, to Terry's surprise she pulled out a miniature Bible.

'I thought you'd thrown that away, Angie! Like we agreed.'

Angie puckered her lips.

'I couldn't, Terry. See, when you're out at meetings I like to – dip into it sometimes.'

'You don't actually read that slop, do you?'

'Sometimes. Can be very comforting. 'Specially round Christmas and Easter.'

She seized his hand and pressed it onto the faded black cover of the Bible.

'Now, Terry, I want you to swear on this that you didn't send round one of your mates to do over the Hampton place.'

'What?'

'Don't say "wot", Terry; just swear.'

The revolutionary, taken aback by the quaintness of the request, chortled.

'Wot's so funny about "swearing", Terry, if you're telling the truth?'

'All right, luv, don't go all sulky. I'll swear on this pile of crap if it'll make you happy.'

'But will that mean you're telling the truth, Terry?'

'Depends what you mean by "the truth", luv,' he said, his eyes continuing to laugh. 'Well, in a country like ours, which is so politically and socially divided, the truth is relative, isn't it? I mean, what I think is the truth, an imperious bitch like Thatcher would say was all lies. In the same way as I would accuse Thatcher of lying every time she evades a question or steam-rollers a questioner – which, let's face it, she's always doing! So who is telling the truth, eh?'

'Oh, don't start that philosophical garbage again, Terry. Just swear you weren't responsible for the break-in and I'll believe you.'

Terry thought a moment, then took a deep breath. He was about to swear when he paused and looked puzzled.

'Angie, why is it so important to you that I didn't organise the Hampton burglary?'

'Because I couldn't marry a man who did a fing like that! Yeah, I know you thieved from Foyles, fiddled your exams and also forced that poor kid to have an abortion. But you were still a student then – and you're supposed to be a man now. And I need to respect that man. So swear!'

For several seconds Terry gazed into his girlfriend's unblinking eyes. Then he leaned forward and gently kissed her forehead.

'Wot's that meant to mean, Terry?'

He smiled.

'I don't need a Bible to swear on, Angie, when I've got *you* to swear on. Which is a damn good thing, because I don't believe in the Bible. Though, heaven help me, I do believe in you.'

To reaffirm his oath, Terry kissed Angie full on the mouth. She didn't respond but she decided to believe him, so harmony was restored to the MacMaster household.

The Hampton household took longer to recover.

Even Liz was surprised how badly she reacted to the burglary. She developed a tic under her left eye, and had a tendency to jump if anyone came into the room without warning, or if someone rang the front door bell when she was alone in the house. She felt as if she had been personally molested.

However hard she tried not to think about the burglary, she couldn't forget the stench of human excrement on the carpet. In her mind's eye she could see the violent hands ransacking the intimate drawers of her dressing table. Sometimes she would wake up feeling as if her own body had been pawed over and soiled. They had stolen all her jewellery, including a Napoleonic bee brooch that Roy had given her as an engagement present, and one of the thieves had torn the cups out of her silk brassiere and ejaculated into her underwear. They had even scattered her sanitary towels over the bathroom, lolled on her bed and spilt gin on her pillow.

It was not only the burglary that had jangled her nerves. She was also very tense waiting for the new Parliamentary session to begin. She was aware that once the MPs returned from their summer recess, the Labour Party's National Executive Committee would be forced to rule on the Hampton/MacMaster controversy. Then the NEC would either find in her husband's favour and brand MacMaster and Keithley as Trotskyites, or they would find in MacMaster's favour and expel her husband from the Party. But although her family did their utmost to comfort her, the nervous tic under her eye continued to trouble her. Roy tried to persuade her to go to the doctor's, but she refused.

'But why won't you even discuss what's eating you, Liz?' he snapped one evening after dinner.

'You know what's eating me. It's this bloody waiting! Especially as I know that at the end of the waiting, there's only disaster!'

OCTOBER

The revolutionary and the Welsh MP sat opposite one another in Zorba's Café, on Lamberton High Street. Terry ordered them both a mugful of tea which the Greek proprietor slopped down in front of them. Then Emrys Glendower, MP, brushed his perfectly trimmed fingernails through his receding hair and glanced round the workman's café. It was already half past nine, but the café was still three-quarters full. Despite the ground frost outside, which was only just beginning to melt, the MP felt compelled to remove his grey herringbone overcoat. The steam generated by the tea machine was making the café unbearably hot. As Glendower sat down again, Terry smiled and remembered that the last time he'd talked with an MP in Zorba's Café had been back in March. And Roy Hampton was on the menu then, as he was now.

Still smiling, Terry studied the Welshman's fine bone structure and physically approved of what he saw. There was not a spare ounce of flesh on either Glendower's face or his supple body. To add to his natural attraction, Emrys had glittering, tawny eyes and an imperious but beguiling mouth. The MP seemed in no hurry to open the conversation, so Terry stirred a spoonful of sugar into his tea.

'Well, I must say, Mr Glendower, it's a surprising honour that an illustrious member of our great National Executive should deign to come out to the sticks, simply to sup tea with yours truly.'

Glendower beamed his best Rhondda Valley smile.

'OK, let's skip the footwork,' Terry said, tracing his finger round the hot rim of his mug. 'Presumably you've come down here to tell me why the NEC persist in dragging their feet on the question of Roy Hampton's expulsion?'

Emrys paused while the Greek proprietor slid a greasy plate

of egg, bacon, tomatoes and sausages in front of him. Then he wrinkled his hooked nose as he noted the underdone fat on the three rashers of bacon. Suddenly the idea of a 'typically English breakfast' ceased to appeal. Terry was becoming impatient.

'Well, you *have* come down here to tell me why the NEC are dragging their feet on the question of Hampton's expulsion, haven't you?'

The Welshman fingered the scratched handle of his knife, then murmured: 'Not exactly.'

'What d'you mean "not exactly"?'

Carefully Emrys cut the fat off his bacon.

'What I'm trying to say, Mr MacMaster, is that I am primarily here as the representative of the National Executive Committee, who are at present considering the possibility of holding an inquiry into the composition of your local General Management Committee.'

'You're going to do what?'

'Are you sure you wouldn't care for some breakfast?'

'Look, don't play funny-buggers with me, Mr Glendower!'

'All right, if you want it spelt out. We on the National Executive have heard that there are some members of your local GMC who may also belong to *other* political parties.'

Terry spluttered into his tea.

'Hampton's put you up to this, hasn't he?'

Emrys was now enjoying the yolk of his fried egg, which was the only properly cooked item on his plate. As Terry watched him eat, he found it hard to disguise his irritation. Unconsciously he chinked the salt cellar against the pepper pot.

'Well, it *was* Hampton who put you up to it, wasn't it?'

'Yes. In fact, one of us on the NEC was planning to come down here a couple of months ago, but we've been snowed under with so much business that we've only just got round to seeing if there are grounds for an enquiry.'

Pointedly Emrys regarded Terry's twitching fingers. The younger man grunted and placed the condiments back in their original position. Terry felt breathless but managed a wry grin.

'If you want to see if there are grounds for an enquiry, Mr Glendower, why don't you come to our GMC tonight and look everyone over?'

The Welshman returned Terry's grin.

'I fully intend to.'

Then Emrys thought for a moment and added innocently: '*You* don't belong to a party other than the Labour Party, by any chance, do you, Mr MacMaster?'

'Course I bloody don't!'

'I see.'

Sweeping the condiments to one side with the back of his hand, Terry leaned forward.

'Are you saying you've got something on me, Mr Glendower? Or on anyone else on our GMC?'

Glendower continued to smile, but his eyes darkened.

'I'm not saying anything yet, Mr MacMaster. I've simply popped down here to see if there are any ... irregularities. Well, you never can tell till you've looked, can you?'

Terry decided it was best to go on the offensive, so he leaned back and deliberately crossed his arms.

'You don't have to look our GMC over, Mr Glendower. We go by the book down here. That's why we want Hampton thrown out; because *he* doesn't go by the book, or believe in party discipline. He's a muck-stirrer, a wrecker and an anti-partyist!'

'Ah, well, that's the other reason I've come down, see. Because we on the NEC want things slowed up a bit, *vis-á-vis* Mr Hampton.'

Terry grinned and took another sip of his sugary tea, then laughed openly.

'So our Great Leader is getting jittery, is he? Doesn't want us little minnows here in Lamberton to make waves.'

Terry went on laughing, because he could see that his sarcasm over the Party's leadership had a chastening effect on the Welshman's confidence. Uneasily, Glendower glanced round the café at the other slurping occupants.

'Look, Mr MacMaster, it's tricky for our leader at the moment.'

'Ever known a time when it *isn't* tricky for our leader?'

'Now you listen, MacMaster! If you push Hampton's expulsion through, it'll create a lot of bad publicity which'll lose us votes!'

'Well, all I can say to that, Mr Glendower, is if you want to gain power, you've got to be seen by the general public to be the complete alternative to Thatcher's authoritarianism. The only way you can do that is by cleaning out the Party's nest first! It's true. And if you, Kinnock, Hattersley and the rest didn't always sit on the Party fence, we could kick all these shitty right-wing traitors out of the nest into the arms of the Alliance, where they belong. Then we could make our Party into the radical socialist party the electorate want us to be, and really get something done in this lousy country!'

The revolutionary's outburst made the Welshman nervous.

'For Godsake, don't get so excited, Mr MacMaster. Everything you want to happen to the Party is happening in any case.'

'It's not happening quick enough!'

Angry blood suffused the Welshman's face.

'That's the trouble with you lot!' he snapped. 'You're in such a bloody hurry to revolutionise the Party, you don't give a fig if you lose the grassroots' support in the process!'

With a flick of his manicured thumb, Emrys indicated the working men in the café, diligently mopping the bacon grease off their plates with slices of processed bread.

'Well, it's the folk in here that provide us with the support we need, Mr MacMaster.'

'Yes, but that's your trouble, "comrade". All you lot care about *is* their rotten support! Because you know damn well if you don't get their scabby votes every four years, you won't be able to jump back on the parliamentary gravy train!'

Emrys tried to interject, but Terry dismissed him with a flourish of his fork.

'You've got no defence, Glendower. Well, to most of you in that antiquated pile laughingly called the Commons, politics is just another career. Whereas we, in the grass-roots, genuinely want to cut unemployment out of this nation and give the workers back their bleeding dignity!'

'Hey, where you going, MacMaster?'

Terry was now standing and counting out the money for his mug of tea.

'I haven't got time to hang around here listening to a Welsh party-hack whose only interest seems to be in slowing up justice. Especially as there are heads to be lopped!'

With a contemptuous flourish, the revolutionary tossed twenty pence on to the formica-topped table. Then he paused by the door as the beginning of a dangerous smile turned up the left corner of his mouth.

'But do come to our GMC tonight, comrade. Well, I'd hate

our Great Leader not to be informed about any little "irregularities" that might occur."

Terry tugged open the café door.

'Plus, of course, I've a . . . bijou motion of my own that I'm going to propose tonight, which might vaguely interest Comrade Kinnock.'

Wearing a scarlet tracksuit, Roy lumbered bearlike along the gravel path bisecting Lamberton Park. Although he felt the jogging was placing a strain on his pounding heart, he was determined to keep up the pace. Besides, he liked the sound of his plimsolls thudding on the frosty ground. The October sunlight streamed into his eyes through the horse chestnuts overhanging the path. The sight of the white plumes of his breath in the cold air made him feel glad to be alive. In the far corner of the park, three middle-aged gardeners shovelled dead leaves on to a bonfire. Closer, two sisters with identical pigtails chased each other down the children's slide.

For the first time for several weeks Roy was not thinking about MacMaster. He was thinking about last night's row with Liz. Recently she had become so highly strung and aggressive that he dreaded coming home in the evening. The strain of waiting for the NEC's decision was also beginning to take its toll on him.

A pair of lanky legs in a blue tracksuit jogged up beside him.

'What's with all this running, then, Dad?'

'I thought a stately little jog would clear my brain, son,' Roy said, smiling. 'That's if it doesn't kill me, of course.'

'You're still worried about the MacMaster business, aren't you?'

'I'm not worried, son, it's just. . . .'

'Oh, come on, Dad, you've got worry written all over your face. You know damn well the NEC won't find in your favour.'

Roy gulped down another frosty lungful of air, then shook his head.

'There's still a chance they might.'

Sebastian saw that Roy was getting puffed so he slowed down the pace. He was longing to ask his father something but didn't know how to phrase it. Then he blurted it out.

'Are you going to smear MacMaster and that woman, Dad?'

Though Roy was experiencing a sharp twinge just below his heart, he was so taken aback by his son's question that he increased his speed.

'Who told you I was thinking of smearing them?'

'Mum told me. She didn't tell me how you were going to smear them, though.'

'She shouldn't have told you anything!'

'Why not?'

'Because . . . well, she shouldn't have. Anyway, I'm not going to smear them! Shouldn't you be at school?'

'Got the day off to revise for my chemistry exam.'

'D'you think you'll get all your A-Levels?'

'Hope so. Worked hard enough.'

They were now running in the open again, but already Roy was wondering how much longer he could keep it up. They passed two snoring tramps on a bench, under piles of old newspapers. Then they jogged by an eighteen-year-old boy who was leaning against a tree and drinking heavily from a bottle of Cyprus sherry. As they ran on, Roy panted: 'That lad looks like he's got a real drinking problem – and he's only your age, son.'

'Is it surprising?'

'What d'you mean?'

'He's obviously one of those school-leavers without a job, isn't he?' Sebastian said. 'People like Thatcher and Nigel Lawson should come and look at places like this. Then perhaps they wouldn't be so bloody callous. Well, every day more and more kids are tipped out of school straight into the trash can. And all because Thatcher and her hit men don't give a bugger!'

Roy gave his son a hard look, but Sebastian was too consumed with anger to recant.

'It's all right you looking like that, Dad, but you've got a job!'

'Only just.'

'Yes, but if you lose your job, it will only be as a result of your political convictions. But those eighteen-year-olds, messing about on the baby-swings over there, haven't been given a choice. They've probably been out of work since they left school in July. What's more, they'll probably still be out of work this time next year.'

'Perhaps they didn't work as hard at school as you've been working, son?'

'Even if I do get all my A-Levels with good grades, Dad, and go to Cambridge, it doesn't mean that in four years' time I won't be in the same situation myself.'

'I know, I know,' puffed his father, labouring to keep up with his son. 'There's no doubt about it, Thatcher's a heartless bitch. And all those schemes her cronies keep setting up are only wallpaper to cover the cracks. You're right. If we don't do something drastic soon, we'll end up with a demoralised, lost generation. If those kids aren't given work, they'll turn to crime, or drugs, or drink – or probably all three! And who can blame 'em? Then they'll be perfect cannon fodder for clever sods like MacMaster. . . .'

Roy trailed off, cursing himself for inadvertently bringing up the subject of MacMaster. Now jogging slightly in front of his father, Sebastian twisted his face round to study Roy's features.

'Dad?'

'Yes?'

'I just want you to know. . . .'

'What?'

Sebastian hesitated and slowed his pace. Then, brushing his floppy hair back with his hand, he said: 'Though I hate politics – and I really do – I still want you to know that I respect you for standing up to the bastards. And especially for not smearing them. Because a lot of people *would* have smeared them!'

Roy smiled at his son.

'Thank you, Basty. I appreciate that more than I can say.'

Still running, Sebastian reached out and touched his father's shoulder. Impulsively Roy seized his son's hand and squeezed it hard.

'Sometimes I bet you want to give in, don't you, Dad?'

Roy grinned inanely.

'Shows, does it?'

'Yes. And Mum should back you up and not keep bitching you.'

'She does back me up.'

'Oh, come on, Dad. . . .'

'As far as she can. You've got to remember she thinks I'm a bit of a class traitor. Mind, that's the trouble with this country. It's obsessed with class. Ouch!'

Roy let out a yelp of pain and brought himself up short. Sebastian, who was striding ahead, turned quickly, then ran back to comfort his father.

'What's the matter, Dad?'

'Got a stitch!' Roy gasped, clutching his side. Then he hobbled forward, putting all his weight on his left foot.

'And I've also got cramp in my big toe. Jesus, I'm a bloody wreck.'

Laughing, Sebastian pointed to a bench.

'Sit down here, Dad, and have a breather.'

Roy was about to follow his advice when Sebastian jabbed a finger at the powdery-white stain on the seat.

'Don't sit there!'

'God, you're right. If it isn't yobbos, it's pigeons.'

With a laugh, Roy limped to the other end of the bench and plonked himself down.

'Dad, do you think that MacMaster and Co. will succeed in getting you thrown out?'

'There's a fair chance.'

'What will you do if you are thrown out?'

'Go on fighting, I suppose.'

'How?'

Roy unlaced his running shoe, then prised it off his cramped foot.

'Don't know yet. Jesus! Not only got cramp but I think I'm developing chilblains.'

'Dad, d'you really believe that if we go on the way we are we could end up with, well, a communist-type government?'

'Certainly on the cards.'

Sebastian was not convinced. He stared at the cold October sunlight on the bed of yellow chrysanthemums.

'Most of my friends at school think the greatest danger is coming from the Tory Party, who are moving farther and farther to the right. They say that as a result of Tory policies we'll eventually end up with some sort of Fascism.'

'That's also possible. But the hard left's alternative is equally undesirable: a siege economy, no nuclear defence, out of Europe and NATO, plus nationalising the banks, building societies and everything else that comes to hand. Whichever way you look at it, the whole thing's out of control.'

Roy paused, noticing a slim middle-aged man with receding hair who was waving at him from the other side of the chrysanthemum bed. Then he recognised the waver and shook his head.

'Good heavens. I don't believe it!'

'Don't believe what?' asked Sebastian.

'Emrys Glendower. In Lamberton.'

Glendower grinned, then undid the top button of his overcoat and extended his hand.

'You gave me a stitch just watching you jog, Roy.'

'What the hell you doing out here in the wilds?' Roy asked, shaking the Welshman's hand.

'Your next-door neighbour told me you'd gone for a run in the park, so I thought I'd join you.'

Glendower's smile was now even broader, which irritated Roy because it showed a perfect set of over-large teeth.

'Aren't you going to introduce me to your lad? Well, you are his son, aren't you, boyo?'

'Sometimes,' Sebastian replied.

Glendower grinned and thrust his hands on his hips.

'Chip off the old ambiguous block, eh?'

'Sebastian couldn't be as ambiguous as you, Emrys, if he tried.'

'Touché, Roy, touché – as we have to say in the Common Market.'

With his customary flourish, Glendower sat down on the bench. Sebastian smirked, for the MP had lowered his posterior onto the flaking pile of pigeon shit. Emrys made himself comfortable, then smiled in the boy's direction.

'Sebastian, would you be offended if I asked for a private word with your Da?'

'Of course not.'

Sebastian stood up and glanced at his father pointedly, then back at Glendower.

'Now you take it easy, Dad. And watch out for yourself.'

Appreciatively Roy smiled at his son's suspicion. It was gratifying to know your own flesh and blood wanted to protect you from Welsh wizards.

'Well, nice meeting you, Mr Glendower,' Sebastian said as he ran off under the horse chestnuts.

'Nice meeting you, Sebastian. Fine strapping boy you got there, Roy.'

Relieved to find he no longer had a stitch, Roy stood up.

'Look, stop playing funny-buggers, Emrys, and tell me what you're doing out here.'

'Oh, c'mon, boyo, you know why I'm here,' Glendower responded, opening his innocent-looking brownish-green eyes to their full. 'It was you who invited me down, remember?'

'Jesus Christ, of course! You've come down here on behalf of the NEC, haven't you? In response to my letter.'

Glendower's eyes smiled weakly.

'That's what I've been trying to tell you since I arrived, boyo.'

Roy clutched his side and a flicker of pain creased his brow.

'Oh, you don't need to look concerned, Emrys. I'm not going to drop dead. I've never felt so fit in my whole bloody life.'

Roy set off at a brisk pace along the path. Glendower caught him up.

'Well, now I'm here, Roy, you can rely on me to see whether there are grounds for an enquiry. For, like you, I am totally against any infiltration into the Party. From whatever source.'

Aware that Glendower was scrutinizing him, Roy went on the attack.

'Presumably you're going to have words with MacMaster and his unholy crew while you're down here?'

'Just this minute have. With MacMaster, that is.'

'And?'

'Looks like you were right, Roy. About the irregularities.'

With a great effort Roy kept walking, though it was difficult to control the excitement inside him.

'I knew it! I knew there were irregularities.'

'Indeed, one irregularity is very irregular,' continued the Welshman, absently nodding at a leaf as it drifted with a seesaw movement out of the branches.

'Well, if it's very irregular, Emrys, it can only be MacMaster himself.'

'No, it's not MacMaster, Roy,' Glendower cooed. 'It's you.'

'Now, wait a minute, Glendower . . .!'

'No, *you* wait a minute, boyo!' cut in the Welshman. 'You're the one who rocked the boat by telling the great unwashed not to vote for that horrible little Trot!'

Roy was dumbfounded. 'Then you agree MacMaster *is* a Trot?'

'Course I do.'

'If you agree, then why the blazes . . .?'

'In private, I agree he is a Trot.'

This was too much for Roy.

'Oh, you two-faced sonova . . .!'

Glendower thrust his hands in his overcoat pockets and smiled.

'Now, now, Roy. Where's your self-control? It's all this name-calling that's going to get you strung up.'

Roy tried to interrupt but Glendower warded him off with a dismissive gesture.

'Stop being so shrill, man. You know as well as I do that even some of the reasonable left wingers, like myself, are under pressure in the constituencies because of the reselection procedures. So there's no way we can witch-hunt these bastards just for their views. No, no, I insist you hear me out, boyo!' he snapped as they set off again along the gravel path. 'Believe me, the only way we can get these bastards out of the Party is if they are stupid enough to proclaim they belong to an alien organisation. But MacMaster's far too shrewd an operator to do that. So if we try to hunt him and his kind out of the Party, it's us who'll be tossed out on our necks. That even includes folk like me who have genuine left-wing sympathies!'

Roy laughed derisively.

'*You* with "genuine left-wing sympathies"? Oh, come on, Emrys, you're just a sit-on-the-fence-I-love-Neil-Kinnock-hack! What's more, you know you are.'

'I'm no hack, Hampton. I'm on the National Executive, for Chrissakes!'

'Exactly. So how dare you accuse those of us who still believe in a democratic Labour Party of trying to witch-hunt the coms and Trots, when the coms and the Trots shouldn't be in the party in the first place? Especially when you know damn well that it's the coms and the Trots who are in fact witch-hunting us!'

'Now, be reasonable, Roy. We on the Executive have stamped on organisations like Militant as hard as we can. . . .'

'You call expelling three-and-a-half people "stamping on" 'em?'

'For Chrissake, we can't do miracles, Roy!' protested Glendower. 'All this witch-hunting has got to stop! Like Neil keeps saying: it's our job now to heal the wounds and emphasise party unity. Otherwise the public will never trust us again. And talking of miracles, I'm going to try to persuade MacMaster not to expel you this November.'

'Oh, thanks a million.'

'Instead, I'm going to suggest they deprive you of your seat in December when you come up for reselection.'

Glendower beamed.

'Be much less messy that way, don't you see?'

Roy snorted: 'You really are a nasty little creep, aren't you?'

Glendower pretended he hadn't heard. With the inside of his foot, he brushed several sodden leaves off the gravel path to reveal some patrolling woodlice. As he crushed the woodlice under his heel, he went on smiling.

'Mind, there is a more sophisticated way of dealing with this little difficulty of ours, Roy.'

Roy raised an eyebrow.

'You mean it would be more sophisticated if I simply tied a millstone round my neck and jumped off Westminster Bridge, waving the Red Flag?'

Glendower scuffed his heel against a stone to ensure that no slimy fragments of the crushed insects were stuck to his shoe.

'Well, I must admit, Roy, that would certainly make things easier all round. But seriously....'

'Oh, there's nothing I like more than being serious, Emrys.'

'Quite. Which is, I'm sure, why you won't mind doing the Party one last service.'

'What service did you have in mind?'

'Your resignation, of course. And the quicker the better.'

With that, Glendower set off across the grass, leaving Roy, stunned, on the gravel path. The Welshman did not look back.

At dusk the same evening, Roy let himself out of the house, clutching his briefcase and car keys. There was frost in the air. He paused by his car to look up at the early stars as the northeast wind rattled the dying leaves in his next-door neighbour-but-one's magnolia tree. He realised the last time he had noticed the tree was in early spring.

Yes, he thought, as he allowed his car keys to clink against his thigh, that was the sunlit morning when I longed to be a tree – if only for a day. So that I could have petals on my fingertips, with all the world and his wife praising my splendour. Unfortunately, now I'm in the same position as that magnolia. What political blossoms I had have been stripped off by the

Marxist wind, or have been left to rot on the bough by the hacks in my own party.

As he unlocked his car, he remembered Helen walking towards him over the lawn at Ufferton.

Perhaps I should call her up now, he thought, and ask her what I should do to gain a victory over MacMaster.

'Off to the House for another late session, eh, Roy?'

Roy blinked.

'I say, are you all right, old chap?' continued Adrian Royce, his next-door neighbour.

Roy nodded, then hovered under the yellowish light from the streetlamp.

'Sorry, Adrian – I'm afraid I didn't catch what you said.'

'I asked if you were off to the House for another late session.'

'Yes. Unfortunately. Though I wish to God they'd do away with these all-night sittings.'

His suave neighbour tipped his black bowler to a more rakish angle.

'Well, rumour has it in the City that soon you won't be attending any more sittings of . . . any kind, old boy?'

Roy grimaced.

'Even the City knows, huh?'

'Yes, so I don't know why you bother to go on pretending.'

Roy unlocked the car and climbed inside.

'Pretending what?'

'Oh, stop being so obtuse, old fellow. You're one of us at heart – and you know it.'

Infuriated by Adrian's drawled vowels, Roy barked at his neighbour: 'I'm not "one of you at heart" at all, Adrian. I may be many things, but I'm no sodding Tory!'

'C'mon, old boy. No one would blame you for being a closest Tory, considering the way your party is treating you at the moment. Surely this is the perfect opportunity to switch parties like Reg Prentice did!'

'Switch parties? Have you gone crazy, Adrian?'

'Certainly not. Everyone knows that our party is the only safe party. At least Mrs Thatcher doesn't spend money we don't have simply to invent ephemeral jobs.'

Roy jumped out of the car and waved his forefinger under Adrian's surprised nose.

'Don't tell me about that unfeeling bitch, Adrian. She not

only thinks she's Queen Elizabeth II – she's now beginning to believe she's Elizabeth I as well! And what you call her "safe" fiscal policy is costing this nation the loss of hundreds of jobs every day. Well, she and Ronald Reagan are so in love with each another, they're both taking their countries on "Maggie's Monetarist Mystery Tour". And it's immoral that our destinies should be decided by the market-place pirates. Oh, I'm not saying that sound finance isn't important. Of course it is. But it doesn't solve everything, and it certainly makes the rich richer and the poor poorer. It's no use you shaking your head, Adrian. In her own way Thatcher is just as doctrinaire as the Marxists. And to make things worse, she never listens to anyone except her own maniacal right wing! So now everything is under threat, the Health Service, education, the pensioners, the unemployed. . . .'

'All right, Roy, no need to have a seizure. I'm the first to admit that some of your criticisms have a grain of truth in them. But whatever else you accuse Maggie of, including those lies about her dismantling the Health Service and ruining education, one thing you *can't* accuse her of is trying to make the power of the state supreme. Which is what a lot of your "comrades" in the Labour Party want to do. And, believe me, anything is preferable to Mr Benn and his inevitable gulag!'

'Yes, on that score I agree with you, Adrian. But I'm saying that we don't need *either* of those extremes. I would prefer a middle way. Something more on the lines of a new type of . . . well, astringent Gaitskellism.'

Adrian laughed loudly.

'What's so funny?'

'The idea of you wanting "astringent Gaitskellism" is bloody funny.'

'Why's it funny?'

'Because Gaitskell's bloody dead, old chap! And so's right-wing Labour. And you bloody well know it is.'

Adrian stopped laughing and placed his gloved hand on Roy's forearm.

'What's more, old boy, if you go on fighting for something that's dead, you deserve all that's coming to you.'

Roy chuckled.

'I'm glad you find it amusing, old boy.'

'Sorry, Adrian, but laughing's less tiring than blubbering,' Roy said, returning to his car.

As he climbed in, he called over his shoulder: 'Well, I enjoyed our little chat, Adrian. Oh, and do give my regards to Sara, won't you?'

He was about to drive off when he noticed a pained looked in his neighbour's eyes.

'Something wrong, Adrian?'

'Yes. Sara's had to go into hospital.'

'Oh, I'm sorry,' Roy muttered, concerned. 'What's she in hospital for?'

'A hysterectomy. And there may be complications.'

'God, I am sorry.'

'Thanks,' muttered Adrian as he trudged up the path to his front door.

Roy called after him: 'It's a bitch of a life, isn't it?'

'Yes, and there's rarely an upturn, is there?'

Then Adrian disappeared into the house, slamming the door behind him.

Terry recognised the girl's slim brown legs the moment he saw them ascend the bus stairwell. Usually he would never have dreamed of going up to the smoking section, but the sight of that chassis moving heavenward was too tempting to resist. Besides, the bus was crowded downstairs and he had already given up his seat for an elderly cripple. So, excusing himself, he manoeuvred his way along the jostling gangway and ran up the stairs.

Seconds later, he was pressing his muscular thigh against the girl's. She was gazing through the bus window at the lighted shops and pedestrians and didn't respond. So Terry fondled her knee surreptitiously. Insulted, she snapped her head round to reprimand him for his sexual impertinence. Before she could voice her complaint, Terry grinned at her.

'Now, now, Joanie. Don't get your knickers in a twist.'

'Oh you bastard!' laughed Joan.

'Well, you always recognise my voice on the phone, sweetie, so I was sure you'd recognise my knee.'

'Christ, you've got a cheek, Terry. Considering the only time I've felt your knee was in a fucking graveyard.'

They both laughed. Then Joan became serious: 'I'm glad we've met up like this.'

'So am I.'

'That's not what I mean.'

Terry studied her solemn face, then raised an eyebrow.

'What's on your mind, lover?'

She hesitated, wishing he would stop his scrutiny.

'I'm worried about what you said to me on the phone this afternoon, Terry.'

'You mean about Hampton?'

'Yes.' Again she hesitated, self-consciously stroking her earlobe.

Terry snorted derisively: 'I see. So that Welsh MP's not only been sniffing around you, he's actually been giving you advice?'

Joan nodded, then thrust her tapered hands into the pockets of her blue denim jacket.

'He insisted on buying me a cup of tea.'

'Join the club.'

'Oh, I know he's a slimy inside-leg merchant, Terry, but tactically I think he's correct.'

'About what?'

Joan cleared her throat and flipped a packet of Gauloise out of the breast pocket of her shirt. She was about to light a cigarette when Terry snatched it from her and threw it on the floor of the bus, then ground it under his heel.

'You don't need drugs to answer my question, comrade. You said you thought Glendower was tactically correct. About what?'

The redhead shrugged, then parted her lips to reply. But Terry came back at her.

'And do keep your voice down, comrade.'

He inclined his head to take in the other passengers who were smoking and chatting on their way home from work. Joan nodded to show she understood. She was about to answer Terry when the West Indian bus conductress asked for their fares. Terry grunted and paid for them both.

'Well, Joan, tell me what Glendower was tactically correct about?'

The girl lowered her slate-green eyes as she angled her body round to face him.

'I think Glendower is right when he says that we shouldn't throw Hampton out of the Party, as you're proposing.'

The revolutionary's eyes narrowed. Joan couldn't be sure whether it was because of what she said, or whether he was screwing them up against the cigarette smoke drifting in layers down the length of the bus.

'Pray continue, comrade.'

'Well, instead of throwing Hampton out of the Party, Terry, I think we should simply dump him at his reselection in December. No, please let me finish. If we throw Hampton out of the Party now, the press will make us out to be the "dangerous extremists" that Hampton says we are. And that could turn the electorate against us come the next election. Whereas, if we wait till December, and then just refuse to reselect him, the electorate will forget about it quickly. Like they have with all the other right-wing MPs who haven't been reselected.'

She paused, in need of a cigarette; but knowing he would only reprimand her, she stroked her earlobe nervously instead.

'You obviously don't agree, Terry?'

'Correct, comrade.'

Terry's eyes glinted dangerously.

'Now listen to me, Joan, and listen carefully.'

The revolutionary leaned forward until his nose was almost touching the girl's. Then, in his most silken tones, he spelled out what was going to happen: 'It's imperative we throw Hampton out *now* because that will scare all the other trouble-making right-wingers shitless! In fact, they'll be so frightened that they themselves are going to be thrown out, that when the pressure comes on them in their own constituencies – as it surely will! – they'll be only too happy to give up the ghost come their reselection. Or they'll simply retire at the General Election like that class traitor, Bob Mellish.'

Terry grabbed Joan's hand and held it in his vicelike grip.

'Not only that, Joan, but as it's our local Executive that will be kicking Hampton out of the Party, it will also shoot a warning rocket up the National Executive's arse. Because then the NEC will realise that *nobody's* safe. So even left-wing-Neil-Kinnock-hacks like Glendower will start shitting themselves!'

Joan winced because of his relentless pressure on her fingers. Then he smiled and released her hand: 'Oh, I know it'll churn up a few hostile waves for a month or two. But the electorate are very fickle. They'll soon forget about it – while the right wingers in our great Party will go on remembering and quivering. Anyway, even if the publicity is bad, it'll soon fade compared to the Tories' bad publicity. We can always rely on Thatcher to keep putting the screws on the nation. She'll eventually force even the Great Placid British Public to rebel. So that in the end they'll have no alternative but to vote us into power. Oh, I know what you're going to say. What about the Alliance? Well, until the Alliance achieve proportional representation, it doesn't matter how many votes they collect, because they'll always be on the sidelines. So in the end, as I say, the public'll have to vote for us. You see, people like us and Tony Benn and the real socialists of this world, Joan, are the only genuine alternative to Thatchernomics and On-Your-Bike Tebbitt.'

Admiring the worn creases on his black leather jacket, Terry folded his arms.

'Yes, there's no doubt about it,' he continued, smiling broadly. 'That's the beauty about having a parliamentary democracy. There always have to be swings and roundabouts because the British are such a fair-minded people. They believe in giving everyone a go at ruling 'em. That's why they'll have no choice but to give us a go. And that's why tonight I'm putting up the motion to our GMC to expel Mr Hampton.'

'Terry, are you sure you're not letting revenge play a part in . . .?'

'Absolutely!'

Again his hand grasped hers and he gazed hypnotically into her eyes.

'So I want your backing in the meeting this evening, comrade.'

The girl sucked at her lower lip, then nodded.

'Of course I'll back you, Terry.'

The bus juddered to a halt. Terry released her hand and got up. Stunned, she followed him down the steps. A moment later they were walking together along the street.

'You can always rely on me, Terry. I just needed to be sure, that's all.'

Terry allowed himself one of his ambiguous smiles.

'I knew you wouldn't forget who pulled the strings to get you on the GMC, Joan. That's why, when the time comes, I want *you* to nail Hampton to the cross!'

Terry draped an arm round the girl's slim shoulders and gave her an affectionate squeeze.

'For if you help me now, comrade, who knows? One day very soon you might be on the New National Executive Committee yourself. With slippery Emrys Glendower on his knees at your feet, drooling for a few crumbs from your table.'

For the first time since they began their conversation, Joan laughed.

'Angie's right about you, Terry.'

'How d'you mean?'

'You do have a way with words.'

At a quarter to eleven, Terry was still in full flow. He leaned forward on his high-backed chair and curled his fingers round the worn edges of the table. Below him, the party faithful waited.

'And so, comrades, as our Member of Parliament has deliberately contravened the Labour Party's Constitution, he must be expelled from the Party.'

Terry paused, then gazed at the depressed-looking figure of Emrys Glendower sitting hunched up at the back of the hall with an unlit pipe clenched between his teeth. Glendower was surrounded by men and women in their mid-twenties who regarded him with hostility. Self-consciously, the MP pulled up the collar of his herringbone overcoat to warm his ears, for the hall was chilly.

'As you know, comrades,' Terry went on, still gazing at the Welshman, 'Hampton could be expelled by the National Executive Committee. But apparently – at least according to Comrade Glendower here – at present the NEC are reluctant to press forward with expulsion proceedings, as it will make things difficult for our Great and Wise Leader.'

As Terry announced this, everyone in the hall turned to stare at the Welshman, who decided to smile bravely. There were cries of 'Typical!' 'Who needs the NEC, anyway?' 'It's all a right-wing plot!'

Terry raised an imperious arm and the disgruntled mutterings subsided. Then he glanced at Joan, sitting expectantly in the front row and still unconsciously massaging her earlobe.

She was worried he was going to call on to her to speak, but he didn't. Instead he gave her a wry smile and continued.

'So, as the NEC aren't going to do their duty to the Party, comrades, it seems we have no alternative but to expel Roy Hampton ourselves.'

'Comrade MacMaster's right!' chorused three acolytes from the body of the hall.

'I was sure that was how you'd feel, comrades,' nodded Terry as he waved several letters at the delegates. 'And as we've already had resolutions from three wards calling for Hampton's expulsion, I feel it is now my duty to put forward the following resolution from the Chair, which, if accepted, will be considered at a special GMC in three-and-a-half weeks' time on October 31st. Then notice of the Resolution will be sent out to the other delegates who couldn't be here tonight.'

Terry looked at Glendower pointedly. 'And, of course, we shall send notice of the Resolution to our MP himself, who we shall then invite to come along to the special GMC meeting so he can state his case.'

The revolutionary peered down at his notes.

'The Resolution is as follows: "The Executive of the General Management Committee puts down the following motion; that the Lamberton North Labour Party hereby resolves that the Member of Parliament for this constituency, having advised electors during the recent Council by-election not to vote for the duly nominated Labour candidates, should be expelled from membership of the Labour Party forthwith. For the Conditions of Membership of the Labour Party specifically state in clause III, section 3, that: 'Each Individual Member must accept and conform to the Constitution, Programme, Principles and Policy of the Party.' As Roy Hampton has failed to do this, he must be expelled." '

Terry paused. The hall was silent, save for the odd smoker's cough.

'If this is agreed upon, comrades, this Motion shall be sent to the National Executive Committee.'

As Terry mentioned the NEC he deliberately avoided looking at Glendower. He knew the rest of the hall would do the looking for him.

'Furthermore, comrades, attached to this Resolution, there will be an appendix of evidence, i.e. the incriminating press statements issued by our MP during the by-election. I now propose this Motion from the Chair. Is there a seconder?'

Immediately a dozen voices shouted: 'Seconded!'

'Right. Those in favour?'

Twenty-seven eager hands thrust themselves into the smoky air. Appraising the situation, the chairman allowed his gaze slowly to traverse the room. Only eleven hadn't moved and seemed uncertain. Terry addressed himself to them.

'Those against?'

For a moment it seemed as if all eleven were going to raise their hands, but Terry smiled at them balefully. Then the moment passed; for the eleven who occupied the back row – mostly tired, old right wingers – thought it safer to fight another day and on another issue. So they all folded their arms and stared into space.

Terry was still smiling as he said: 'Carried unanimously.'

Then he turned to Glendower and winked.

It was the third week in October. British Summer Time had ended, so dusk fell an hour earlier than usual. As the dark enveloped Kensington, it brought with it heavy squalls of wind and rain. The wind was so fierce that Roy wasn't sure whether he was fighting his umbrella or his umbrella was fighting him. Either way he was losing. There was a sudden, metallic crack as two of the umbrella's labouring stays snapped.

Cursing Taiwanese handiwork, he discarded the broken brolly and hurried down the rainswept cul-de-sac opposite Kensington Gardens. Relieved, he dodged under the narrow porch of 6, Paradise Mews. With water trickling down his neck, he seized the bronze doorknocker and was about to rap on the door when he decided against it.

What the hell am I doing here? he thought, as large drops of water spattered on to the exposed shoulders of his raincoat and the back of his head. She shouldn't have rung me at the Commons – and I certainly shouldn't have agreed to come.

He turned to beat a retreat, but paused as the clear, seductive opening bars of Rimsky-Korsakov's *Scheherazade* called to him from inside the mews house. Sighing, he pressed his rainwashed cheek against the door. As the exotic music unrolled its Arabian magic carpet behind the lamplit window, Roy remembered the first time he'd heard the ever-beguiling tales of the Sultan's bride. It was the night he possessed Helen in the Euston bedsit, four days after they'd met at the LSE coffee bar. They made love six exhilarating times to the music of Rimsky's masterpiece.

Why has she asked me to come and see her tonight? But how could I refuse? She sounded distracted, almost confused – as if she needed help.

Lulled by the music, he conjured up the fragrance of Helen's skin when they made love at Ufferton Hall. In the moonlight, her overwide, green eyes demanded he sheath himself even deeper inside her as he rode her through the spring night. Scented memories of their ecstatic breathing dissipated the effects of the rain buffeting his neck, and even *Scheherazade* was relegated to sensuous background music.

Christ, how I want her, he brooded. I try to persuade myself I don't. But recently, with Liz's incessant moods and our interminable rows, I continually dream of losing myself between Helen's breasts. Yet I know I'm wrong to betray Liz, even in my thoughts. But I do long to possess Helen. . . .

He gasped at the shrill, ringing sound by his left ear. Then he realised in dismay that during his sojourn in the past, he had inadvertently leaned against the front-door bell. Before he could recover, the door opened and Helen's green eyes materialized in the doorway. But the flush of excitement he expected to see on her face wasn't there. Her generous mouth was bloodless and taut. He glimpsed something yellow in her hand.

'Yes, aren't they beautiful?' she said, extending four saffron autumn roses, beaded with raindrops. 'I saw them being battered by the storm, so I had to pick them. Well, don't stand there getting soaked, darling. Come inside and dry off.'

Moments later, Roy found himself seated on her snow-white sofa, nursing a large Scotch. As she finished arranging the roses in a cut-glass vase, he glanced round him. This was his first time in her domain. Three walls of the elegant Edwardian room were crammed with books, from the dark-chocolate carpet to the gilded mouldings on the ceiling. The fourth wall was dominated by French windows, with swagged, snow-white curtains, leading to a thriving, walled garden.

Helen broke his reverie by crossing over to the gramophone and turning off the music.

'Why did you do that?' Roy asked, puzzled, as he moved towards her, intent on embracing her.

He reached out to persuade her into his arms, but she warded him off with a shake of the head.

'You're had all your hair shorn off, Helen!' he blurted, registering her new pageboy haircut.

'Shows how much you notice, darling, doesn't it?'

Again he opened his arms to her, but again she refused him.

'There's no point in us going through all that again, darling,' she smiled, her eyes clouding with regret. 'It'll only make you feel unnecessarily guilty, and whet my appetite to no purpose.'

'Then why did you ask me to come round tonight?'

She looked beyond him at the rain-furrowed windowpane, where beads of water were chasing one another down the darkened glass.

'I'm leaving England on Thursday,' she said, turning back to adjust a yellow rose in the vase. 'Probably for ever.'

'You're doing what?'

'England's hopeless.'

Stunned, Roy jabbed his hands into his trouser pockets in search of cigarettes, but found none. This wasn't surprising, for he had not smoked for over two-and-a-half months – though when the pressure was on, as now, the old habit died hard.

'I've plenty of ciggies if you need them,' Helen said, offering him a black lacquered box with a crimson dragon on its lid.

Roy shook his head, then brushed several strands of damp hair away from his eyebrows.

'Why are you leaving England?'

'This country's had it. And I've been offered a teaching post, with a lucrative stipend, at Stanford University.'

'But . . .' Roy trailed off, to pick up his discarded tumbler of Scotch. He gulped down a third of it, then waved the glass at her in a vague semi-circular motion. 'But what about you and the SDP? Surely you believe there's still hope for this country? I mean, if the Alliance gains power . . .?'

'They won't gain power!'

'How can you be so sure?'

'That's one of the main reasons I'm leaving,' Helen sighed, subsiding on the white sofa.

Roy sat down beside her, wanting to touch her but knowing

it was probably too late. He had to content himself with stroking his chilled glass of Scotch.

'So after all your proselytizing on behalf of the SDP, Helen, you now don't believe the Alliance will ever form a government?'

'I'm afraid not.'

'Why?'

Helen sighed again, then smoothed her dress over her knees.

'The reason the Alliance has had it, my darling, is because people like David Owen are ambitious for themselves, rather than for the country. Oh, I believe Owen is bright, charismatic, and one of the best speakers in the House, with all the qualities of a leader. But unless he starts putting the needs of the nation before his own career, the SDP will end up nowhere. And until the leaders of the Alliance realise that the SDP and the Liberals must eventually amalgamate into one *single* party, there's no chance the populace will ever vote them into power. Who wants to vote for two silly little parties who are forever squabbling about who should be leader and who should have which particular parliamentary seat? And as the Alliance is the only real hope for radical moderation in this country – and yet the Alliance is hopeless! – what's the point of me hanging around here when I've got the chance to start a new life in the States?' She paused, then smiled wryly. 'Because whatever else the States is, darling, it isn't a self-destructive anachronism like England, forever intent on ending its days in an extremist's knackers' yard.'

'This conversion to the States is very sudden.'

'Mm. Isn't it wonderful?' beamed Helen.

'You say that Stanford University has given you a teaching post?'

'Yes. For a year initially.'

'So they haven't offered you tenure, then?'

'Of course not.'

'Then at the end of your year at Stanford, you'll have to come back here, because without a green card you won't be allowed to go on working there.'

'I won't have to come back.'

'But . . .?'

'During the summer vacation I met an eligible Professor of Semantics from UCLA who had the good sense to propose to yours truly.'

Roy gripped his glass with both hands to prevent himself shaking.

'Did you accept his proposal?'

Helen's eyes glinted mischieviously.

'Not exactly.'

'Then . . .?'

'I told him it would depend on whether I liked the American way of life. Mind, if I do, I'll probably marry him. I haven't had a husband for over eight years now. And as Chester's wife, I'll be eligible for a green card. Then I'll be able to work anywhere I like in the US of A – and for as long as I like.'

Helen's eyes were now probing his, but no longer with a glimmer of mischief.

'Why shouldn't I marry a semantic hunk of Maryland beefcake?' she protested, her restless fingers coursing through her closely cropped hair. 'There's no point in me waiting around for you, darling. Your grammar school morality will always enmesh you in guilt. Even if we went to bed this instant, in the morning you'd slink out of here like a beaten puppy, and go straight home and confess your "sins" to your beloved wife. And why shouldn't you? You may lust after me, but you love her. And you always will.'

She paused to give his knee a sisterly pat, then added: 'And that's how it should be, my dear. You see, your mother was right when she pushed you away from her after your aunt's funeral. You don't need to lean on me any more, either. Or Liz. I'm just sorry I won't be here to applaud you when you beard your Trotskyite lion in his den. Because you will beard him. You have to.'

She stood up with her hands clasped tightly together.

'I think you should go now, darling. Anyway, you'll be better off without my shadow haunting you. As I'll be better off without you haunting me.'

Roy remained motionless on the sofa. He couldn't think of an appropriate response. Then the opening fragments of Eliot's *The Burial of the Dead* came to his lips. Smiling at Helen, he whispered: 'Eliot was wrong, you know. For it's not "April" but October that is the "cruellest month" of the year, breeding not "Lilacs" but roses "out of the dead land, mixing Memory and desire. . . ."'

He sighed wistfully: 'Yes, that's all we have left, isn't it? Memories and desire.'

Helen shook her head, then crossed to the half-open door.

'Forget all your quotations, Roy. It's too late for them now. They will only make the hurt deeper, and make it last longer. But if and when you ever think of me again, think of me as a determined ex-patriot who, in the end, never completed her biography of the Great Pragmatist.'

'You mean, you're not even going to finish writing . . .?'

'Why should I? Wilson doesn't deserve a biography! All history owes him is ignominy. But one day, if you hold on to your belief in England and freedom, unlike Wilson, or me, *you* may merit a biography. Well, it's a funny old world that gets funnier by the hour. So you never know. Do you?'

As October went into decline, the days got rougher, at least as far as Roy was concerned. Despite his appeals to delegates on Lamberton North's local GMC, he knew that on the night he would not have a majority in his favour, and that unless a miracle occurred on October 31st he would be expelled from the Labour Party.

At mid-afternoon on the thirty-first, Roy was spending what could well be his last afternoon in the august chamber of the House of Commons. As he leaned back against the olive-green leather bench, he allowed his gaze to sweep over his fellow MPs for the thousandth time, as he considered his future.

If I'm expelled tonight, which seems likely, he thought, I can either hang on as an Independent Labour MP, or I can join the Liberals, as de Quincey's always threatening to do. Or, failing that, there's always the SDP. Or I can simply retire into private life. Yes, maybe I'll accept Winner's offer and take up management consultancy. The money's reasonable, and I'm sure the prospects are rosy. Well, everyone's consulting someone about something these days.

As he contemplated his future, he was propelled once again into his past. Embarrassed, he remembered delivering his maiden speech in this very chamber, at three o'clock in the morning fourteen years ago. Not only had most of the Members been asleep or inebriated, or both, but he had had the gall to pontificate on 'the social advantages of high-rise dwellings in the derelict urban areas of my constituency....'

God, I was so naive and blinkered in those days. I even praised Harold Wilson and his 'technological leap forward' speech, believing it would revolutionize Britain. If only I could have accomplished more and verbalised less! And I've watched so many famous faces haranguing one another with warning fingers from these benches; Heath, Barber, Powell, Walden, Home, Grimmond, Crossman, Crosland, Marsh; and lately Wilson, Callaghan, Steel, Foot and many, many more; some dead, some disabled, some retired. And those that have survived are generally disillusioned, neurotic and exhausted. . . .

Is it worth it? he thought. Is the hassle and the heartache worth the parliamentary candle?

As his internal flame began to gutter, he forced his thoughts back into the present: yes, I suppose it is worth the heartache. And Parliament is the only way – at least, it's the only way for me.

Then his eyes flickered round the half-full chamber. On the Government benches, 'Tarzan' Heseltine, sporting his Lex Barker hairstyle, was in the middle of one of his habitual performances, counterpointing with sweeping gestures and a shrill resonance on his upper register. Close by Heseltine, Peter Walker was purse-lipped and obviously disgruntled. Whereas Margaret Thatcher, the new 'Queen of England', despite her honey-coloured bouffant looked every inch a king. Clustered round 'Her Majesty' was her sycophantic court, in the unctuous personages of Nigel Lawson, Leon Brittan and the rest of the toadying Tory, well-heeled, over-oiled smoothies. Only the fanatical skulls of 'Death's Head' Tebbit, and that other tormented aesthete, Sir Keith Joseph, broke the courtiers' mould.

Roy began to superimpose faces of the past on the faces of the present. Instantaneously the ghostly visages of Churchill and Attlee, Eden and Bevin shimmered in their iridescence before his amused eyes. Then Heseltine waved an imperious finger and the spectral statesmen slunk back to their graves, knowing their time was past and would not come again. For this was the decade of the mediocre 'media' men, who had no time for yesterday's 'gentle'-men. . . .

Mind, after tonight, I may also be one of yesterday's men.

And though I have often abused this historical edifice, God help me, I shall miss it. That, of course, presupposes I should decide to leave this theatre for ever, to step back into real life.

Roy knew that if he stayed any longer he would probably weep like an overwrought schoolboy tormented by the first love of his life. So covering his cheek with his hand to disguise his feelings, he edged out of his seat. To his consternation, he bumped into Denis Skinner, who had just entered the chamber. Then he hovered in the centre aisle to say a silent half-farewell to the Speaker, whose face was still shrouded in his full-bottomed wig. His eyes smarted, but he refused to give in to tears.

Instead, he took a final, long, hard look at his own Front Bench. There, sure enough, was the purple, bloated face of Denis Healey, the parliamentary Cardinal Wolsey of our time. And over there was Peter Shore, who was still desperately trying to square the right-wing circle, and who to a degree had succeeded in holding on to more of his political principles than had most of his peers. But even he, with his lank comma of hair curtaining the right side of his long face, had the look of a man who wished he could be elsewhere. Which is more than could be said for the smug middlemen like Silkin and Kaufman, or the passionately ebullient Great Leader of the Party and his equally ebullient Deputy.

But Roy had had enough of his bumptious compatriots. Part of him admired his adversaries in the Party, such as Meacher, Heffer, Mikardo, Skinner and Benn, far more. At least they were fighting for what they believed in. They had never trimmed their political sails when the prevailing wind had blown from the right wing.. They had always kept faith with their hard-left beliefs, and had not betrayed themselves merely to grasp the illusory tiller of power.

Once outside the chamber, he moved trance-like past the bronze, bulbous statue of Churchill. Moments later he was on the Terrace, nursing a glass of chilled orange squash and staring at the Thames, which winked at him in the autumn sunlight.

He glanced to his left to see de Quincey peering at him fondly. As Roy returned David's smile, he sensed there was also someone on his right. He turned and looked into the kindly, grey eyes of Charles Derwent, the young Tory MP.

Then, as Derwent held out his hand, Roy remembered their last meeting on a long-ago May evening on this very Terrace.

'I just want to say, Roy, that I've heard via the grapevine about what you're going through. And I want you to know that I still admire you for the consistency of your stand against the Marxists. No, please, don't turn away. You taught me a great deal about communism that night, for which I'm very grateful. But in case things don't work out the way you want them to this evening, I'd be privileged if you'd let me shake your hand. You know, in case we don't happen to bump into each other ... for a little while....'

He grasped Roy's hand and shook it firmly. Roy was too embarrassed to respond. But as the young man turned to go, Roy reached out and touched his retreating elbow.

'Thank you, Charles. I appreciate your good wishes. But do take my advice and go back to managing your estate while you've still got one. You don't belong in this theatrical jungle.'

Charles smiled, then said: 'Do *you*, Roy?' and was gone.

For several seconds Roy gazed blankly at the rolling water below him. Then de Quincey broke the silence.

'Christ, a human Tory! Whatever's happening to the world?'

Roy was too upset to laugh. David placed a comforting arm round his friend's shoulder.

'I'm sorry, Roy. Actually it was a compassionate action on his part, and I agree with every word he said.'

David gave Roy's shoulder an intimate squeeze.

'We know my problems, David,' countered Roy, gently disengaging himself. 'But you're in the same trouble yourself, surely? Isn't your Trot going to unseat you in January?'

De Quincey pursed his lips, then studiously brushed a grey hair from his lapel.

'Isn't he going to unseat you?'

Another pause while David watched the river.

'You're going to join the Liberals, aren't you,' persisted Roy, 'like you threatened in Dartmouth?'

'Well ...'

'Oh, I see! You've changed your mind and you're going to join the SDP instead?'

'No.'

'Then ...?'

Roy trailed off, amazed, as David twitched a packet of Mannikin cigars out of his trouser pocket.

'Care for one?'

'No!' Roy said emphatically. 'Anyway, since when have you started puffing on cancer sticks?'

David didn't reply. Instead he cupped his hands against the late October wind which suddenly gusted from upriver.

'If you're not going to join the Liberals *or* the SDP, David, then . . .?'

'It's not that I don't want to join them, Roy!' David blurted. 'It's just I can't afford to join 'em. I've got Wendy and the twins to think about, remember. Not to mention my gargantuan mortgage. Well, I didn't buy my house while the market was in the doldrums like you were fortunate enough to! So . . .' David took a break, then made a testy, stabbing motion with his cigar. 'So until I can find another job with an equivalent salary, well, I've decided to. . . .'

'To what?'

'To eat humble pie! Like my Trot wants me to. That way I can still keep my seat.'

'And he's going to allow you to keep your seat if you eat humble pie?' Roy asked in disbelief.

'Yes. See, he's a clever, sadistic sod. He knows that time and history are on his side. So he's quite happy – for the time being – to let me go on representing my constituency as a yes-man delegate for the left.'

'Jesus Christ!'

'Unfortunately He doesn't come into it very much.'

Perturbed, Roy turned his head away from David's beseeching eyes. De Quincey, sensing his friend wanted to leave him, grappled his fingers around Roy's wrist.

'And if you've got any sense, Roy, *you'll* eat humble pie tonight, too.'

'But. . . .'

'You've got no time left for "buts", old friend. Believe me, if you agree to all their terms tonight and then publicly recant your misdeeds, it'll take the puff out of MacMaster's sails completely. That way you'll save yourself from being purged. You might even find a way of holding on to your seat. If you can do that, you'll have a chance to regroup your right-wing forces on the quiet later. Oh, it may take a couple of years.

But if you can hold on to your seat you can secretly begin to promote Gaitskellism in your constituency . . . Hey, where are you going?'

'Home.'

'Roy, listen to me, for pity's sake! Can't you see I'm trying to save you from yourself? I've thought it all through and it's the only way we can live to fight another day, because the SDP and the Liberals will never get their act together. Even if they do, it'll take years. Then it'll be too late! By that time the whole fucking country will have been ripped apart by the crazy polarisation of the two major parties . . .!'

David slithered into silence, for his friend was no longer with him. No one was listening – save his own autumnal shadow.

From the moment Roy wrenched his shoes and socks off and threw himself onto the double bed, the telephone never left his hand. The cup of tea Liz had made him had gone cold, and he gave up trying to drink it. Then he answered the right-wing trade unionist on the other end of the phone who was bewailing the Labour Party's present situation.

'Yes, I know that, Joe; but what can we do when the Constituency Party's been taken over? I've chatted up everyone I could these last three weeks, but MacMaster's got such a majority on the GMC that the whole thing's been a waste of time!'

Roy did not hear the man's answer, because he was distracted by some flame-coloured roses in an earthenware vase on the windowsill. Despite himself, he was transported to another room where Helen was fondling the rain-streaked petals of a saffron rose. Fiercely he rubbed his earlobe. This triggered a different memory: after the cricket match when Helen kissed him an overlong goodbye . . . then Alexa noticed her lipstick on his ear. But now Helen had fled to the States, and, by his own admission, de Quincey was on his knees to his Trot. So now Roy was alone.

'What was that, Joe?' he said, fighting to keep up his interest in the telephone conversation. 'Now, don't get me wrong. I appreciate that you and some of the boys are going to be backing me up at the GMC tonight, but I still think the result will be a foregone conclusion. . . . It's going to take a bona-fide,

Church of England miracle to save me. And there's been a shortage of them recently.'

Roy was so preoccupied with trying to make Joe smile at the other end of the phone that he failed to notice Liz standing in the doorway.

'Look, Joe, don't worry, I've still got a couple of explosive jokers up my sleeve. So you can rely on me to go out with a bang tonight, and not the usual Manifesto Group whimper! Well, see you there then in a couple of hours, and thanks again for calling.'

Roy hung up, then fell back against the pillow. He was closing his eyes when Liz spoke.

'You're not really going to go crazy tonight and go out with a bang, are you?'

'What have I got to lose?'

'For a start, you'll lose the little political credibility you've got left!' Liz rasped, brushing a strand of grey hair away from the bridge of her nose. 'Well, you're bound to make an embarassing spectacle of yourself which we'll have to live with afterwards. For I'm sure you've invited the press to talk to you after the meeting, haven't you?'

Roy sat up abruptly, then pummelled his fist into the squashed pillow behind him: 'Sebastian's right!'

'About what?'

'About you always bitching me when I'm having my head kicked in! Instead of supporting me like. . . .'

'A compassionate, loving spouse?' Liz demanded, folding her tired arms across her breasts.

'Surely a little support from your wife is not too much to ask?'

Before Liz could snap back, Roy pushed himself off the bed and studied himself in the dressing-table mirror. He was haggard about the eyes, his mouth set in a hard line and his red tie rumpled.

Despite herself, Liz was moved by his distraught image in the mirror. She crossed to him and stroked the curls at the nape of his neck, murmuring: 'I'm sorry, love.'

'Funny way of showing it.'

She brushed her lips against his earlobe. 'I know. It's just, well, whether you realise it or not, during these last few months you've changed so much. . . .'

Roy didn't move but continued to stare at their reflections.

'I'm not the only one that's changed, Liz.'

'Oh, maybe I am a fraction more to the left than I was when I first joined the Party, but that's only to counter-balance your extremism.'

'Oh come on, Liz, stop fooling yourself!'

'No, *you* come on, Mr Hampton, and you stop fooling yourself! You know damn well I've never been a left-wing fanatic and never will be. Anyway, you seem to forget that when you joined the Party, you supported left wingers like Bevan, too. And *not* right wingers like Bevin! It's only in the last five years you've turned into an unreconstructed Gaitskellite. You certainly didn't support Gaitskell when the poor sod was alive!'

Roy wrenched his strained face away from the mirror and stood up to challenge his wife.

'So I've been wrong for a long time, darling. It still doesn't mean I should chicken out now. That's the trouble with this bloody country. No one ever admits their mistakes. That's why the Labour Party is now in deep trouble.'

Impatiently Liz pulled the pins out of her flaxen bun to loosen her hair onto her shoulders.

'It's not just the Labour Party that needs to change,' she said bitterly. 'What about the bloody Tories? But then, as you supported Thatcher over the Falklands, I suppose you approve of her Iron-Man leadership now?'

'Don't let's start on the Falklands again! It's got nothing to do with what I'm talking about.'

Liz barged past him to pick up the Ponds Cleansing Cream from the dressing table. As she pursued her argument, she rubbed cream into her skin to remove her make-up.

'Well, I think the Falklands has got everything to do with everything!'

'Don't be ridiculous.'

'I'm sorry, Roy, but until "General" Thatcher had her little war with the Argentines, she was about the most unpopular prime minister on record. That's why some of our best young soldiers had to die in order that she could be re-elected.'

'Liz, that's garbage!'

'Well, if she hadn't been ill-prepared and ill-advised by Carrington and the like, the Argentines would never have dared to take those rotten islands. Then she wouldn't have had her "patriotic" war and she wouldn't have beaten that tin-pot Fascist junta. So she would never have become the "popular" leader and won a landslide second term in office. But then you only approve of her "patriotic" spoutings because that's just the kind of "patriot" you are!'

Seething at the thought of Liz's injustice, Roy closed his eyes to steady himself. Then he snatched the Ponds Cream away from her and hurled it onto the bedspread.

'Now you listen to me, Liz, and you listen carefully. You're right I thought Thatcher did a pretty good job during the Falklands – with the exception of the sinking of the *Belgrano* – but her kind of patriotism isn't mine. Because mine isn't a hawkish patriotism. And I'm no dove, either! But my patriotism has got nothing to do with how "superbly" we beat the Argentines – whom we only beat by the skin of our teeth anyway! Christ Almighty, I'm aware – even if Mrs Thatcher isn't – that what we did in the South Atlantic was pitiful compared to the War. But I believe, along with a few Labour MPs like Peter Shore, that under the circumstances we had no choice but to fight.'

He paused to see if Liz was listening, because she was laboriously wiping the cleansing cream off her face with a piece of tissue. He moved closer to her, lowering his voice.

'What I'm trying to say, darling, is my kind of patriotism isn't bellicose. I'm a romantic patriot. So whenever I rant on about being patriotic, it is the soul of Englqnd, plus the basic goodness and decency of the English people, that I feel "patriotic" about.'

Liz discarded the make-up-stained piece of tissue and reached for her hairbrush. Roy hoped she was listening.

'That is why I agree with you, darling.'

He paused to see if she would respond. Slowly she dragged the brush through a painfully tangled knot in her hair.

'You agree with me about what?'

'I hate the fact that only the demagogues and the extremists of either political persuasion have the courage of their convictions. Trouble is, most people in this country believe that if there is a rotting corpse plastered up in their living-room wall, the stench will eventually go away. But it won't, Liz! Because eventually that rotting corpse – or, in England's case, the corpses. – will ooze out of the wall and breed a plague that poisons everyone it touches.'

Roy broke off to laugh at the lines of concern in his wife's face.

'Yes, perhaps you're right,' he agreed, still laughing. 'Perhaps I am crazy. But is it surprising? I've been in active, crazy politics all these years, whereas you've only ever been on the sidelines.'

Liz stared at him, hurt welling up in her eyes.

'And it's because I've been active all these years, darling, that I'm now crazy enough to believe that something's got to be done about the rotting corpse in our Party while there's still time. That's why I've got to go *really* crazy tonight and expose the corpse.'

Without waiting for her reaction, he pulled a tie out of the wardrobe and draped it round his neck.

'And the only way to go really crazy is for me to dispense with my inhibitions. Then I can kick those pseudo-working class layabouts on that GMC where it really hurts!'

As he struggled with his badly-tied Windsor knot, Liz moved away from the bed. Then he saw the despair in her face.

'Come to think of it, my darling,' he said cheerfully, 'it's a shame that you're not a delegate on our GMC. Then you could come along with me now and be a "real supportive" wife and actually vote for me!'

'It's a bloody good thing I'm not a delegate, Roy. The way I feel at the moment, God knows what I'd do.'

Then she laughed.

'You're not going to wear that black tie, are you?'

Roy pulled on his jacket, gave his tie another tug, then opened the bedroom door.

'As you keep telling me: it's my funeral!' he said, then ran down the stairs.

Stunned by the abruptness of his departure, Liz didn't hear Alexa wishing him good luck as he climbed into his car. Nor did she see Sebastian hugging his father on the pavement.

As Roy drew into the car park, he noticed the shadowy figures of two children hiding in the alleyway opposite. Sensing the children were peering at him, he climbed out of the car and locked it. He couldn't understand why they were watching him, and before he could ask them, they ran off down a darkened alleyway. Still puzzled, he squared his shoulders, switched his briefcase to his other hand, then headed towards the worn steps leading to the Labour Party rooms. Already some reporters, who were representing national as well as local papers, loitered at the entrance. They were soon joined by two outside-broadcast camera teams from the BBC's 'Newsnight' and ITN.

As Roy approached the hall, he saw that most of the hard-left delegates had arrived before him, all pointedly refusing to answer the waiting reporters' questions. Roy was only two-hundred yards away from the newsmen when Terry MacMaster, surprisingly dressed in a white, rollneck sweater and tight, black corduroy pants, beat him to it. As always Terry was surrounded by his entourage.

'Well, I must say, gentlemen,' Terry announced with relish, 'it's nice to see the Tory press here in full strength tonight. Especially as you're about to witness the result of some genuine democratic proceedings for a change.'

Roy increased his pace, unable to believe his luck. Though MacMaster didn't realise it, the revolutionary had set himself up to be humiliated publicly. Swiftly Roy moved forward into the centre of the television lights. Before Terry could escape into the hall, the MP produced his first 'joker'.

'Just one moment, Mr MacMaster.'

Terry turned at the top of the steps, flanked by his praetorian guard. He was blinded temporarily by the television lights. Then, shading his eyes, he focused on the MP.

'Sorry, Mr Hampton, but this is not the time for a debate.'

Roy smiled and nodded.

'I wasn't suggesting we had a debate, Mr MacMaster, but I would like to see your Labour Party membership card.'

Terry looked bewildered.

'You must be joking, comrade?' he rasped, laughing and turning to his acolytes for support. 'Our MP's really clutching at straws, isn't he?'

Before Joan Keithley or Alf Spencer could respond, the BBC reporter seized the initiative.

'Are you saying that you *don't* have a Labour Party membership card then, Mr MacMaster?'

The two cameras edged closer to Terry.

'Perhaps you're not a fully paid-up member of the Labour Party, Mr MacMaster?' probed a local journalist.

'Of course I'm a fully paid-up member of the Labour Party! As our MP well knows.'

The ITN reporter was about to fire another question at Terry, but Roy was too quick for him:

'If you are a fully paid-up member, Mr MacMaster, then perhaps you'll be good enough to show me your membership card?'

Terry started to protest, but Roy advanced on him. As he came level with Terry on the top step, Roy deftly produced his own membership card from his wallet and brandished it under the revolutionary's nose.

'Here's mine, Mr MacMaster, which has been fully paid-up now for over twenty-five years. So, as you intend to expel me from the Party, surely the very least you can do is show me your membership card which you say you have held for the last, what, eight years, is it? And which may or may not be paid-up?'

Terry grinned.

'If the sight of my membership card will bring you some solace, Mr Hampton, I'll be only too happy to. . . .'

He trailed off as he thrust his hands into his trouser pockets, only to find them empty. He was aware of the cameras, the hand-held mikes and the eager faces, but there was no sign of the card. Not even in his back pockets. Or his shirt pocket. He started to sweat.

'Well,' said Roy, 'I think before we start these momentous proceedings, Mr MacMaster – and they're certainly going to be momentous for me – you had better go home and find your card.'

'I left it in my jacket!'

'I only have your word for that. Until I see your card with my own eyes, I refuse to attend the proceedings tonight. If, however, you go ahead without me, the NEC may well declare my expulsion null and void – as then I will have been expelled under the chairpersonship of a non-card-carrying member of the Labour Party. At least I assume you're a member of the Labour Party?'

Terry decided to 'tough' it out.

'OK, Mr Hampton, you've made your point. I'll go home and get my card. Then perhaps we can finish with this time-wasting and get shot of you once and for all!'

Terry ran down the steps, barely controlling his impulse to smash the television cameras. As the revolutionary flagged down an idling taxi and stumbled into it, the amused media converged on Roy to ask him more questions, which the MP was only too happy to answer.

'So where the hell is the fucking thing, Angie?' Terry screamed as he hurled his crumpled leather jacket onto the bed.
'I thought you said it was in your inside pocket, Terry.'
'Well, it fucking isn't, is it?'
Angie looked on, wide-eyed and helpless, while the revolutionary stormed round the room as if he were Lenin in Zurich. For the fourth time he tugged out the pockets of his paint-stained jeans. Then he flipped through his wallet again. Still no sign of his membership card. He let out a roar of frustration. Then Angie clapped her hands to her mouth.
'Shit!'
Frenziedly, Terry turned on her.
'Have you remembered where you saw me put it, Angie?'
'Arseholes!'
'Look, will you stop sucking your fucking thumb and help me look for the fucking thing!'
'You'll never forgive me, Terry!'
Nervously Angie backed towards the bookshelf.
'I meant to tell you, Terry, but . . . I forgot.'
'Where the hell is it, then?'
Angie turned to the bookshelf and came face to face with Leon Trotsky's forbidding pince-nez. Gasping, she rummaged through the books until she found what she was looking for: the hardbacked edition of Trotsky's *On Lenin, Notes For A Biography*. In a fury Terry snatched the book off her. He was about to hurl it at the wall when she bleated:
'Don't chuck it, Terry! That's where I've hidden your card! I had to put it somewhere when it dropped out of your pocket, didn't I?'
Dumbfounded, Terry shook the book open. To his amazement his membership card fluttered onto the carpet. As he picked it up, Angie pointed to the discarded Trotskyist masterwork.
'Well, it were the perfect place to hide it, weren't it, Terry?'

Terry stormed out of the room, clutching his membership card in his talons, and Angie was wise enough to let her dragon go. But as she switched on the telly to watch her favourite programme, *Dallas*, she did wonder whether she would enjoy being married to a whirlwind.

Because we certainly will get married once I've plucked up enough courage to tell him I'm six weeks pregnant! she thought.

Then she pouted and addressed the man everyone loves to hate on the TV screen: 'Well, he won't have any choice but to marry me, will he, JR?'

JR nodded, then winked.

Terry fell out of the taxi and for the first time in his life told the cabby to keep the change. Then he brushed his angry fingers across his sweating hairline. He had no time to compose himself, for immediately Hampton and the BBC and ITN cameras pressed in upon him. Gnawing his lip, Terry thrust his dog-eared membership card at the widening camera lenses. Then he beamed at the viewers at home: 'I trust this will satisfy our frivolous MP.'

To Terry's consternation, Roy snatched the membership card away from him.

'What the devil . . .?'

'It's out of date, comrade!' Roy interrupted, pointing to the numerals on the card.

'What d'you mean it's out of . . .?'

'It's last year's card.'

Chuckling, a local journalist pushed his way past the TV reporters and thrust his florid face in front of the camera, demanding: 'Does this mean, Mr Hampton, that Mr MacMaster will not be allowed to be the chairperson on the GMC tonight?'

'Absolutely!' Roy assured him, unable to hide the 'joker's' gleam in his tired eyes.

'That's where you're wrong, "Comrade" Hampton,' Terry intervened, alternately grinning at both cameras. 'Here!'

With a flourish, he produced two shining pound coins from his jeans' pocket. Before Roy could refuse them, Terry pressed the coins into the MP's reluctant palm.

'What's this for?' protested Roy.

'That, comrade, is my subscription, as an unwaged person, to renew my Labour Party membership.'

'Why have you given it to Mr Hampton, Mr MacMaster?' asked the BBC reporter.

'Because I know of no safer repository in England,' grinned Terry. 'Oh, don't worry, Comrade Hampton, I won't assume my seat as chairperson until my new membership card has been fully made out. That shouldn't take more than a couple of minutes. Should it, Comrade Keithley?'

In front of Roy, on the crimson tablecloth, a Hitachi tape-recorder whirred to itself. To his left was Reggie Kirkpatrick, the official representative of the NEC from the regional office. Roy knew that Kirkpatrick couldn't help him in his fight to stay in the Party, for Kirkpatrick was only present in an advisory capacity to ensure that the local GMC followed the correct procedures for expulsion.

Roy glanced beyond Kirkpatrick to Terry MacMaster who, as the reconstituted chairperson, was addressing the delegates in the already smoke-filled room.

'So now, comrades, we come to item two on tonight's agenda: the Motion from the Executive Committee for the expulsion of Roy Hampton, our Member of Parliament, from the Labour Party.'

Terry paused for effect, then turned his cool gaze onto the Party Secretary, who was taking notes and monitoring the GMC's own tape-recorder. Then Terry leaned forward and continued.

'So I now formally move the Motion in front of you, comrades. Is there a seconder?'

From the body of the hall voices echoed: 'Seconded!'

Terry nodded: 'The Motion is now open for debate. First I will give Comrade Hampton the right to defend himself. Then, at the end of the debate, he will have the right to sum up.'

The chairman inclined his head towards the MP but didn't look at him.

'The floor is yours, comrade.'

Roy stood up, allowing himself a secret smile, for his 'joker' had delayed the opening of the meeting by over an hour and a quarter. He was aware it was only a trivial victory, but any victory was better than none. Then he held up his arms until a grudging if uneasy silence descended on the hall.

'Comrades! I would like to thank you for giving me this opportunity to defend myself against this malicious Motion.'

As he hoped it would, his opening remark was greeted by vociferous heckling. But he seized the moment by the throat and found a new resonance which momentarily quietened the hecklers.

'But this *is* a malicious Motion, comrades! For it seeks to deprive me of my membership of the Labour Party which I have belonged to for over twenty-five years. Unlike most people here who have only been members for three or four years!'

Waving both arms, Dave Pickles screamed: 'You rotten scab! You class traitor!'

'Calling me "scab" and "class traitor" won't change the truth, Comrade Pickles.'

Now the delegates were bellowing like oxen. With a scything gesture, Roy pointed at Terry MacMaster, who was already adopting his arms-crossed stance.

'And the silence of our chairman doesn't help the meeting, either!'

The clamour continued. It was obvious Terry had no intention of calling the hall to order, so Roy stared pointedly at the regional representative of the NEC. At first Kirkpatrick refused to intervene. But then the mindless baying became so deafening that he clapped his hands to his ears, and Terry MacMaster was forced to call: 'Order! Order! Let the man finish, comrades. You'll have your say in a minute.'

Gradually the frenzy subsided.

'Pray continue, Mr Hampton.'

'Thank you, "Mr" Chairperson,' Roy said, as he studied the seventy-three members of the jury and sadly missed his old friend Harold Bunting.

'Let me explain, comrades, why I advised the electorate not to vote for Mr MacMaster here and Miss Keithley at the recent Council by-election. But before I go into the details, I want to make it clear that I only took this momentous step after a great deal of heart-searching. And the reason I could not in all conscience advise the electors to vote for Comrades MacMaster and Keithley was because they are both avowed Marxist-Leninists.'

Again Pickles pushed himself to his feet.

'Yeah, you're right, Hampton. Comrades MacMaster and Keithley *are* Marxist-Leninists! And that's wot makes 'em *real* socialists!'

'Wrong!' Roy fired back. 'Marxist-Leninism has never been a legitimate strand of British democratic socialism, whatever people like Benn and Scargill say. Indeed, there is nothing "democratic" at all about Marxist-Leninism. Lenin denounced the very concept of democracy. By his own admission he believed in the one-party state. Which is how and why he created the Soviet Union and everything it stands for today. And it's because I am opposed to our having a totalitarian regime here in Britain that I advised our supporters to reject MacMaster and Keithley. But it's not just people like myself in the PLP who are against the Marxist-Leninists. Trades-union comrades, like Duffy and Chapple, are always warning the Labour Party not to flirt with people and policies that will lead to the establishing of a mini-Soviet-type state here in England.'

At the mention of Frank Chapple, the *bête noire* of the hard left, the delegates chanted: 'Traitor! Traitor! Scab! Scab!'

Roy's voice rang out: 'If Keir Hardie, one of the founders of our Movement, were alive today, he would also join me in attacking the Marxists in our Party.'

'That's a blatant lie, Hampton! Keir Hardie was a great believer in Marxism!'

Roy shook his head emphatically: 'I'm afraid you're wrong, comrades. Again! Hardie only believed in Marxism at the beginning of his career. But when he actually became an MP, Hardie wrote – and I quote: "I am repelled by much of the work of Karl Marx. Because Marxism does not touch one human sentiment or feeling. Marx was also wrong about Class-War; for human feelings of Brotherhood can never grow out of a propaganda of Class-Hatred." And Keir Hardie also said: "Life is already barren enough for most people without our voluntarily adding to its bitterness."'

A grudging murmur of respectful bewilderment.

'Comrade Hampton?'

'Yes, Comrade Chairman?'

Terry paused to roll up the cuffs of his white sweater, then murmured:

'Forgive me interrupting you, but what exactly have these

picaresque quotations from Keir Hardie got to do with your defence?'

'Everything!' Roy snapped, moistening his dry lips with a sip of water from his glass. 'Because, you see, Comrade Chairman, Hardie went on to say: "Mankind in the main is not moved by hatred, but by the love of what is right." '

Then Roy lowered his voice and placed his typewritten quotations under his glass.

'That is why, comrades, I ask you tonight not to let your hatred of me blind you against the truth. And the truth is, if you throw me and the other moderates out of this Party, this Party will degenerate into a dictatorial Marxist-Leninist party. And once the British people realise this has happened, they will turn their backs on this Party. Because the British people are a moderate people. But if, instead, we throw the extremists out of the Party, then the man in the street will once again support us. If, however, we listen to the likes of Ken Livingstone and Arthur Scargill, and take to the streets in potentially violent extra-parliamentary activity, then this Party will continue to wither away into a wilderness of its own making. For I repeat that most people in this country believe in and basically trust parliamentary democracy. Therefore, it's up to us to uphold the sanctity of Parliament. Then we will have the right to save this nation, and hurl Queen Margaret into her own inhuman, fiscal abyss!'

To the chairman's consternation there was a strangulated cheer from the back of the hall. His eyes glittering, Roy seized the initiative.

'So that is why, comrades, in the name of moderation, I ask you to continue to support me as your Member of Parliament. In which capacity I promise to go on working for democratic reform in this country. At the same time, I promise to go on fighting against extremism of whatever political persuasion and wherever I encounter it. Thank you, comrades.'

Terry gave the MP a half-smile.

'And thank you, Comrade Hampton, for your original defence.'

Then Terry addressed the delegates.

'I will now open the Motion for discussion from the floor.'

A man thrust his arm into the air. Roy recognised the man as Joe Dipperling, the delegate from the General Municipal

Boiler Makers and Allied Trades Union. It was Joe who had been talking to Roy on the telephone earlier that evening. Instantly the hands of several hostile delegates shot up around the trade unionist. For a moment Terry pretended to be uncertain as to whom he would choose. Then, to Roy's amazement, Terry pointed to the dapper trade unionist.

'Comrade Dipperling, the floor is yours.'

'Well, comrades . . . all I'd like to say, as the delegate for the GMW, is that I've also been a member of the Labour Party for thirty-odd years.'

From the hall erupted predictable cries: 'All right, we know your record, comrade!'

'The point is, comrades,' Dipperling continued, 'that though I don't always agree wiv everyfink our MP says, particularly on defence, I *do* agree that we've got to watch out for extremism!'

The heckling grew in volume and intensity, but Dipperling refused to be shouted down.

'And wot's more, comrades, we've got the right to be heard! So why don't you cut this crap out? Because, believe me, there's no hope for the Labour Party unless we all stand together! – like Kinnock and Hattersley keep telling us. We've got to be tolerant of other people's views. Oh, I know Hampton may have bent the Rules a bit, but I believe he did it for the best of motives.'

'Bent the Rules?' screamed the hecklers. 'He didn't bend 'em, he smashed the fuckers!'

Dipperling gave his moustache a frenzied scratch, then shouted back: 'No, he just bent 'em a bit. Out of principle! And, let's face it,' he urged hoarsely above the waves of barracking, 'Comrade Hampton's been a damn good constituency Member of Parliament for the last fourteen years. And he never said anyone should vote for the Tories! Or them Liberal Social Democrats! Or any other rubbish, did he?'

As the trades unionist slumped down on to his seat, Roy's spirits slumped with him. It was obvious MacMaster was only allowing him a token defence. And so it proved. For the next three delegates called were the O'Hara girl, the woodwork teacher and a well-groomed plasterer. During their harangues against him, Roy encouraged his imagination to swim through the cigarette smoke and the dissonance of hatred around him.

If this is the England of the future, he thought, then God help us all!

With effort, he was able eventually to refocus on a bearded social worker, new to the MP, but who nevertheless was wearing the statutory black leather jacket and faded jeans.

'Well, Comrade Chairman,' hissed the social worker. 'I only want to reiterate what the last three comrades have already said. And that is: don't be taken in by Dipperling and his right-wing union gang! They whitter on about "tolerance" and the like. But underneath they're itching to start a witch-hunt against all of us who support Benn, Heffer, Livingstone, Scargill and real socialism!'

As the social worker spat out his words, he flared a glance at the trade unionist.

'You may well sneer, Dipperling, but you know you'd purge us all if you bloody could! But it's too late now. Because with every day that passes the political balance of this Party moves farther to the left. You can't stop it now! A permanent majority of the left on the NEC is inevitable! We also control nearly ninety per cent of the Constituency Parties! And there's already a left-wing majority in the PLP! So the future belongs to us, comrades – the future belongs to us!'

His sunken eyes glittered as he raised his fists.

'That is why we mustn't go soft now, comrades,' he urged. 'Our moment of glory is approaching. At last, we real socialists are getting our hands on the levers of power. Then, by God, we will . . .!'

'I doubt whether God will have much say in it, comrade,' interrupted Roy.

'Oh, you cheap . . .!'

'Order! Order!' Terry intervened.

The social worker opened his mouth to berate the MP, but Terry shook his head.

'And by "order", I mean you, Comrade Winters! You've had your five minutes, so I'd like you to give way.'

Then, unfolding his arms, Terry jabbed his thumbnail against his white sweater.

'Now, comrades, as I . . .' – he prodded his chest again – '. . . was one of the two candidates that our Member of Parliament denigrated to the electors, I feel it is only right that I speak my piece.'

He smiled in Roy's direction and continued: 'So, in accordance with our standing orders, I will now vacate the chair and speak in the debate from the floor.'

Terry turned to the secretary sitting next to him.

'Will you be so good, Comrade Smithers, as to stand in for me a moment?'

'Certainly, Comrade MacMaster.'

Terry descended the two platform steps and a quiver went round the room.

'Right, comrades,' Terry began, 'I'd like to start by saying how very good it was of our MP to come here tonight to explain his reasons for betraying our great Party. Because there is no other word but "betrayal" for what he did, comrades. What's more, he did it consciously!'

Terry paused while the delegates cheered.

'Not that we don't appreciate that he worked hard for the Party in the past. But unfortunately . . .' – Terry raised a judgemental finger – 'unfortunately now, in the present, Comrade Hampton has wilfully broken the Party Rules – which is something he would never have dreamed of doing if he was truly working-class!'

The revolutionary swivelled round, his finger aimed at the MP's heart.

'But Hampton isn't working-class, is he? He's a middle-class intellectual from the polytechnic. So to all intents and purposes he's slumming here with us! If you scratched him, you'd find he had a Roy Jenkins attitude towards the working class, and towards every one of us in this hall tonight!'

After uttering his pronouncement, Terry swung round to conduct the baying below, for the revolutionary had transformed himself into a demonic Stravinsky conducting *The Rite of Spring*. Then, as the blood-clamour echoed round the faded posters, with a dismissive flourish the great conductor silenced his timpani. Etching his features with sorrowful lines, Terry modulated his voice to express his disappointment.

'Yes, it's very unfortunate, comrades, that Mr Hampton has this superior attitude towards us. Because it's us, in the real working class who are the ones who do the real work for the Party. Well, let's face it: the real work for the Party is not done in places like the House of Commons!'

Again Terry focussed his considerable energy and sense of grievance on Roy.

'No, the real work is done on the doorsteps and in the Party offices. What's more, it's done twenty-four frigging hours a day! Typing out letters! Doing the duplicating! Licking envelopes! Arranging the meetings! The rallies! The protests and the sit-ins! And taking the class war out onto the streets, like Tony Benn, Scargill and Livingstone want us to!'

Most of the delegates were now on their feet, cheering their conductor and demanding an encore. With a world-weary shrug Terry obliged.

'And we do all this, comrades, because we loathe the class-ridden and barbaric tutelage that is continually foisted on the working-class by the fascist Tories!'

The adulatory pandemonium in praise of the conductor was deafening. Roy closed his smarting eyes. He was reminded of a similar experience the previous April in this very hall. Then, as now, he had felt he was drowning in a sea-fog, with the albatross of the Labour Party dragging him down into a plummeting nightmare. But even in his waking desolation he couldn't escape 'Pied Piper' MacMaster, who called the tune as he lead the predators on the blood trail.

'And it's because we passionately hate the Tories and everything they stand for that we know how working-class we are!' Terry roared. 'That's why we could never betray our life's work out of malicious spite – like Mr Hampton up there has done!' His voice swooped to a theatrical whisper. 'Well, is there a greater crime against the working class, comrades, than breaking the basic rules of Labour Party loyalty?'

His whisper was so huskily deep that the delegates had to lean forward to catch what he was saying.

'No, comrades. There *is* no greater crime than breaking the Rules. Therefore it is with a heavy heart,' the revolutionary solemnly placed his right hand upon his left breast, 'that I go along with the wishes of my working-class compatriots and must insist that Roy Hampton be expelled forthwith from the Party he has so wantonly betrayed.'

Roy opened his eyes and stared blankly in front of him. The revolutionary continued to ooze compassion.

'So, comrades, we can only hope in the forthcoming months that Mr Hampton will see the error of his ways and recant his sins against the working people of this country. Then, after a decent period of *public* repentance, he can once more rejoin the fold of progressive socialism, and help us create the New Society.'

Although Roy's eyes were open, his mind was dazed by the swelling noise around him. Then Terry returned to the platform and assumed his official role as chairman. For several moments Roy could only make out the blurred outline of the next speaker. Then he realised it was Joan Keithley, but all he was aware of were her expressive eyes. There was a sadness about them which was belied by the curl of her lip. Then she narrowed her gaze at the bemused MP.

'Comrades, our Comrade Chairman is right about our so-called Member of Parliament. We've always known that Hampton's really a closet-Tory. A secret supporter of Reg Prentice and George Brown!'

As Joan shouted this she knew she was exaggerating, but her fear of MacMaster was such that she had to go through with it. Again with a look she tried to signal to Roy that she only meant half of it. But she could see the MP was in his own myopic world and unaware of her contrition. This angered her, and she spat abuse at him like tin-tacks from a blunderbuss.

'So I say, comrades, if Hampton doesn't believe in socialism – which he obviously doesn't! – why doesn't he have the guts to become the Labour Party's Enemy Number One, like Reg Prentice? Yes, why doesn't he join all those other fascists in the Tory Party?'

The delighted screaming from the hall provoked her to surge on with her swingeing sarcasm.

'Or if the Tory Party's too "extreme" for Hampton, why doesn't he join the other Tory Party: the SDP – along with the Gang of Four and those other class-traitors? Then he can go on guzzling his claret in the House of Con-men – or do I mean Commons?'

There was another burst of cheering laughter. Joan's eyes glistened with triumph.

'That's all he's interested in, isn't it, comrades? Claret and poncy dining! Mind, in that respect he's like so many other MPs in our Great Party. He's spent years using the working-class movement to feather his own nest.'

Joan paused for effect, then speared her forefinger at Roy's throat.

'In fact, some of us believe that Mr Hampton has never been a genuine socialist at all. He's been lying to us for years. If not, why has he got the Tory press lined up out there in the street? Because we all saw that gutter filth waiting for him as we came in, didn't we? You can be sure he'll go running to them with his lies the moment we pass sentence. And being the kind of class-traitor he is, he's probably going to announce to the press that he's planning to join the SDP/Liberal Alliance, the Tories *and* the National Front all at the same time!'

This brought the house down. The applause and cheering even exceeded that bestowed on Terry, which did not please the latter-day political Stravinsky.

When the laughter eventually subsided, Roy couldn't resist a riposte: 'Yes, I must concur, Comrade Keithley, that was pretty witty.' Pause. 'For a closet-com.'

'Oh, you ...!' screeched Joan, as his remark provoked pockets of laughter. 'You're rotten through and through, Hampton!'

Then, because of her strenuous harangue, she found herself inexplicably near to tears. Her head pounding, she yelled out the uppermost thought in her mind: 'You're so rotten, Hampton, you didn't even support our movement in our struggle to get Denis Healey to remove the VAT on tampons!'

Only as Roy tipped his chin back to laugh did she realise how embarrassingly pathetic her accusation was. Then, before she could counter-attack, the MP took the initiative.

'I don't mean to laugh, Mr Chairman, but here I am about to be burnt alive and all she can do is whitter on about tampons!'

The women delegates reacted by hissing, booing and screaming: 'Chauvinist pig!'

Terry, who had had more than enough of Joan stealing his ever-diminishing limelight, pounded his fist on the table and demanded: 'Order! Order!'

The hubbub gave way reluctantly to sporadic coughing, followed by the flicker of cigarette-lighters which fuelled even more coughing. Then Terry gestured towards the still-smiling MP.

'Comrade Hampton, before the seriousness of this Motion deteriorates any further, you had best sum up your case. And briefly! We need a decisive vote on this Motion. Order, comrades, order! The floor is yours, Comrade Hampton. Order, I say!'

Roy stood. 'Yes, and by the sounds of it, Comrade Chairman, the floor is mine for the last time.'

Laughter and cheers.

Roy shook his head. 'I wish to God it were a laughing matter, comrades.'

Another flurry of laughter. For the first time, Terry was moved by the stricken look in his adversary's eyes. Knowing he had destroyed Hampton, he suddenly wanted to make token amends. With a rush of anger Terry flailed his words at the delegates as if he were winnowing chaff in a cornfield.

'Order, comrades! Order! Let the man speak! This is not a Soviet show trial! This is the Labour Party – and Roy Hampton has every right to Labour Party justice!'

Instantly the delegates were stilled by the whiplash of Terry's tongue.

'So, comrades, we will listen in silence to what Comrade Hampton has to say. Well, we don't want him telling the press that he's not had a fair hearing, do we?'

Several delegates laughed. The rest nodded in assent. Roy rubbed the back of his hand over his lower lip to stop himself shaking.

'The reason I said it was no laughing matter a moment ago, comrades, was because I feel that what is about to happen to me is only the *beginning* of the final purge of the rest of the moderates in our Party. Oh yes, I know what many of my friends have said: that I have left my attack on the extremists until it's almost too late. But surely to God it is better to put my beliefs on the line when it is almost too late than never to put them on the line at all. Well, I could easily have taken Comrade Keithley's advice and made things much easier for you all by resigning. But instead I prefer to be thrown out of the Party that I have been a member of for over twenty-five years. Because that way the whole country will see for itself the dangerous intolerance, the alien philosophy and, above all, the envy and hatred that drives these so-called "real" socialists in their messianic lust for total and *continuous* power!'

Despite their chairman's earlier admonition, the delegates

began to stir again. But Roy, now grim-faced and relentless, overrode the growing disquiet.

'But the real tragedy, comrades, is not what is happening to me, but what is happening to Britain! For it's a fact that until very recently the Labour Party was the only party that genuinely represented the working people of this country. But because the Labour Party is being destroyed from within, and because it continues to espouse policies like unilateralism and even more nationalisation, in desperation the working people end up voting for the Tories and the Alliance. And is it surprising? For unless we quickly return to being a constructive, compassionate and popular left-of-centre party, by the end of the decade there will be no party left to represent the working people of this country. At least, no party that's capable of achieving power under our present electoral system. So the Thatcherite years will continue ad infinitum. And what a horrible and fearful thought that is!'

Roy paused as more and more delegates jeered at his message.

'Oh, I know what you think, comrades,' he called out above the clamour. 'You think that you'll all take to the streets or have a general strike – or both! And you probably feel that that desperate state is all but here. But believe me, when that day dawns, when *force* rather than Parliament becomes the law, it is not only parliamentary democracy that will be crushed in the pitched battle, but also the British way of life! Because on that day, you'll find to your cost that there are more than enough extreme right-wingers who'll be only too happy to bloody it out with the extreme left wingers, whether it be on the streets or the picket lines. And whichever political extreme is the better organised and the more violent, that extreme will take the day. *And* the country! And you will have helped those undemocratic, militaristic extremists to march into the political vacuum which even now you are creating! Because democracy, comrades, is a very rare and extremely delicate orchid.'

'Democracy a fuckin' orchid?' jeered a bearded giant from the side-aisle.

'Yes. And what's more, comrade, it's a hot-house orchid,' insisted Roy, completely unmoved. 'And Kier Hardie would've been the first to say that if you allow the orchid of democracy to be trampled on by the black, or red, jackboots of intolerance, then you will have deserved the nettles that will spring up in democracy's place – in the form of bully boys, roughnecks and murderous thugs. And believe me, they will be only too happy to police your brave new world for you!'

Roy now abandoned all caution, and with open arms he pleaded with the smoke-hazed faces below him.

'So for pity's sake, comrades, if not for the Labour Party's sake, give your malice a holiday for once. And cast your vote for democratic, parliamentary moderation instead, while there is still time! So that at least there will be a remote chance that our children, and our children's children, can inherit some kind of democratic future.'

As Roy's anguished plea poured out, the delegates in the hall seemed to him to be no more than statues in a misty garden. Desperately he tried to grapple with the turbulent reality below, but now they were no longer even statues, but merely an amorphous mass of tendrils clutching at his doubtful sanity.

'Hey, look at Hampton!'

'Yeah, the old bastard's actually got tears in his eyes.'

'Yeah, he's like Shirley Williams, crying for himself!'

'Order! Order!' snapped the chairmen, his hand drumming on the table. 'We have now had over three hours of debate on this contentious Motion. So without more ado I intend to put the Motion to the vote. Please give your ballot papers to the tellers.'

As the tellers passed the ballot box to the nearest delegates, Terry allowed his eyes to swivel in Roy's direction. But the MP did not answer his look. He was enveloped in his recurring nightmare, but this time the nightmare was about to become a reality.

As the delegates voted, Roy swayed back in his chair. Crimson billows tumbled over him ... over the dappled wood decked with spring leaves ... over the bluebells ... the flag flapping on the spire ... the English pub and the locals listening to the nightingale ... the lovers in the leafy lanes ... over the freshly-cut grass and the butterflies ... the apples thudding on last year's leaves ... and still the red waves rolled on and on and on ... over his mother gardening, his father digging, his brother fighting, his sister crying, his son running, his daughter yawning, his wife smiling, Helen kissing, Harold dying ... himself drowning ... and his beloved England weeping. ...

Then Roy heard Terry's voice, like Noah calling above the

bloodstained flood – only the revolutionary's voice was quiet and inexorable. Roy knew that this time he would not wake up from his nightmare, clutching his wife's hair and screaming. This time the nightmare was for ever.

'The tellers have counted the votes,' Terry said. 'The result is as follows. There are sixty-five votes in favour of expulsion and seven votes against. So it is my sad duty to confirm that Roy Hampton is no longer a member of the Labour Party.'

As soon as the meeting was over, the quietly triumphant revolutionary pursued the MP down the worn steps into the media-ridden street.

Terry was just in time to prevent several of the more hostile GMC delegates from harassing Hampton, who was clutching his briefcase and forcing his way towards the expectant journalists. As Terry brushed his fervent acolytes imperiously aside in his attempt to catch up with Roy, the BBC and ITN cameramen converged on the protagonists. Within seconds the competing cameramen had framed MacMaster and Hampton in overlapping two-shots, with the jeering delegates providing a restlessly blurred background.

Before either reporter could fire a question at the MP, Terry took the initiative and leaned farther into frame. With his eyes blazing with candour he said: 'I trust there's no hard feelings, Roy. I'm afraid what happened tonight was simply an integral part of the historical inevitability of the triumph of socialism. And, anyway, I'm sure even you will acknowledge that your expulsion from the Party tonight was carried out in a totally democratic manner.'

Immediately both cameramen swivelled slightly to the right and adjusted their lenses to embrace the MP in a large close-up. With growing astonishment Terry realised that his adversary was smiling.

'Of course it was "totally democratic",' Roy murmured, the corners of his lips now edging towards the lobes of his ears.

Terry looked mystified. Roy's overt cheerfulness disturbed him. The TV reporters were quick to realise that Hampton was about to lob a political Molotov cocktail at the revolutionary's bewildered feet. After exchanging significant looks they decided not to intervene.

'Indeed, my expulsion tonight from the Labour Party was so "democratic",' continued the beaming MP to the thousands of sleepy 'Newsnight' viewers in their armchairs, 'that even a child could see that it had been "democratically" rigged from first to last.'

Terry gasped audibly, but before he could make a cryptic rejoinder, Roy smiled on with: 'In fact, my "democratic" expulsion tonight had all the hallmarks of Soviet "democratic centralism". That is, it smacked of the kind of "democracy" in which the chairperson uses so-called "democratic" procedures for his own very undemocratic "centralised" ends! But then, as I'm sure all our viewers are aware, Comrade MacMaster's "democratic centralism" was invented by the most famous Marxist "democrat" of them all: Joseph Stalin.'

Still smiling, Roy reached out and seized Terry's right hand, forcibly tugging him into shot. The revolutionary tried to extricate himself, but Roy tightened his grip on Terry's fingers and pumped them vigorously.

'But I've no hard feelings, Mr MacMaster. On the contrary, I'm grateful for everything you've done for me tonight.'

'You're grateful?' blurted Terry as he finally snatched his hand away.

'Absolutely. You see, if you Marxists hadn't thrown me out of the Party tonight, I probably would have ended up eating humble pie like the rest of my right-wing Labour colleagues. But now, thank God, I have no choice but to fight you and all extremists like you – whether of the hard left or the hard right – until one or other of you nail a coffin over my face!'

This was the cue the reporters had been waiting for.

'So what are you going to do now, Mr Hampton?'

'Yes, what are you going to do'?

Roy beamed into the jostling cameras.

'If it's all right with you, gentlemen, I shall discuss my future plans with my family, but on camera.' Roy paused, then ostentatiously pulled back his shirtcuff to scrutinise the wristwatch which his father had given him on his twenty-first birthday.

'Yes, in exactly thirty minutes' time, I shall hold this discussion in my living room. So, gentlemen, if you are interested in the opinions of an ex-member of the Labour Party, perhaps you'll be good enough to follow me?'

Without waiting to see if he had any followers, Roy strode

off in the direction of the car park, leaving a thunderstruck Terry staring after him, his mouth ajar.

Fifteen minutes later, the media clambered out of their cars with their equipment and bustled up the steps into the Hamptons' unsuspecting household. As they whirled round Liz and the children, Sebastian and Alexa gaped at them in wide-eyed incomprehension. Liz, in a state of shock, simply stood in everyone's way, hands on hips and glowering furiously at her husband.

Twice she thought of intervening when the two rival lighting technicians were arguing about where they should set up the wrought-iron standard-lamp. With an understanding smile Roy shook his head at her. In desperation, she tugged at her complacent husband's sleeve.

'Look, darling, I know you've been thrown out of the Party, but is all this really necessary?' she hissed under her breath, as the ITN sound technician waved at her to be quiet so that he could adjust his tape-recorder to get the right level.

'Yes, it is, darling,' Roy whispered back, encircling her tense shoulder with a protective arm and leading her into the relative privacy of the hallway. Equally as bewildered, Sebastian and Alexa followed their parents hurriedly out of the room.

'Yes, why have you brought these dreadful newsmen home, Dad?' snapped Sebastian, once they were alone in the hallway.

'Because I'm going to discuss my future – on camera.'

'You're going to do what?'

'Darling, you must understand that I've got an opportunity tonight which only comes once in a lifetime: to tell the public what I intend to try and do to ensure we all have some kind of democratic future.'

'But why've you brought the newsmen home, Dad? Surely you could've done that outside the hall after the meeting?' countered Alexa.

'I could, Lexi, but I want the people who are watching us to hear your views as well as mine.'

'You want *us* to take part in your interview as well?'

'Yes, darling.'

'You mean, if we disagree with you . . .?' Liz persisted, with a dangerous shimmer in her eyes. 'You actually want us to tell the viewers that we disagree with you?'

'Of course.'

'But surely . . .?'

'If we can't be democratic at home, darling, what hope is there? So why don't you girls nip upstairs and powder your noses while Sebastian and I go and make ourselves comfortable in the bullring. Don't argue! From now on life can only go upwards.'

Liz shook her head as he pushed her gently towards the stairs.

'This interview could ruin your career, darling!'

'It probably will. Still, if the worst comes to the worst, I can always take the consultancy job. But tonight I'm going to make a stand. When you hear what I've got to say, if any of you disagree with me, just tell the world, OK?'

'You're crazy, darling!' Liz cried, immediately clamping her hand over her mouth in case she was overheard by the BBC presenter who was now beckoning Roy from the doorway.

Roy opened his arms impulsively and crushed Liz against his chest. He whispered something in her ear which the presenter and the children failed to catch. Then he patted her bottom affectionately and pushed her onto the first stair. Laughing, she ran up the stairs. Then she turned at the bend and silently mouthed: 'You're crazy – but I love you.'

Roy and Liz sat on their sofa, with Sebastian and Alexa on either side of them. As Roy stared steadfastly into the lenses of the two cameras, the expressions on the faces of Liz and the children flickered between embarrassed amusement and growing tension. To the left of the sofa, the tape-recorders on the carpet whirred silently to themselves. The interview was now fifty-five seconds old. The BBC presenter edged forward slightly.

'So what are you going to do, Mr Hampton, now you've been expelled from the Labour Party?'

Roy glanced briefly at Liz who was unconsciously kneading her fingers on her lap. Then he took in the looks of concern in his children's eyes. Still smiling, he leaned forward and said:

'I'm not going to fight my expulsion. Though, of course, I could if I wanted.'

'How could you fight your expulsion, Mr Hampton?'

'I could refer my case to the Labour Party's National Executive Committee. But although some of the members of the NEC would probably be on my side, in the end I'm sure the majority would uphold the expulsion decison of my local GMC.'

'So what are you proposing to do?'

Roy spread his hands on the coffee table.

'Before I answer that question, I'd like to make a statement which I believe will explain my answer.'

The BBC presenter glanced shrewdly at his ITN counterpart, then said: 'Please make your statement as brief as possible, Mr Hampton, and then answer the question.'

Roy nodded, then refocussed on the cameras.

'First let me say I am now absolutely certain that the Labour Party is finished. At least, the Labour Party that I believed in and supported all my life is finished.'

Liz opened her mouth to protest, but surreptitiously Sebastian squeezed his mother's elbow. She folded her arms and waited for the worst.

'I'm fully aware that this is coming as a shock to my family,' Roy continued, still gazing at the cameras. 'To make things worse, as my wife has often inferred, I'm responsible as much as anyone for what has happened to the Labour Party.'

He turned to Liz. Then, before she could prevent him, he grasped her hand.

'You see, for the last ten years I have watched the extremist "moles" infiltrate the Party. During those years I should have fought them tooth and nail, but I didn't. For it is these "moles" who are fast taking over the Party. And they will finally ensure that the Party becomes merely a tool of the Communist Party. Indeed, I believe that by the end of the decade the Labour Party will be the Communist Party, in all but name!'

The BBC presenter raised a quizzical eyebrow.

'Are you really suggesting that the Communist Party, with its meagre membership, has such an influence over the Labour Party?'

'Absolutely. You see, despite popular opinion, the Communist Party is much more dangerous here in Great Britain than it is in Italy or France. For in Italy and France, the Communist

Party is out in the open. But here in Britain, as Lenin instructed them, the majority of British communists are not card-carrying. Indeed, most of them deny that they are communists. In fact, they pretend to be just ordinary supporters of the Labour Party and its democratic ideals. Thus they are able to infiltrate the Party in order to *subvert* the Party, so that they can eventually sweep away democracy once and for all.'

Roy raised an accusing finger.

'And most of the right wingers in the Labour Party, like Healey, Shore and Hattersley, know what I'm saying is true! Yet publicly they pretend that organisations like Militant Tendency and Socialist Action, not to mention the Communist Party itself, are not serious threats to the Labour Party. But communism, in its various "democratic" disguises, is a continuous threat, and it grows more dangerous by the hour. Anyone who has got eyes can see that the Marxist left will ultimately take over the NEC. As it has already taken over many of the powerful trades unions. But it's the hard left's control of the constituency Parties which is by far the most frightening aspect of the whole business. For it is the constituency Parties that choose the MPs. And it's the constituency Parties that insist that these MPs should be unthinking delegates, i.e. mouthpieces of the hard left. So I prophesy that by the end of the decade – no matter who is leader – the Labour Party will be more communistic in its policies than the Communist Parties in Italy and France.'

His eyes glittered with excitement as he surged on.

'And I also prophesy that the Tory Party under Thatcher and her lunatic monetarists will continue to move inexorably to the hard right!'

The BBC presenter smiled mischievously: 'Let me get this straight, Mr Hampton. You say the hard left are driving the Labour Party into becoming the Communist Party?'

'That's right.'

'So are you equally suggesting that Mrs Thatcher and her right wing are driving the Tory Party into becoming a Fascist Party?'

Roy considered a moment, then said: 'That is less likely, but still possible. Well, there is no doubt that Thatcher now believes in her own "charismatic leadership" propaganda. And you must remember that although she won an electoral landslide, she did this with only forty-two per cent of the vote. And of those who did vote for her, at least a third did it as a tactical, negative vote because they understandably feared the totalitarian lunacies of the far left. So the number of people who voted for her out of genuine Tory conviction was probably no more than twenty-five per cent of the voters! Yet, though our Queen of the Market Place has in fact only a moral minority, nevertheless she claims that she has been given an overwhelming moral mandate to privatise everything that comes to hand and implement her most controversial right-wing policies. It is unfortunate that our parliamentary system can at times saddle us with democratic dictatorship. And when the Opposition are so totally outnumbered as they are at present, then someone like Margaret Thatcher can really perpetrate whatever craziness she likes. And as she hates to listen to moderate advice, God knows where she will lead the country!'

The presenter raised his hand to interrupt, but Roy hadn't finished.

'The tragedy is that while the right-wing Tories and the left-wing socialists wage their ideological war, the *majority* of our nation is completely *unrepresented* by *either* of them. So most people in this country, who are neither extreme right-wing nor extreme left-wing, are forced to sit on the sidelines and suffer, with little or no say in their own destinies.'

Roy paused for breath. Then, to the presenter's surprise, Sebastian challenged his father.

'If you dislike the Tories and the Labour Party as much as you say, Dad, I can only assume you're about to join the SDP!'

The MP smiled at his son, then murmured: 'I'm afraid it's the only alternative on offer, son.'

'What about the Liberals?'

'Well, the Liberals have also got a pseudo-Marxist lunatic fringe, which if it isn't nipped in the bud will lead them into concocting a crazy manifesto like the 1983 Labour Manifesto. And with the same probable results.'

'You can't join the SDP, Roy!' Liz protested, shaking her head. 'There's nothing more despicable in the world than swapping Parties simply to hold on to your parliamentary seat.'

'I don't intend to swap parties, dear.'

'But . . .?'

'Tomorrow morning I will resign my parliamentary seat. Thus I will be the first politician to resign his seat on the same day that he joins a new party. And that includes Winston Churchill.'

Irritably Sebastian flicked his hair away from his eyebrows.

'But, Dad, if you join the SDP without keeping your seat, then you'll be forced to stand against someone like MacMaster who'll doubtless be representing the Labour Party in Lamberton.'

Roy grinned: 'That's right, son. Only this time everybody will know that MacMaster is a Trot before we start. So if the SDP accept me as their candidate, I've got a helluva good chance of beating him. Well, most people round here, thank God, are still old-fashioned, moderate Labour. So they may well prefer to vote for me than for a known communist.'

'And if they don't vote for you, Mr Hampton?' intruded the BBC presenter.

'If I lose, I'll stand again. And again. And again. Until I win.'

Clenching her hands to control her impatience, Liz turned on Roy.

'For Godsake, Roy, we can't go through all that again! Anyway, it'll take years for the Alliance to come to power. If ever!'

'You may well be right, dear. But I'm sure you'll admit the Alliance has done remarkably well in a very short time. It got nearly twenty-four per cent of the vote in the 1983 election, and it only came into being about eighteen months before the election.'

'Yes, but. . . .'

'You must remember how long it took the young Labour Party to gain power after its birth pangs with Keir Hardie and the rest. Mind, I believe the Alliance could become the Government in a far shorter period of time than that. But this will only happen if the SDP and the Liberals amalgamate into a brand-new party. What's more, they've got to do this as quickly as possible. Oh, I know there are still a lot of problems ahead – not least the young lunatic Liberal fringe and the die-hard, old Liberals. But then the SDP isn't a bed of roses either, with the overweening ambition of its leaders, plus all the middle-class schoolteachers, accountants, journalists, advertising executives and media people that still make up most of its membership. But these problems are soluble if the Liberals and the SDP forget politicking and their own personal ambitions for once, and instead concentrate on the desperate plight of the nation.'

The ITN presenter, who had been fretting impatiently, stepped forward.

'Yes, but even if the two parties do eventually join forces, Mr Hampton, the new party will never have a chance of achieving power without there being some form of proportional representation, surely?'

'Right!' agreed Roy, leaning farther into the pool of light cast by the standard lamp. 'That's why we must fight like hell for proportional representation. For that's the only way the millions of moderates in this country will ever get the kind of moderate government they crave. And we *should* have a moderate government, because the majority of people in this country are moderate. That's why I have now, belatedly, come round to believing that a Liberal Democratic Party – or whatever else we eventually decide to call it – is the only hope for political and social sanity on this island.'

'And you're willing to put everything on the line to fight for this new party?' Liz asked, unconsciously presenting her profile to the camera.

'Absolutely. To get the new party elected as our Government is the only certain way we can prevent ourselves forever being ruled by either the authoritarian right or the totalitarian left. That's why, first thing tomorrow morning after I've resigned my seat, I shall start to recruit for the Alliance.'

'Recruit who, Dad?' Alexa chimed in, determined to make her mark in case one of her bluestocking schoolfriends was still watching.

'I shall start by recruiting my friend, David de Quincey,' Roy said, trying to mask his grin, 'who, I'm sure, is watching this programme now, and who, despite his protestations to the contrary, is dying to join us.'

Roy addressed the camera directly: 'Aren't you, David?'

'Yes, but that's only one MP, Dad!' protested Sebastian, ostentatiously holding up his forefinger to get in on the act. 'Who else are you going to recruit?'

'Yes,' asked the BBC presenter with a cynical twinkle. 'Where are the recruits to your amalgamated new party going to come from?'

'I shall work night and day to prise all the disillusioned great men out of the Labour Party, of course.'

'Great men?'

'Yes. Denis Healey, Roy Hattersley, Peter Shore, Jim Callaghan, to name but four. Not to mention everyone in the Manifesto Group, and all those right-wing trades unionists like Chapple and Duffy. You see, it's very important that the Alliance has a strong working-class base. It needs some real people as members, and not just trendy folk from the middle classes. What's more, I'm sure that those I have mentioned know in their hearts that the Party of their youth has been destroyed. And secretly they're all dying to join a new radical party. They simply haven't the guts! Or they're too worried about their careers and pensions. Or at best they're simply deceiving themselves. Mind, they're no different to the left-wing Tory "Wets", like Sir Ian Gilmore, Jim Prior, Ted Heath, Peter Walker and Francis Pym, who are equally disillusioned with Thatchernomics and Tebbittitis. And they could equally be happy in a new, radical Centre Party. So I shall do my damndest to recruit *all* of 'em!'

'How will you do that?' demanded Liz in disbelief.

'The way Cassius recruited Brutus to kill Julius Caesar, of course.'

'I beg your pardon?' said the TV presenters in ragged chorus.

Roy laughed: 'Well, Cassius – at least according to Shakespeare – sent Brutus lots of letters and missives until he convinced Brutus that Caesar had to go! So I shall follow in Cassius' inspired footsteps – but I shall use the telephone as well. Either way I will be the secret whisper in their ears, spelling out the choices.'

'Which are?' interrupted Liz.

'Either all these illustrious gentlemen join us, or they'll be trampled by history. And I intend to start on them tomorrow. Oh, I'm fully aware that most of them will laugh in my face, but some will listen. A few may even act on my advice. You see, I believe that the situation in this country is potentially so serious that I don't care if a few politicians think I'm a paranoid clown, because I'm certain there are millions of *real* people who agree with me. But they are *silent* millions who are only allowed to express their opinions once every four years at the ballot box. Then they generally vote negatively because they are so disillusioned by the gobbledegook and mindless dogma of both so-called "major" parties. So, because I'm in politics and they're not, it's my duty now to fight for moderation and commonsense, in their name.'

Roy stopped, then turned to gaze at each member of his family. 'I can only hope that my family is going to support me in this endeavour.'

'Are you going to join your husband, Mrs Hampton, on his political crusade?' challenged the ITN presenter.

Liz unknotted her fingers slowly. Then, aware that both cameras were focused on her, she reached out and grasped her husband's hand.

'Of course I shall join him!' she said sharply.

'But I didn't fink you agreed wiv Dad, Mum.' Alexa cried in surprise. Then she bit her lip when she heard the shrillness in her voice.

'I don't know yet whether I agree with your father or not, dear,' Liz murmured. 'But I'm now certain of one thing. My feelings for your father and our family life are far more important to me than bloody politics! I'm sorry, but. . . .'

She broke off, her eyes glistening. Frustrated at her inability to express herself, she brushed her free hand fiercely over her eyelids.

'What I'm trying to say, Alexa, is . . . I'm willing to stand by your father for as long as he wants to go on fighting for what he believes in. He used to be a great fighter in the old days, but recently he's suffered a lot. We both have. But what we . . . share together has kept us together. And I realise now that he needs all the support he can get.'

Liz trailed off as she saw the tears welling up in her son's eyes.

'I can't bear any more of this!' she cried, waving a defensive hand at the unblinking cameras. 'It's too painful.'

The cameras edged closer, eager to photograph the drawn faces and moist eyes, for this was television at its best. Distraught, Liz pleaded into the widening lenses.

'All I can hope is that everyone who is watching us tonight also believes that moderation is worth fighting for. Well, it's not just up to my husband. It's up to us all, isn't it? It's up to all men and women in this country who want to live good and decent lives, and want their children to grow up in a free and fair society. The only way we can ensure we get the kind of government we want is to cast our votes at the next election for such a government. We've got to put our votes where our hearts and minds are!'

'Amen to that!' whispered Roy as he squeezed his wife's hand.

'I'd just like to add a couple of things to what my wife has said. And they are: I can only pray that our new party will be worth your voting for. But more important, if and when it is, I hope your votes won't come too late. For if a new moderate party doesn't become the Government very soon, and the dogmatic polarisation between the two nations of the haves and the have-nots continues unabated, then in the end only mindless violence will be the ultimate arbiter. And one morning you'll all wake up to find that the violent winner, whether of the left or the right, has crushed democracy, stamped out freedom and imposed some form of police state during the night. And I'm sure none of us wants that. So our future and our children's future depends on *us*. Every democratic nation gets the kind of government it deserves. And the time is short. So we must act *now*. Good night.'